SEDUCTION AND SURRENDER

Julian turned to speak to Mme. Devereaux, but she had disappeared, leaving him to his own discretion. A wry smile tugged at his mouth. This was hardly his first visit to a School of Venus, as they were often called, but certainly the most surprising.

Sipping brandy, his gaze shifted back to the women across the room. Ah, here was a notable difference from polite society, for they did not look away or pretend a modest indifference, nor were there chaperones hovering protectively over them. Instead, as his eyes moved over each one, a smile was offered, some coy, some sultry, all inviting. There was something to be said for eliminating the uncertainty, but he'd always been a man who enjoyed the chase and seduction as much as the eventual surrender.

Not that it mattered. He was not here to be titillated, he was here to choose a mistress to establish in a house. It would have to be a woman he could tolerate, for he would of necessity spend a certain amount of time with her or the subterfuge would be for naught.

The violins had stopped and someone played a pianoforte. He glanced toward the dais, his brows lifting in surprise. A young woman with glorious deep red hair entwined with white roses and ribbons sat on the bench, graceful fingers flying over the keys. She seemed absorbed in the melody. Intrigued, he moved closer. She was exquisite.

BOOK YOUR PLACE ON OUR WEBSITE AND MAKE THE READING CONNECTION!

We've created a customized website just for our very special readers, where you can get the inside scoop on everything that's going on with Zebra, Pinnacle and Kensington books.

When you come online, you'll have the exciting opportunity to:

- View covers of upcoming books
- Read sample chapters
- Learn about our future publishing schedule (listed by publication month *and author*)
- Find out when your favorite authors will be visiting a city near you
- Search for and order backlist books from our online catalog
- Check out author bios and background information
- Send e-mail to your favorite authors
- Meet the Kensington staff online
- Join us in weekly chats with authors, readers and other guests
- Get writing guidelines
- AND MUCH MORE!

**Visit our website at
http://www.kensingtonbooks.com**

UNTIL
YOU'RE
MINE

Lisa Higdon

ZEBRA BOOKS
Kensington Publishing Corp.
http://www.kensingtonbooks.com

ZEBRA BOOKS are published by

Kensington Publishing Corp.
850 Third Avenue
New York, NY 10022

All Kensington titles, imprints and distributed lines are available at special quantity discounts for bulk purchases for sales promotion, premiums, fund-raising, educational or institutional use.

Special book excerpts or customized printings can also be created to fit specific needs. For details, write or phone the office of the Kensington Special Sales Manager: Kensington Publishing Corp., 850 Third Avenue, New York, NY 10022. Attn. Special Sales Department. Phone: 1-800-221-2647.

First Printing: March 2004
10 9 8 7 6 5 4 3 2 1

Printed in the United States of America

In memory of Maurice Gibb, of the Brothers Gibb.
Your music defined a generation and will never be forgotten.

PROLOGUE

London, 1813

"Divorce is out of the question, my lord."

"I hardly need to be reminded of that." Julian Norcliff, the sixth Earl of Lockwood, spared a glance toward his secretary before turning back to the bank of windows overlooking London's dingy streets. Cold rain wet passing carriages, and a brisk wind stripped skeletal tree branches of leaves, tossing them into sodden heaps. Smoke from a forest of chimneys hovered just above rooftops, only adding to the bleakness of the day and his dark mood. He braced a hand against the window frame and stared through the leaded glass. "If that were possible, I would have long since been rid of—that woman."

His wife.

He refused to say her name aloud. He'd accepted the marriage for what it was, even before the vows had been exchanged. Theirs was not the first union arranged by wealthy, titled parents looking to better their own standing and insure the family holdings for one more generation.

But he wouldn't allow any woman to make his life a living hell. God knew he expected little enough of her, made no demands on her, provided a generous allowance, and even looked the other way while she dallied with whatever man caught her fancy. Anything to keep her away from him.

Now things had gone too far, even for Eleanor.

"The doctor assures me she'll be able to travel after a few

days of rest." Malcolm coughed discreetly, a subtle reminder that he had, as usual, intervened in the midst of chaos and prevented a full-blown scandal.

A good, faithful watchdog, Julian thought cynically, always putting himself in harm's way to protect the Lockwood reputation. His hand knotted into a fist against the window frame. It should never have been necessary.

"When she recovers, my lord," Malcolm continued, "I shall see that Lady Lockwood is quietly spirited out of the city. A few weeks at Shadowhurst will give her time to recuperate and time for the gossip to die down."

Julian wheeled abruptly to face him. Gray light through the window gleamed on his hair, turned thick gold strands molten, blending with the darker hues. His eyes narrowed into hard, brittle amber. "No. She is *not* going to Shadowhurst."

"You mean to keep her in London?" Malcolm's voice rose slightly, and sketchy eyebrows shot up as the secretary blanched, incredulous at the suggestion. "With all the talk going about? My lord, there's even been mention of a coroner's inquest."

Julian stalked across the library to an inlaid marquetry table set with cut-crystal decanters and glasses, and poured himself a brandy. He held it up and inhaled the potent bouquet. "A man is dead. Someone will have to answer for that."

"But it was self-defense, my lord, pure and simple."

Julian flinched. There was scarcely anything pure about it.

Eleanor's *intruder* had been a well-known scoundrel, infamous for trouble, but much too well off to resort to burglary. Still, she had insisted that Fielding forced his way into the house and threatened to kill her if she didn't give him all the money and jewels on hand. Then she'd swooned and been conveniently unable to say more.

There were many questions left unanswered. No doubt, they would remain unasked.

Malcolm cleared his throat. "Lady Lockwood's remaining in the city would not be advisable, my lord."

"I realize that." Julian tilted the brandy and it warmed his throat, chased away the chill that pervaded the room and his bones. "I intend to see that she's out of London. Preferably, out of the country."

"Out of the country, my lord?"

"Wherever she would like. Rome, Vienna." His hand tightened on the crystal snifter. "She cannot remain in London, and I will no longer tolerate her presence at Shadowhurst."

"I see. Ah, is this to be—permanent?"

"I'm sure she will miss me even less than I'll miss her." He drained the rest of the brandy and watched Malcolm's angular face, expressionless again as befitted an excellent secretary. Julian shrugged. "You handle my accounts. See that she has a monthly allowance that will support her sufficiently but not lavishly."

"Yes, my lord. But perhaps we should consider—"

"I've considered all I intend to consider. Either she accepts living abroad, or I'll leave her to face the coroner's inquest without my protection."

And a bloody fine vengeance that would be. He almost wished she'd refuse his offer.

CHAPTER 1

Covent Garden, 1814

" 'Ere, can't I tempt you wi' one o' me pies, love?"

Laura Lancaster knew she should turn away, but couldn't resist leaning over the barrow of small meat pies. They were still hot from the oven, and heady with the tempting fragrance of sage and onion. Her stomach clenched, a reminder of how empty it was, and her mouth quivered in anticipation as she fingered the few remaining coins in her purse. A veritable fortune, a tuppence, a ha'penny, and a farthing, but could she spare coin for a pie?

"Me meat pies are the best you'll come across. Fresh, they are."

She bit her lip, wavering. "How fresh?"

Blinking, small eyes seemed to disappear in a sea of wrinkles as the vendor grinned. He wore a wool cap atop grizzled gray hair, wisps sticking out like straws to frame his rumpled face. " 'Ere then, mebbe you'll fancy a nice apple tart, love."

What she would really prefer was a side of beef and fresh, white bread, soft and yeasty and slathered with butter, but that was beyond her means. Every penny was important. If she wasted her money, she'd never be able to buy passage on a ship home.

That yearning was almost as sharp and painful as the bite of hunger.

Then grubby fingers pushed forward a tray of tarts. Her

stomach growled loudly, and Laura surrendered to the inevitable. She couldn't resist the heady aroma of cinnamon-laced apples and hot pastry. Wrenching her gaze from the tarts, she looked up, clutching the small, worn purse tucked beneath her coat. Pie men loved to haggle.

"A farthing?" she said hopefully.

"One ha'penny, love." There was the spirit of barter in those beady little eyes that watched her closely.

"A ha'penny for two," she tried.

This time a grin split his face nearly in half as he chortled. "A ha'penny for one, and I'll gi' you this broken one wi' it."

Smiling, Laura fished a coin from her purse. A ha'penny. Utter extravagance. When the exchange was made, steaming tarts lay in her linen handkerchief. Cupping her hands together, she savored the warmth as well as the spicy fragrance. The heat flushed her cheeks, and a strand of burnished copper hair escaped from her cap to fall onto her brow. If she closed her eyes she could almost hear her grandmother humming a popular ballad as she took a hot pie from the hearth for Sunday dinner.

A wave of homesickness washed over her, mixed with aching despair. So far away now, as if in another lifetime. Or someone else's life. Had she ever really lived so simply? It didn't seem so special then, but now she'd give anything to be back where the sky was often blue and it was warm and safe and she was loved. . . .

No, enough of that. She couldn't mire down in sentimentality or she'd lose everything.

It was late. The bells of St. Giles had chimed the hour, and she still had to make her way through the crowded streets of Covent Garden. By sunrise the markets were always crowded with green-grocers and costermongers. Great piles of cabbages, cauliflowers, and turnips rose twice the height of a man, quickly depleted by Londoners. By eight o'clock the produce would be gone, little left but wilted cabbage leaves and other debris. At least the rain had stopped, though the sky was still the thick color of lead.

Scurrying down Longacre, she turned onto Bow Street and passed the Covent Garden Theatre with its covered portico for carriages and the statues of Tragedy and Comedy decorating the beautiful facade. She'd peeked in once, used to the bare boards and cramped pits of the small theaters, and been nearly overwhelmed by the opulence. It certainly made Greene's Theatre pale by comparison.

She hurried toward Greene's, nibbling at the edges of a tart as she wove through the throngs of pedestrians and dodged the occasional slop pot tipped out an upstairs window. It was as crowded here as near the Seven Dials district where she had lodgings, but the pinched faces and tattered garments were fewer. A beer wagon rumbled past, horses straining and the barrels rocking. She hardly noticed the smells or the noise of London anymore. She did notice the well-sprung landaus that often passed, ornate carriages with gold-embossed crests on the doors, with uniformed footmen clinging to the rear, and drivers in their boxes handling the ribbons of smartly stepping horses. Reminders of another world, one where she didn't live in a room with three other lodgers, where there was enough to eat and coal for the fires.

Navigating the pavement, she sidestepped a large puddle, then turned the corner onto the side street that ran behind Greene's Theatre. As she rounded the corner, she caught sight of a small crowd gathered outside the stage door. A hum of apprehension seared her. The building couldn't be on fire— there was no smoke or screams. Everyone should be inside, getting sets ready, studying lines, and fighting for space to put on their costumes for the dress rehearsal, not standing outside in an angry knot. She could feel the tension long before she reached them, heard a few voices rise in anger.

Laura reached the fringes of the crowd, a little startled to hear them muttering about Tom Costley. She edged closer, and put a hand on Jeremy Pinch's arm. "What's the trouble? I can't believe Tom is the one who's late, when I was worried he'd be angry at me for—"

"He's not late. He's gone."

"Gone?"

Jeremy nodded, directing her attention to the printed notice nailed to the door. "Gone. Read for yourself."

Swallowing hard, she stared in mute disbelief. *Notice! By order of the Mayor of London, this property and all assets seized for failure to satisfy outstanding debt and taxes. £5 fine for trespassing.*

She was barely aware of the others around her, jostling each other and rumbling about the injustice of it. Some seemed resigned, others shocked into silence. After a moment she looked up, her eyes finding Jeremy. He stared at her solemnly, and her heart sank. *No*. She was out of work. They were all out of work.

"What about our wages? We haven't been paid in weeks." A futile question. The answer lay in Jeremy's eyes, in the tight faces of those around her and the resignation that slumped spines and filled the air. She'd been counting on her wages. Weekly rent was already due, and McFinn, her landlord, would be waiting with outstretched hand when she returned to her cramped room.

Four pennies a week secured her a room she had to share with only three others, instead of the fifteen or twenty that often crammed into drafty rooms. Now she had a ha'penny less, and just enough to keep a roof over her head, certainly not enough to waste on fruit tarts. She looked down at the handkerchief in her hand, carefully wrapped around her extravagant apple tarts. She could have rented a room for a shilling a week and lived alone, but she'd sacrificed to save money for her passage, and now she was out of work. And rent was due.

"Here, now." Jeremy chucked her on the chin just as a quiver threatened her lips. "None of that. I know just what to do."

Clearing his throat, Jeremy spoke loud enough for the other cast members to hear. "We've suffered this before. It's off to the Angel with us, hey. We'll drown our sorrows in as much hot rum as our pennies will buy."

A murmur of agreement resonated among the players, and the group turned as one to traipse back down the alley. A resilient lot, one of them made a ribald joke and several laughed.

Jeremy slipped an arm around Laura's shoulder and turned her toward the mouth of the narrow alley that ran between buildings. "There are other theaters in London, love. And they pay better wages, I warrant."

"Some pay in stale bread and cheese," she said gloomily, and as there was no good reply to that truth, Jeremy ignored it.

"Aye, tomorrow you'll go on an audition, and another and another after that, love. You'll take whatever role you're offered, just like the rest of us."

Stumbling forward, she nodded. He was doing his best to comfort her, but he had to be as worried as she was, as the others were. She thought of her few coins, so precious, and the fruit tart that would be her only meal for a while. She had a small cache of money saved, more than the few coins in her purse, but it would be quickly gone unless she found work soon. Her goal slid further from her grasp. Passage home to America came dear.

Unshed tears stung her eyes, and she blinked them away furiously. "What good will going to another theater do if they close down all the time? This is the third one in a year."

"Laura, my lass, it's all part of being a player."

"Charming. I don't think I like this part very much. You go on to the Angel without me. I think I'll go back to my lodgings for the day. I'd rather be alone."

Jeremy grinned, and looked almost handsome, with his sandy hair and bright blue eyes. He struck his chest with his open palm and said dramatically, " 'Sweet Phebe, do not scorn me; do not, Phebe; Say that you love me not, but say not so in bitterness. . . .' "

An unwilling smile curved her mouth. " 'I would not be thy executioner: I fly thee, for I would not injure thee.' Act four, scene five of *As You Like It*."

"Act three. Be my shepherdess for the day. You'll feel better."

"I've not the coin for it."

"A little blue ruin and we'll be chirping merry," he said cheerfully, "and I've the coin for us both. I'll not take no from you, Laura lass, not today. Come along, there's a good lass."

The truth was, she dreaded the thought of returning to her dreary lodgings, a garret on the edge of Seven Dials, an area frequented by prostitutes and the flotsam of society. The three other women in the garret worked as seamstresses and were decent enough, just poor drudges fighting for survival in a world that seemed hopeless. Day by day, Laura saw herself becoming one of them, gray and anonymous, lost in St. Giles rookery.

"I'll come," she said, "but I shan't stay long. You know I won't."

Jeremy affected a wounded expression. " 'How now, my love! Why is your cheek so pale? How chance the roses there do fade so fast?' "

" 'Belike for want of rain . . .' " she said, Hermia to his Lysander.

"Or want of hot rum," Jeremy put in, his arm sliding around her back. "We'll put that right soon enough."

It was, Laura reflected, a better choice. It was warm in the crowded pub as she wedged between Jeremy and another actor, the heat from their bodies and the rum doing far more than the pathetic efforts of a fire across the common room. The rum made her a little light-headed, but the laughter of the others eased her bruised spirit. They were accustomed to this, but she found it more difficult. Still, by the time they left and Jeremy and Celia walked with her toward Carrier Street, deep shadows masked the gutters below leaning buildings. It was late, and tomorrow they would meet at one of the other playhouses.

"Drury Lane, Haymarket, Sadler's Wells—there will be room enough for good actors," Jeremy said firmly.

"Not everyone can be Master Betty," Celia said with a sigh, and slid Jeremy a soft glance. "Though you come close enough."

"Master Betty was a prodigy, and he retired to go to Cambridge," Jeremy said, but he looked pleased at the comparison to one of London's famous actors.

Jeremy was a vicar's son, defiantly running away from his village to come to London and be an actor, but Celia and Laura were quite alone. Celia orphaned by death, Laura by fate. It lent them a strong bond.

Tomorrow, she told herself when she was in her shabby room where the wind seeped through cracks in the walls and whistled down the cold, dark chimney, *I will find work again*.

"Start over. The line after the mother insists her son is innocent. And this time, *try* to impart a little emotion. Unless you like dodging rotten apples."

Laura bit the inside of her cheek in vexation. Arrogant little toad. He even looked like one, with his big, bulging eyes and wide mouth, but he held her future in his hands so she only nodded and found her mark on the rough wooden boards of the stage.

A sea of empty seats stretched beyond, but she spoke as if to a crowd, her voice lifting to sail into the void.

"'Prithee, how can you *do* this?'" she began, pouring her own frustration and anger into the words. "'Tis an abomination that you would lie for him when you know he killed my husband!'"

"'Because he is my beloved son.'" The assistant assigned to read with her picked at his teeth with a broken thumbnail. He looked unimpressed and bored. "'If 'twas your son, you would do the same as—'" He stopped, looked up from the script with a frown. "Your accent is off."

Laura faltered, noting the stage manager's frown and shake of his head, but desperation drove her on. "'Yea, and what will you do when he kills again? When another luckless soul—'"

"That's enough."

She flinched at the harsh interruption, recognizing a dismissal. She'd heard enough of them in the past few years. Chin held high, she swivelled to look at the men standing just beyond the rack of candles that lit the stage.

"You're unsuitable, Miss Lancaster." The stage manager gave an indifferent shrug. "This part demands an actress with presence. The scenes require . . . a bit of a jolt."

"Then I suggest you begin with a new playwright," she said sharply. "This is pure drivel."

Astonishment and outrage mixed on his face, and the playwright who watched from the pit shouted an insult, but she didn't acknowledge it. She made a grand exit, sailing serenely across the stage to the wings, where a stagehand flashed her a grin of approval. It eased the sting of failure, but did little to console her that she was still without a paying part.

As she descended the side steps and slipped out the stage door, she braced for the blast of icy wind. Her best wool cloak was threadbare in places but clean and mended, and she tugged it more firmly around her and weighed her options.

Barely noon, and the second audition of the day, though she hardly counted the first, since she'd been summarily dismissed for being female. The role called for a burly Roman soldier, not a slender woman. Frustrating, that men were allowed to play women but women must never play men's roles.

A tattered handbill sailed down the alley toward her like a bird, flapping loudly. In the inky shadows below dank walls, rats glared out at her, hovering protectively over a meal of refuse and occasionally indulging in a squabble. Shuddering, she moved on, passing the open door of a pub. Laughter and warmth whooshed out like so much steam from a tea kettle before the door closed again. The promise of warmth and company was seductive. She knew she'd be welcomed, for the pub was a common gathering place for players "between roles."

Steeling herself against temptation, she continued on her path, ignoring the sharp twinge of her empty stomach. One more playhouse and audition, one more chance to secure a paying role. She thought of Jeremy and Celia, and wondered how they fared. Celia always seemed to snag roles quickly, her bright beauty as infectious as her ready laughter. She never seemed to be so hungry her very bones ached, never seemed to be desperate, and Laura wondered how she managed. Jeremy had suggested Celia had other avenues of support, but offered little explanation. Whatever they were, Laura was near desperate enough to ask for details.

Acting was not her goal in life, and didn't consume her as it did the others. Perhaps that's why she didn't do well. Her heart and soul wasn't in it. It was only a paying position, a profession that was better than most for a solitary woman without means of support or letters of character to recommend her. *Better than the choice Maman made . . .*

Enough of that. This was no time for melancholy. If she didn't find a role soon, she'd be forced to take a position as a scullery maid if she was fortunate enough to find one. Even the enclaves of servants to the wealthy seemed to close ranks against outsiders, and the traces of her accent still created suspicion. It was not the time to be an American in England, with war between the two countries still dragging on. At least Napoleon was exiled to Elba and no longer swept across Europe, leaving as the primary concern the American blockades that chipped at British commerce with crippling efficiency. Victory Summer was behind London, Wellington was created a duke, and talk of a treaty with America promised to end hostilities.

The Thames snaked through the city not far away, teeming with swaying spires of ships that often sailed across the Atlantic. When the war ended she could go home. Passage would be cheaper then. *Home.* The lure dangled tantalizingly, images of green fields, neat houses, and blue Virginia skies seeming only a dream at times until she reminded herself that it was very real.

Galvanized by reminders of home, she forged ahead with

greater determination. The next audition would be the one. She'd not end up like so many of her fellow actors, lulling themselves into the pleasant delusion that fame and riches lay just beyond the next role. Acting was the means to an end, a better way to earn her way home than scrubbing floors. Inhaling deeply, she trudged through the noisy, dirty streets toward Figg's Playhouse.

Laura sank to a stool in front of the dressing table and propped her elbows on the rough, cluttered surface. Pots of paint were scattered in disarray: white powder for the face, lampblack to line the eyes, and alkanet root to color lips. Bottles of scent nestled by jars of vinegar. Sighing, she stared into the mirror before reaching for a brush. Pink cheeks flushed from the cold air made her green eyes look bright, and even the circles beneath her eyes were less noticeable. Around her, the chaos of opening night was a loud clamor that she barely heeded. It was always like this. And she had a role in the play, albeit a small one, thanks to Celia Carteret.

Shrugging off her cloak, Laura lifted her arms to loosen the pins holding her hair atop her crown. It tumbled down in a wayward mass of dark red curls, wild and unruly, defying taming with brush or comb. She glared at her image, then lifted the hairbrush to attack.

Behind her, the dressing room door burst open and a wave of noise and shrieks of laughter and foul oaths entered with Celia. She slammed the door with a flourish, and the noise abated. "Hullo," she sang out, cheery as always, looking like a lovely, exotic bird with her pale hair and exquisite features, "are you ready?"

"I know my two lines, but my hair is not at all the image of a shepherdess," Laura replied. "It refuses to obey."

"Then we shall discipline it severely," Celia chirped. She slung her cloak onto a hook. "It may be no larger than a pie cupboard, but at least we have a dressing room of sorts."

"*You* have a dressing room. I'm just fortunate enough to have you as a generous friend." That was true. If not for Celia, Laura might not have had this role, and she definitely wouldn't have access to a dressing room, a scarce commodity.

"Nonsense. We must look out for one another. You would do the same for me. Now here, give me the brush. I barely escaped being seen. He's such a fusspot, when I've never missed an opening scene."

The *he* she referred to was Roscoe Throgmorton, playwright, producer, and stage manager of the theater production, and nervous as a cat. He relentlessly hounded Celia about being late for curtain call or missing rehearsals. More than once, he'd threatened to sack her, but it was only an idle threat. She was a favorite with the men in the audience, and they all knew it.

Celia plopped a tiny bundle wrapped in cloth on the dressing table. "For you, ducks."

A tempting fragrance wafted from the cloth. Laura hesitated, but hunger won out. She unfolded the linen napkin and inhaled the enticing aroma rising from the pastry. A meat pie, and this one looked to be very fresh. Lifting her gaze, she met Celia's eyes in the mirror.

"Bless you."

Celia smiled, her fingers deftly stroking through Laura's curls, pulling her hair back and dragging the brush ruthlessly through it until she had it snared in two neat braids on each side of her head. "There you go, ducks. Now eat. I don't intend to see you starve, even if you seem determined to do so. It would be disruptive were you to swoon upon the stage."

"I must watch my pennies," Laura murmured. She picked at the flaky crust of the meat pie and broke off a bit. Her stomach growled impatiently, but if she ate too quickly she risked being ill. It had been two days since she'd had more than ale and a crust of hard rye bread. She brushed her fingertip over embroidered letters. "This linen is so white and soft . . . an expensive napkin. Whose initials are these?"

Celia's hand stilled on her shoulder, and Laura looked up. A fleeting expression of indecision flickered on Celia's face, then was gone.

"Viscount Belgrave. He's a new acquaintance."

A new acquaintance. Laura immediately understood. That's what Jeremy had meant then, when he'd said she had other means of support. It was common enough, but not usually for those in the smaller theaters. Celia's star was obviously rising.

"Oh," Laura said after a moment, a soft sound, and Celia laughed.

"Didn't you know, ducks? I thought everyone knew. A woman cannot get far in this world without a man's protection, unless she's born to the manor. I wasn't, but I always knew I'd do what I must to survive. Don't you ever tire of being hungry and cold?"

It was a brutal question, and Laura almost choked on a bite of meat pie. Swallowing, she nodded. "Of course I do. I hate it."

"Then do something about it," Celia said practically, and turned to the costume chest to pull out a heavy satin gown. She stripped out of her loose dress down to her corset and hose, and stuck her arms into the sleeves of the costume, a period gown that had seen better days.

Laura rose to fasten the hooks in the back, uncertain how to respond. Celia watched her in the mirror. "Look here, ducks," she said when Laura had fastened all the hooks, "it's a man's world, and we do what we must to survive." She moved to the dressing table and wound her hair into a tight knot on her crown, then settled a high, powdered wig atop her head and pinned it in place. Leaning forward, she began to paint her face with swift, expert strokes of a hare's foot, then outlined her eyes with lamp black, blinking away the soot carefully so as not to irritate her eyes. As she reached for the alkanet root to color her mouth, she sighed. "Just last night, I was told two gentleman have inquired about you. Companions of my . . . protector."

"Viscount Belgrave."

"Aye, ducks." On occasion, a trace of Celia's origins slipped into her careful speech, the accent harkening back to her childhood in the slums of St. Giles rookery.

"I knew he was an ardent admirer," Laura said cautiously, "but I didn't know it was more serious."

"Serious?" Celia looked surprised, and turned to stare at her. "Belgrave isn't serious about anything but whist and hazard, and blooded horses. But he likes his pleasure, and he appreciates being told how handsome and virile he is, even though he's fat and old and boring as a stick. But he's also rich and kind, and that quite makes up for the other."

"A practical viewpoint."

"It's a matter of survival. I've been where you are, spent the first six years of my life in the stews of St. Giles, and I've no intention of ever going back. I may not have been manor born, but I was born with a gift for being what others want to see, whether it's on the stage or in the bed. And my bed these days has soft, clean sheets."

A luxury. Laura bit her lip. "Belgrave is married. What will happen when he . . . moves on?"

"I'll move on as well. Oh, I'm fond of him, I am, but we both know that one day he'll find a new attraction, and who knows? I may find one richer and more generous before he makes that decision."

"These friends you mentioned . . . they are married, as well?"

"Of course they are, ducks." Celia covered her face with a mask and shook a fresh dusting of powder on the wig, then peered at her reflection in satisfaction. "There we go. Now you see, married men make less demands. They usually have responsibilities, while some young buck that fancies you can be a great deal of trouble."

"Trouble?"

"Aye, always randy, trotting upstairs fumbling with the buttons of his breeches."

Laura laughed. As Celia moved aside, she took her place

in front of the mirror and applied a coating of face paint. It made her itch, but was necessary.

"But, Celia, what if you want to get married someday?"

"No danger of that, I assure you. I've been wed and found it not to my liking." She helped Laura into the shepherdess's short skirt and buskin, then stood back to look at her critically. "You're sure to snare some man's attention in that tonight. Roscoe was right. You've lovely legs."

A little embarrassed, Laura smoothed the skirt, feeling awkward. "It's only a small role."

"Mark me, there will be a gentleman or two at the door after tonight's performance. Now come along. Take your shepherd's crook and hope no one's eaten your lamb."

Standing in the wings and holding a squirming, unhappy lamb in her arms, Laura heard the loud noise of the audience subside, then rise when Celia made her entrance on the stage. It was always the same—she garnered instant attention. But that was Celia, not Laura. They were not at all alike, despite Celia's suggestion.

If she had wanted to barter her body for money, she'd have listened to her mother.

CHAPTER 2

"Christ above, Malcolm, this is nothing more than common gossip. I refuse to stoop to their level with a defense against such ridiculous drivel."

Julian heard Malcolm inhale a deep breath, then exhale again. He looked up, saw lines of concern crease his steward's normally placid face.

"Gossip or not, my lord, people are listening and wondering how much might actually be true. I felt it my duty to keep you informed."

"I'm grateful for your concern." Julian looked at the mound of unopened correspondence neatly stacked on the leather blotter in front of him, his desk nearly obliterated with it. Devil take Eleanor! Curse her, and his own distaste for adding to gossip by letting her skewer herself on the sharp sword of rumor. There she was, safely tucked away in Europe, leaving him to deal with the avid rumor mill of London society. And the vultures gathered to eagerly await details of such a juicy scandal. Or, at the very least, a titillating reaction from her husband.

Left to their own speculation, the *ton* usually wasted no time in assuming the worst. It was the second season Eleanor had missed, and only the most dire of circumstances would justify her absence from the glittering balls and sumptuous banquets. It wasn't like her, and they all knew it. She loved being the center of attention. Vain as a peacock and voracious as a shark, she'd never willingly miss a London season, even the little season.

Malcolm coughed politely. "Most suspect you're living apart."

"Do they. How perceptive of them." He picked up the top letter, already neatly slit open, and extracted the contents, a boring letter reciting Lord Havering's list of grievances against the Whigs.

"Yes, my lord. Still, they wonder at the reason."

"And mortals wonder at the reason of the gods. Let them wonder. It occupies their often empty minds."

"Yes, my lord. That is true." Another polite cough earned Julian's attention. He looked up with a frown to find Malcolm staring at him with something like embarrassment. His complexion was mottled. "It is another concern that moves me to mention such distasteful matters to you, my lord."

"What? Spit it out, man, before you burst."

"Your . . . comportment."

Malcolm fidgeted when Julian's brows lowered. Reining his temper in sharply, he said softly, dangerously, "Explain that, if you will."

"With your permission, my lord, it is being said that a wealthy, powerful man in the prime of his life must have a reason to deprive himself of . . . life's most basic pleasures."

"Is it. How quaint. And solicitous that there are those who worry about my needs. Here I thought there was a surfeit of matters to concern the populace, such as Napoleon, or the prince's consort running amok in Europe, or the Americans attacking English merchant ships at will, but now I see that those are merely unimportant trivialities. How foolish of me."

Malcolm stood steadfast, not retreating from Julian's sarcasm. "There is speculation that you pine for your lost love."

That brought him upright. "Pining? *For Eleanor*?"

"Yes, my lord. Or worse."

"What could possibly be worse than being thought to pine for Eleanor?"

Malcolm stared at a spot on the wall behind him. "That your interests run . . . shall we say in a more perverse nature, as of those who prefer young men in ladies' stockings."

"Ah. No need to expand upon that topic. Spare me the details. God, a rum state of affairs when I'd rather be known as a Sodomite than to be pining after my faithless wife."

"My lord . . ." Malcolm still stared at a spot on the wall. "It seems that . . . that a partner has been named in your . . . suspected activities."

"Really. Fascinating. Is it someone I know?"

"Yes, my lord." Hot color stained his cheeks, and Malcolm's eyes shifted back, miserable and bewildered. "Your secretary."

Julian's brow shot up. "You? How droll. Oh, I see that this gives you much distress. Curse those with nasty little minds and even nastier wagging tongues." He sighed. "See here, Malcolm, there's not much that can be done about it. Denying such ludicrous accusations only lends them a form of credibility, as you must know."

"Yes, my lord. I understand, my lord."

It was obvious he didn't. Julian regarded him for a long moment. This was not just about a love of rumor and gossip. There were political overtones here, shading a vicious desire to bring him down, to lessen his effect in Parliament.

Damn politics. If a man had no dirty laundry to air, it would be fabricated for him. And the innocent were frequently trampled. He'd seen it happen far too often, one of the reasons he much preferred a quiet life in the country. Shadowhurst, his refuge. His sanctuary.

"I'm sorry, Malcolm," he said, and his secretary nodded.

"Yes, my lord. I find it . . . distressing."

An understatement. Julian smiled and shook his head. "I know of no way to counteract such vile rumors, other than to call out those repeating them, and that may well eliminate half the population of London. I can't imagine it would sit well with the Regent were I to challenge his current favorite to pistols at dawn in Hyde Park."

"No, my lord. It would not."

Malcolm looked utterly miserable. He stood erect, his thin shoulders squared as if to fend off blows, and Julian realized that the man had gone his entire life without a hint of reproach in his direction. He was a squire's son, and had been captain of the rowing team at school, an excellent scholar and exemplary employee. This must be devastating for him.

"Shall I have tea brought up for you now, my lord?"

He studied him for a moment. "Malcolm, have you any notion on a method of contending with these rumors?"

Dark eyes lifted to his face and lingered. "A suggestion only, my lord."

"A suggestion. Very well. What do you suggest?"

"Make no attempt to deny the rumors of our . . . liaison." He nearly choked on the last word. "Instead, counter them with your own actions."

"What, shall I go a round or two at Gentleman Jackson's to prove my manly inclinations? I've no notion that being beat senseless by a formidable pugilist will help much, but if it will ease your mind, I'll step up to the mark."

A faint smile curved Malcolm's mouth. "I've a less . . . violent . . . suggestion, my lord."

"Ah, excellent."

"Choose a suitable mistress to squire about on your arm, be seen in public with her, dote on her, if you will, so that none will be able to say your tastes run . . . elsewhere."

Julian recoiled. "Out of the question. I've no desire for a mistress. I've enough unwanted baggage at the moment and no inclination to embroil myself in another tangle."

"It needn't be a permanent arrangement." Malcolm held his gaze, and there was a hint of pleading in his eyes that was absent from his careful words. "A demi-rep, perhaps, someone who would never expect or desire anything but temporary ease of finances. Such females come with very few entanglements."

"Tell that to Prinny." His remark wrung a faint smile from

Malcolm, as it was intended to do, for after all, the Regent was known to have abysmal discretion when it came to choosing a suitable paramour or love interest. Or wife. It was appalling that he had the latter in common with the prince.

He turned abruptly, and stepped out from behind the massive oak-and-brass desk that had been his father's at one time. "Actually, it's not an unreasonable suggestion," he said, and saw the light leap in Malcolm's eyes. "While I've no intention of allowing myself to be blackmailed into acting against my own wishes, neither do I intend to allow the perpetrators of such vicious rumors to succeed in maligning an innocent man. That would be you, Malcom. You should not suffer for my cause. You've been a good and loyal employee, and one that I respect. If this would ease you and end the speculation concerning my carnal preferences, it seems a harmless enough thing to do. Am I to understand that you have a prospect in mind for me?"

Malcolm flashed him a startled glance, and his pale skin reddened. "Indeed, my lord. I've been privy to certain . . . facts . . . in my endeavors in the city."

"No doubt." Julian regarded him with amusement.

"I've been told the, uh, young ladies are very discreet, my lord."

"Not a worry, as I have no intention of being intimate with females who find it advisable to barter their bodies for profit. In retrospect," he mused aloud, "that would entail every female now living, as that seems to be their primary goal in life. A pity. It would be refreshing indeed to meet an honest woman, as unlikely as that may be. Still, I foolishly hope."

Too many men had made the mistake of trusting unwisely, revealing military secrets to courtesans, and even selling army commissions to appease a cajoling mistress. There had been a great furor when the Duke of York had allowed Mrs. Clarke to wheedle commissions from him in their bed, marring an otherwise excellent military career. Ridiculous. He'd never be so foolish, and not only because of his position. His enemies sought to bring him down by any means at their disposal, and he'd be damned if he'd stand idly by and allow it.

Those who sought his destruction would learn their mistake too late.

Angry shouts backstage nearly drowned out the unruly crowd still in the theater. Roscoe Throgmorton's face was beet-red and his jowls shook with rage.

"Are you daft? Do you know who you've just insulted?"

Laura regarded him steadily, unflinching in the face of his anger. "Yes, I know very well who he is—a drunken pig who has no business backstage, let alone hiding in my dressing room!"

Still shaken, she refused to let him see her distress. Behind Throgmorton, a bleeding baron lay draped over a stack of crates, nursing his head and shouting expletives that made her shudder.

"He's Lord Emory, you brainless baggage!" Roscoe snarled.

Her eyes narrowed ominously. "He assaulted me. Is this a theater, or a bagnio, that you let any drunken lout commit crimes against your players?"

Throgmorton swelled up dangerously, his face purpling as he sputtered incoherently, and she shook her head. "I did nothing to invite his advances, nor did he have the courtesy or restraint to even inquire as to my interest. He leaped at me from behind that screen when I was changing costumes and wearing nothing but my chemise."

"You nearly killed him," Roscoe got out in a strangled gasp.

"Nonsense. I hit him with a jar of powder. He should be grateful there was nothing heavy to hand, or as frightened as I was, I would no doubt have skewered him with one of the props."

Her gaze moved past Roscoe to the baron, still shrieking curses and batting at those who tried to help him. Pompous ass. He'd terrified her, leaping out at her like a cutthroat from behind the ratty old screen being stored. She'd caught only a glimpse of him in the mirror as he came at her with outstretched hands, crowing, "I've got you now, my girl!" It had been enough to send fear surging through her so that she'd reacted on instinct. Now he was covered with a liberal dose of white face powder that contrasted nicely with the bright red flow of blood from a cut on his forehead. He resembled Grimaldi, she thought, the clown who painted his face in red and white.

Still opening and closing his mouth like a landed fish, Roscoe gaped at her, then seemed to collapse like wet sugar cake. "We're ruined," he moaned, "ruined! You stupid, stupid girl—Lord Emory is our major patron."

Laura drew in a deep breath. *Disaster*. Roscoe nearly sobbed as he plopped onto a three-legged stool in front of the dressing table. She stood uncertainly.

It was a relief when Celia pushed her way toward them, assessing the situation with a single glance. Her lovely mouth thinned into a taut line.

"Stop carrying on like a fishwife, Roscoe," she said briskly. "I'll handle Emory. You'd best tend to the night's receipts. Asa has taken charge of the cash box."

That piece of information propelled Throgmorton to his feet in an instant. When he reached the door he paused, turned to look back at Laura, and said, "Never darken these doors again."

Laura exchanged glances with Celia as Roscoe stormed off. "Well, melodramatic but final, I suppose."

"Nonsense," Celia said briskly, and beckoned to the man behind her. "Do see what you can manage with Emory, my lord, while I soothe Roscoe's temper."

Charles, Lord Belgrave, leaned lazily in the doorway with a big grin on his rather pudgy face. "I detect dissension."

"As always, my lord, you are perceptive. Lord Emory seems to have met with a mishap and needs assistance. And a lesson in comportment. He assaulted this young lady."

"Did he now." Belgrave gazed at Laura with interest, and

she was suddenly aware that her gown was unfastened in places, having been hastily dragged over her head after Emory was repelled. She stared back at him coolly, unwilling to accept any blame. He smiled. "Then the fellow deserves a set-down for insulting such a lovely and talented lass. I shall see to him."

When he'd gone, moving to Emory and helping him to his feet, speaking to him in low tones, Celia smiled encouragingly at Laura. "There's a bottle of brandy in that chest, ducks. Help yourself, and I'll go soothe old Roscoe's ruffled feathers."

Laura nodded, but didn't really have much faith Celia could accomplish a miracle. Roscoe was furious with her. She'd seen it in his eyes, the frightened anger and sense of helplessness in knowing that his fate depended upon the patronage of powerful and wealthy men. She knew well enough how he felt, for she'd felt it herself far too often.

With a trembling hand, she found the brandy and poured a liberal amount in a cup. It was expensive stuff, coating her mouth and throat and slicking a fiery path to her stomach. Fortified, she finished dressing and put away the shepherdess costume and crook. She doubted she'd need it again.

It was much quieter in the theater now that the audience had departed. Stagehands and actors finished their duties and drifted away, leaving echoes in their wakes. Footsteps were loud, and she recognized the clack of Celia's heels on the scarred wooden floors as she returned to the dressing room.

"Well, ducks, Roscoe sees the sense in your defense against Emory, even if he isn't quite happy about it."

She looked up in amazement. "Then—"

"I suggested that his lordship would not want it known that he'd been bashed in the head by an actress. Of course, I also suggested that you have a much more powerful protector than Emory, who would be exceedingly displeased were you to be sacked, much less assaulted. It was the last that persuaded him, I think."

Laura laughed incredulously. "You are amazing!"

"Yes, so I've been told." Celia grinned impishly. "Now come, let's have a drink to our triumph over Roscoe and that nasty bit of work, Emory. Belgrave tells me he's a loutish fellow anyway. I've no doubt there are others who'd love to do what you did."

Laura's smile faded and she shuddered. "I've incurred the enmity of a powerful man, and I don't have a protector, unfortunately. No gallant knight to rescue me from the dragons."

Celia shrugged. "That can change quickly enough. While it's true the peerage make bad enemies, the trick is in knowing who to risk offending."

"So it seems." She took the cup of brandy Celia held out to her. Curving her fingers around the pewter bowl, she held it a moment, inhaling the potent fumes. "How do you decide that?"

"Learn all you can about them, who runs with who, who's engaged in a feud, and most importantly, who's related to who. They're all related in one way or another, it seems, either by marriage or blood. One has to be careful not to speak unwisely. It can be fatal to aspirations."

"How do you do it," Laura asked suddenly, letting the brandy soothe her frayed nerves, "how do you fit in so well with them? You weren't brought up in Mayfair, yet you converse so easily."

Celia raised a brow, hesitating, then smiled slightly. "I was apprenticed at the age of six to the household of a certain earl. I started in the kitchens, and worked my way up. I paid attention, I listened when I cleaned bedrooms, I watched what the ladies wore, I practiced the way they spoke. I taught myself to read well enough to be able to read the society pages. The world of household service is intricate, and just as brutal and strict as the stews. One doesn't step over a certain line. I was bright, and fortunate enough to have a way with me. By fifteen, I was warming the earl's bed."

"Fifteen." *The same age I was when my world changed so drastically . . .*

"He taught me a lot. He was kind and generous, and when I left, he settled a nice purse on me." Celia tipped her head to the side, gazing shrewdly at Laura. "You may live now in St. Giles, but I'll warrant you spent your childhood in a soft bed with clean sheets. And I'll wager that you are running from a man."

Startled, she nodded before she caught herself. It wasn't a tale she'd shared with anyone. It wasn't something she wanted to remember. Not now. Not until she was safely home.

"A husband?" Celia guessed, and Laura shook her head. "Ah. A determined suitor. Or perhaps even a ruthless pursuer." It was so close to the truth that Laura began to tremble, and Celia knelt beside her, a hand resting on her arm. "It's all right."

"No, no, it's not all right. It may . . . never be." She looked up, sucked in a deep breath, and forced a shaky smile. "I know that you've made the best of what life gave you, and I admire you for it. You're smart and beautiful and brave. I'm not. I'm . . . afraid."

Celia laughed softly. "Oh aye, afraid enough to douse Lord Emory with a jar of face powder! You could enlist in the Royal Guard."

Laura met her eyes. "He threatened me. I reacted instinctively. If I'd had time to think, I may well have just run from him."

"And that's not always a bad thing either. Flight has saved my bacon on more than one occasion. Here now. You don't have to tell me anything. If ever you want to talk, you know I'm not going to judge you."

Suddenly it seemed all right, and the burden of keeping her shameful secret seemed lighter and less shocking. "I know. You may be the one person who truly understands. It's just that I've lived with it for two years—no, more than that. Seven. I just didn't realize at first . . ." Her voice trailed off as images flashed into her mind, seen from an adolescent's viewpoint at first, then from that of a young woman, the shock and shame and fear and ever-present yearning for a life that had disappeared. A life that had been an illusion.

Celia was quiet, sipping her brandy, patiently waiting, and it all came pouring out then, as Laura's words tumbled into disjointed sentences that betrayed her pain. "Since I was born I'd heard of Paris, what a lovely city it was, and how she—my mother—wanted me to live with her there. Then Papa died. Virginia was so far away, and I was only five, and with my father dead, Maman no longer wanted to stay in the colonies. I think my grandparents were relieved. She was different. So beautiful, but . . . restless. Being away, I understand now how homesick she must have been for her own country, the life she'd always led. So she went back. When my grandparents died, I joined Maman in Paris. Then—I came to London because I didn't want to live that way."

"Live in what way?" Celia prompted, and Laura's face burned at the memory.

"Maman . . . it seemed so exciting at first, the lovely *maison,* the elegant balls, and silks and satins and jewels . . . I thought her life was so perfect. And then . . . then I learned that the man I first thought was her husband was—not. My maman was a courtesan, lovely and desirable, and for sale to the highest bidder. It was—a shock. But not as shocking as the comte's suggestion that his son be my protector." She looked at Celia, who nodded understanding. "I was brought up by my grandparents after Maman went back to France, and we lived simply if comfortably. I suppose I was naïve. It was so unexpected. And Maman—"

"She thought you should agree," Celia said after a moment of silence, and Laura bent her head to stare at her empty cup.

"Yes. She was surprised at first that I refused, then she became angry. She said I was an ungrateful chit, that I was near twenty and should know by now how the world worked."

"And did you?"

"It was a swift education. The comte's son came for a visit, and he . . . he was worse than ever I thought a man could be, arrogant and cruel." She shuddered at the memory.

"Why fight it, little pigeon? You'll be like your mother, a whore. Women like you always end up as some man's pleasant diversion."

Celia's fingers tightened over her hand. "He forced you."

"Oh no. But he would have. He . . . tried." She'd never told anyone about the night she fled Paris, wishing she could put it from her mind. "Maman and the Comte had gone to a grand fête in Napoleon's honor—it was just before he left for that disastrous march in Russia. Everyone was so gay and excited. By then, I was so unhappy. War was imminent between England and America, and I wanted to go home . . . it wouldn't be the same, of course, for my grandparents are dead and my uncle inherited the estate, but it's familiar. I was so restless that night, and went down to the library to find a book. It was late . . . lamps were low and the servants asleep in the garret." She twisted her fingers around the cup, gripping it tightly. "Then . . . he was *there*. In the library, staring at me with such a smile I knew he'd been sent. Oh God, it was terrifying. He came toward me, saying all these things—when he got too close I struck him with the book. It must have taken him by surprise, for I was able to get away. I hid in the larder, behind a stack of cheeses." Unwilling laughter rose in her throat. "I smelled like cheese for days afterward."

Celia stared at her sympathetically, smiling. "Did he find you?"

"No. But he was furious. I heard him, swearing, saying that Maman had the good sense to know what was best for me, that I'd never escape what I was. . . ."

"What a cod's head," Celia snapped. "Did your mother turn you out for it?"

"I never gave her the opportunity. When he finally left, I packed a valise and left as well."

"How did you manage without coin?"

"I had a little, and sold my jewelry, but it wasn't enough for passage to America. And then war was declared, and passage became even more dear." Naïve and alone, she'd quickly learned a valuable lesson on survival. "If not for a troupe of players leaving Paris for London, I may well have ended up with the comte's son," she reflected. "I fell in with them one rainy night at a café, and one of them saw my plight and gave me a post as her understudy. She said I have talent, but apparently, it's largely unnoticed."

Celia shook her head. "You do have talent, but it's plain to see your heart isn't in it. Listen to me, Laura. Men notice you. What brought Emory backstage is not your role as a naïve young shepherdess, but your beauty. You can make that work for you, take you far beyond the stage. Pretty girls are common enough in London, but you have a quality about you that's different. A dignity, and . . . presence."

Laura thought of the stage manager who'd told her she lacked presence, and smiled. "You seem to be alone in that opinion, I fear."

"Am I? I don't think so. Emory didn't think so. And Belgrave doesn't think so. He said you are a prime article. You're no longer in Paris. Here, you can have your pick of protectors, men who will cosset you and keep you well. I have clean sheets and an abundance of good, white bread if I like. Belgrave is very good to me, and he passes the time pleasantly. If I wished, I could leave the stage, but I like being here. I don't have to be here. I name my own terms in life now. There's a difference."

Yes. There would be a vast difference. Weariness settled over Laura, the past years of dire circumstances weighing her down like a heavy stone. Constant struggle for survival left her numb most of the time, save for those moments of utter despair. Even hope had begun to dim, her faith that she would be able to return home slowly fading into bleak inevitability.

"I would be what Maman is," she murmured, "what I fled in Paris. I'm twenty-two, and I have held onto my virtue all these years not just for my future husband, but for my own sake. It's been a matter of pride. Of honor. I've resisted offers, kept to myself and not encouraged any man because I knew that one day I'd go home again. How can I go home if I've compromised my own principles?"

"How can you go home if you die of hunger in the stews?"

Celia said brutally. "There are always choices, Laura. It takes courage to live."

Lifting her eyes, Laura searched Celia's fresh, lovely face, the honest blue eyes so open and shrewd, for all that she looked a brainless bit of muslin. It was part of her masquerade. Celia was the consummate actress offstage as well as on.

"If I were to . . . choose . . . a protector, how would I find one suitable?"

Celia smiled reassurance. "Just leave everything to me, ducks."

"Milk or lemon?"

"Milk, *s'il vous plaît.*" Laura watched Mme. Devereaux pour cream into a delicate teacup, her movements graceful and assured. The exquisite china rattled slightly as she accepted it, steam curling up. "*Merci,*" she murmured.

Mme. Devereaux beamed at her. "I find it delightful," she said in her elegant English, "that you are French, is it not so? English gentlemen dote on beautiful Frenchwomen, despite the recent war. Such an unpleasant business, that, but hopefully it is over."

"I am only half-French, madame. My father was born in the Colonies of English parents."

Dismissing Laura's unfortunate Colonial ancestry with an airy wave of one hand, Mme. Devereaux leaned forward. "That is of no consequence. For our purposes, you shall be very French, *n'est-ce pas?*" She was a tiny woman with artfully arranged pale hair and bright, shrewd eyes that she fixed on this newest prospect. "Celia has told you, has she not, of our arrangements?"

Laura slid a glance toward Celia, sitting in a Hepplewhite chair next to the settee, her tea balanced on her lap as she nodded encouragement.

"*Oui,* madame," Laura murmured.

"Excellent. It is most important that you understand my

goal. I provide discreet, beautiful, and intelligent companions to certain members of the *ton* who pass my stringent inspection. All must come with a strong recommendation from their peers. And, of course, from the Bank of England." She smiled when Laura shot her a startled glance. "One must be practical. I offer a valuable service to influential men, and cannot risk their displeasure. Therefore, I also require that the ladies who attend my functions behave impeccably and adhere to my rules. I succeed because I do not countenance infractions."

A nervous tremor rattled Laura's teacup in the saucer, and she set it carefully in her lap. "Yes, madame."

"Delightful. Your accent is charming, soft and rich, a little husky so that a man has to lean close to you to listen. That, of course, is very desirable. And your hair—such lovely curls the color of fine brandy. Flawless skin, and eyes like emeralds . . . yes, you will find a protector very quickly." There was a brief, delicate pause before she asked, "Are you still a virgin?"

Laura spilled her tea, and recovered while she dabbed at her skirt with the napkin Mme. Devereaux tactfully provided.

"It is necessary to ask, you understand, Mademoiselle Lancaster. I must know all."

"Yes, I understand, of course. I've not . . . I mean . . . yes."

"*Bon!*" She smiled reassuringly. "That is most excellent. It is a valuable asset. Gentlemen all wish to be the first. They will swarm to you . . . we shall call you Laurette. Is that agreeable?"

Confused, she didn't know quite what to say, and Celia chimed in. "A lovely name. Easy enough to answer to, I think, not like mine. It took me several weeks to adjust to Celia Carteret, but now I can barely recall when I used to be Maggie Buttons."

"When we take on new names, we take on a new life," Mme. Devereaux agreed. "It is so much easier then. Now Laurette, I must take you at once to my modiste for new garments. I think a willow green silk with the new shorter waist and flared skirts. No ruffles, though perhaps a delicate gold embroidery . . ."

A little dazed, Laura sat quietly for a moment. An ormolu clock on the mantel ticked away several minutes while she considered her options. Coal hissed heat in the grate, warming the small sitting room furnished simply and elegantly. There was nothing at all crude about Mme. Devereaux, and she was not at all what Laura had envisioned.

As if reading her thoughts, Mme. Devereaux smiled. "My father was a marquis, my mother the daughter of a comte. They were killed in the Terror, and I barely escaped with my life. I am an exile from my homeland. Now England is my home. One must learn to adapt to circumstances. So, *ma petite,* what shall you do?"

Celia nibbled at the edges of a brioche with tiny, delicate bites, nodding when Laura looked at her indecisively. "I predict you will have men fighting duels in Hyde Park before long. You are lovely, and a virgin. I admit, I had not thought it. As for a gown, madame, I think white muslin, or a rich white velvet to signify her purity."

Mme. Devereaux clapped her hands in delight. "Of course! With tiny white roses and thin ribbons wound in her hair . . . a Grecian goddess."

While Celia and Mme. Devereaux discussed what she would wear, Laura sat numbly, her hands knotting the linen napkin in her lap. She'd not yet voiced her agreement, though it seemed understood that she would. These past two years since she'd fled Paris, all for naught. What did it matter if she gave herself to the Comte's son or to a stranger? The result would be the same. She would be a whore like her mother, just as Aubert Fortier had said. *Oh God. . . .*

Closing her eyes, she let it all wash over her, the wasted effort, the flight, the fear, the long struggle against fate. She'd been foolish to think she could escape it.

CHAPTER 3

"Lord Lockwood, it is a pleasure to meet you."

"And you, madame." Julian bowed easily over her proffered hand, hiding his impatience to have the evening behind him. He must be mad to even consider attending this thing. Worse, he'd actually agreed to such lunacy. No doubt, they'd soon find him baying at the moon and slavering in the garden. He had no desire to be at what was essentially a Cyprian's ball, a soirée given by Mme. Devereaux to procure wealthy protectors for her Fashionable Impures.

It was a personal distaste that made him avoid such affairs, for he detested being used or allowing others to be used. He'd had mistresses before his marriage, but under very different circumstances. A mutual understanding between consenting adults, a heady flirtation that ended in bed. That was what he preferred. Malcolm's insistence that he attend Mme. Devereaux's soirée was the only reason he was here.

He'd been assured by Malcolm it would be pleasant and discreet. It was not. There was nothing pleasant about young ladies arrayed like so many porcelain statues about the large room, like wares for sale at a market, and discretion vanished the moment he recognized Lord Sartain in deep conversation with a young woman who looked the age of one of his own daughters.

The urge to depart was diverted by Mme. Devereaux's tactful summons of a butler bearing a tray. "I believe you prefer brandy, my lord," she said, and he didn't ask how she knew that. Malcolm again, no doubt. The secretary was thorough.

He looked down at Mme. Devereaux with slightly narrowed eyes. She dressed stylishly but discreetly, an older woman probably in her early forties, but it was difficult to tell these days. So many women hid their age well, but Mme. Devereaux's elegant bone structure gave her a timeless beauty. Only about the eyes did she show her age, faint lines fanned out as if she laughed a great deal.

"It seems to me that you prefer a more discreet atmosphere, my lord," she said, her English tinged with a French accent. "Am I correct?"

"You are very wise, madame."

She smiled acknowledgment. "There is genteel music in the drawing room that you might appreciate."

There was no mention of the reason he was there, only her subtle guidance to a drawing room papered in pale yellow, with potted plants by long windows, and musicians on a dais at the front of the room. Soft lighting illuminated stuffed chairs and small settees, and several young women chatted quietly together. A young baronet he recognized from White's was deep in earnest conversation with a petite brunette who seemed to hang upon his every word. Even from a distance, it was evident the baronet had been imbibing freely of refreshments. A green pup, with no head for drink.

He began to relax slightly. Malcolm was right. Mme. Devereaux was very discreet, even if he didn't find it particularly pleasant to be here. But he'd never been one to shirk unpleasant duty or responsibility, and he had no intention of allowing vicious rumor to impair his effectiveness or injure his secretary.

Violins sobbed a haunting tune by Haydn as another gentleman entered the drawing room, moving directly to a smiling young woman who detached herself from the others to greet him. It could almost have been any home in Mayfair with a night of polite entertainment. There was none of the expected bawdiness or coarseness, and these fair women were garbed enticingly but not brazenly.

Malcolm rarely erred, and this seemed to be no exception. He turned to speak to Mme. Devereaux, but she had disappeared, leaving him to his own discretion. A wry smile tugged at his mouth. This was hardly his first visit to a School of Venus, as they were often called, but certainly the most surprising.

Sipping brandy, his gaze shifted back to the women across the room. Ah, here was a notable difference from polite society, for they did not look away or pretend a modest indifference, nor was there a chaperon hovering protectively over them. Instead, as his eyes moved over each one, a smile was offered, some coy, some sultry, all inviting. There was something to be said for eliminating the uncertainty, but he'd always been a man who enjoyed the chase and seduction as much as the eventual surrender.

Not that it mattered. He was not here to be titillated, he was here to choose a mistress to establish in a house. It would have to be a woman he could tolerate, for he would of necessity spend a certain amount of time with her or the subterfuge would be for naught. What, he thought as he sipped his brandy, would Eleanor say when she learned of it? No doubt, she'd be shocked, then furious. She'd never appreciated sharing any man's attention, and rather smugly considered her husband to be far too chagrined by her behavior to retaliate in kind.

The violins had stopped and someone played a pianoforte. He glanced toward the dais, his brows lifting in surprise. A young woman with glorious deep red hair entwined with white roses and ribbons sat on the bench, graceful fingers flying over the keys. She seemed absorbed in the melody, though two gentlemen hovered about her like eager puppies. They elbowed for space and gave one another harsh looks, but the woman ignored them.

Intrigued, he moved closer. She was exquisite. Where did Mme. Devereaux find young women like this?

"Impeccable manners and negotiable morals," Malcolm had promised, and he smiled at the apt description.

Looking up as he smiled, the woman's gaze met his, and he was startled at her immediate smile in return. Green eyes fringed by dark lashes widened slightly as she stared at him, but her fingers never faltered. His gaze dropped to her mouth, her lips still curved, lush and sensuous, yet the gown she wore bordered on demure. White muslin embroidered in gold thread skimmed her slender frame but couldn't hide the gentle swell of her breasts. Short sleeves left shapely arms bare, and a gauzy shawl looped gracefully from her arms to drape at the small of her back. She looked . . . virginal. Pure. A Cyprian goddess. He blinked.

Then one of the young men hovering over her leaned close, and her attention shifted to him, though the smile faded. Julian took another sip of brandy, leaning against a faux marble pillar flanked by potted palms. A surprise, to find a woman here who actually seemed out of place.

"Good evening," a soft voice said at his side, and he straightened, turning to the willowy blonde who smiled up at him. "She plays well, doesn't she?"

"Yes, she does."

"My name is Sophia. Shall I fetch you another brandy?"

A faint scent wafted from her, not unpleasant but musky, and her smile was wide but not genuine. There was a brittle quality to her, and a sense of boredom that she could not disguise.

"Yes," he said so she would leave, but she beckoned to a uniformed servant who approached with a tray. Reaching out, she plucked a crystal glass from the tray and held it out.

"For your pleasure, my lord." When she'd placed his empty brandy glass back on the tray and the servant faded away, she tilted her head to one side to smile up at him, blue eyes rather hard. "This is your first visit here. How do you find the . . . entertainment?"

"Discreet."

Her brow shot up in amusement. "Madame would allow nothing less."

"No, I can imagine that she would not. She seems formidable."

Sophia laughed, the sound abrasively loud. "Madame is indeed formidable. But so, I'll wager, are you." Her lashes lowered, then lifted again flirtatiously, her eyes bolder now.

This was more expected, the woman's innate coarseness surfacing through the facade no doubt carefully created and coached by Mme. Devereaux.

"Yes," he said, "I've been said to be formidable. Excuse me."

He moved away from her, and found himself closer to the dais and the exquisite creature now surrounded by no fewer than four gentlemen. The two younger ones were outranked by the age and title of the newest admirers, and it made them louder and more determined. Beethoven's Sonata for violin and piano continued despite the jostling around her. She seemed composed and unperturbed if one didn't notice her eyes, the quiver of long lashes betraying distress.

Fascinating. A melodrama of sorts.

Apparently desperate, the young baronet hovering over her reached down to grasp her arm and lift her from the bench. The music stopped abruptly. She did not withdraw her arm, but she did not respond to his entreaties, either, eying him with what seemed to be genuine distress. Not at all the correct response for a demi-monde, Julian mused. She should be simpering and smiling, not resembling a frightened doe.

One of the other men protested, but the baronet steered his prize toward a secluded corner off the dais, half-hidden from view by a length of drapery and a potted palm. The three thwarted men on the dais glared in that direction for a moment, then abandoned the dais for the company of more available prospects.

Amused, Julian thought it excellent theater. Mme. Devereaux should be commended for her masterful tutoring in the seductive arts. It had certainly succeeded in enticing the baronet, and he wondered if Stokely's father would appreciate his heir's patronage of such an establishment. It was unlikely, unless the elder Stokely had altered his personality a great deal. He remembered him as a staunch Reformer and an annoying dissenter. Of course, his own admission to Mme. Devereaux's "soirée" had required an oath not to divulge names of any he recognized. Not that he was inclined to admit his own presence.

A sudden oath rent the air, shattering the subdued conversation and muted melody of the violins, and Julian turned in time to see Stokely stumble backward from the alcove. He held a hand to his cheek, and anger resonated in his voice.

"You teasing bitch!"

Without realizing it, Julian was only three feet from him by the time Stokely lunged for the woman trying to avoid him.

"A bit strong, Stokely," he said, and grasped the young man's collar firmly. His fingers dug deeply into his shoulder when the baronet attempted to pull away. "Very unwise of you to be bad-tempered."

"The doxy slapped me!" Outrage thickened his voice as he glared at the woman. "As if she thinks she's a diamond of the first water instead of a—"

"I'd watch my language were I you," Julian warned softly, and something in his tone earned Stokely's abrupt silence. "Since there seems to be a misunderstanding, I suggest you take yourself off to a woman more appreciative of your advances. You appear to have done some damage to this one."

It was true. A strip of embroidered gilt on her bodice hung by several threads, and a mark reddened on the pale white skin of her throat and breasts. Clumsy pup. He must have grabbed at her like an unlicked cub, pawing exquisite flesh instead of caressing it.

For a moment, it seemed that Stokely would refuse; then he gave the woman a final glare and wheeled away, stalking across the drawing room and out the door. Julian turned his attention back to the young woman, but she wouldn't meet his eyes. A flush stained her cheeks, and she shook her head, dislodging a curl that dangled becomingly over her forehead.

"My apologies, sir, for such a scene. I . . . oh, I apologize."

"No need. It's Stokely who should apologize, the impatient whelp." He thought she might look up at him then, but she kept her face averted and edged away from him, the draperies behind her shifting in a whisper of heavy gold velvet. It struck him more strongly that she seemed out of place here, that her actions were not those of a woman accustomed to dalliance with the peers of London society. There was an elusive quality in her voice, a soft drawl that was alluring and vaguely familiar. Where had he heard that accent before? Those peculiarly rich inflections that made each word seem intriguing?

Curious, he wanted her to speak again, and smiled encouragingly. "Are you harmed?"

She shook her head, and the carefully pinned riot of curls on her crown quivered. Tiny white roses were tucked cleverly into the cluster, and creamy ribbons vied with soft tendrils on each side of her face, framing her exquisite features.

Still easing away from him, she made him think of a graceful deer poised for flight, nervous and quivering with fear. It contradicted what he'd surmised about Mme. Devereaux. Madame was no Covent Garden abbess, abducting helpless young girls and forcing them to prostitution. No, he knew that was not her style. Yet this young woman seemed terrified.

Before he could form another question, Mme. Devereaux appeared at his elbow, her eyes sharply assessing her protégée. "Laurette, come with me, *s'il vous plaît*. My apologies, my lord, if you have been witness to some unpleasantness. It happens on occasion, though we strive to avoid it."

"Apologies are unnecessary, madame."

He didn't interfere, but watched silently as the young woman called Laurette was escorted across the drawing room. Her words floated back to him, sounding plaintive and desperate.

"I'm sorry, madame," he heard her say in French. "I just cannot do this. I cannot!"

His brow rose. Strange, indeed. Mme. Devereaux spoke soothingly, but Laurette shook her head so violently one of the white roses fell from her curls to the floor. It lay abandoned on the textured design of a Persian carpet as the two women passed from the drawing room, and Julian found himself drawn to retrieve it.

Holding it in his hand, the velvety soft petals exquisitely formed by a talented modiste, he inhaled the subtle fragrance of rose water, suitably alluring. There was something quaint about a courtesan who used such an old-fashioned scent instead of one of the stronger, more popular blends of orange blossoms, frankincense, and cloves. Most extraordinary.

Cynicism dictated that he disbelieve what had most likely been a contrived and convincing performance by a demimonde with a talent for play-acting. A masquerade, no doubt for the benefit of any man green enough to be fooled by it.

Closing his hand over the fabric rose, he pivoted abruptly and strode from the drawing room to call for his coach to be brought round. There must be another solution to his problem, for this sort of farce could not be tolerated.

"*Non, non, monsieur,* you must not!" Laura pulled away from the too-eager hands of the drunken marquis leaning over her and leering. Her head throbbed with tension. She hadn't allowed Mme. Devereaux to coax her into remaining, and not even the practical reminder that it would take only one assignation to assure her passage to America had swayed her. Now this foul-breathed lord had followed her flight from the house, cornering her near an alley.

Fear knifed through her more keenly than the cold wind as the marquis gave a harsh bark of laughter. "Stupid chit, I saw you inside. I know what you are. This is nothing new to you, no matter what madame may say. It's not as if I won't reward you for your favors, so stop playing coy, my cunning little jade."

"*No*," Laura said, abandoning any pretense in her desperation to escape him, "I am not what you think—"

His hand closed on her throat, squeezing lightly to cut off her protests. Leaning against her, his weight cumbersome and heavy, he laughed softly. The stench of unwashed body and stale wine washed over her, and she turned her face away, bile rising in her throat. Her back pressed painfully against the brick wall, with escape impossible. Street lamps shed a soft glow that seemed reluctant to enter the alley where the marquis had cornered her, small pools of light appearing like dots before her eyes as she struggled for air. So this is how it was to end, in the squalor and fetid shadows, while a member of the peerage unbuttoned his breeches to take her virginity. . . .

Then, abruptly, she was able to breathe. Choking and gasping, the thundering rush of air and blood to her starved lungs and brain drowned out the words exchanged by the two men, but she recognized the fair-haired earl from the drawing room who had come to her rescue with young Stokely. She closed her eyes and leaned weakly against the wall, but her legs would no longer support her and she felt herself sliding slowly downward.

Shame scalded her. She'd fled before a carriage could be called for her, humiliated by her cowardice and the knowing stares from men assessing her as if she were no more than a prize mare to be bought and mounted. Galling, that she had yielded to temptation, and even more galling that the bitter disappointment she felt was more for the loss of funds than her compromised morals. What a fraud she was, and Mme. Devereaux had known it.

"Return," she had urged her softly, "for you have snared the attention of Lord Lockwood. He is no paltry baronet, but an earl, *ma petite*, and you will gain your heart's desire and enjoy the company of a handsome peer of the realm. It is the answer to everything—do not be foolish!"

But she had not, the memory of the baronet's hand on her breast too vivid and shameful. Sighing with regret and impatience, Mme. Devereaux had said sharply that she would give her one more opportunity to reconsider, that a lone woman in London had few options and she'd rue it if she allowed this golden chance to pass. It had been prophetic, it seemed.

Now she slumped in the filth of an alley while two men fought over her like the rats she'd seen fighting over scraps of food. It was over quickly, the battle one of harsh words and not swords, and Lockwood returned to her as the marquis scurried angrily away.

He put out a hand to help her to her feet, and after a brief hesitation, she laid her fingers in his warm, broad palm. He wore no gloves despite the cold night, and his head was bare, golden hair a muted gleam in the weak light behind him.

"Did he hurt you, mademoiselle?" he asked politely, and she shook her head though it gave an unpleasant throb at the motion.

"No. Just my pride."

"You'll have bruises in the morning," he said, eying her throat, and she looked down to see the lovely white muslin was soiled and torn, a flap of embroidered bodice dangling and leaving nearly bare her left breast. Before she could, he'd reached out to tuck up the torn material, and the brush of his fingers against her cold skin was warm and reassuring. "Have you lost your cloak?"

"I . . . I forgot it." Shaking with cold and reaction and the looming regard of the earl, she fought a wave of tears. No use weeping now. "You have my gratitude, my lord," she said before he could speak again.

"No doubt. I confess, I rather enjoyed it. I've often longed to see Whitfield speechless with rage, and at last have realized a dream. Here now, watch your step. Have you transportation to your lodgings?"

The thought of returning to Mme. Devereaux made her shudder, and once again before she could reply he said, "I'll summon a hack. No, do not refuse. Whitfield and Stokely must have left you with a distasteful impression of the British peerage."

She stole a glance up at him. They'd reached the fitful light of the street lamps. His face was softly illuminated, all stark angles and planes, strong and resolute. Despite the cynicism of his comments, he'd come to her rescue twice in the space of an hour. And he requested nothing from her. His hand on her elbow was courteous, and the brief brush of his fingers against her breast had been only to repair her modesty. Yet he'd been in attendance at Mme. Devereaux's, so obviously had come with the intention of choosing a companion. A contradiction, this Lockwood, and very intriguing.

True to his word, he summoned a hack and assisted her inside, instructing the driver to take her where she indicated. He pressed a coin into the driver's hand, then he stepped back, his gaze cool and assessing. "*Bonne nuit, mademoiselle.*"

The hack lurched forward, and when she glanced out the open window, Lockwood was gone. Oh yes, a very intriguing man.

CHAPTER 4

"Roses . . . in winter!"

Laura gazed at the creamy white flowers with an emotion akin to awe. Delicate buds and gracefully opening blossoms nodded in a sleek vase on the dressing room table, reflected in the wavering glass of the mirror behind them like a double bouquet. Celia moved closer, then leaned to breathe in the heady fragrance that seemed to fill the tiny, dank dressing room.

"These cost a bloody fortune. Roses in winter come dear. Who sent them, ducks?"

Shaking her head, Laura said, "There was no card, and the footman was gone by the time I arrived. Jeremy saw him, and said he wore green-and-gold livery."

"Ah. A conquest from the soirée. That's heartening."

Laura didn't reply. Celia had been stricken to learn the events of that night a week before. Mme. Devereaux had sent around a messenger to deliver several cards from gentlemen who'd met her that night, but none of them was from Lord Lockwood. Not that she'd expected him to contact her in any way, for he'd been coolly polite and distant, kind to a distraught courtesan. And he'd never connect that courtesan with a little-known actress.

Reaching out, she touched the velvety furring of a rose petal, soft and snowy, with a hint of pink in the center, a delicate shading. So lovely, so fragrant. If she closed her eyes, she could smell the roses that grew in Longacre's garden, feel the warmth of the Virginia sun on her face, and hear her grandmother's lilting voice singing a merry melody. A lovely, pleasant dream of time long gone now.

Celia leaned back against the dressing table, a brow arched. "Madame extended an offer for your return, ducks. Your situation has not changed. What do you intend?"

Drawing in a deep breath, she looked up. "I cannot return. It was . . . humiliating. I wish I could be more like you, Celia, but I'm not. You're . . . courageous. Smart. Resourceful."

"You underestimate your talents, Laura. Madame tells me you charmed several lords that night, even the notoriously elusive Lockwood."

"Elusive?" That didn't seem like the same man, but Celia was nodding.

"Elusive as the devil in a vicar's parlor. His wife's off in Europe creating scandals, and he's said to be devastated. Of course, there's also a rumor that he prefers his secretary to feminine company, but if that's true, he wouldn't be at Mme. Devereaux's soirée."

"No," Laura agreed faintly, "he wouldn't." She tried to reconcile the man she'd met with a man devastated by his wife's infidelity, and couldn't imagine any woman foolish enough to betray him. That must be another vicious rumor.

"Laura, I don't think you realize how valuable you are." When her head snapped around to stare at Celia, she continued in a rush, "You offended a baronet, but had four other lords dangling after you. Stokely is no one. Ffft! Lockwood, however, is—"

"Married."

Celia sighed. "Yes, and you do recall that I told you the married men are always better than young, randy bucks, don't you?"

A weak smile curved her mouth and she nodded, but Laura felt hot and cold at the same time when she thought of Lockwood in that way. Ridiculous, yet it might not be as unpleasant if he were the one to touch her.

Jeremy rapped sharply on the door and stuck his head inside, grinning at them. "Nearly time, me loves. The rabble is restless tonight. Sherman was pelted with apples when he missed his cue, and his wig fell into the pit."

Unperturbed, Celia adjusted the fichu and frills of her satin gown. "Sherman is a farce at any time. He never remembers his lines. Too bad he didn't go into the pit along with his wig."

Laura glanced at the mirror to assure herself the shepherdess costume was fully hooked, and the lovely white roses nodded slightly as if in approval. Smiling, she followed Celia out the door.

The theater had been renovated years ago, so that the audience was now confined only to the auditorium, removing them a bit from the players but not curbing their critical tendencies and accurate aim. Perhaps Drury Lane or the Royal Theater had a more sedate audience, but those who attended these productions were a rowdier crowd. A small budget didn't allow for many dioramic scenes, but what the play lacked in sets and costume, it made up for in energy and cheek. It felt good to stroll onto the stage with the lamb under her arm, her lines really no more than a wink and a nod to the audience that always reacted with laughter and hoots. Hers was a small role and her lines few, but she never failed to earn enthusiastic applause. It was a welcome change from the last play, where she'd portrayed a witch.

When her last scene was finished, she faded into the wings with the lamb tucked under her arm; it had bleated so loudly she'd had to shout to be heard over it. "You'll be mutton stew if you don't learn better manners," she scolded the wriggling beast as she put it in the small pen and fed it a bit of hay, then as a treat, a piece of bruised apple from Sherman's pelting. Patting the woolly head, she turned away to go to her dressing room, and came to an abrupt halt.

Leaning against the wall, arms crossed over his chest and a faint smile curving his mouth, Lord Lockwood watched her with a lifted brow. "It's my opinion the lamb is a better actor than the mutton-head who lost his wig."

Her heart thumped loudly, and she couldn't think of a response.

"Perhaps a similar threat might work best on him rather than the lamb," he added when she just stared at him. "Have I inconvenienced you, Miss Lancaster?"

Finding her tongue at last, she shook her head. "No, my lord, you just surprised me."

"Are you not accustomed to gentlemen at your dressing room door?"

"Perhaps, but certainly not a man of your consequence."

"Ah." He smiled.

"How . . . how did you know where to find me?" His brow shot up in obvious amusement and she flushed. "Of course. It would be simple for a man of your—"

"Consequence," he supplied helpfully when she halted, and she nodded, eyes narrowing at him. It didn't help that he made her so nervous, that in the light of bright lanterns, he was even more handsome than he'd been in the yellow drawing room. Strong light streaked his hair with gold and she saw now what she'd not seen in the shadows, that dark brown strands were woven through as if artfully painted. Strong eyebrows were also dark brown, but with sprinkles of gold dusted through, and his lashes were long and thick, tipped with gold on the ends. Amber eyes were flecked with gold as well, and gazing at her so steadily that she felt the urge to touch her face to see if soot marred her cheek.

"It was simple enough," he said, and one corner of his mouth tucked slightly inward to indicate his amusement. "I inquired of Mme. Devereaux."

"Oh."

"Pardon my impatience, mademoiselle, but is it necessary that we remain here in the wings with the livestock? There's rather a stench."

Heat flushed her cheeks, and she forced her feet to move. "Of course not. There's my dressing room—Celia's dressing room."

"Celia. The exquisite creature who swooned so magnificently in the third act. Very well. Carry on, if you will."

It was nerve-wracking to know he was right behind her, and she felt the heat of him even though he'd not touched her. Why did she feel so young and foolish in his presence? A green girl, that's how she felt, awkward and clumsy and unable to form proper sentences.

When they reached the dressing room, it was even worse. He filled it with his presence. It was disconcerting. Ducking, as the ceiling was low and he was so tall, he slouched against the wall and looked about him curiously.

"I've never been in an actor's dressing room before," he said. "Quite interesting."

Aware of the clothes strewn about and cosmetics cluttering the dressing table, Laura tried not to consider what he must truly be thinking. It looked a tip, with the garments she'd worn to the theater flung carelessly over the ratty screen against the wall, and powder coating the surface of the dressing table, and the glorious white roses spicing the air with sweet scent. The roses . . .

She gave him a sharp glance. He met her eyes coolly and crossed his arms over his chest. Dressed casually in buff breeches and knee-high black boots polished to a high sheen and fitting snugly to his calves, he looked every inch the elegant lord of reputation, an earl with a hereditary seat in Parliament, influential and above reproach. Save for the rumors that swirled about his wife.

He flicked an invisible speck of lint from the sleeve of his brown kerseymere coat and murmured, "I request the pleasure of your company at a small supper, Miss Lancaster. Would you be so good as to oblige me?"

She blinked. This man was no Emory, demanding and expecting her submission. Yet he was no less dangerous for the fact that he employed subtlety rather than crudeness.

"Supper, my lord?"

"Yes, it's a meal taken in the evening, usually consisting of several courses and some fine wine."

"I know what it is," she snapped, and recognized the amusement in his eyes. Turning away, she moved to the dressing table and toyed with one of the roses, drawing it from the vase and holding it to her nose as if considering his invitation. What did he want? He hadn't come here on a whim, it was obvious. Had *he* sent her the roses? It would be embarrassing to ask, for if she was wrong, he'd think her presumptuous for expecting it of him.

"So," he said when the silence stretched too long, "have you decided yet what it is I truly want with you, or if I intend to force myself upon you in some dim corner?"

"No," she replied frankly, "I cannot fathom your reasons. Pray, share them with me."

For a moment, he watched her carefully, then he shrugged. "You are quite unique, Miss Lancaster. Your speech is cultured despite your Colonial accent, and your French is excellent. I'd wager that your mother is French, or that you spent a great deal of time in France. You arrived in London with a troupe of players traveling from Paris, and before this theater, you played the part of a crone at Greene's Theater until it closed down when the investor gambled away all the money and the city seized the building. Your lodgings are in Carrier Street—a particularly unhealthy area in which to live, I may say—and you share a room with three other women, seamstresses for a small tailoring shop off Bond Street. As wages are overdue, you are in great need of funds. Is that why you were at Mme. Devereaux's soirée?"

Gaping at him, she had the wild thought that somehow he knew everything, that he knew why she'd fled Paris, and who her mother was . . . then she realized he could not. How had he found out so much about her? And why?

Aware that he was waiting, his head tilted slightly to one side as he watched her, she weighed her words carefully.

"You know a great deal, my lord. I didn't know you found me so interesting."

"Miss Lancaster, there is a world of things you cannot know about me. Have supper with me and I shall enlighten you on some of them."

How arrogant!

"It would be extremely beneficial to you," he added, "and if you refuse, then you may never know if you should have taken the opportunity to listen."

"Very well," she said, and wondered if she was making a grievous error in judgment, "I'll have supper with you. But I wish to choose the place."

He smiled. "Excellent."

Her heart beat a little faster at that smile, and she felt as if she had just stepped off a high precipice and found nothing beneath her feet.

"A charming place," Lord Lockwood said, looking around the Angel with a lifted brow. "Do you come here often?"

Laura stifled a laugh. No doubt, the earl had never in his life been in a common pub—not like this one, where actors and actresses came after their performances and ale flowed freely. He would inhabit elegant clubs with exquisite appointments and linen tablecloths, where the music, if there was any, would be discreet and subdued. In the far corner by the fire, a group of musicians played a bawdy tune, singing drunkenly, and smoke lay in a thin haze near the low, half-timbered ceiling. Tankards of ale sloshed as weary performers found seats on the long, scarred benches, some of them looking curiously toward Lockwood.

"Often enough," she replied, a lie for she could never have afforded it. Only when Jeremy insisted upon buying her a rum or ale could she join her companions.

The buxom serving wench, harried and untidy, served their meal, and despite her efforts to appear composed, Laura gazed at the steaming steak-and-kidney pie and tried to stem the flow of saliva that filled her mouth so it wouldn't spill over onto her chin. Celia's bounty was often cold, and of necessity, eaten quickly. Here was heaven on a pewter plate, curls of steam rising from slashes in the crust. Her stomach growled, and she hoped Lockwood hadn't heard it.

It took all her restraint not to wolf down her food, and she barely noticed anything but the plate before her as she began to eat. Thick gravy and a nice crust, small peas and pieces of turnip quickly disappeared. When she looked up at last, Lockwood was watching her with a bemused expression. She flushed, wondering if her table manners had deserted her completely.

"You have a healthy appetite, mademoiselle."

"Yes," she said simply, and he smiled.

"Excellent. An honest reply. I admire a forthright woman."

She kept her silence, uncertain if she wanted to know why he had brought her here, only glad to be full for the first time in so long. If her stays weren't laced, she'd have eaten even more, but there was no point in confessing that. Nor was there reason to delay longer. Once he'd divulged his reasons for seeking her out, she could go home to her narrow cot and the warm wool blankets that Celia had insisted she accept as a gift.

Pushing aside the meal he'd barely touched, half a roast chicken that would have kept her fed for three days, he leaned forward and said clearly, "Miss Lancaster, I propose a mutually beneficial arrangement that is worth your consideration."

Her stomach lurched, and she almost regretted devouring an entire pie. Almost. "Please go on, my lord," she said, "with emphasis on the mutually beneficial portion."

Lamplight glittered in his eyes and his brow rose. "Indeed. It seems that I desire a suitable companion, and you are in obvious and dire need of a protector."

She waited silently, certain she knew what he would say next, and the feeling of warm contentment that came with a full stomach ebbed slowly away.

"I'm prepared to offer you a comfortable situation," he continued, "and when my purpose is served, I'll settle a handsome sum upon you."

"And what would this . . . situation . . . require of me, my lord? To be at your beck and call, to satisfy your every . . . need?"

"Miss Lancaster, if I desired the services of a whore, I know full well where to go for one," he said coolly. "I specified *companion* for a reason."

"Companion."

"Yes, that is all I would require of you. You would be expected to attend the theater and the opera with me, of course, and any other social function of my choosing, but your bed will be your own."

She stared at him. He looked perfectly sane. And serious. "This . . . why do you need me as your companion, my lord?"

"My reasons are my own, and I have no need to divulge them to you. It is a business proposition, not an offer of marriage."

"I see," she said, though she didn't see at all. "You ask me to masquerade as your whore, but I'm to be one in name only. An attractive offer indeed, my lord."

His mouth tightened slightly, and something flashed in his eyes. "When first I saw you, you were being offered to the highest bidder for your virginity, Miss Lancaster. Don't come the high road with me now. I'm offering not only the highest bid, but I'm leaving you with your maidenhead intact. When our association is ended, you're free to peddle it where you will."

A gasp stuck in her throat at his bluntness, and worse, she could offer no argument. She'd been willing to prostitute herself for passage home—why would she not accept an offer that would leave her with her dignity if not her reputation?

Her head began to pound, and the thick smoke stung her nose and eyes. She had to think, had to delay, for the wrong answer may well be fatal.

"I'll consider your generous offer," she said finally, and he nodded.

God help me . . .

"Stop here, Franklin." At Julian's command, the driver slowed the carriage to a halt. No street lamps illuminated this section of London, at the edge of one of the most notorious slums in London. A little further, and they would enter an underworld of footpads and murderers, whores and thieves.

Laura Lancaster's lodgings were in a shabby, ramshackle building that leaned over the narrow street as if too weary to stand straight. Gutters ran thick with offal, and in the alleys that cut between rows of houses, sinister sounds warned away the unwary. He'd insisted she allow him to see her to her lodgings, citing her safety and his conscience. The last had earned him a scathing glance of disbelief. Clever girl.

She sat stiffly on the velvet seat across from him, a warm brick at her feet, her misery and shame like a banner on her expressive face. The coach lights flickered over her, and when the footman opened the door to help her out, Julian murmured, "It has been a pleasant evening, Miss Lancaster. Do give my proposition some consideration."

"Yes, my lord, I certainly will. And . . . thank you."

He inclined his head slightly, watching as his footman assisted her. Thin clouds drifted in the night sky, slivers of moonlight filtering through to shed just enough light that he could see her approach the steps of her lodgings. A trunk and valise perched on the bottom step. He signaled his driver to wait.

"What is this?" he heard her say to the man standing on the top step. "Why are my things out in the street?"

Burly and sullen, the landlord growled, "Behind in yer rent, ye are. Ye're evicted."

"I most certainly am *not* behind! I paid you in advance for this week, and it's not up until Sunday next—"

"Four pence a week, and I've nought from ye this seven days past."

Distress thickened her voice, and a trace of panic made it rise higher when the landlord just shook his head obdurately. "You know I gave you that money!"

Julian watched impassively. He should feel guilt for his part in this charade, but after seeing where she was forced to live, it was considerably diluted by relief. No woman should live like this, nor human being either, for that matter. Passage of the Poor Laws had done little to alleviate the plight of these wretches. Cows at Shadowhurst lived much better.

Signaling to his footman to go to her aid, he swung open the door and stepped down from the carriage as the man moved forward. The landlord was acting as instructed and blustering about her rent money, threatening to hold her belongings until he received it.

"Ye can take the blankets, but the trunk stays wi' me, it does," he said, and Laura's reply was a hiss of fury.

"You sorry oaf, I'll have the magistrate after you for this!"

"See here," Julian said calmly, "I'll pay for the lady's lodgings."

Moonlight glittered in his small, dark eyes as the landlord shook his head. "Already rented out her bed, I have."

Turning on him, Laura snapped, "You'll not pay him a farthing! He's been paid and he knows it. I don't know why he's doing this, but I won't have it." She wheeled back around. "See here, McFinn, if you'd not received your payment you'd have put me out days ago. You know I paid."

McFinn kept shaking his head and finally Julian said, "Your bed has been given to another. There's no point in continuing this discussion. There must be better places for you to live."

"Of course there are," she said sharply, "but none I can afford. This . . . this was the most decent place I could find on my wages."

"We'll find you another. Charlton, load Miss Lancaster's trunk while I settle with Master McFinn."

Despite Laura's stony-faced silence, he paid off the landlord, who took the coins hastily and retreated into the house as if afraid they'd be snatched away. He'd been paid handsomely to evict his tenant, and seemed more than satisfied with Malcolm's arrangement. For his part, Julian was more than satisfied to get her free of such a derelict building.

She still stood as if turned to stone, staring at the closed door as if unable to comprehend what had happened. He put a hand out to touch her shoulder. "It's late, Miss Lancaster. Come along, and we'll decide what to do with you."

Slowly turning, she looked up at him, and errant moonlight gleamed in her eyes, betraying the silvery sheen of tears. Oddly, he almost believed Mme. Devereaux's claim that she was virgin. An impossibility, of course, but an alluring illusion. She looked so—despairing.

"It seems that you've gotten what you wanted after all, my lord."

He nodded. "I always do.

CHAPTER 5

"I trust the room is satisfactory, miss."

It was only a polite comment not meant to imply her approval was necessary, Laura knew, as the silver-haired butler who'd shown her to the third-floor room of Lockwood's town house radiated disapproval from every pore. He stood stiffly at the door, watching her as if he expected her to make off with the silver candlesticks.

"It's quite satisfactory," she said calmly, refusing to acknowledge his disapproval. She was not unacquainted with the balance of power between servant and master, and knew that any hint of servility on her part would be met with icy disdain. It would be said below-stairs that she was a fraud, but that was likely to be said at any rate. Still, she'd no intention of giving them fodder to use against her.

Inclining his head slightly, the butler backed from the room, closing the door behind him, and she was alone at last with her thoughts. Silence closed in around her, the household asleep save for the butler and a sleepy-eyed chambermaid summoned to lay a fire to warm the room for his lordship's guest. A warming pan had been slid between the sheets, and the coverlet on the wide bed turned down, all duties performed under the watchful eye of the butler, who'd stood like an obelisk just inside the door. He'd dismissed the chambermaid with a flick of his hand.

Sighing with weariness, Laura had the thought he'd just as summarily dismissed her as an opportunist, no doubt. The opinion of servants would be harsh, their hierarchy as rigid as that of the aristocracy. Not that it mattered. She'd not be here long.

Despite the welcoming comfort of the room, elegant and luxurious beyond anything she'd experienced in two years, Laura refused to allow herself to think beyond the night. Tomorrow she would seek new lodging. If she stayed here too long she'd be like Persephone trapped in the underworld, bound for all eternity to dwell where she didn't belong. Enjoyment of the warm fire and soft bed would be her version of the pomegranate seed that had doomed poor Persephone.

Oh God, but it was so seductive: the thick carpets on the floor beneath her feet, the cheery blaze in the grate, and the high bed with a feather mattress that would cushion her aching muscles with all the softness of a cloud. Damn Lockwood. He'd known how she yearned for this. He knew far too much about her, and it was disconcerting.

Still standing in the middle of the room as if turned to stone, she forced herself to move at last to her trunk and the battered valise McFinn had evicted so rudely. Of all times for him to be so greedy, it had been when Lockwood was a witness. *Curse McFinn for a greedy sod*, she thought with a curl of her lip. He'd tried to evict her once before, claiming she'd not paid, but another tenant had come to her defense and he'd backed down.

Her small leather trunk sat forlornly out of place against the backdrop of these elegant furnishings, and she knelt in front of it to unbuckle the straps, not expecting to find any of her meager belongings inside. McFinn had been known to keep what he fancied of a tenant's things, discarding only what would bring him no coin. Hinges creaked lightly as she lifted the lid, and she stared in surprise—and instant suspicion.

Neatly folded were the fine lawn nightdress she'd brought from Paris, her buckram-and-whalebone corset, a pair of drawers of elastic India cotton and one of fine lawn that she saved for her return home, as well as pink stockings, a cambric petticoat, and a linen chemise. These would have fetched a fine price should McFinn be so inclined, and she knew at once that he'd not been the one to pack her trunk. Nor would his slatternly wife have allowed such fine garments to leave her possession. Who then? One of the seamstresses? She couldn't see those timid souls defying the ogre McFinn or his mistress. Holding her breath, she dug beneath the undergarments to find her good dress, a white muslin with delicate green sprig and satin ribbons, and a deeper green pelisse trimmed in fur. Sewn into the lining were her precious coins, and she breathed a sigh of relief to find them still there. Through every deprivation, she'd managed to cling to these things, not wanting to return to America penniless and in rags.

Upon opening the valise and finding her silver-backed hairbrush and comb, small mirror, and an almost empty bottle of rose water still intact and carefully wrapped in strips of cloth, her suspicions were confirmed. Lord Lockwood. More specifically, his footman, had packed her few possessions. There could be no other explanation. McFinn would not have relinquished them.

She sat back on her heels to consider Lockwood's reasons. Had he found her evicted and merely rescued her belongings, or had he been behind McFinn's sudden loss of memory? It was a question she intended to ask him at the first opportunity.

She should be furious, yet strangely enough she was only weary and grateful for a warm fire and soft bed. Perhaps it was true after all that one's soul could be cheaply purchased, for at this moment, she knew that she was not at all sorry to be here.

Rising to her feet, she gazed down at what was left of her former life, most sold during the past years to buy lodging and food, then began to disrobe. Tomorrow she would decide what to do. Tonight, she would sleep safely and comfortably for the first time in two years.

* * *

Sunlight poked through a crack in the heavy velvet curtains, moving stealthily across the room to shine in Laura's eyes. Her lids fluttered open, and she stared up at an unfamiliar canopy overhead in bewilderment. Then she remembered, and lay for a long moment in the fat feather pillows, relishing the warmth of the coverlet over her. The fire had gone out, and the room would be chill, but not the icy cold of her St. Giles lodgings, where her breath came out in frosty clouds and she woke shivering every morning. Ice crystals often formed on her nose and lips. The garret was cold in winter, stifling in summer, rarely bearable at any season. This was luxury, indeed, and she intended to absorb what she could to give her strength for the day.

Lockwood must be dealt with immediately. He'd tricked her. She was certain of it, and it made her angry. He'd presumed too much, but then, he'd admitted that he always won. Now she knew why. He arranged circumstances to his benefit with an arrogant highhandedness that was infuriating.

He thought he could manipulate her. He would soon be disabused of that notion!

Rehearsal was at three o'clock, the only performance began at six, and before then she had to find new lodgings. Celia may take her in temporarily, though she lived in a small house paid for by Belgrave, so it would of necessity be only a brief stay. Men who kept mistresses did not pay for the support of two without some sort of benefit in return.

A light, discreet tap on the door jerked her from contemplation, and she sat up in the bed, wishing she had a dressing gown. Alas, it had been sold months before.

"Enter," she called, pulling the coverlet up to her chin.

The faint rattle of china preceded the appearance of a uniformed footman bearing a tray, his expression carefully blank. "His lordship thought you might prefer taking your morning meal in your chamber, miss," he said, and set the ornate silver tray on a japanned table near the window. "Shall I draw the curtains?"

"Yes," she said, her nose quivering at the delicious odors

seeping from beneath silver covers. Her stomach growled loudly, and she pressed her hands to it in a vain effort to stem the eager rumblings.

Unperturbed, the footman drew back the curtains to a sunny morning, light instantly flooding the room. He seemed to avoid her eyes, and she wondered if he'd been the one to pack her undergarments. Without comment, he laid a fire, feeding it curls of paper until it was a bright blaze, then turned to Laura, his gaze riveted on the wall nearby.

"Will there be anything else you require, miss?"

"Not at the moment." She hoped she sounded more certain than she felt. A wave of hunger so intense as to be debilitating rendered her nearly immobile, and she could hardly wait for the footman to depart so she could attack the tray. How could she be so hungry after eating an entire steak-and-kidney pie the night before?

When the door closed behind him, she threw back the covers and slid to the floor, her toes curling up from the cold boards as she leaped to the warmer carpet. Lifting each cover, she closed her eyes and breathed in the seductive aroma of hot sausages, coddled eggs, several apricot tarts, a generous portion of kidneys and bacon, and a basket of croissants glazed with butter. There was even poached salmon. A pot of tea and small pitcher of cream completed the meal.

It would be much easier, she decided as she pulled up a tapestry-cushioned stool, to do battle with Lockwood on a full stomach. Much easier.

Julian arrived at No. 81 Piccadilly on the east corner of Bolton Street much earlier than his normal hour, nodding to several acquaintances, some of whom looked to have spent the entire night gambling. Watier's, named after a royal cook, owed its origins to the Regent's desire for decent food to be served at the gentlemen's clubs, and so the fare here was always excellent.

Deeming it prudent to be absent when Miss Lancaster emerged from her chamber, he'd left the house early, and now took a seat at a table in the corner. There had been fire in the lady's eye the night before when he'd made his proposition, but he suspected once she thought over her prospects, she'd see reason. Cranford would see to her needs as he'd instructed, and Malcolm was set to ensure that she remained safely ensconced in the house until his return.

Wounded pride would fade with the hours, he hoped, and she'd see the sense in accepting his offer. Why shouldn't she? It was reasonable and more than fair. He required a lovely escort, and she required lodgings and protection. He was offering her far more: a tidy sum for her return to America once the charade ended and he no longer needed her.

Any other woman in her position would have leaped at the suggestion, but she'd stared at him with genuine affront. It'd occurred to him to wonder why she'd fled Paris. Despite her accent and current situation, it was plain she'd been properly reared. If Mme. Devereaux was correct, she wasn't fleeing an unhappy husband or lover. Her reluctance to put a price on her supposed maidenhead gave her a certain cachet, in his opinion. She had standards, where so few did these days. Those of his experience, at any rate. Deuced unpleasant, to have such a jaded view, but he'd not made the acquaintance of many women who possessed the courage of their convictions. Did *she*?

Laura Lancaster, a contradiction. A genteel female of gentle birth, and an actress capable of offering the illusion of her virginity to the highest bidder. A contradiction, indeed. Which was her true nature? Or was she just a consummate actress attempting to fool them all?

A puzzle, but one he meant to solve. He enjoyed unraveling puzzles, especially when there was a prize at stake. A lovely prize, with sea-green eyes and Judas hair—

"Hullo, Julian."

Jerked from his reverie, he looked up from his plate, eyes

narrowing. "Up early, are you, Randal? What brings you out before three o'clock?"

It wasn't really a question, and his younger brother forbore a reply, taking a chair opposite him without an invitation. "Is there tea left in that pot?"

"I'm drinking coffee." Julian regarded his brother's slightly disheveled appearance with a jaundiced eye, smiling wryly when Randal grimaced.

"How Colonial of you. Chocolate would be better if you're not civilized enough to drink tea, old boy. All these coffee houses in London—"

Leaning back in his chair, Julian raised a brow. "Did you come to criticize my breakfast preferences, or is there another reason I'm graced with the pleasure of your company?"

"I'll confide all if only you'll feed me. I'm famished."

Julian beckoned and a waiter appeared, soon returning with Randal's tea and toast. Faint lines of dissipation marked the young man's face, a scourge of younger sons. Heirs must behave with propriety, but younger sons were left to their own devices far too often. It was not a pleasant thought.

Stuffing the last of his toast into his mouth, Randal followed it with another cup of tea, then sat back with a sigh, unperturbed by his brother's silence as he regarded him lazily.

"Imagine my surprise to learn that while your wife is on an extended tour of Europe, you have taken up intimate company with your steward."

Julian didn't pause in cutting his sausage. "You must visit low places indeed to hear such vicious—and unfounded—rumors, Randal. I wonder that you'd have the courage to repeat them."

"Low places indeed, I fear. I only report what I hear. Any other man would suffer a facer for being fool enough to repeat them to you, I'm sure."

"Don't consider yourself immune," Julian said mildly. "A hard blow to your face has a certain allure at the moment."

Randal only grinned. "That's what I admire most about you, Julian, your commendable restraint."

Enough of the verbal fencing. He leaned forward. "What are you doing here?"

"Cranford told me I'd find you here."

"You've been there this early?" Julian eyed him narrowly. Randal toyed with his spoon, turning it bowl to handle repeatedly, a certain sign he was nervous. "Tell me what you need, and without a Canterbury story, if you please."

"Simply enough, I'm in dun territory again. Shall I bore you with the details?"

"Spare me. How much do you need?"

"Five hundred pounds, unless you're feeling particularly generous."

"Only five hundred? I'm astonished. You must have left the tables early."

"Macao," Randal said gloomily. "Brummel had the devil's own luck. I lost a thousand, but couldn't come up to scratch with the last of it."

"Brummel holds your marker?"

"I said I'd pay him today." Randal flicked a glance up at him, affecting nonchalance. "I could always borrow from a cent per cent."

"Excellent notion. Go deeper in debt with a notorious usurer." Disgusted, Julian shook his head. "I'll give you the money, but it comes out of your proceeds from the estate."

Instantly in good humor again, Randal grinned. An engaging scamp, handsome and generous and a complete greenhead, he drove Julian to distraction a great deal of the time.

"In your debt once again," he said with a laugh, "but you should be well-accustomed to it by now, Julian."

"Far too accustomed. I'll have Malcolm settle your account."

Nodding, Randal stretched his long legs out under the table, regarding Julian with a lazy smile that didn't quite hide the sharpness in his gaze. "Ah yes, Malcolm. A jack of all trades, if the whispers are to be believed."

"Enough," Julian said quietly, and his brother's smile vanished.

"Yes, more than enough. I hate it when your name is bandied about so loosely. Why don't you do something about the gossip? Call Eleanor back, then send her to the country, lock her in the wine cellar, anything to stop the vicious gossipmongers!"

Julian studied him for a moment. The flush of anger on Randal's face was genuine. There were times Julian forgot he was still a youth, ten years younger than his own thirty years, a boy still for all that he played at being a man of the town. And it wasn't, he realized suddenly, the debt to Brummel that had brought Randal in search of him, but his concern for his brother's reputation.

"It will pass soon enough," he said then, nodding when Randal shot him a doubtful glance. "I'll be old news before long. Someone else will transgress and divert attention from me."

"Not bloody soon enough," Randal muttered, and raked a hand through his blond hair, the soft, pale strands like silk falling over his forehead and making him look even younger. His collar was disheveled, the points rubbing against his jaw on one side, his ear on the other, and his once intricately folded neckcloth looked as if it had been hastily retied.

Julian rose from his chair. "I'm going to Tattersall's, if you'd like to accompany me."

Chair legs scraped against the floor as Randal eagerly rose to his feet. "Buying a fast trotter always puts me in a decent mood."

"I'll buy, *you* look," Julian said, and Randal only laughed.

Laura had just finished dressing when a light tap sounded on the door. Her heart leaped with sudden anticipation, and she smoothed her wrinkled skirts with one hand, palm against the flat plane of her stomach and her fingers splayed. Nerves thrumming, she started to go to open the door, then hesitated, then settled for calling permission to enter.

It was not Lockwood, but a slender man of medium height with dark, thinning hair and a narrow, austere face. Brown eyes rested briefly on her, and he inclined his head politely.

"Good morning, Miss Lancaster."

"Good morning." She waited, and he smiled, supplying his name.

"I am Malcolm, Lord Lockwood's steward. I trust you have found all to your satisfaction, Miss Lancaster?"

"Exceedingly satisfactory." She was uncertain how to address him. Was Malcolm his first or his last name? She'd thought such informality was frowned upon in the upper classes, and tried to recall what she'd learned about proper titles and forms of address. He'd introduced himself as Malcolm, and if required, that's how she'd address him, she decided, all this flashing through her mind in the time it took him to advance several steps into the room.

"I see your breakfast tray has not been retrieved. Very remiss. I'll send someone for it directly. Apparently, there's been a miscommunication below-stairs."

Certain he'd not come to discuss the breakfast tray or introduce himself, Laura waited, and after a moment, Malcolm coughed discreetly.

"Lord Lockwood has requested that I present you with an offer for your services. I believe he discussed this with you in some form, but it is my duty to outline certain expectations should there be any question."

Coward, she thought furiously, *that he'd send his steward to ask for my answer!*

"Indeed," she said aloud, lifting her brow to indicate her distaste with the subject.

"Indeed, Miss Lancaster." He gave her a perfunctory smile. "It's my understanding that you are an actress by profession."

As he seemed to expect a response, she nodded warily, uncertain how he intended to ask her to be his employer's mistress without sounding like a procurer.

"It's a simple enough business arrangement, and I have

drawn up an agreement for you to peruse so that you may decide for yourself if you wish to participate. His lordship requires only that you accompany him to various functions—that you, in effect, play the role of his mistress in public with no expectations as to future commitments of any kind other than monetary. In return, he will settle upon you an agreed-upon sum when your association with him is ended."

Very smoothly done, she thought, and not a hint of impropriety. He'd managed to skirt the moral issue quite neatly.

Taking a deep breath, she said, "I've often thought of myself as a forthright person, so will not mince words with you now. As to the matter of duties I'm expected to perform, I'd require assurance that my presence in his bed is not one of them."

Malcolm's brows shot up so high they almost disappeared into his receding hairline. For a moment, he remained speechless, but seemed to recover quickly. Then he tilted his head in an acknowledgment.

"If you prefer, I shall specify that in writing, Miss Lancaster."

"I prefer." His answer was unexpected. She'd thought he would insist, or at the least, say he would have to consult Lockwood, giving her the opportunity to refuse and retreat.

"Are there any other suggestions?" He gazed at her politely, but there was an assessing gleam in his eyes as if he were trying to decide her reasons for the stipulation.

"That one is sufficient for the moment, but should anything else occur to me, I'll be most happy to relay it to you. And please, do not think that because I'm considering his lordship's proposition, I've accepted it. I'm merely giving him the courtesy of my consideration in return for rescuing me last night."

"Of course, miss." He bowed slightly, the perfect example of a stoic major domo, head of a household of servants, his master's devoted servant and usually an educated young man of good background such as a cleric's son or a businessman. Malcolm was perfectly suited for the post. He backed out of the still-open door and before closing it quietly behind him, said, "I'll draw up the necessary documents forthwith, and bring them to you for your perusal."

When he was gone, Laura stared at the solid oak door and wondered if she'd just made a grievous error. To even consider such a proposal . . . but then, would it be so dreadful? It wasn't as if she had a reputation to uphold here, and she'd no intention of ever returning to England once she was safely back on American soil. The prospect of a respite from the ever-present worry of utter ruin would be so wonderful, even if only for a while. And she'd not have to compromise her morals, just her principles. Was it a beneficial bargain—or a deal with the devil?

Oh God, she wished she knew what to do but it was all so overwhelming, the long months of struggle so depleting, and she was so weary of it. So very weary of not knowing if this was the day she'd be out on the street in the cold, with no coin, no food, no roof over her head, as shabby as it might be. She thought of those in Covent Garden, her neighbors as they were, the pinched, hopeless faces, the weary, dull plodding through lives as miserable as the souls in hell must endure, and the inevitability of their fates.

Then she thought of Lockwood, tall, handsome, a golden-haired Apollo offering her an escape from that fate— offering her the pomegranate seed Pluto had offered Persephone in the underworld. And she knew that if she accepted it, her life would change as irrevocably as had that poor, doomed Persephone's.

Moving to the window, she gazed out thick leaded glass to the street below, where the cold wind bent trees and sent a gentleman's tall beaver hat sailing through the air so that he had to chase after it. Trees and gentlemen, not slops and cutpurses, as she was accustomed to seeing out her window. No icy wind through cracks in the wall, and a cheery fire warming the room; a wide, comfortable bed, and the remains of her morning meal left on the silver tray when she'd not been able to eat it all. Closing her eyes, she inhaled deeply. Her pomegranate seed . . .

A light rap on the door jerked her from her tortured reflection, and her heart lurched as she turned to call permission to enter. Again, it was not Lockwood. A small, curly-haired girl with a white lace cap atop her crown and an apron pinned to her dress stepped into the room, eyes cast downward.

"Beggin' yer pardon, miss, but I've come for the tray, I 'ave."

"Of course," Laura said, and smiled encouragingly at her, but the girl kept her head down and didn't see. Moved to sympathy at the almost frightened way she skittered across the room, as if afraid she'd be reprimanded, Laura said, "What is your name?"

Startled, the girl glanced up, huge doe-eyes widening with surprise. "Becky, miss," she blurted. Her face was thin, her lips slightly quivering. A red welt burned freshly on her cheek.

Upon closer inspection, Laura realized that this was not a child as she'd first thought, but a girl of perhaps fourteen, small and undernourished for her age, but showing the beginning of maturity in her thin chest. And sporting a fresh blow upon her face.

Frowning, Laura abruptly demanded, "Did Malcolm strike you, Becky?"

"Mal—oh *no*, miss, he would never hit any o' us. He don't even talk to *us*. It's Cook who gives us our orders, she does. And I . . . I forgot yer tray, I did. Beggin' yer pardon, miss."

"The tray is of no consequence, Becky. I'm sorry it's caused you trouble."

Becky stared at her in blatant disbelief, then bobbed her head and reached for the tray. It was huge and heavy, the ornate silver covers solid and large. Thin arms strained as Becky slid the tray toward her, and Laura recognized the pinch of hunger in the girl's face as she gazed at the leftover fruit tarts. It was a hunger she understood, for she'd tucked several into a linen cloth and put them in her own valise for later, not quite daring to take them all.

"Becky," she said on impulse, knowing she was trespassing on proper conduct but unable to withstand the girl's obvious yearning, "those tarts will only go to waste if they're not eaten. Put them in your pocket."

Silver rattled loudly, and Becky paused, giving her a sharp glance. "Oh no, miss, it's not permitted. If Cook found out, she'd slap me smartly, she would."

"Would she. Cook sounds as if she likes them for herself."

An unwilling smile hovered on Becky's mouth, and she ducked her head. "I wouldn't know about that, miss."

I'll bet you wouldn't, Laura thought. *I bet Cook is a greedy old harridan.*

Aloud she said, "Before you take the tray, please be good enough to put more coal on the fire for me."

Becky slid the tray safely back onto the table, and crossed to the hearth, where she fed the fire that was already cheerily blazing. When she turned back, Laura held out two of the apricot tarts.

"Let's trick Cook this time, shall we?" No doubt, it was Cook who'd already given her that blow on the cheek, Laura thought angrily.

"Oh *no*, miss, I couldn't."

"Of course you can, if I insist. Aren't you sent to tend my wishes?"

Becky's head bobbed, and there was such hunger in her eyes when she stared at the tarts, that Laura felt a bond with the child. Is that how *she'd* looked whenever Celia brought her tarts or meat pies? It's how she'd felt—she knew that well enough.

"Then here," Laura said firmly, "I insist that you have these tarts. Both of them. Eat them here, if you please, before the fire, while I pour myself another cup of tea."

Glancing nervously toward the door, Becky hesitated still. "If Cook or Cranford finds me 'ere eatin' tarts—"

"It is at my request, Becky." She moved to the door and turned the key in the lock. "That should prevent any nasty surprises, now, shouldn't it?"

Hunger finally overrode Becky's instinctive caution and fear, and she took the tarts with a trembling hand, devouring the first one so quickly it was like watching a starving dog bolt down an unexpected meal. The second tart was eaten more slowly, the bites savored, and something akin to utter joy gleamed on the girl's face.

"There, that wasn't so difficult, was it?" Laura said with a smile, and Becky's answering grin was instant if rather fleeting, her brown curls bobbing as she nodded.

"No, miss," she said, "not 'ard at all."

"I thought not. I've been hungry myself, and know well enough how it feels."

"Yes, miss."

"Now then," she said briskly, "if Cook should ask, you may tell her that I kept you here to feed the fire for me."

"Yes, miss."

When Becky had gone with the tray, Laura returned to the window to gaze out at the street below, so different from those in St. Giles. Once, she'd read the plays of Hannah More with only a distant sympathy. Now she felt much in common with the heroine of *The Story of Sinful Sally*, the moral tale of a young woman who took her first step down the slippery slope toward depravity by becoming a kept woman, and who then suffered complete moral collapse after reading novels. It was far too close a situation for comfort, and now she felt more sympathy for poor Sally than she ever could have before.

CHAPTER 6

"I trust the documents are satisfactory, Miss Lancaster."

Laura shuffled the pages for a moment, unwilling to answer, uncertain and apprehensive. The terms were simple and brief, and far more generous than she'd ever thought possible.

"You're very efficient," she replied when the moments passed without comment, and looked up at Malcolm with a faint smile. "I'd like a few moments to read over them and make my decision. I'll give you my reply before I leave for the theater."

"Of course." If Malcolm thought the arrangement unusual in the extreme, his expression didn't reflect it. Instead, he seemed to take it all in stride, that a peer of the realm would put into writing an agreement to the support of a Covent Garden actress in return only for her presence on his arm at social functions. Discreetly worded, the document specified that any intimate acts were neither required nor desired. For some reason, that last rankled a bit.

"As it's nearly time for me to leave," she said, folding the documents and moving to place them on the table in front of the window, deliberately avoiding saying anything else that could be misconstrued as acceptance or refusal, "I'll have to hurry to avoid being late."

"His lordship has instructed me to provide you with transportation," Malcolm replied. "You have only to ask. Also—" he put a hand to his mouth and coughed discreetly, "should you so desire, accommodations have been made for your lodgings in anticipation of your acceptance of his lordship's proposal."

"Indeed?" Lodgings of her own . . .

"Indeed, a small house has been made available for your use. Staff will be provided upon your acceptance—only a small staff, but efficient. All is in readiness for you, should you be in agreement, Miss Lancaster."

She nodded. Malcolm's tone made it clear he thought she'd be foolish to refuse. And she had to agree it was tempting. The proposal was entirely to her advantage. Should she agree to pose as the earl's mistress throughout the political season, she'd receive a monthly salary equal to what she'd earn in a year at the theater, a residence of her own, and all living expenses. At the end of Parliament's current session, first-class passage would be arranged for her return to America, in addition to a bonus equaling three months' salary. *Home*.

It was a tantalizing lure, and like Persephone with the pomegranate seed, she found it impossible to resist.

Celia Carteret brushed rice powder over her cheeks with the soft tip of a hare's foot, her eyes on Laura's reflection in the mirror. Poor child, she looked so miserable and so young though they were only a year apart in age. Celia felt her own age keenly at times, a lifetime of struggle crammed into her twenty-three years. Determination to rise above her origins in the stews of St. Giles was all that kept her going at times, and Maggie Buttons had been forgotten by all but her restless dreams at night, when she was once more that hungry, frightened child.

But now her attention was on Laura, who wouldn't quite meet her eyes.

"Hullo, ducks."

"You're here unusually early," Laura replied, removing her wrap and tossing it over a stool without looking at her. "I didn't expect to see you until right before the curtain rises."

"Being unpredictable is useful," Celia chirped, and turned on the stool to stare at her with a faint smile. "All right, ducks, give over."

"What do you mean?"

"Don't come the sly with me, ducks, I know Lockwood bought you dinner at the Angel last night, and that you left with him in his plush coach. So?"

Laura sank onto a pile of old curtains stored in the corner by the rickety screen. "McFinn evicted me."

"No! That bran-faced clunch," she said, reverting to the vernacular of her youth as anger made her tone sharp. "You can stay with me until you find other lodgings, ducks, never fear."

"It seems that I've already found other lodgings," Laura said slowly, and lifted her head to gaze at Celia with green eyes that looked dark with uncertainty.

"Capital!" Celia clapped her hands together and gave her a cheeky grin. "Lockwood, I trust?"

Laura nodded. "He's offered a proposition."

"No doubt. I heard that he seemed quite smitten with you."

"Not at all." Laura leaned back on the moth-eaten velvet curtains that had once hung over the stage. Dust poofed into the air. "He doesn't desire me in his bed, but on his arm."

Celia blinked. "You jest."

"Not at all. I slept quite alone and undisturbed last night."

"Where?"

"Mayfair, if you will. An elegant room, certainly enough, warm and tidy." She shrugged and leaned forward as if confiding a great secret. "I confess I enjoyed it immensely."

"No doubt." Tilting her head to one side, Celia narrowed her eyes. "Lockwood may not have come to your bed last night, but he will, ducks. No man offers his protection without an expectation of return."

Laura looked down at her hands, pleating folds of her dress between her fingers. "Perhaps you're right."

Something was amiss. Celia knew it. Had Lockwood hurt

her somehow? These swells of the upper class were not always the gentlemen they claimed to be, and it wouldn't be unusual at all for a man to be rough. They seemed to view women as the same possessions as blooded horses bought at Tattersall's, though the horses normally fared better.

"As lovely as you are," Celia said, "you've not got to suffer with an unsuitable protector. If Lockwood harms you in any way, you—"

"Oh no." Laura's head jerked up. "He hasn't harmed me. I'm just . . . not sure this is the right decision."

Celia leaned forward to curve her fingers over Laura's trembling hand. "You made the right decision, ducks. It's a matter of survival. And no man can own you, though he may think he does."

"I hope you're right," Laura said softly, and the sheen of unshed tears in her eyes reminded Celia of the tears she had shed so long ago. A bitter realization of how her life would be had come to her at fifteen in the bed of the earl who'd taken her maidenhead. It'd not taken her long to recover, nor to realize that he'd done her an enormous favor. Practicality had erased doubts, and since then, she'd known how the world worked and accepted it. It was always better to be a willing participant than a victim.

"Lockwood seems a decent sort," she said, and turned back to the mirror, "and except for the scandal about his wife, I've not heard anything bad about him."

"Tell me about his wife," Laura said.

Celia turned back with a frown. "See here, ducks, men like Lockwood never marry girls like us."

Laura flushed. "I'm well aware of that."

"Yes, of course you are—sorry." Still, there was something so intense in Laura's lovely face that Celia wondered why. Ah well, when she was ready to confide in her, she would. So she shrugged and rose from the stool, reaching for her costume. "It's said she's living in Vienna at the moment, dallying with first one, then the other man, living quite a scandalous life on the earl's blunt. There were whispers that he sent her away at first, but now it seems that she ran away to be with some lover after an intruder was killed in Lockwood's town house." She paused. "And, of course, there were the rumors that the intruder was really her lover and Lockwood killed him. No one ever actually accused him of it, but after Lady Lockwood fled the country, it was whispered he was somehow involved."

Laura paled and Celia shook her head. "Don't worry, ducks, if Lockwood really had killed the man, his enemies would have shouted it from the rooftops. There's nothing Whigs love more than bringing down a Tory."

A rattling knock at the door signaled it was nearly time for the curtain to rise, and Laura stood up, reaching for her shepherdess costume.

"I hope you're right," she said, and there was something so vulnerable in her voice that Celia rushed to assure her all was well.

"You'll be fine, ducks. Lockwood is rich and handsome. All your problems are over."

It was a lie, but a kind one, and Celia hoped it would prove to be the truth.

A chill wind swept over them, and Laura shivered as she and Celia emerged from the backstage door into the alley. Dank air smelled like snow. The lantern had gone out, and it was dark in the passageway between the theater and the next row of buildings, so that they scurried toward the mouth of the alley and Celia's waiting carriage.

"I'll have Belgrave's driver see you home, ducks," Celia said, her words muffled as she pulled the fur-trimmed hood of her cloak more snugly around her face. "Lockwood's lodgings?"

Before Laura could reply, they saw the coach lights of another carriage directly behind the familiar vehicle belonging to Belgrave. A footman in green and-gold livery stepped forward.

"This way, please, Miss Lancaster."

It was Charlton, Laura realized, the footman who'd packed her belongings, and no doubt delivered the white roses to her dressing room as well. Lockwood was thorough. Or was it Malcolm who claimed such efficiency?

"God above," Celia breathed in a frosty cloud, "you're to travel in style, ducks!"

That was true enough. Belgrave's carriage was a small tilbury that held only two people, but the carriage sent by Lockwood was a town coach, a large, impressive conveyance with four wheels and pulled by four horses. Painted on the sides of its enclosed body were the Lockwood heraldic arms. It could hardly be more conspicuous.

As Laura's footsteps faltered, Celia grasped her arm, fingers digging in tightly even through the wool folds of her cloak. "Don't be a fool, ducks," she hissed in her ear, "this is better than scrubbing floors or tending the yowling brats of the peerage."

Then she was gone, hieing off to her own vehicle with an airy wave of one hand, leaving Laura to be handed into the coach by the footman. When she was seated on the plush velvet squabs, before he could close the door she leaned forward to ask, "Where are we going?"

"Frith Street, miss." Without further explanation, he closed the door and took his station at the rear of the coach, and it lurched forward, huge wheels rolling toward her new home.

Frith Street. A discreet avenue on the fringes of Mayfair, within easy distance of the earl's residence.

Heated bricks warmed her feet, and Laura sank back against the tufted upholstery. How drastically her life had changed from one day to the next, from being homeless and penniless to a life of riding in opulent carriages and sleeping on fat feather beds. She could quickly grow used to such a life, she thought wearily, leaning her head back against the velvet squabs. It only went to show how easily she could trade her principles for comfort. A depressing thought if she were to dwell on it. But too late now. She'd agreed to the proposition with a calmness she'd been far from feeling, and had looked up to find Malcolm gazing at her with an enigmatic expression. It was almost one of—relief. How strange.

All too soon the coach slowed to a halt in front of a small house that was no less lovely for its size. Her eyes widened. A two-story building of plain buff brick and elegant windows was alight with welcome, a glow in the windows that promised warmth and comfort inside, and when Charlton opened the door for her, she stepped out into the cold night air with more energy than she'd thought she had left.

Lamps flanked each side of the door, burning brightly, and she ascended the wide steps with her stomach churning nervously. This was it. There would be no retreat once she stayed a night in this house, and she wondered again if she'd made the right decision.

The door opened when she was only halfway up the steps, and Laura saw young Becky in the doorway. When she reached her, Becky held out her hand for Laura's cloak, head up and her expression one of nervous delight.

"I'm to serve ye, miss, until proper help can be found."

"I'm pleased to see you, Becky." She allowed the girl to take her cloak, looking around the entrance hall with what she was certain was the same nervous delight on her face as on Becky's.

Though small, it was comfortable, with a parlor to the right, easily visible from the entry hall, and an angled staircase to the left. Beyond were more rooms, no doubt a kitchen and pantry, and perhaps a room for the servants. There was even a small garden in the rear, glimpsed through a window. While not lavish, it was more than she'd had for so long, and comfortable and clean.

"There's tea, miss," Becky said, "and biscuits. Cook sent a small supper, until ye 'ave yer own cook. Yer trunks are in yer bedchamber."

So quickly, and all she owned in this world now waited for her upstairs in a bedchamber that belonged to someone else. Lockwood . . . had he chosen the house for her? No, of course he'd not done so. Malcolm would have taken care of all the arrangements—it's what a steward did for his employer. It had been Malcolm who'd chosen this house, the furnishings, and no doubt even the servants. But Lockwood had chosen *her*.

Oddly, that thought was cheering, and Laura allowed Becky to show her up the stairs to her new bedchamber. The girl possessed more confidence this evening than she had earlier. Though her glances were still shy and her manner diffident, she didn't cringe.

A fire burned brightly in the small grate, and snug windows looked out over the street. A four-poster bed stood against the wall opposite the hearth, and a thick carpet cushioned the bare wood floors almost to the walls. A wardrobe stood in one corner, and several chairs and a small dressing table comprised the rest of the furniture. Cozy, cheery, and feminine. Paradise after the hell of St. Giles.

Then Laura noticed the bouquet of white roses in a vase on the mantel, and unexpected tears sprang to her eyes. A caring touch that made her think she meant more than just a business arrangement, that Lockwood recognized her as a woman as well as part of his mysterious charade. It was comforting.

"Miss," Becky said, and Laura turned toward her, "I . . . I thank ye kindly for askin' for me to be in yer service."

Laura smiled. It had been part of her acceptance, the condition that Becky be allowed to serve her, and though rather startled, Malcolm had swiftly agreed to it.

"I'm sure we'll deal together splendidly, Becky. You seem a bright girl."

Becky's cheeks reddened. "Thank ye, miss. Cook wasn't going to let me come, said it were silly, but Cranford gave her a smart set-down, he did, told her that it was what Malcolm 'ad said do, and she was to hush about it or find herself sacked. I never saw Cook's face go so red! It was worth gettin' another smack, it were."

"I can imagine." Laura allowed Becky to help her unfasten her gown, the girl's clumsiness an indication that the post of ladies' maid was unfamiliar to her. It was a relief to be out of the constrictive corset and into her own nightdress at last.

"I'll brush yer 'air if ye like, miss," Becky said when Laura was seated upon the small stool in front of the dressing table mirror, "and not 'urt ye, I won't. I'm quick to learn."

"I'm sure you are, Becky." She allowed her to unpin her hair and drag the silver-backed hairbrush through it in long strokes, closing her eyes at the unfamiliar luxury. Becky's touch was gentle and sure. After several minutes, the tension in her shoulders had eased and she was lulled into an almost somnolent state. It would be far too easy to become accustomed to this, a warning voice in the back of her head reminded her, but she stuffed it firmly into the farthest recesses.

Not tonight. Later, she'd worry about what must be done. About Lockwood. But tonight she'd enjoy one more worry-free slumber. It'd be enough to see her through the days ahead, she hoped.

Becky brought her up a tray of cold chicken, cheese, and soft white bread that was still warm, and a pot of chocolate that was rich and heady.

"Have you eaten?" Laura asked her, and when she shook her head, insisted that she do so. "I cannot have you hungry and cold and be easy myself. Take sufficient coal for your fire as well."

Speechless, Becky nodded, but Laura saw in the girl's eyes what she felt herself, that she'd somehow fallen into a wonderful dream. She only hoped it lasted long enough for both of them.

Coals hissed in the grate, spreading warmth into the parlor while outside, sleet beat against the glass panes of the windows. Seated before a small secretaire, Laura dipped a quill into a pot of ink and signed the last of the documents with a determined flourish, breathing a prayer that she wasn't making a huge mistake. After a moment, she carefully blotted it, then looked up.

Malcolm regarded her solemnly. "If you have any questions, Miss Lancaster, now is the time to ask them."

"No," she said, and handed him the documents that he placed into a leather case, "the time to ask them was before I signed."

A faint smile hovered at the edges of his mouth. "Quite right. However, I merely wish to avoid any misunderstandings that may cause unpleasantness later."

Becky arrived with the tea tray, her thin arms straining with the burden but a look of grim determination in her eyes, and Laura waited until she'd placed it on the small table set before the settee before she said, "I'm not certain I understand you, sir."

Malcolm stirred a generous portion of milk into his tea, and added a lump of sugar. "Miss Lancaster, I deem it imperative that you have no illusions this arrangement might lead to a more . . . lasting association with the earl."

"Do you consider me a complete fool, sir?" she demanded with rising indignation.

"I consider you a young woman of good background whatever your current condition, but one who may think that the interest of a gentleman is permanent. I offer you a caution, that is all."

"What would you know of my background?" His arched brow indicated a polite refusal to reply, and she leaned forward. "You're correct in the assumption that I was properly reared, sir, but pray, do not also assume that I have designs upon the earl. I want only to go home, and this arrangement cannot end too quickly for me!"

Malcolm inclined his head to acknowledge her comments. "Indeed, then we are of the same mind, I see. I'm pleased to hear it, Miss Lancaster."

"In future, please be frank and that will avoid any misunderstandings."

"Very well, in the interest of frankness, I have a list of requirements the earl has provided for you. First, there must be sufficient staff here so that when he is in residence, his comforts and needs are tended. The maid you've already chosen may stay, of course, and if you have any other preferences as to staff, feel free to inform me. If not, I shall provide you with a cook, post boy, and a driver for your carriage. His lordship deems it necessary that you have proper transport to and from the theater should you wish to continue your . . . performances."

"I do intend to continue," she said when he paused and glanced up at her from the slip of paper he held. "As this situation is temporary, I have no intention of giving up secure employment for the whims of a man, even an earl."

A flicker of surprise passed over Malcolm's face before he masked it. "Very wise of you, Miss Lancaster. Now. Ahem. Perhaps I'll just read these off quickly. An appointment has been made for you at a reputable modiste, with necessary visits to seamstresses, milliners, and furriers required, of course, for your new wardrobe. His lordship desires that you are turned out in the manner that befits his companion." He glanced up at her again and continued, "If there are any other areas in which you need instruction, I am authorized to see that you have the necessary tutoring."

"Tutoring?"

"Indeed." He gave a discreet cough. "While in Lord Lockwood's company, you will encounter certain powerful people. It is imperative you make the proper addresses should they be required."

She was silent for a moment. She knew well enough what he meant. In the two years she had been in London, she'd managed to untangle the often confusing list of titles and forms of address for the peerage, but as she'd not been called upon to speak directly to barons or earls or marquesses, it would be far too easy to make a mistake.

"Very well," she said stiffly when it seemed as if Malcolm expected a reply, "I admit I find titles and forms of address confusing. However, perhaps I should inform you of my educational background so *you* won't be confused in future. I attended Mrs. Spentwell's Academy for Young Ladies in Virginia, and at seventeen, traveled to the Continent to live in Paris, where I studied music and French under the tutelage of Mademoiselle Villiers. I learned to sew a delicate seam, paint watercolors, and dance the minuet, cotillion, quadrille, and the waltz. I have an excellent seat and am well acquainted with horsemanship. I was taught deportment, and have read Mrs. Chapone's collection of polite letters. I am well versed on *Regulation of the Heart and Affections, The Government of the Temper,* and *Politeness and Accomplishments.* I play piano and have been told I have a lovely singing voice. Should there be any other instruction required to round out my education, I cannot imagine it would much interest the earl, can you?"

Malcolm blinked at her in silence, and she felt a spurt of fierce satisfaction that she had at last managed to wring some reaction from him. *Stuffy old sod*, Celia would have said about him, and she'd be right.

After a long moment, during which Malcolm opened and closed his mouth twice without speaking, he cleared his throat. "No, Miss Lancaster, I cannot imagine the earl would require anything else of you. Indeed, you surpass even my expectations."

"Really. I shudder to think what those expectations might have been." She rose to her feet to indicate that their interview was ended. "Inform the earl that I am comfortable and will strive not to disappoint. Nor do I expect to be disappointed in him. Good day, sir."

"Good . . . day, Miss Lancaster." Bundled into his greatcoat and hat, he left the house and went out into the cold, scurrying down the short walk to the waiting carriage with his shoulders hunched against the wind, and Laura had the thought that every word of their conversation would be repeated verbatim to Lockwood.

Good!

CHAPTER 7

"Oh, miss," Becky said from the window, "'is lordship's carriage is 'ere! It's time to go!"

Outwardly calm, Laura's stomach was a tight knot and her heart sent blood pumping so fast and hard through her veins that she could barely hear anything but the thundering beat. Still, she managed to say steadily, "I'm ready."

Was she? Properly dressed, yes, and with a week's worth of tutoring in rank and address behind her as well as the whirl of visits to seamstresses and glovers and cobblers, she had as much preparation as was humanly possible for a night at the opera. Yet it was Lockwood whom she had not been able to prepare herself for, seeing him again, listening to his amused, rich drawl as he spoke to her, the assessment in his gaze more important to her than anything else right now. Only because of her situation, she told herself, the need to earn his approval and her passage back to America. Yet there was a tiny voice in the back of her mind that echoed Celia's pithy remark that snaring an earl like Lockwood was the same bloody prize as finding the Holy Grail.

"Cor, miss, ye're the loveliest thing I've ever seen."

Laura smiled uncertainly at Becky. "You've a talent for hairdressing that quite amazes me."

It was true. Becky had pulled her hair into a cluster of curls atop her head and wound gold ropes of tiny seed pearls through the strands, leaving a fringe of curls on her forehead and wisps of hair dangling in front of her ears and the nape of her neck. It gleamed with a rich color that an egg wash had produced. A glance in the cheval mirror to reassure herself that the lines of her new gown were perfectly arranged, and Laura sailed down the staircase just as the post boy opened the door to Lockwood's footman.

Becky bustled after her, helping her into a wrap that covered the deep green drape of her gown with a cloud of gold-spangled satin. The newest thing, the seamstress has assured Laura, was rich, bright colors for evening wear. And of course, a display of bosom was *de rigueur* for a night at the opera, the corset thrusting her breasts up to reveal a deep cleavage. Daring, almost brazen, the gown was very Parisian.

Pulling the satin wrap around her shoulders, Laura drifted down the steps and out to the waiting carriage with head held high and her back straight. Lockwood would know at once that she intended to keep her bargain with him. And she prayed he'd never know how absolutely terrified she was at the prospect of appearing in public as his mistress.

The luxurious town coach with its heraldic arms on the doors was attended by four footmen, and one of them held the door for her and handed her up into the softly-lit interior where Lockwood waited. Surprising her, he took her hand to assist her as well, and when she was seated opposite him on the plush velvet squabs, he smiled.

"You're exceedingly lovely tonight, Miss Lancaster."

"Indeed I am, my lord," she said primly and was rewarded by his soft laugh.

"Ever frank, if not modest, I see. How refreshing."

"If I were to play coy, it would only belittle your efforts to see me properly turned out, would it not, my lord?"

"A practical view, and quite true." The smile still softened the hard line of his mouth, and she had to catch herself to keep from staring.

How had she not remembered just how handsome he was? Like a great, golden cat, with his tawny hair and amber eyes, and that limber posture that disguised how quickly and suddenly he could pounce. She'd seen him not once, but twice, exercise his ability to bring up short those who displeased him. First that impetuous young Stokely, then Whitfield, who had been far more determined and thus dangerous.

Looking down and away from his golden regard, she smoothed her skirts with nervous fingers, her matching gloves of green India cotton masking the way her hands trembled.

"It has been some time since I've attended the opera," she said.

"Has it. And do you enjoy it, mademoiselle?"

"Very much. Madame Catalani is a favorite."

"Indeed." His brow rose. "And you have been privileged to hear her?"

She looked up to find his skeptical gaze on her, and flushed. "I have. In Paris, of course."

"Of course."

It was obvious he thought her a complete fraud. A hot retort trembled on the tip of her tongue and she looked out the window to keep her temper from boiling over. Yet even with her gaze averted, she felt his intense regard and it made her nervous. He looked every inch the lord tonight in his white waistcoat and black cutaway tail coat, barely visible beneath the warm surtout over all, and a snowy white cravat draped in simple elegance, his collar points not so high they looked ridiculous as many wore. Snug-fitting breeches clung to well-muscled thighs, and gleaming black kid shoes and silk stockings were understated elegance. A top hat perched on the seat next to him beside a pair of smooth leather gloves.

Julian Norcliff, sixth Earl Lockwood, had chosen her for his companion and she wondered for what must have been the tenth time just what his wife must be thinking to leave him. What would cause a woman to flee her husband for a lover's arms and certain disgrace?

And what, Laura wondered, glancing at him through her lashes to find him gazing at her with a faint smile, would she do if he *did* desire her in his bed?

Her pulse leaped and she felt oddly breathless, air leaving her lungs in a soft whoosh at the very thought of it. It was a relief when the coach finally halted in front of King's Theater.

Julian found his gaze continually straying to his little protégée during the evening, a pleasant surprise as Malcolm had warned him she'd be: spirited without being cheeky, desirable without being coarse, and he'd found himself nearly at a loss for words. There was a freshness in her beauty that he found infinitely more alluring than the jaded expectations of the courtesans at Mme. Devereaux's soirée. And it was intriguing that Mme. Devereaux insisted the girl was a virgin as she claimed. Unlikely, but intriguing.

At intermission, Julian rose from his velvet upholstered seat and held out his arm for Laura to tuck her hand into the crook of his elbow. Well aware of the avid gazes in their direction and the whispers behind open fans and gloved hands, he intended to give them a good show. He held her wrap for her, a frothy bit of gold-shot satin that couldn't be warm but was certainly lovely, and let his hand linger a moment upon her arm when he'd pulled it around her. She shivered.

"Deuced cold," he murmured close to her ear, "and a perverse sense of fashion that requires that ladies wear no proper wrap in the evenings. You should have a warm pelisse."

"And so I do, my lord, at your expense. However, I didn't wish it to crush my gown."

He laughed softly. "Your gown is saved at the expense of extreme chill. I commend your fortitude."

She slanted him a saucy glance from green eyes almost the same deep shade as her gown, and it was definitely flirtatious, as befitted a mistress. Yes, she'd play the part well.

Leaning into him, she said softly, "Your concern is warming enough, my lord."

He found himself grinning as they exited the box and entered the crowded corridor where the noise of laughter and conversation filled the air. In the light of glittering chandeliers and new gas lamps on the walls, he could see the change in her from the hollow-cheeked waif to a woman no longer gaunt but glowing. There was color in her cheeks and jeweled eyes, and animation in her mobile face that was positively entrancing. She captured attention, and he saw eyes swivel toward her from every direction. Malcolm's plan had merit, indeed.

"Ah, Lockwood, a pleasant evening, what?"

Stepping from an alcove, a burly man in a stained waistcoat barred their path so that Julian had to pause. "Good evening, Sandridge."

Lord Sandridge smiled broadly, and his gaze shifted from Julian to the lady on his arm. "I don't recall seeing you here often. Didn't know you as a devotée of the opera, hey what?"

"I do attend functions other than Parliamentary sessions." He slid an arm around Laura's back to press his palm lightly against her spine, urging her forward as he nodded at Sandridge and attempted to move on. Sandridge, however, did not take the subtle hint.

"No, no, can't say that I've seen you out and about, hey. Lovely company you're keeping these days, what?"

Julian relented. "Lord Sandridge, may I present Miss Laura Lancaster."

"Hey, what? Not of the Yorkshire Lancasters, hey?"

She smiled sweetly. "No, indeed, my lord."

Amused at her self-possessed reply, Julian saw the speculation light Sandridge's eyes, and knew that it would be all over London within two days that Lockwood had taken a new bit of muslin to his bed. It couldn't be working more perfectly. How fortuitous that it would be Lord Sandridge who stopped him first.

By the time the intermission was over, gossip buzzed throughout the five tiers of peerage and the ever-present ladies of the evening who came to see and be seen. The vast gallery seated over three thousand, and it seemed as if every eye turned to watch when Julian and the object of their speculation returned to his private box as the last act of the opera began.

"I think you're enjoying this greatly, my lord," Laura said when he'd seated her and took his own chair close beside her. She lifted the opera glasses he'd lent her and stared down at the pit below. "So many, and they all seem to be watching you."

"No, I believe they are watching *you*," he said with a faint smile.

She gave him a surprised glance. "Do you truly think so?"

"Indeed, I'm convinced of it." After a moment, she turned back to the glasses and her perusal of the crowd below. He watched her, studying her profile, the clean lines of her nose and cheek and throat; then his gaze drifted lower, to the soft swell of her bosom thrust up in the green bodice decorated with gold gilt embroidery. Fetching. Most fetching.

"Oh!" she said, leaning forward with a smile, lips parted and her breasts pressing against the green satin. "There is Celia with Belgrave in a box opposite us!" She lifted a slender arm and waved, her laughter bubbling up. "She's staring at us through her glasses, too."

"Is she. Saucy Celia."

It was amusing to watch her watch those staring at them, and when the lights dimmed and Catalani returned to the stage, he was almost disappointed as Laura sat back in her chair and turned the glasses back to the opera. Hardly any need for the glasses, as his box was quite near the stage and the sets were easily viewed, but she seemed to enjoy using them.

And he enjoyed watching her.

Too soon, the opera ended and it was time to continue Malcolm's carefully orchestrated evening designed to restore his damaged reputation.

Again, he was accosted when he escorted her from his box into the wide, carpeted hallway crowded with glittering lords, ladies, and curiosity.

"Lockwood," a young baronet more bold than most said as

he approached with a smile, "not seen you about in a good while."

"I've been rather occupied of late, Ellsworth."

"Have you." Young Ellsworth's eyes shifted at once to Laura, who remained cool and poised on Julian's arm, her fingers tucked over his sleeve as if accustomed to being with him. "I can well understand."

"No doubt. Good evening."

As he moved past, Ellsworth gave a start, and called after him. "P'raps we'll see you later at White's, then."

"Not this evening, Ellsworth." Julian nodded at those they passed who spoke to him, and continued a slow progress through the throng and down the steps, ignoring the curious gazes as they left King's Theater. His footman stood waiting, the carriage door open, the line of vehicles in front of the theater long and twisting through Haymarket like a snake.

Once seated in the warmth of his coach, Laura looked up at him expectantly, her eyes a soft gleam in the dim interior. "That was most entertaining," she said, "though I'm not at all certain if Catalani appreciated the crowd's distraction."

He grinned. "If there's one thing London loves more than opera, it's the human comedy. Tonight, we were the players and all the theater our stage. Did you enjoy it?"

"Immensely." Her lashes lowered over the speculation in her gaze. "An elaborate charade, and to what end, I've found myself wondering."

"To my own purposes," he said easily, leaning back to watch her, the smile hovering still at the corners of his mouth. "You play the part well, as if born to it."

"I shall take that as a compliment, my lord, though to be sure, it's not the most flattering remark to make, comparing me to a courtesan."

He laughed, amused at her spirit. "It was meant as a compliment, Miss Lancaster. Your talents are wasted as a shepherdess on the Covent Garden stage."

"Yet that role has been more kind to me than the last. I was not at all pleased to play the part of an ugly crone with a hump in the last production."

"*Macbeth,* I presume."

She nodded, then smiled mischievously. " 'When shall we three meet again, In thunder, lightning, or in rain?' "

" 'When the hurlyburly's done, When the battle's lost and won.' Were you the first witch, then?"

"Yes, with the most lines of the three, but still . . . I rather wished to be Celia. She was Lady Macbeth, of course."

"And now you are a shepherdess with few lines, but the best legs."

She stared at him a moment, eyes wide. "Yes, that's quite true, my lord, though Jeremy does have a nice turn of leg himself."

"Jeremy?"

"Jeremy Pinch, one of the players."

"I shall have to watch for him when next I attend the production, to see this well-turned leg for myself," he said solemnly, and saw her smile return.

"Then rumors shall fly, my lord."

"So they would." To his surprise, he found himself quite entertained with her. She'd begun to blossom now that there was adequate food and a sense of security, no longer looking as if she expected the ceiling to fall upon her head or the next word to be a blow. He rather liked the metamorphosis, like watching a butterfly emerge from a cocoon.

By the time they reached their destination, he had decided that he'd chosen the perfect woman to play the role of his mistress. Anyone who knew him at all would know he could never suffer a silly chit for long, and Laura Lancaster was exactly what he would have chosen were he inclined to take a mistress. Exactly.

Lockwood's coach halted on Bennet Street, St. James, in front of a corner house with a red baize door. Laura accepted the footman's hand-down from the vehicle, and glancing up at the door, had the distinct impression this was not at all a gentleman's club, not in the true sense of the word *gentleman*. Though there was a uniformed servant at the door regulating those admitted, the caliber of the players was not confined to the peerage.

Smoke drifted in thick layers in the large room to which they were shown, coming from an ill-laid fire in the grate. A sharpness marked faces of men crowded around green baize tables, as faro and hazard consumed those playing. No ladies were present, though there were women of obviously low morals moving through titled barons, merchants, and any who had money to wager.

A gaming hell.

No *lady* would be found here. A sense of shame sent heat beating through her as Laura fought to hide her dismay. It was to be expected, she supposed, that Lockwood would want her exact role in his life known by those of his acquaintance, but she'd not considered he'd be so forward with it as to parade her through such an establishment. She would have much preferred a fashionable assembly of nobility discussing politics and world events over tea and brandy in an elegant drawing room.

But it wasn't her choice. She'd agreed to play the role of his mistress, and so set herself to make the best of the situation, keeping a smile pasted on her face that felt stiff and false as she remained at Lockwood's side.

"Do you play, Miss Lancaster?" he murmured when they paused before a hazard table, and she shook her head.

"Since arriving in London, I've never had money enough to wager."

"There are gaming tables in Paris, I understand."

She looked up at him and smiled. "So there are, but not for a child."

"Ah well, you're a child no longer. Come. I'll teach you the rules and you can try your luck." He reached out and palmed a pair of wooden dice, turning them with his thumb. "This is a good game for one who can master the odds, so listen carefully. Two dice are thrown until one scores five, six, seven, eight, or nine. The first one thrown is called the main. The second toss is the chance. If the second die equals the main, the caster—or player—has nicked it and won all the stakes. If the caster throws two, three, eleven, or twelve, he's thrown crabs and lost. If the caster neither nicks it or throws out, he must continue casting until the chance nets a win. Now here. See what you can do."

Laura threw out almost at once, and laughing, tried again. This time her luck was better, and she nicked it on the second score. Smiling, Lockwood placed her bets for her, his presence at her side an encouragement, though he offered no advice. Soon there was a crowd pressed close to the hazard table, watching the play.

"'Pon my word, Lockwood," one gentleman grumbled finally, "the children in the wood will see me done up before long. Deuced fine luck your *fille de joie* is having, what?"

Faltering slightly, Laura threw out, and the man's smile widened with satisfaction.

"Do you by chance refer to Miss Lancaster, Harrowby?" Lockwood asked in the soft tone she'd heard him use the night he rescued her from the drunken advances of a marquis. An instant hush fell over those at the table, a sort of avid curiosity and excitement at the prospect of a quarrel between gentlemen.

At the center of it, Laura wished only to sink through the floorboards and into the cellar below. Bad enough being thought a whore; to have it remarked upon in her presence was worse.

"Heh, what? Miss Lancaster? How the devil am I to know your doxy's name?" Harrowby seemed oblivious to the nuances of his transgression until Lockwood leaned forward to fix him with a narrowed gaze.

"You have just been informed of it, Harrowby, and will be pleased to beg her pardon for your rude words in her presence."

Harrowby looked astonished. The same emotion was reflected in several faces around the table, and Laura wished nothing had been said. Now it would be repeated all over London, and those who'd not known her name before, would certainly know it soon.

"I'll do no such thing, Lockwood! Have you run mad?" Harrowby demanded indignantly. "If you've made the mistake of bringing a decent woman into a gaming hell, you cannot expect me to know it."

"Perhaps you're right," Lockwood said after a moment. "It's too much to expect a man of your consequence and rank to express common courtesy not only to a peer, but a young woman in my company."

Looking thunderstruck, Harrowby's jaw dropped, and a glance around him at the faces reflecting disapproval made his heavy gray brow lower. "By God, Lockwood, you've gone too far now."

"Indeed?"

"Indeed!" Giving him a harsh look, Harrowby stomped away from the hazard table, leaving a wake of interested onlookers behind.

With supreme indifference, Lockwood turned back to the hazard table. "Ah no, my love, you've thrown out, have you? Here's another quid to bring you up to snuff."

Play resumed, but Laura found little pleasure in it now, feeling instead the sting of rumor that would be spread all over town on the morrow. No doubt, with morning tea and the *Times*, her name would be on every tongue. If he'd planned it, the earl could not have assured notoriety more neatly.

After several moments of desultory play, he took her arm in his warm hand, fingers curling over her wrist lightly. "Lost interest now, I see. Never mind. Come see how you do at faro."

Laura's attention was distracted, and she missed most of his instruction on playing faro, but stood mutely by the table painted with representations of the thirteen cards on its green baize surface. A dealer drew from a box placed faceup, while players bet against the house on the card representation, winning if their guess was correct. The earl won several times, and juggled his winnings in his palm carelessly. Just the amount of the wagers made would have been enough to support her in comfort for a year, and it was appalling that children starved while barons played, she thought, but held her tongue and kept her face carefully blank.

"Does the entertainment pall?" the earl asked her softly, and she looked up with a start to find his golden gaze resting on her with an enigmatic expression.

"Not at all, my lord," she replied promptly. "I merely find myself speechless with delight."

A curl of his mouth indicated frank disbelief, and she couldn't help a returning smile at the amusement in his eyes. "You're a dreadful liar, Miss Lancaster."

"One of my virtues, my lord."

"No doubt. It occurs to me to wonder about your other . . . virtues." He reached out to tuck a dangling curl behind her shoulder, his fingers brushing against skin bared by the low vee neck of her fashionable gown, and she suppressed a shiver at his touch.

"Cold? Come, we'll stand by the fire as long as we can bear the smoke."

It was better to let him think her chilled than to know his touch affected her, and she went quietly with him to stand by a tiled hearth where heat spread a few feet into the room. Her head ached, and her eyes itched, and she thought longingly of her small parlor that had become a sweet refuge these past two weeks. Too quickly, she'd grown accustomed to comfort.

Beckoning to a waiter, he secured them both a drink—brandy for himself, a slender glass of champagne for her—and she sipped it slowly, savoring the heady tickle of bubbles on her tongue. It was soon gone, and he replaced her empty glass with a full one and a smiling caution not to let the bubbles go to her head.

"Too late, I fear, for I'm quite liable to swoon any moment."

"You're not a woman prone to faints," he said with a laugh, and she tilted her head to one side to study him with a smile.

He could be so charming when he chose as now to play the part, but there was something in his eyes that was . . . restless. A constant searching, as if for someone he knew or expected. His wife, perhaps? Did he think she could be here, or should be here? Did he miss her on his arm, and played the part of attentive lover only as vengeance? There had to be a logical reason for his offer of support in return for her masquerade as his mistress instead of the reality. No other explanation made sense.

"Sweet Christ!" Lockwood's sudden oath made her eyes widen, and she saw he was staring with narrowed eyes at a table near the fire. Following his gaze, she saw only a handful of gentlemen seated at the table, intent upon their cards and play. "Devil take him for a green gull," he muttered savagely, and strode toward the table with her in his wake.

Upon reaching the table, where the play was so intent none took notice of those around them, he clapped a hand on the shoulder of one of the players, and the man gave a sudden start and glanced up. His face went pale, hazel eyes widening.

"Norcliff."

Lockwood nodded grimly. "I see you recognize me. What I fail to see, is why you are here instead of where you'd said you'd be."

A guilty expression flickered briefly on the young man's face, followed by annoyance. "It's hardly the time or the place to discuss it, old boy."

"On the contrary. I think it most appropriate." Leaning forward, he put a hand over the stack of chits at the man's left side. "Shall we discuss it privately, or do you prefer to remain at the table?"

After an instant's hesitation, the young man rose and bowed to his companions. "As all here must be aware of my brother's impatience, I beg your indulgence for a brief absence."

Across the table, another man grinned, leaning back in his chair. "Carry on, Faraday. We'll await your return."

"It may be of necessity a lengthy wait," Lockwood interjected smoothly, and the glance he shot his brother stifled any retort from that direction.

Feeling oddly in the way, Laura stepped a short distance from the two men as they moved across the room, though the earl's hand cupped her elbow and drew her along with them.

The younger man halted in an alcove and swung to face his brother angrily. "Do you intend to humiliate me?"

"No, I intend to stop you gaming away your inheritance."

"It's mine to do with as I please," Faraday shot back at him, tension marking features very similar to Lockwood's but lacking maturity and a certain strength of character. He was young, it was plain to Laura, and obviously trying to bluff his way out of their argument, and failing.

"Yours, yes, but not to do with as you please. You have responsibilities to go with that title you inherited, not just coin to spread among the rabble."

"Don't come the swell with me, when you're here in a gambling hell yourself. I thought you never frequented these places." Faraday glared at him, and then his gaze moved to Laura and his brows lifted in surprise. "And with a woman! I'm flummoxed."

"I've no doubt of that," Lockwood replied coolly, "but you'll do well to keep your remarks to yourself at the moment. Instead, explain to me how it is you're here instead of at your estate in Surrey seeing to the matter of the flooded cellar."

Dragging his gaze from Laura to his brother, Faraday shrugged. "Beastly weather, cold enough to freeze any water before it can do more damage. I sent Darby."

"You sent your valet?"

"My steward." His chin lifted, square like his brother's but as yet irresolute, and there was a defensiveness to his posture that betrayed his youth and uncertainty. "I've not the vast staff you employ, nor the coin to pay them."

"My point exactly." Lockwood gave a grim shake of his head. "Viscount Foolscap, what were you thinking?"

"That I'd the ready to wager, and a run of luck that would see the cellar repaired and the tradesmen's bills settled, of course."

"The ready to which you refer is actually my money, on loan to you at the moment in the vain hope you'll spend it wisely, not put it in the pockets of those sharps at your table."

"Those sharps are my comrades," the viscount responded stiffly. "And they are waiting on my return. Unless you intend to stop me by force, I'm committed to finish the game."

"Finish then, but remember that I won't be so generous with my purse the next time you ask."

For a moment, indecision filled his hazel eyes as Faraday studied his brother, then he slid a glance to the table and those watching with knowing smiles, and seemed to shake himself like a dog. He inclined his head slightly. "I'll remember."

As he walked away, Lockwood muttered, "Young fool."

"A boy still," Laura murmured, "and desperate for your approval."

He shot her a narrow glance. "If he were desperate for my approval, madam, he'd not be sitting down at the table to be fleeced."

"On the contrary, my lord, he'd like nothing better than to earn your respect by winning and proving to you he's not a fool."

"Instead he'll prove he is. Hardly a strong recommendation." He stared at the far corner of the room where his brother had returned to the table. "Just when I think he's listened to me, he behaves with stunning stupidity."

Laura stood silently. Nothing she said would sway the earl, and in truth, it wasn't her quarrel. If she spoke out of turn, he'd take her to task for it. It really wasn't her business, she reminded herself when Lockwood turned back to the faro table, his mood irritable. She stood at his side while he played, boredom settling on her as time passed. Then she happened to glance up and see a familiar face on the opposite side of the table, and smiled in surprise.

Rex Pentley, an acquaintance of Celia's, tipped his head in her direction and waggled his brows as if to ask what she was doing there on the arm of an earl. His infectious grin made Laura laugh softly.

"Excuse me, my lord," she murmured to Lockwood, who nodded absently as he wagered a gold guinea, and slipped away to stand in front of the fire. As she expected, Rex appeared at her side within moments.

Holding her palms out to the fire as if only there to warm them, she said, "I see you're up to your old tricks, Rex, here to fleece the gulls. Did you tire of swindling lonely married women out of their jewels?"

"Laura my darling, you malign me. Those women were paid handsomely for whatever baubles they bestowed upon me for my . . . attentions." A handsome enough rogue, though a bit coarse, Rex grinned down at her, leaning against the mantel. "And you here with a swell like Lockwood, running your own game? Have you given up chastity for a more lucrative profession? Or are you just toying with him?"

She rapped him smartly on the arm with her reticule, but didn't take offense. It was the natural assumption, and she'd chosen to put herself in this position. Besides, an idea had occurred to her. "I've an offer of my own for you, Rex, if you're game."

"Ah, for what prize?" His eyes sharpened, gaze raking over her quickly before returning to her face.

"Not that." She thought of the coins she'd won at hazard. "A gold guinea if you succeed."

He laughed. "Hardly worth my time, love. What else?"

"My gratitude."

"Ah, that's worth much more. What is it you want me to do?"

Glancing toward the table where Lockwood's brother sat, she leaned forward to say in a soft murmur, "Cheat at cards."

Pentley laughed. "Delighted to oblige!"

* * *

Julian downed the last of his brandy and shook his head at the waiter to refuse another. "I fear I'd give in to the overpowering urge to drag Randal from the table and into the alley for a sound thrashing, but he's more likely to get one from those sharps," he said when Laura glanced at him, and she smiled.

"Perhaps he'll play well, my lord."

"It would be a welcome change from his usual run of luck. Young fool. He's gambling away his future and I'm damned if I'll replace it."

She held her tongue, understanding his frustration if she didn't agree with it. Oddly, she understood the impetuous, rebellious viscount. She'd recognized the expression in his eyes for what it was—a desire to prove himself to a man he admired. Once, she'd felt the same need for her mother's approval, long ago as it was, until she'd learned shattering truths.

A crowd had gathered around the table where his brother was playing, and Lockwood moved across the room to watch, Laura trailing behind. Two new players had taken seats, one of them Rex Pentley, who looked up at her without expressing recognition. Nothing registered on his fleshy, handsome face, save a somber regard for the cards in his hand.

After the first two hands, Viscount Faraday slumped lower in his chair, and Laura felt Lockwood's tension. She put a hand on his arm, fingers resting on his tensed muscles, and kept her tongue. The whisper of pasteboard cards seemed overloud in the smoky room, though there were still the sounds of dice thunking against green felt, and the *clack clack clack* of the E.O. wheel spinning round. Laura felt some of Lockwood's tension, but put her trust in Pentley. He'd not fail her.

After a moment, she heard Lockwood make a sound deep in his throat; then Faraday won a hand neatly, raking in a pile of money. Two more hands passed and his stack of coins grew high as play continued; two players threw in their hands in disgust, leaving only two. Pentley glanced up at Faraday, a flicker of his eyes assessing the other man.

"Another round, my lord?" he asked politely, and for a moment, Laura thought Faraday might agree. But then he shook his head, a faint smile of relief on his handsome mouth.

"It's bad form to stop when winning, but I've enough for the night."

Pentley inclined his head, then spread his hands to the sides. "My pockets are to let, so it's just as well." As the viscount scooped up his chits, Pentley looked directly at Laura, the ghost of a smile on his lips as he rose from the chair.

Laura turned, and found Lockwood gazing at her with narrow speculation. Her heart gave a peculiar thump. Had he seen? Did he somehow know? If he did, he didn't mention it, but turned instead to his brother.

"Well done, Faraday."

A look passed between them before the viscount nodded. "A good run of luck."

"My carriage is outside. I'll give you a lift."

Once outside, a wide grin split Faraday's face. "By God, I've never had such a turn of luck! It seems a shame to cut the evening short."

A light snow had begun to fall, drifting down to powder streets, horses, and carriage. "Get in the coach," Julian said as the footman held the door open for Laura, and the viscount followed her inside, settling on the seat opposite as the earl climbed in after them. When the door closed, Lockwood turned to his brother. "Don't you know when you've been gammoned?"

"Gammoned?" Faraday looked incredulous, then angry. "Don't you think I can win at cards without being gulled?"

"Yes. I do." Lockwood looked across the coach at Laura. "But tonight, you didn't."

Laura met his gaze steadily, aware that Faraday had turned to look at her as well. His brow knit into a frown. "I don't understand."

"Perhaps Miss Lancaster can enlighten you."

"I only meant to help," Laura said after a moment. "You were being cheated, so it seemed fair enough to cheat them in turn."

"But how . . . what . . . who are you?"

Ignoring the last, she said, "I recognized a friend and enlisted his aid. He merely arranged the cards to your benefit, as his lordship has surmised."

"You have most intriguing friends, Miss Lancaster," Lockwood said softly, "and very adept. I almost missed it."

"Yes, he's very good. Rex used to perform card tricks at the theater, but found a better way to earn a living, it seems."

"So it seems," Lockwood observed dryly.

Crestfallen, young Faraday recovered quickly from the shock of finding he'd been fooled. He smiled at Laura, and slanted a sly glance toward his brother. "I find the lady more intriguing than her friends. Has my staid old brother abandoned his stuffy rules at last?"

"There's a difference between being stuffy and being stupid," Lockwood said sharply. "It would behoove you to learn that."

Leaning back, the viscount lazily cocked one leg over the other, resting a gleaming boot atop his knee. "There's no need for me to learn it with you always hovering about to remind me," he drawled, and despite the softness of his tone, anger darkened his eyes. "You set such an excellent example of moral turpitude. And this young lady is . . . ?"

"My companion," Lockwood replied shortly.

"A lovely choice. I admit I'm astonished, but then, you've always shown good taste when allowed free rein. Eleanor was Father's decision, after all, and a bloody bad one as it's turned out, hey?"

Laura sat in horrified silence as the coach rocked through the streets at a fast pace, and the silence that fell was thick with tension.

"Don't go too far, Randal," Lockwood said at last, a soft

warning that fell on listening ears, for his brother nodded agreement.

"Sorry, old boy." He seemed genuinely contrite, and the tension eased. "I confess to being cup-shot or I'd never have said it."

"I recommend a good night's sleep before you leave for Surrey."

Faraday calmly acknowledged the veiled command. "Darby will be relieved to see me, no doubt. Ah, here we are at my lodgings." His glance slid to Laura, and he grinned suddenly, all anger forgotten. "Should you ever require more lively company, Miss Lancaster, you've only to arrive on my doorstep. I'll be most pleased to offer my services."

"Devil take you," Lockwood said amiably before Laura could form a response, then the coach halted and the door opened. The viscount stepped out, then turned to lean inside, his eyes alight with laughter.

"Julian's not as dreary as he seems, Miss Lancaster, just devilish good at hiding it."

Lockwood gave his brother a push and he stumbled backward, laughing as the footman caught him. Then the coach door swung closed and the vehicle lurched forward again, leaving them alone in the enclosed shadows. Silence hung heavily for several minutes.

She opened her mouth to offer a comment just as a wheel dipped into a deep rut, rocking the coach to one side and throwing her from the seat. Before she landed in a heap on the floor, the earl caught her, his arms going around her instinctively, holding her up.

Suddenly aware of the tension in his arms, she glanced up at him, and her heart leaped. He seemed surprised to find her in his embrace, but did not immediately release her. Instead, his hold tightened, and the warmth of his arm beneath her breasts burned into her. She hung there, her face only inches from his, so close she could count his lashes, see her reflection and pinpoints of light from the interior lamps in his amber eyes. Then another light flared that had nothing to do with the lamps, and before she could anticipate it, his head lowered and his mouth found hers, hot and consuming, covering her lips like a burning brand.

Shivering, she clutched at him blindly, fingers digging into his arms, the taste of brandy on his tongue as heady as the press of his mouth on hers, igniting an unfamiliar blaze deep in the pit of her stomach that threatened to turn her to ashes. When finally he lifted his head, staring down at her with darkly shadowed eyes, she could only cling to him in bewildered confusion. Her heart beat rapidly, her pulse thundered and she felt hot and cold at the same time, flushed and shivering.

"We've arrived at your lodgings, Miss Lancaster," he said, and she slowly became aware that the coach had halted, and a footman was opening the door.

Flustered, she pulled away and smoothed her skirts, awkward and feeling foolish. What should she say? Do? Did he mean to come inside with her? And oh God, what if he did? What if he kissed her again . . . ?

Charlton stood politely, hand outstretched to help her down, and she put her fingers into his gloved palm and accepted his assistance, stepping from the coach. Snow whirled in drifting gusts, cold against her heated cheeks, and she looked up at Lockwood still inside.

"Good night, Miss Lancaster," he said in the same composed tone, and she managed a nod that felt stiff and fraudulent.

"Good night, my lord."

Charlton escorted her the few steps to her door, and Becky opened it to admit her inside, and by the time Laura turned back to look, the coach had begun to roll away, the footman leaping to catch hold of the rear handles and climb on. It quickly disappeared into the shadows down the street, leaving her to stare at streetlights diffused by snow.

CHAPTER 8

"I trust all is well, my lord."

"Indeed." Julian rustled the pages of the *Times* and didn't glance up. "I expected to find you at my chamber door with the morning paper. Your restraint is commendable."

Malcolm's polite cough indicated agreement. "It does seem to be working splendidly, does it not?"

"You're referring, of course, to my appearance at the opera with Miss Lancaster."

"Indeed I am, my lord." Malcolm beckoned to a footman to pour hot coffee into the earl's cup. The fragrant brew served to lure Lockwood from behind his paper, and he lowered it to fix his secretary with a steady gaze.

"My name is in several articles, and no doubt, as of this morning, on every tongue. This should set the rumors to rest about my preference for the company of young boys. Or for my steward, as fine as he may be."

"Indeed it should, my lord." An expression of satisfaction eased the normal severity of Malcolm's features. He looked like a cat in cream, and Julian smiled.

"You deserve to feel quite pleased with yourself, Malcolm. I've been most satisfied with the results of your ploy."

"And the young lady, my lord? She pleases you as well?"

"A pleasant enough surprise," he said after a moment's reflection. Not the least of which was his surprise at his own actions the night before, the surrender to a startling temptation to kiss her. He'd run the gamut of emotions during the evening, and his irritation with Randal had put him in a dangerously irrational frame of mind. There was no other explanation for his actions.

"I understand she was quite a surprise to others as well," Malcolm said as he placed a tray of letters and cards near Julian's plate as instructed. "She conducted herself with a proper degree of comportment. A fine actress, it seems."

"Perhaps." Julian folded the paper and set it aside. Weak sunlight through the glass panes of the morning room windows gleamed on silverplate; the snow had stopped some time during the night. He thought of Laura's face, the pure lines so lovely and delicate, and her innate modesty even in a gown that displayed her soft white breasts almost to the point of immodesty. "Though I suspect your assessment of her as being gently reared lent more to her performance than merely an ability to mimic the actions of others," he said after a moment. "What were you able to learn about her life before she came to London?"

"At this time, very little, my lord. She just seems to have appeared on stage with a troupe of players from France, and lingered after they moved on. Her closest companion is another actress, Celia Carteret, whose protector is Lord Belgrave."

"Another protégée of Mme. Devereaux?"

"No, my lord, not to my knowledge. Miss Carteret is merely another actress. No doubt, there are many such acquaintances of low class."

A faint smile curved his mouth as Julian thought of Laura's deception the night before, her effort to extract Randal from a blunder of his own making. It had worked quite neatly, and he'd not thanked her for it but been angry. More at his brother than at her—still, she deserved more than a few sharp words and a clumsy embrace. God, *that* had the power to embarrass him. He'd ignored his own rule and given in to the temptation her parted lips and wide eyes provoked, the feel of her soft breasts against his arm erasing any restraint he thought he possessed.

A restless night had been his reward for it.

Looking up, he saw Malcolm staring at him expectantly. "Yes?"

The secretary coughed politely. "I asked, my lord, if I should have the footmen clear away the dishes now."

"Yes. I'll read the morning post in my study."

Damned inconvenient that he'd moon over an actress like a schoolboy and be caught at it, and he took himself off to the privacy of his study before he embarrassed himself further.

Pale drifts of snow cloaked the alley by the theater in a mantle of white and hid the piles of refuse. Laura thought it coldly appropriate, this fraudulent beauty.

"Are we to return for you after the evening performance, miss?"

"Yes, Trenton," she said, lifting her skirts so they wouldn't drag in the damp, dirty ruts worn into the snow by carriage wheels. She hurried the few yards to the stage door, fading light entering the theater with her as she stepped inside. Dark came so early now, only a few hours after the noon hour, but soon the days would grow longer again.

Lamps shed pools of light in the musty corridors, and groups of players who'd been talking loudly suddenly grew silent as she entered. Laura faltered at their scrutiny.

"Hullo," she said, and no one answered, the silence strangely ominous. Uneasy, she went past them and into the small dressing room shared with Celia. It was empty, Celia late as usual, and she shrugged out of her warm pelisse, a simple wool garment unadorned with fur, and hung it on a hook jutting from the wall. Why were the other players so sullen? They'd stared at her with such strange expressions, almost angry.

Celia provided the answer when she arrived, whirling in with her usual exuberance and flinging a newspaper down atop the cluttered dressing table. "Look at you, then, famous as Mrs. Fitzherbert, I vow! How'd you do it, Laura? Your name is on every tongue in London, from St. Giles to Westminster!"

"Oh God." She snatched up the paper and scanned the articles. "How can they write this?"

"Easily enough." Celia flung her cape at the hook and it missed, sliding to the top of the old draperies in a rustle of wool. "They don't dare use Lockwood's name, of course, but have no scruples about using yours. Still, anyone with half a brain can deduce that L——, an earl whose wife is said to be taking the air in Vienna, is Lockwood. And that his lovely new companion is an accomplished actress in Covent Garden, who can be seen nightly playing the part of a shepherdess with bare legs. The rest of the company is near mad with envy, and Roscoe is delighted. I hear the evening performance has been sold out, and all because of you. All of London will be here to see the girl who has—what did it say?—'charmed the elusive lord from his lofty perch to her snowy bosom,' or some such drivel as that. Wonderful, isn't it?"

Laura had listened to Celia with only part of her attention, the rest trained upon the lines of newsprint now smudged beneath her fingers. Lurid innuendoes. The entire city thought she was no more than his trollop. But hadn't she known that was inevitable? Just not like this, not so public and so blatant, and so . . . humiliating.

Groaning, she buried her face in her hands. "I can't go out there tonight," she said, her voice muffled by her palms.

"Nonsense." Celia moved to pat her shoulder. "You're famous. Besides, you knew this would happen once you consented to Lockwood's proposition. Just one more juicy bit of scandal for the idle. If he were a mere viscount like Belgrave, I daresay no one would care, but he's an earl and an MP, and there you have it. Instant fame. Enjoy it, ducks. It won't last."

She looked up. Celia stood in front of the mirror, winding

her hair into a knot atop her head and securing it with pins. "I can't," she said to Celia's reflection, "I'm not like you. I can't go out there with everyone thinking I'm warming the earl's bed at night."

"Don't be a goose. Of course you can. Did anyone care that you had no warm bed at night before now? No. Believe me, it's far better that people think you've the good sense to take proper advantage of an offer than that you're muddle-headed enough to sleep in the gutter. Come along, now, be a good girl and put on your costume."

Rather wildly, Laura sat still as Celia donned her wig, then pulled on the satin period gown and arranged the frothy fichu and ruffles. Finally she rose to her feet and tossed the paper to the floor. "I suppose you're right," she said in resignation. "I just didn't expect it to be so . . . so . . ."

"Sudden?" Celia supplied helpfully. "Yes, that is a surprise. Almost as if someone had the intention of putting it about, but there you have it. The gossip mills must need new meat. Shall I help you with your hair?"

It went better than she'd thought, and Laura was relieved when at last the performance ended and she could escape the theater. So many people, louder even than usual, voices rising in calls and hoots and a wild clapping of hands when she made her entrance with the lamb, and after the first moment of near paralyzed fright, she'd sauntered boldly across the stage and said her first line with a saucy grin so that the roar grew even louder. Aware of Celia's smiling encouragement from the wings, she'd turned once to face the audience with a sly wink and cheeky lift of one shoulder, then left the stage to thundering applause. It was not really for her they cheered, she knew, but for the part she played as Lockwood's mistress. All the world loved a good scandal.

And Roscoe beamed from ear to ear as he filled the cash box to overflowing, and caught her before she left for the night. "You'll not be leaving me now, will you, now that you have a protector?" he demanded, and she shook her head.

"No, I'll stay the rest of the play's run."

"There's a good lass—only another week, and even Emory will have his due."

"And, of course, I'll have a bonus as well, I'm sure," she said, nearly laughing aloud when he gave her a startled glance, then sighed in resignation.

"How much?"

"An extra shilling a night for every player," she said promptly, and ignored his horrified squeak of protest.

"A shilling a night! For every player? Impossible!"

"A week then," she said, and he nodded. She smiled. A shilling a week more was a tidy sum indeed. "I'll have your promise in writing," she added, and from the glum expression on his fleshy face, she knew she was wise to insist.

The play was to run until Christmas Eve, and that would put more into the players' purses than they could have hoped, she thought as she climbed into her carriage, a smart tilbury drawn by a pair of matching bays. Only two more weeks and she'd be out of work again, save for her role as Lockwood's mistress.

The first flush of humiliation had faded. In retrospect, she could have expected no more or less. Yet she'd not thought it would be so instant or encompassing. Rumor was one thing, to have it in print was quite another.

When she arrived home, Becky met her inside the foyer, an anxious expression on her face. "Ye've a visitor in the parlor, miss."

"Really?" Her stomach lurched, and she fumbled in pulling off her gloves. "Who is it?"

"Malcolm."

Unexpected disappointment knifed through her, and she nodded. Of course. Had she really expected Lockwood? How foolish she could be. "Tea would be nice," she said, and Becky gave a brisk nod.

"It's near done, miss. D'ye want I should serve *'im* tea and biscuits?"

"No, tea will be fine." A modicum of civility was all that was required for Lockwood's steward, and he'd not expect her to serve refreshments to him.

He stood up when she entered the parlor, his expression smooth and assessing as always. "You've made quite a cozy home, Miss Lancaster."

"With your direction, sir. Please be seated." She perched on the edge of the settee, near the fire so that it warmed her left side, facing Malcolm.

He smiled slightly. "His lordship was most pleased with your . . . performance last night."

She only nodded, and when he sat down opposite her, said, "It was an interesting evening. I always enjoy the opera."

"Indeed. I trust you've found your household arrangements satisfactory?"

"Yes, most satisfactory. The cook is excellent, and the groom and driver capable, as is my maid. She has a deft hand in arranging hair."

"Does she now. She was certainly ill-suited to service in the kitchens."

Becky arrived at that moment with a silver tray bearing a pot of tea, and placed it silently on the table between them, shooting a narrow glance at Malcolm.

Laura smiled. "I find her most adept. What brings you out on such a cold evening, sir?"

"Ah, a matter of business. His lordship wished me to inform you that your services will be requested again in three days time, at an evening function."

"He sent you as a messenger?" Her brow shot up, and color splotched Malcolm's cheeks at her assumption.

"No, of course not. A mere message could be conveyed by a postboy. I was sent to deliver this to you." Reaching into his jacket, he produced a small black velvet box. "You are to wear this at the function, and proper evening clothes. His carriage will arrive for you as last night, but at the theater when your performance is ended. You may inform your driver he'll not be needed."

After a brief hesitation, she took the box and opened it. A slender rope of pearls nestled on velvet, and she lifted it to find a small ivory rose dangling from the center. Her fingers trembled slightly.

"A Lancaster rose, I presume," Malcolm remarked, and she looked up at him with a faint smile.

"Hardly. Yorkists had the white rose, the Lancastrians the red." No, she knew the white rose meant something else to Lockwood, but she wasn't certain just what it signified.

And in three days, she would see him again.

"Your trousers, my lord."

Julian glanced over his shoulder as Cranford delivered the freshly pressed pair of breeches, then turned back to the mirror. Lifting the razor to his jaw, he saw Cranford watching him.

"What is it, Cranford?"

Silver hair gleamed in lamplight as the old man shook his head. "Nothing, my lord."

"The devil, you say. Then don't distract me, or I'm liable to cut my throat."

"Indeed, my lord, if you would allow your valet—"

"To cut it for me? I think not." Cranford's hand was not as steady as once it had been, and Julian had no intention of allowing him near his throat with a sharp implement. "You know I much prefer doing this myself. I didn't have you to shave me at Trafalgar, and if ever there was a need for a proper valet, it was in His Majesty's Royal Navy."

"Indeed, my lord." Cranford's tone dripped disapproval. Reared in the old school of proper service, the butler combined his duties as valet and groom of the chamber, which included his services as barber. Only in a gigantic household would those duties be performed by separate servants. Once, the Lockwood household had been such a size, when Julian's parents were alive and their children still young. Now, it was only Julian, and on occasion, Randal, so the necessity of a large staff during the year was ended.

"I've cleaned your evening coat," Cranford said after a moment, "and there's a proper shine on your boots, if you still intend to wear them."

"Where I'm going, Cranford, evening shoes are not required."

Amused at the old servant's disdainful sniff, he grinned. There was no more snobbish creature on earth than a gentleman's butler. But one more night in public should cement his reputation, and that of his supposed mistress. With Randal safely in Surrey, the evening should pass without incident. A relief, and an opportunity to study his little Covent Garden actress more closely.

It wasn't his imagination that she'd kissed him back, and with enthusiasm if not expertise. While he wasn't a man to make a habit of seducing virgins, he'd almost swear that her trembling and clumsiness were genuine, not the actions of an actress. Tonight, he meant to learn the truth.

After shaving, he patted his face dry with a clean towel, and allowed Cranford to assist him in dressing. Few in London could tie a cravat with the old man's elegant touch, though Beau Brummel's valet exceeded him by the slightest margin. The Beau may be in disgrace with the prince, but he still set the fashions. Julian, however, had little patience with the ludicrous fashion of neckcloths starched so stiffly and high a man could barely turn his head, and restricted Cranford to a sedate replica of Brummel's cravats.

Bitter cold greeted him when he stepped outside to his waiting carriage, and the interior wasn't much warmer. Heated bricks cooled quickly in this climate. He had Charlton bring more of them before they left for the theater. He arrived in time to see the last act of the play, and stood in the rear as the crowd cheered the little shepherdess with the short skirt and legs clad in blush-colored stockings that made them look bare.

The lamb under her arm had grown, and she managed it with some difficulty, finally setting it down and using her shepherd's crook to guide the balky creature. Her role had altered since he'd first seen it, and now she invited the audience to laugh at her saucy observations, a hand on her hip as she swayed across the stage and spoke her lines.

"'If all the world were paper, and all the sea were ink, and all the trees were bread and cheese, what should we do for drink?'" Pausing, she looked back over her shoulder, hand still on her hip and her crook guiding the lamb as she said, "'Why then, we all should perish, aye, if not for that noble soul, who with one hand put a penny in the urn of poverty, and with the other took a shilling out.'"

As the audience roared at the sly inference to those noble lords who professed to give to the poor while taxing them to perdition, Julian laughed softly at her impudence. He'd wager a gold guinea she'd added those lines, and not the dullard playwright.

He was still grinning when he met her backstage, surprising her in the cramped dressing room she shared with Celia Carteret.

"My lord," she said, a little breathlessly as she struggled with the wayward lamb, "I didn't expect to see you quite yet."

"So it seems. Here. Give me the future mutton chop or you'll find yourself sitting on the floor in a moment."

"Her name is Phoebe, and she's hungry." Laura relinquished the lamb to him doubtfully, and he managed to steer the beast out of the dressing room and into the corridor.

"Phoebe? You named it?" He gave her an astonished glance and her chin lifted defensively as she met his gaze.

"I've grown attached to her. When the play ends, Roscoe said she's to be butchered for his table."

"Did he. And you protested, I assume."

"I did, my lord. I paid him dear for her."

"You can't keep a lamb in the garden," he pointed out sensibly, but she shook her head.

"Celia knows a farmer who'll take her when she grows too big."

"Take her to market, no doubt." He looked down at the bleating lamb. "I'll send her to my estate, if you like. My steward there has a child who'll no doubt appreciate a pet lamb. You've ruined her for any proper purpose, I see."

The lamb chewed delicately on the ribbon around her neck, and when Laura smiled at him happily, he knew he'd committed himself. He escorted the beast to her pen with the lure of a piece of apple, and fastened the gate latch to leave Phoebe contentedly munching straw.

When he returned to the dressing room, Celia was fastening Laura's gown, nimble fingers buttoning it securely around her. Shrewd blue eyes regarded him speculatively, and Celia smiled as she turned her around.

"There you are, my lord, a more lovely sight you've never seen."

"I'm inclined to agree with you," he said, and noted the flush that brightened Laura's face. She was lovely, indeed, in the white and green-sprigged dress caught just beneath her breasts with a satin ribbon that tied snugly; the green fur-trimmed pelisse she wore over it lent her eyes a brilliant sheen. The pearls circled her slender throat, the white ivory rose nestling in the shadowed valley between her breasts, drawing his eye to the tempting swell of pale flesh. A fierce surge of heat beat through him, unexpected and unwanted. When he looked back up at her face, he wondered if she knew the effect she had on him and hoped not. Damned inconvenient.

Once in his coach, with the bricks still warm and radiating heat, he sprawled on the seat across from her and watched her smile widen as her feet rested atop the cloth-covered bricks.

"You spoil me, my lord," she said with a sigh, and his brow rose.

"And myself. I happen to like warm feet as well."

Her lashes lowered, then lifted. "That was presumptuous of me, wasn't it?"

"Not nearly as presumptuous as the lines you spoke during the last act. Do you think all peers steal from the poor box?"

"Oh no, my lord, not at all. I daresay there are those too old, ill, or feeble who must send their servants for them." She gave him a saucy smile; he was now convinced she was responsible for the added lines as he'd suspected.

He grinned. "You tempt fate, Miss Lancaster."

"Just by breathing at times, my lord."

"Hypocrisy is a dangerous charge," he said, still smiling. "There are those who'll not be pleased."

"'To beguile the time, Look like the time . . .'" she quoted, and he shook his head.

"'Look like the innocent flower, But be the serpent under't.' I see your logic."

"Do you? If it amuses, perhaps it will linger in the minds of those who might otherwise ignore it. There are so many who suffer, and so few who see it."

"You cannot save the world, innocent flower." It was a gentle reminder, and her smile faded as she turned her face to gaze out the window. There was something oddly naïve about her despite her chosen profession, an actress and courtesan and willing escort. A woman who could quote Shakespeare, and probably Greek philosophers, who could masquerade as a whore and claim to be a virgin. An enigma, a contradiction, a mystery. He wanted to delve into her mysteries and solve them, uncover the clues layer by layer, like the petals of a rose, to reach the heart of what made her who she was. God above, he was falling into fascination with her. It'd been so long ago, when he was still at Eton, since he'd felt this same rush of excitement, this eagerness to know more about a woman, and impatience to see her when she was elsewhere. Extraordinary.

It could be that Malcolm had been more right than he'd

known, that a mistress was just the antidote to the ennui he felt so often. And a more lovely antidote he'd yet to see, even when she was garbed in the guise of a lowly shepherdess.

"I believe you were mistaken, Miss Lancaster," he said, and she tipped her head to the side to smile at him.

"In what, my lord?"

"While it is true that young Jeremy Pinch has a fine turn of leg, he cannot hope to match the beauty of yours."

She laughed, a soft, husky sound that seeped inside and warmed him. "Jeremy would be most distressed to hear it."

"I have the distinct notion that he must suspect the truth. Any man with decent eyesight can see it for himself."

He'd thought there may be constraint between them with the memory of their embrace and kiss so sharp and fresh in his mind, but apparently it'd meant little to her. She was composed and easy, as if there had never been that damning kiss.

"Jeremy has never been accused of being observant," she said with another laugh, and his brief tension eased into a conversation that reminded him of the Wilson sisters, who were known for their witty repartee and good companionship. Amy Wilson's house was always overflowing with titled lords, some of whom paid a hundred guineas for a few hours' dalliance with her sister Harriette, but most cared more for the witty conversation and congenial company.

It was surprising to find Laura Lancaster conversant in politics as well as banter, and she gave her opinion of Napoleon's abdication with a deprecating smile.

"Elba will not hold him long, my lord."

"No? You think the little Corsican will escape?"

"Indeed, I think it most likely. He will tire of his studies of science and mathematics, and the governing of Elba will pall quickly to a man intent upon ruling the world instead of an island. France's liberties, so hard won during the revolution, are being leached away from the people. The emperor will not sit idly by and watch from a distance while France reverts to the same horrid condition as it was under the Directory."

"And you approve of his escape?" He asked it idly, but saw her hesitation, then the quick shake of her head.

"No, but my approval is unnecessary. It's only my opinion, of course, but a man of his nature, accustomed to great power, will not remain content to do nothing."

"Yes," he said softly, "I've said the same myself. Yet few will listen. Most are so relieved to think the war with France at an end, they refuse to consider the possibility that France's current unrest is dangerous."

"We can only hope to be proven wrong," she said after a moment and he nodded, then turned his attention to the carriage door as the vehicle slowed to a halt and a footman leaped down to open it for them.

It occurred to him that she'd spent time in Paris, that she'd fled to England only two years before, at a time when Napoleon was marshaling his troops for the ill-fated invasion into Russia. What did he really know about her? Her French was fluent, her connections mysterious.

She spoke of Napoleon almost as if she had intimate knowledge, and she had an obviously educated background. How strong were her French connections? He'd have Malcolm investigate at the first opportunity.

Amy Wilson's house was lively, with a buffet spread for those so inclined, the drawing room cluttered with more lords than usually attended Parliamentary sessions, and dark-haired, dark-eyed Harriette holding court near the fire. No one remarked on his appearance with Laura, though many slid sly glances in their direction. To be seen at the Wilsons', it was said, was just as important as being seen in White's or the Argyle Rooms. It would seal his reputation as having a new mistress quite firmly. His goal would be accomplished, her presence in his life unnecessary.

What would he do about her then? For this young lady was no practiced demimonde, but no doubt as virginal as she claimed. It was both astonishing and irritating. He wanted her with a ferocity he found most disturbing, yet found himself reluctant to ruin her. It was maddening. More maddening was the decision he'd recently made.

For the first time in five years, he found himself in London at Christmas instead of in the country. He wondered why.

CHAPTER 9

"Hurry up, be ready now. It's a sellout!" Roscoe ran a hand through his sparse hair, stringy strands sticking up like broomstraws as he looked around with a wild expression. "A full house! For two months, we barely sell enough tickets to keep the curtain up, and now on the last night, the house is so full we cannot fit another person inside— I've outdone myself, I have!"

"It's not you who brought in all the swells," Jeremy muttered, "it's *her*." He glanced at Laura with a lift of his brow. "Since she took up with an earl, all the swells want a look at her."

"Not just any earl," Celia said coolly, "but Lockwood. Jeremy's quite right. She's the one bringing in all the interest. And you know it, Roscoe. Give Laura her due."

Not to be outdone, Roscoe shrugged away any hint of sharing credit. "It's this play that's brought 'em 'round, it is—I knew it would. The new lines I added—"

"That Laura added," Celia broke in, "you insufferable toad. It's closing night. If you want the curtain to rise on time, you'll get out of our way and let us dress. Get along with you both now, leave us be."

She shut the door behind Roscoe and Jeremy and leaned against it, eying Laura with a lifted brow. "Are you all right, ducks?"

Laura looked pale as milk, green eyes so huge and dark

they seemed to swallow her face. Celia smiled reassuringly at her, struck by how frightened she looked.

"Yes," she said faintly, "I'm fine. I just . . . they've all come to see *me*?"

"Don't worry. You've done this for two weeks now. You're nearly as famous as Harriette and Amy Wilson. Did you know that Sophia, their younger sister, landed a lord as husband? I've heard that Fanny is the nicest one, though, and Harriette always going from one lord to another is quite a success—are you all right, Laura? You look so—distressed."

Laura had risen to her feet, her pallor alarming, and Celia put a hand on her arm. Her skin was cold and clammy, and she drew in a sharp breath.

"He . . . tonight it's . . . he'll be here."

"He?" Celia echoed, then guessed. "Lockwood?" At Laura's tight nod, she smiled. "And you're nervous because he'll be watching you, ducks, I know. It's all right. I think he means more to you than you're telling me, you know. For the past two weeks you've been . . . scatty. Has he still not come to your bed?"

Laura gave her a startled glance, and Celia knew her guess was right on that, too. So, the earl was her protector by reputation only, and had not yet sampled the wares he paid handsomely to keep as his own. Interesting.

"He stayed all night only last week," Laura said, but the flush on her face and the way she looked just past Celia put the lie to her inference that they'd enjoyed the same bed. Whatever her reasons for keeping her true relationship with Lockwood secret, Celia hoped she'd not be hurt by it. Laura was so naïve, for all that she'd managed to survive on her own for two years in London.

"Jolly good," was all Celia said, and she turned to the mirror and brushed rice powder over her face with the hare's foot, eying Laura in the mirror.

A knock on the door was swiftly followed by its being opened, and Jeremy Pinch stuck his head into the dressing room, a scowl on his normally cheerful face. "You'll miss your cue," he said to Celia, then turned his gaze on Laura. "And you'll no doubt be too busy after tonight's performance ends to join us at the Angel."

"It's . . . his lordship has made other plans," Laura said, frowning when Jeremy glared at her. "But perhaps—"

"Oh no, wouldn't want you to get in a twist about it. Go on and rub with the swells. We'll drink your health, though it's bloody rude of—"

"Really, Jeremy," Celia said, turning to face him, leaning back against the dressing table as she gave him a pointed stare, "it's bloody rude of you to be in here going on at her when you've got yourself in a twist because Laura's found herself a good situation."

"And what would you know about it?" he shot back, face turning red with indignation. "I don't see you at the Angel lately."

"No, but it's not *my* absence that makes you mad. You're just jealous, so give over. Let her alone about it."

She was right, she knew, and she'd watched these past few weeks every time Jeremy got into a sulk when Lockwood's name was mentioned. It was obvious to anyone who cared to look that he was besotted with Laura, and had been for months. But she'd no intention of allowing him to make her suffer for it.

"Sod off," she said rudely when Jeremy spluttered a denial, and moved forward to push him back out the dressing room door. Then she looked at Laura's stricken expression. "Come to the party at the Angel if you like. And don't worry about Jeremy. Rex will be there, and he'll take care of him if he gets out of hand."

"Rex Pentley?" Laura managed a smile. "Yes, I can imagine he'd handle what needed to be done, but still—I had no idea Jeremy felt that way about me."

"He's not alone, ducks. You don't give yourself enough credit. Look in the mirror. Now come along, or Roscoe will be here shrieking about missing my cue. Fetch your lamb. I'll see you after the last act—and remember, the crowd loves you. Give 'em what they came for."

Celia gave her a smile, then made her way toward the stage. It was true enough that the crowd now came for Laura instead of for her as they had done, but she was practical enough to know that soon their fickle attention would be diverted to a new pleasure. Laura would move on, go back to America or elsewhere, but she'd still be here with a saucy smile as long as her looks held up. And if she played it right, she'd do as Sophia Wilson had done and land herself a titled gentleman as husband and never have to worry again.

Pasting a bright smile on her face and straightening the fichu of her costume, Celia paused in the wings and waited just a beat after her cue, until the attention would all be on her, and sailed out onto the stage to a thundering round of applause. Oh yes, she'd do just fine. She knew how to lie back and wait, just like a butcher's dog.

Still shaking, Laura put the lamb in her pen and fed her an entire apple, then made her way to the dressing room. It had gone off nicely, she thought, the crowd roaring with appreciation of her sly innuendoes, and she was glad she'd made Roscoe let her add them. The lines always got a reaction, as she'd known they would. Now she had to hurry. Lockwood would arrive soon, and she had to beg his leave to attend the celebration at the Angel before they attended the function he had planned for them. Despite Celia's sharp set-down of Jeremy, she felt guilty. She'd suspected he felt more for her than she did him and done nothing to encourage it, but neither had she tried to discourage it.

Stripping off the short shepherdess frock, she draped it over a stool and reached for her own gown, hanging on a wall hook. A sharp rap sounded on the door. Oh no, not Lockwood already, and she only in her chemise and stockings! Snatching up her gown, she held it in front of her as the door swung open, prepared to plead for more time. Yet framed in the doorway was not the earl, but the sly, arrogant face of her nightmares.

Too late, she lunged forward to slam the door, but he anticipated her reaction and blocked her effort with his sizeable frame.

"*Mais non, ma petite chou*," Aubert Fortier chided. "That is no way to greet an old friend who has come far to see you."

Blood beat loudly in her ears, and panic constricted her lungs so that she had to struggle for air. That familiar gloating expression, the dark eyes and face and hair, all just as she recalled though it had been over two years since she'd seen him.

"Get out of my dressing room," she demanded when she found her voice, and it came out much more strongly than she'd thought she could manage.

"Ah, I think not, *chérie*. You are so lovely . . . even with all that paint on your face. The past two years have been kind to you after all. Your maman has been concerned."

She stiffened. "Did she send you for me?"

"Alas, no. I found you quite by accident." Beyond him, in the corridors backstage, could be heard the rising sound of activity. Soon someone would come. Lockwood, perhaps, or Celia. She had only to delay, and the last act would end and she would be rescued.

As if reading her thoughts, he smiled, a curve of his full lips into a caricature of amusement that made her shudder. "It is the final night. They will linger for the last applause to end. We have a few moments of privacy."

"I don't need privacy with you. Leave at once, or I'll call for you to be removed." She stuck her chin in the air, still clutching her gown to her chest, refusing to allow him to see how he still frightened her.

But Fortier merely chuckled, a nasty sound, and stepped inside, closing the dressing room door and leaning back against it to cross his arms over his chest. "Little pigeon, you amuse me more now than I'd remembered. So brave, a cocky little bird, eh?"

Retreating, she felt the edge of the dressing table press into her hip, but didn't dare take her eyes off him. He radiated power and danger, and made her flesh prickle with fear. She drew in a deep breath for courage.

"Tell me what you want here, then go."

"Ah, and if what I want is—you? Will you still tell me to go?"

"If what you want is me, you are doomed to swift disappointment."

His eyes narrowed slightly but his smile remained in place. "Then it is fortunate that I am not here for you. No, I have other . . . interests. Shall I enlighten you?"

"I'm not concerned with your interests."

"Oh, *petite poule*, you'll be concerned with these, I assure you. Or perhaps I should be so cruel as to not tell you, but confide in his lordship? Would that be better, do you think?"

"Tell him what? He knows of my past."

"Does he? I think not, perhaps, not all of it."

"Really, I cannot think you so foolish as to believe you can come in here with wild threats and frighten me."

"But I do, don't I," he said softly, and leaned forward, brushing the tips of his fingers over her chin, laughing at her instinctive flinch. "I've thought of you these past years, you know, and how foolish you were to flee my bed. Are you not curious about your mother? Do you not wish to know how she fares?"

"I trust she fares quite well. Maman seems more than capable of landing on her feet."

"Or her back. *Le chat* . . . yes, so she does. A remarkable women, your maman, and one who knows how to seize an opportunity." His eyes narrowed slightly. "She also knows when to yield the moment, if not the day."

"And you suggest what? That I yield to you what I would not yield two years ago? I think not, my lord!"

"Do not be a fool, Laura," he said cuttingly, "I did not come here for that. I can find many willing women for my pleasure—I do not need to pursue one silly girl for a few hours' pleasure."

Her fingers curled more tightly into the velvet folds of her new gown, a deep burgundy trimmed in black fur. There was something so malicious, so malevolent, about Fortier . . . and he was confident she would yield whatever it was he demanded. Thank God for the dressing table at her back, for she didn't think her legs would hold her if she didn't have it to lean on.

"Tell me what you want," she said crisply, "so we can end this farce! I have other plans for the evening."

"No doubt." Fortier leaned back against the door, his heavy-lidded eyes raking over her in a slow inspection that made her grit her teeth. Then he laughed. "Indeed, I can see Lockwood's interest in you. You've filled out since last I saw you. Very well. I shall explain what I require of you, then you may go to your protector and beg prettily to see that my requirements are met." He pushed away from the door suddenly and she swallowed a gasp at the unexpected movement as he leaned closer. "My esteemed father has deemed it prudent to cut off my funds of late. I have incurred a few debts at these infernal gaming hells in London now, and in order to pay the vowels must have money. You will get it for me."

"You're quite mad," she said calmly, though her heart thudded so loud she was certain he must be able to hear it. "I have no money."

"No, but Lockwood has much more than he needs. He's provided you with a house, and, no doubt, some kind of allowance. I require two thousand pounds to begin with, then regular payments of five hundred a month, or I shall be in the regrettable position of confiding the true circumstances of your past."

It was so outrageous that she laughed, a mistake she quickly realized when his face grew dark and ominous. "Not only could I never get that amount from Lockwood even if I wished to, I hardly think his lordship will care that my mother is a courtesan. Look at my own position. Do you truly think he'd care?"

"That your maman is a courtesan? Not a bit. But perhaps, as one of the leading Tories in Parliament, he might care a great deal that your maman is now the *fille de joie* of Louis's chief ambassador. After all, how would it look if the *Times* were to report that Lockwood's paramour is the daughter of a high-ranking French official's whore? Especially in light of the king's brother selling army commissions not so long ago, and now, of course, with Napoleon exiled to Elba and making noises about the unrest in France . . . well, you can see where it might put the earl in an awkward position, can you not? I daresay, it might even ruin his political career, if not see him accused of treason were it to get out that his current mistress exchanges secrets with her French mother. The political situation is still so volatile. . . ."

Laura stared at him in horror. Of course it was. And it didn't need to be the truth to do a great deal of damage to Lockwood's reputation—it needed only to be plausible. What could she do to get out of this? There must be a way to delay him, even if only for a little while, until she could find a way to protect the earl from vicious lies. She shook her head and looked at Fortier.

"I . . . I cannot possibly manage that much. A few hundred at most, perhaps . . ."

"Do what you can. I'll send a messenger to your lodgings. Frith Street, am I correct? Keep in mind that if you displease me, I'll see that the *Times* has a full account of the situation. I trust you will be able to get me the entire two thousand within the next two weeks. I'd hate to see Lockwood suffer for your failures."

As noise in the corridor grew louder, he opened the door

and stood framed in the opening for a moment, smiling at her. "His future is in your hands, *petite chou*. Do what you must."

Disaster, she thought, staring at the closed door for several long moments after he'd gone, and felt as if she were balanced on the very precipice of complete ruin.

"I'd be intrigued to hear how the pub earned the misnomer of Angel," Julian observed as they entered the crowded common room, "when it resembles the anteroom of Hell."

"We don't have to stay long, my lord," Laura replied quickly, and he glanced at her once again, puzzled as to her unusually pale face and somber demeanor. She'd been amusing and saucy on stage, but chalk-white and melancholy after the play ended.

"We'll stay as long as you like," he said with a shrug. "The play was a resounding success in no small part because of your performance."

"I don't think it was my performance that drew the curious, my lord." Her tone was flat, with none of the wit and playfulness he'd grown accustomed to hearing from her. It could be that she was just sad the play had ended, but he suspected there was a deeper reason for her manner. She didn't look just sad, she looked—haunted.

Immediately upon entering the pub, they were surrounded with the other players, none of whom seemed to mind that the newest member of the cast had stolen the show these last few weeks. Instead, they seemed enthused, and whispers of another production starting soon were reason enough for the excitement.

Celia Carteret pushed her way through the throng toward Laura, followed by a man Julian recognized. He smiled slightly, and wondered if he looked as out of place and uncomfortable as did Belgrave.

"Dashed crowded in here," Belgrave muttered, and despite the cold outside, beads of perspiration dotted his forehead and upper lip. Gray flecked his brown hair, and he looked like a burly pouter pigeon with his barrel chest and waist most likely cinched by a corset, but his face was pleasant and uncomplicated, and rather than looking irritated, he looked merely resigned. "Celia does love the theater," he offered by way of explanation for his presence, and Julian nodded understanding.

"So it seems. There's quite an unusual crowd here."

Belgrave nodded. "Not so very different from a week at my hunting box, to be frank. I lack only decent wine to feel as if I'm in my own parlor."

Grinning, Julian appreciated the brutal assessment of many of their crowd. They spoke for several minutes about horses and hounds, and whether the hunting was better at Melton in Leicestershire or with the pack at Belvoir, though both admittedly prime.

"I've a flying leaper that's cracking good," Belgrave enthused. "Never among the McAdamites with that one—no, no, not at all. Over the bullfinches first, I am, nearly always." He paused, watching as Celia and Laura stood near the far wall in deep conversation, then turned to Julian. "I've invited a few out to my hunting box next week, Lockwood. I'd be honored if you'd join us. You know, after Boxing Day and before Parliament convenes again."

Julian followed Belgrave's gaze to the two women, and the viscount smiled.

"Bring her with you, if you like, Lockwood. Celia will be there."

"Will she now."

"Indeed. I deem it vital to remove myself from a surfeit of family and visiting relatives at this time every year. Amazing how many of my acquaintance feel the same pressing need."

Laughing softly, Julian could well recall his father's exasperation during the holidays when old maid aunts and cousins from the country gathered at their house for a few weeks' visit; then the earl would disappear for a few days, and upon his return—usually timed to coincide with farewells to the guests—he was always in a much better mood. Now he understood the reason for it.

"Amazing, indeed," he said. "My own house is now crowded with two elderly aunts from the country, as well as my brother and his staff, and a covey of cousins that have required my attention at the most inconvenient times. They're family, but wearing on the nerves."

"Then a few days in the country with the foxes and the muslin can only be beneficial."

Julian was surprised at how enticing it sounded, and he heard himself agree, even while he wondered if Laura would like the country. He imagined her sitting amidst a bower of spring blossoms instead of white roses, and thought that perhaps when spring finally arrived, he'd take her to Shadowhurst.

"Laura, what is it?" Celia leaned close, her voice low and confiding, her brows drawn into a frown and her blue eyes worried. "You look so pale, and you're so quiet—is it Lockwood? Has he distressed you?"

"No, no," Laura murmured, "the earl is, as always, a perfect gentleman. It's . . . my head. It aches abominably." That much was true enough. A pounding behind her eyes throbbed steadily and relentlessly. Fortier's unexpected appearance had rattled her badly.

"I have a powder that will give you ease, if you like," Celia said, and Laura shook her head.

"No, it will fade soon enough. Perhaps a cup of wine—"

"Take mine." Celia pressed a cup into her hands, her brow still furrowed. "Is it because the play has ended? Are you upset about that? Another one will be starting soon. Roscoe told me that he intends to expand. I'm sure there'll be a role for you as well if you want it."

Managing a smile, Laura nodded. "That would be lovely. I feel much better."

Celia's gaze was disbelieving. "Stuff," she said rudely, hands on her hips. "You're not very good at lying, Laura. What ever is the matter with you tonight? I thought you'd be quite satisfied with yourself, turning out the star and landing yourself an earl—yet you look as if you're on the cart to Newgate."

Prison would be the least of her problems, Laura thought, if Fortier made good on his threat. She could be executed for treason, hanged on Tyburn Hill and dispatched without a thought. At the least, Lockwood's reputation would be tarnished; at the worst, he risked the same fate. Did they hang earls or take them to the block? She tried to recall, but then Rex Pentley chose that moment to join them, grinning down at her and winking.

"The lovely Laura, the fairest Lancaster rose of all," he said, and presented her with a red rose in a dramatic flourish. "Quite the smashing success, you are, love."

"Thank you." She took the rose, not surprised it was made of fabric—another of Rex's illusions, no doubt. He had many. If only he could make Fortier disappear. . . .

"Ah, and a gold guinea behind your ear," Rex teased, his deft hand producing a coin from her cluster of curls. "I believe it's the same one I earned in your employ not so long ago."

"I doubt that," she said. "You'd have spent it too quickly."

"Or turned it into ten guineas," he said easily, laughing. "A most intriguing play that night, the gulling of a viscount. No wonder Lockwood glowered at him. The man has dismal luck."

"Until you joined the play." Laura smiled. "You have my gratitude, Rex."

"Do I? How grateful are you, lovely Laura?"

Still smiling, she tapped him lightly with the rose. "Grateful enough not to involve you in any more schemes."

Seizing her hand in his, Rex shook his head mournfully. "I confess I'm devastated at the dashing of my hopes."

"You great barking oaf," Celia said, shaking her head. "You'd best leave off your play. The earl does not seem amused at your attentions to his lady."

Indeed, Laura saw with some surprise that Lockwood stared at them with cold eyes, and his mouth had thinned into a straight line. He stood across the crowded common room with the Viscount Belgrave, looking so handsome and golden he made her shiver. She had to do what she must to keep him from Fortier's vicious scheme. But where would she get two thousand pounds? It was a staggering sum. Oh God, if only he'd never found her, if only he'd just go away. . . .

Rex laughed, bowing over Laura's hand, and looked up at her mischievously. "I'm at your service any time you should require my help, lovely lady. Magic? Illusions? You've only to ask."

"It's too bad that you cannot truly make people disappear, for that's all I need at the moment. Now go, before Lockwood decides *you* need to disappear."

Straightening, he turned in the earl's direction with a smart salute, then said over his shoulder, "But I *can* make people disappear, my dear. You've only to tell me who and when."

Then he was gone, moving through the crowd, and Laura stared after him. "Can he?" she asked Celia. "Can he truly make people disappear?"

"Only in the conventional sense. Why? Oh no, ducks, you don't mean the earl—"

"Of course not. But . . . oh Celia, I do need your advice, I think."

"I knew there was something wrong—here comes Belgrave and Lockwood, but later we'll talk, when we have privacy."

Laura nodded, and pasted a bright smile on her face for the earl as he and the viscount reached them. Lockwood's brow lifted.

"You seem in better spirits now than earlier. Is it the wine or the company?"

"Hardly the wine, my lord. And the company has just improved drastically from a moment before."

"Ah, the perfect answer." He patted the hand she tucked

into the crook of his arm. "Ever the diplomat, I see. You'd be a lovely ambassador to France."

A shudder ran through her, and she wondered with a sense of desperation what he would say if he learned that her mother slept with the current French ambassador. Oh God, such a tangle now, when it had seemed so briefly as if she might at last have found good fortune.

I should have known better. . . .

CHAPTER 10

"Indeed, miss, it seems you've quite enough here for only a few days."

Laura looked up over the still-open lid of the trunk, and Malcolm's brow lifted higher, an event she'd thought nearly impossible. Any higher, and he'd tip over backward from the sheer imbalance of the extra weight on top of his head.

"I was instructed to be prepared, Malcolm, so I am. I've been told it's cold in the country, and that I should take warm garments."

"Ah yes, of course. I only anticipate how many footmen will be required to load your extra luggage atop the coach. I do like to be prepared, and I like to know all. Fortunately, I usually do."

Her eyes narrowed slightly. Pompous little man. She began to dislike him excessively. He was too smooth, too . . . smug. Almost as if he knew her thoughts, knew what she'd had to do to get rid of Fortier. Had one of the servants told him? Had she been betrayed?

"Then if you know all," she said after a moment, "you know that I have no intention of embarrassing the earl by being improperly dressed."

"Yes, though I hardly think it to be that discreet an affair." His tone conveyed his opinion quite neatly, and she flushed at the subtle reminder that she was, after all, only a courtesan going to the country with her protector.

She consoled herself with the thought that Celia would be

there as well, and she could talk about her ongoing problem with Fortier. Oh God, she prayed Lockwood wouldn't expect her to wear the pearls he'd given her, for they were gone, sold to pay Aubert what he demanded. It was only a temporary solution, for he'd be back. She knew that. She couldn't expect to purchase his silence for long. He was too greedy, too dishonorable. She had to find a way to rid herself of him for good. Perhaps he could be exiled back to France, or lured from London by some means, or even impressed into the British Navy. The last was preferable. Let Fortier see what it meant to truly suffer!

For now, she was just relieved to be away from the city, where she expected to look up and see him leering at her from around every corner. Curse him.

Becky waited on her at the door, helping her into a matching green velvet wrap, quivering with excitement at the prospect of going to the country.

"I've never been out o' the city," she said with wide eyes and a delighted smile, "never gone farther than the banks o' the Thames!"

"Then you'll enjoy this, I'm sure," Laura assured her, "for I understand it's quite lovely, even at this time of year."

Charlton stepped into the entry, eying the two trunks with resignation. "Put them on the boot of the tilbury," he told the other footman, "as his lordship intends to travel quickly."

There were to be two coaches traveling, Laura realized when she was handed up into a well-sprung landau, smaller than the town coach, and faster. Becky and the earl's valet were to follow behind with most of the baggage.

Lockwood looked up when she seated herself across from him, and her heart skipped a beat at the faint smile curving his hard, handsome mouth.

"I see you're well prepared for any millinery emergency," he said, indicating her trunks with a tip of his head in the direction of the footmen bearing them toward the other vehicle.

"I've found being prepared at all times to be an excellent motto, my lord."

He laughed softly. "It is one Charlton should employ. He needs a sturdy postboy to help him bear the load."

Smoothing velvet skirts with a gloved hand, she met his gaze briefly before looking away. He always made her so nervous lately, even when he was as affable as now. It was probably guilt that made her so tense in his presence, the knowledge that Fortier could ruin them both if she didn't find a way to stop him. How could she laugh and be the gay company the earl expected her to be when doom hung over her head like a sharpened sword?

"I see you brought work with you, my lord," she said when silence fell, indicating the sheaf of papers he had in his lap. "To while away the hours until we reach Belgrave's hunting box, I presume?"

"Your delightful company notwithstanding, these need only my immediate attention so I'm free to enjoy the next few days. But you are not to be left out. Malcolm included this envelope for you as well. Apparently, it's information you requested."

A little surprised, she took the thick envelope, laying it in her lap while she removed her gloves, then flexed her fingers. It was cool in the landau but not frigid despite the chill outside. As she opened the envelope and slid out a folded sheaf of paper, she was aware of Lockwood's gaze on her. Her hand shook slightly as she unfolded the paper. It was a list of purser's agents, as she'd requested from Malcolm when she'd signed the agreement. There was also a short list of tracts of land for sale in Maryland and Virginia, gathered from a local firm, no doubt in anticipation of the success of truce talks in Ghent. She looked up at the earl.

He regarded her with lazy nonchalance. "Malcolm mentioned to me your desire to secure passage to America when the hostilities ended."

"Then--"

"Yes, a treaty was signed at Ghent on the eve of Christmas. No doubt, it will be in all the papers tomorrow, but a messenger brought word around to me last night."

"That's excellent news, my lord."

"Yes. One more damnable difficulty resolved. Now parliament can address other matters, home concerns." After a moment's more regard, he turned his attention to the papers in his lap again, and she stared at the top of his head.

It was to be done that easily then, that quickly. When her presence was no longer required she'd be cast off like an old boot. But wasn't that what she expected? *Wanted?* Yes, of course it was, and since Fortier's malicious reappearance in her life, the sooner it was over the better. They would both be safe then, she on her way to America, the earl secure in his position as esteemed MP. It was for the best.

So why did she feel suddenly as if it was too soon? Silly of her, foolish and completely ridiculous that she felt like dissolving into tears of disappointment. Folding the papers, she slid them back into the envelope and turned her face to gaze out the window.

London was soon left behind, the landau speeding over the London-Birmingham Road at a brisk pace. Northamptonshire lay some fifty miles northwest, and Belgrave's hunting box was situated in Wicken, near the bordering county of Buckinghamshire.

Soot and crowded buildings were replaced by sloping fields and small, neat villages that reminded her of Virginia. Dry stone fences and hedgerows enclosed grazing sheep and cattle, and the only smoke in the air was tendrils coming from pleasantly scattered chimneys. Dense trees fringed the roadside in places, stripped now of leaves and their limbs frosted with lacings of snow. At midday they stopped in the village of King's Langley for a change of horses and brief rest at an inn. A black-and-maroon coach with scarlet wheels and undercarriage and Royal cipher on the door stood in the innyard. The Royal Mail.

Wheels dug deeply into frozen ruts as the Royal Mail prepared to leave. The guard blew his yard of tin to summon passengers from the cozy warmth back to the coach, and people scurried out bundled against the weather, only a fortunate four climbing inside the vehicle, most relegated to precarious perches atop. Clothed in royal scarlet, the guard leaped onto the rear of the coach as it lurched forward, the mail tucked safely away in the boot beneath his feet.

Lockwood's landau yielded the right of way, then took the spot just vacated by the Royal Mail. At once, ostlers hurried out to secure the earl's horses, and Charlton opened the door to allow them to go inside. There was no sign of the baggage and tilbury, as they'd been left behind fairly swiftly after reaching the open road.

Laura picked her way carefully over the icy ruts, and after asking discreetly where to find the necessary, was directed to a small building just behind the inn. She stared at it in some dismay before Charlton appeared at her side.

"Miss Lancaster, I've been instructed to inform you that the earl has made arrangements inside for your comfort," he said, and there was only the slightest trace of embarrassment in his face when she looked up at him. Blue eyes met hers briefly, then glanced away.

She understood, and was relieved. "Thank you, Charlton."

Lockwood had immediately procured a private room for dining and more private functions that needed tending, and tactfully remained outside until she'd had the opportunity to avail herself of the most urgent use of the chamberpot. By the time he joined her in the small, dark-paneled room, a meal had been served of cold ham, kidneys, beef, game pie, bread and cheese, and a tankard of foamy ale for their refreshment.

Laura sat near the fire, the welcome heat at her back as she filled her plate. "Shall I serve you, my lord?"

"I think I can manage." He pulled out the narrow-backed chair opposite her and sat down. "Though there are those who prefer to think me incapable of it, I've been known to serve my own food at times, and while in the Royal Navy, even mend my own boots."

She looked up at him through her lashes, uncertain if he was teasing. "You have a talent for cobbling, my lord?"

"I do. If not born to another station, I'd have made an excellent cobbler. I could give Hoby instruction, if I chose."

Her mouth twitched in a smile at the mental image of the earl bent over a cobbler's bench with an awl in his hand and boot nails sticking from his mouth.

"Perhaps Hoby should take you on as apprentice," she said, and Lockwood grinned.

"He could do much worse. It takes him too long now to deliver boots ordered a month in advance. He's all the crack, and that makes him slow." His gaze fell on her plate. "I see that your appetite has returned. Excellent."

Thick slices of ham and pigeon pie crowded her plate. She shrugged, and cut another bite of ham. "It never really left, was only curbed for a time."

He looked up at her face, his gaze lingering for a moment too long. "It pleases me to see you eat."

"And would it please you as well, my lord, were I as big as a beer barrel?"

Laughing, he shook his head. "Even if that were to happen, it'd not change that saucy mouth, I fear."

"And I thought you appreciated my wit."

His eyes found hers. "I do. Oh, I do, more than I expected. You are . . . unique."

Her breath caught, so that she couldn't swallow the bite of ham for a moment, trapped by his amber gaze and the sudden leap of her heart into her throat. There was a low, husky quality to his voice now, while in the hours spent traveling he'd barely looked at her, had spoken only at rare intervals. He sounded almost intimate now, and she was suddenly aware that across the room on the far side stood a bed. Heat flushed her cheeks, and she wondered if he'd changed his mind about their agreement, wondered if perhaps he expected more of her now than he had at first. And if he did? What would she say?

Then the moment was gone as a light rap on the door preceded Charlton's announcement that his lordship's horses were ready.

"Finish your meal," Lockwood said with a faint smile, "for we'll not stop again until we reach Wicken."

Laura finally swallowed the ham, her appetite for food gone. In its place instead, another hunger had ignited, and it was one she dared not ease. Not with the earl. It would be her ruin.

They arrived at Belgrave's hunting box not long after dark. It was a small place by usual standards, with perhaps only thirty rooms. Snow mantled the ground, laced trees and bushes, and glittered under a cold, clear sky with stars so bright it hurt the eyes to look at them.

Julian followed Laura inside, admiring the slender curve of her back as her cloak was taken by one of Belgrave's servants. She had to be weary after the day's arduous travel, but held her head high. Endearing curls framed her pretty face, gleaming like dark fire in the lamplight.

Celia Carteret swooped down a curved staircase to greet her, and took Laura with her up the stairs, calling down an apology to Belgrave.

"I'll see her settled until her maid arrives, my lord, and we'll be down for the late supper."

With that, Laura disappeared in a graceful drift of green velvet, and he was left standing in the entrance hall staring after her.

"Brandy in the drawing room," Belgrave said, "and good company. Westbury is here, and so is Langston. More to come. Damnable weather, I say, but never too bad to hunt."

Julian had his own opinion of that, but kept it to himself as he followed Belgrave into the large drawing room. Westbury he knew fairly well, but Langston only by sight, and he nodded at both men as he took the offered brandy from a uniformed butler.

Talk turned from politics to hunting and the new horse the Duke of Rutland had bought for his stables. It was said to be all the crack, a flying leaper of fame and repute. Then the viscount said he had his own flying leaper, and Langston and Westbury went with him down to the stables to view the horse, leaving Julian to his brandy and brief solitude. He cherished it while he could, knowing that soon enough more guests would arrive.

The fire was warm, the silence unbroken except for a clock upon the mantel, and Julian stretched out his legs and studied the toes of his boots while sipping good brandy. Not a bad decision at all, coming here, he thought idly. There'd be nothing to do other than hunt, drink, play cards, and admire their respective ladies. A welcome break indeed, before he had to return to the city and the usual parliamentary quarrels.

Perhaps here, with her friend close by, Laura would lose the haunted shadows that had been in her eyes these past few days. Whatever disturbed her could be forgotten in the country. He thought then of Shadowhurst, the elegant house and rolling meadows, his interest in draining marshes and enriching sandy soil with marl, and rotating crops, and the increased yield his acres had produced, benefitting not only his own household, but those of his cottagers. His tenants lived in houses of wood and stone, not mud and sod, and all were warmly clothed and well fed. It was a matter of personal pride that he'd accomplished most of this in the five years since inheriting the title. His father had experimented, but with only sporadic interest, and left it to his son to bring about vast changes, though he'd complained bitterly that Julian was an enigma.

"A yeoman," he'd once sneered, looking at his heir with an expression that was perplexed and exasperated at the same time. "You'd be nothing but a yeoman with dirt under your nails and mud on your boots if not for my prodding."

"And a damn sight happier," Julian had retorted, and both of them knew it was a lie. While he loved Shadowhurst, he wasn't fool enough to think he'd be happy without money to support the land and his own lifestyle. Nor would he be able to ease the burdens of his tenants if he couldn't support the estate.

He'd tried to convey that to Randal, but it never seemed to soak in that he'd not be the first young lord out on the town to lose his entire inheritance at the gaming tables. No, Randal seemed to think the money would always be there, that there was an inexhaustible supply, if not in his own pockets, in his brother's, and in the inheritance he'd receive in only a few months when he reached his majority. There would be no helping him then. And, Julian had warned him, he'd not jeopardize Shadowhurst or the lives of those who depended on his careful husbandry for their very existence. But would Randal listen?

It was doubtful. He'd not seemed fazed the night Laura had arranged for her friend to be sure he didn't lose all his money, but instead had been more interested in her than the fact he'd narrowly escaped penury. So how had Laura convinced her friend to forego what would have been a tidy sum?

He'd first noticed the man across the faro table, his regard of Laura surreptitious until she looked up at him. Then she'd met him by the fire, and he'd still not understood until he'd seen the man sit down at the table with Randal. It was then he'd realized that Laura had sent him, and his first suspicions were that she intended her companion to cheat Randal. Until he'd seen the sleight of hand that gave Randal the trick and a tidy amount. Then he'd known what she intended, if not why. That still puzzled him. Why would she care enough to do that?

Lost in thought, he didn't hear her at first, then became aware that Celia Carteret had come into the drawing room, and she was looking at him with a faint smile.

"Good evening, my lord. I see you resisted the enticing lure of viewing Belgrave's newest addition to his stables."

"With utmost difficulty. And relief." He rose to his feet as she moved past him to the fire and held out her hands as if to warm them, but he knew she hadn't come here for that. There was no sign of Laura, yet her absence was louder than her presence would have been. He waited.

"Once," Celia said after a moment of silence, "I cleaned drawing rooms. Now I drink tea in them. If I'm very lucky, I'll never have to dust or clean another coal bin." She turned to face him. "But if I did, it wouldn't kill me. I'm not certain about Laura."

"You underestimate her, Miss Carteret. I believe her capable of doing anything she decides to do." He set his empty brandy glass on the table next to the settee. "Is there something of note you wish to tell me?"

"Yes, of course there is. I believe you to be fairly decent." When his brow shot up she let her mouth twitch into a wry smile. "It is not an opinion I have of many in your position, my lord, so while it may surprise you, it would truly astonish you if you knew what low esteem I have for certain members of your rank."

"It may surprise you to learn I hold the same low opinion of certain members of my rank, but I still don't think that's what you've come to discuss."

"No, my lord," she said, "I came to discuss Laura with you, as I'm sure you've guessed. I am quite fond of her, and I worry."

His eyes narrowed slightly. "Is she ill?"

"Not at all. She'll be down soon." She paused in what he suspected was uncharacteristic hesitation, then blurted, "I merely came to assure myself that your wishes are being followed."

Her lifted brow seemed to indicate that he should know what she was talking about, but he was mystified. "I presume they are, as my staff is fairly efficient."

Celia made a chuffing sound and turned to face him, hands on her hips. "My lord, is it your intention to sleep in the same bed as Laura?"

"Really, Miss Carteret, I cannot see where it's any of your business to inquire about my sleeping arrangements."

"Quite true. However, I feel it *is* my business to ask about hers."

Amusement mixed with irritation. A surprising little baggage; now he knew what drew Belgrave to her. Along with Celia's saucy wit and fair face, she possessed a high degree of loyalty not found in most Covent Garden actresses. Before Belgrave there had been Sir Rupert, an elderly knight of some distinction who'd been her protector for well over a year, and before him, there had been an elderly banker who, it was rumored, had died in her bed with a happy smile still on his face. Celia Carteret was an opportunist and demimonde, but not basically dishonest. It was a fine distinction he recognized.

"I admire your loyalty, Miss Carteret."

"That does not answer my question, my lord."

"No," he said, "it does not."

Chagrin flickered on her lovely face, but whatever she might have said next remained a mystery to him as Laura sailed into the drawing room with a bright smile. He turned toward her, unable to resist an answering smile that seemed to please her.

"Not out at the stables, my lord? I'm shocked. I thought you'd be with Belgrave admiring his newest horse. As you see, Celia has told me all."

"As enthusiastic as I am about fine cattle, I find I'm more enthusiastic about a warm fire this evening. Have Cranford and your maid arrived yet?"

"Not yet, my lord. Celia played the part of ladies' maid for me, so that I no longer resemble the crone from *Mucbeth*."

"That," he said honestly, "you could never do."

"Really, my lord, you've become quite the flirt in my brief absence." Pretty color flushed her cheeks. He smiled.

"Here in the country we can be less formal, I think. I grow weary at times of the 'my lord' continually tossed at me."

"I was instructed in the proper use of titles and address, and Malcolm admonished me most strenuously not to grow too familiar." She moved to the fire and held out her hands; long, slender fingers bare of jewelry quivered slightly as if chilled. He resisted warming them himself.

"Malcolm is an excellent secretary and well versed in many areas, but there are some things he cannot anticipate. My close friends call me Norcliff."

Before he could say more, Celia laughed softly. "I call Belgrave Charley when we're alone, and he likes that tremendously."

"Please don't call me Charley," Julian said with a pained expression, and both women laughed.

Then there was a stir at the front door, and Belgrave's butler opened it to admit a flurry of noise and activity as more guests arrived, and hard on their heels, the tilbury with Cranford and their baggage arrived.

"I'll direct Becky where to put my trunks," Laura said, and with a swift glance in his direction, crossed the drawing room and went into the entrance hall, with Celia close behind. He heard their soft voices, the greetings exchanged, and thought of Celia's question. What did he intend? He knew what he wanted. Oh yes, he knew quite well what he wanted, and it was surprising and inconvenient and damned awkward.

But inevitable.

CHAPTER 11

"Are you certain there's not been a mistake?" Laura studied Charlton's face, and saw from his expression there was no error. "Never mind. Leave it here, of course."

The footman left Lockwood's trunk next to her own, a silent indication that they were to share a chamber. Looking up, she met Celia's curious gaze.

"Something wrong, ducks?"

Laura shook her head. She wouldn't discuss it now, not with Becky nearby and Charlton still in the room. Why had she not thought the sleeping arrangements would be different here? She hadn't even considered it. Not until now. Until the certainty that she would be sharing a room and possibly a bed with the earl was in front of her. She inhaled a deep breath, and when Charlton had gone and Becky was sent below to fetch hot water, she turned to Celia.

"You didn't expect him to share your bed, did you?" Celia said, and Laura shook her head.

"No. I should have, I see. But I just didn't think—think he would renege on our . . . our agreement."

"It's not the worst thing that can happen, ducks."

"No, I suppose not."

But it was, of course. She felt too strongly about him, dreamed about him at night when she slept, and when they were together, she found herself studying him, watching the light in his hair, or his strong hands, lost in a rapt admiration that may well be her undoing.

"Your *agreement*?" Celia echoed belatedly, her blue eyes wide. "What kind of agreement did you make with Lockwood?"

Laura bit her lip, knowing it would sound foolish. "I daresay you'll think me silly, but I only agreed to be the earl's escort in public, or at private functions, not . . . not intimately."

"Good God," Celia blurted, "you mean he didn't insist on bedding you?"

Flinching slightly, Laura nodded. "Not only did he not insist, it was part of the bargain he made. In writing."

Celia stared at her in astonishment. It was plain she'd never heard of such a thing. She abruptly sank down onto a tufted stool. "His idea? Not yours?"

"His idea, but one I much prefer, of course. I know. It rather shocked me, too. I couldn't understand why he'd set me up in a house of my own, treat me as his mistress, without the . . . his . . . my . . ."

"Bedding him," Celia said absently, her gaze now narrowed and riveted to the door as if expecting Lockwood himself to burst into the room and confirm it all. "Amazing. No one would believe it. And I wonder why he'd go to all that trouble, unless—" She paused, and looked back up at Laura. "Has he ever mentioned his wife to you?"

"No. Never. I've heard the gossip, of course, that she's in Europe and leading a rather scandalous life. It seems to be the thing for spurned wives to do, since the prince's consort is also creating a lovely scandal."

"Yes, but have you heard all the gossip? I mean, *all* of it?" When Laura shook her head, Celia leaned forward, tone lowered conspiratorially. "It's said he married her under protest, that his father nearly had to force him to the altar at swordpoint. They've hardly spent a night under the same roof, it's said, and detest one another. So much so, he cannot bear to produce an heir as he knows he must. The disappointment of it all is said to have killed the old earl, Lockwood's father." Celia shrugged. "I don't know if I believe that, for from all accounts he was a doughty old bird, but there you have it. Just another *on-dit* for the *ton* to feast upon, I daresay."

"Then it would seem likely that the earl would take a mistress, I'd think," Laura said after a moment.

"Yes. It does." Celia looked up from arranging her bodice, eyes suddenly sharp. "He's had his occasional fling, I understand, but never taken anyone under his protection. You're the first."

Laura closed her eyes. "I cannot," she whispered, "I cannot share his bed. It would ruin me."

"Don't be a gudgeon," Celia said calmly. "You're already ruined."

Her eyes snapped open. "I don't mean that way. I had little enough reputation before, so risking it by being known as his mistress is hardly damaging. I meant . . . I could not for another reason."

"One of the first rules you should learn, is that you cannot fall in love with a man of his position. It will do you no good, and quite likely ruin you. Have you, Laura? Oh, do tell me you haven't been that foolish!"

"Of course, I haven't," she assured her, but knew it was a lie even as she said it. Silly, indeed, but she felt more for Lockwood than she should. She knew it. Until today, however, she'd not dared acknowledge it. The realization they were to share a chamber should horrify her, anger her, but instead she thought of how lovely it would be to remain in his company, to feel his mouth on hers, his hand on her . . . oh God, she had to stop!

Frankly disbelieving, Celia blew out a lengthy sigh. "Of course not. God, what to do now? How do you deal with this? Tell me—do you have someone waiting for you in America?"

"No. The only relative I have left besides my mother is an uncle, and when he inherited the house and land, he put me out with nothing. If not for Maman sending my passage to France, I would have been there as I am here—quite alone."

"You're not alone here," Celia said softly, and Laura smiled.

"No, I have you. Thank God, you've been a true friend to me. I can't imagine what would have happened to me if I hadn't met you."

They were quiet for a moment, the soft silence broken only by a log popping in the grate. Finally Laura said, "How do you know all these things about him?"

"Charley, of course. Belgrave loves to repeat gossip. I swear, he must take scandal-broth with every old tabby in London. He likes you more than he admits, you know."

"Belgrave?"

"No, goose girl, Lockwood. *Norcliff*." She laughed softly. "Before we leave here I predict you'll be calling him Julian."

When she turned to look at her, Celia smiled knowingly, and Laura's spirits rose. Was it true? Did he like her? Oh, she knew he liked her companionship, and there were times she thought he might regard her with something more, but then she recalled the vast difference between them and knew she must be wrong. While it wasn't as if it had never been done, marrying beneath one's station wasn't at all common. And, of course, Lockwood was already married anyway. The only thing she could ever be to him was his mistress. An impossible situation.

"Now come," Celia said, "I heard the bell ring for dinner, so Belgrave must be back from the stables. We'll talk more later."

Yes, Laura thought, for she still hadn't confided to Celia her problem with Fortier. She had to find a solution. Celia would help her think of something. Perhaps Rex Pentley could make Fortier disappear. Then she could leave England and not worry about Fortier or the earl. She never had to think of Lockwood again. But she would. She knew she'd never forget him. *Never*.

* * *

After-dinner conversation palled quickly. Julian had lost patience with the discussion of Rutland's new horse at least an hour before, the retreat of the ladies taking any pretense of his interest upstairs with them. He rose finally and made his polite apologies, though it was obvious he'd not be missed. Brandy lent conviviality to his companions, as well as a tendency to talk. But none of them had Laura in their bedchambers, as he did.

What did she think of the sleeping arrangements? If she protested, there'd been no hint of it during dinner. She'd seemed as always, lovely and witty, though subdued when in company. He much preferred her company confined to the two of them. Then she was saucy, even cheeky, parrying his verbal innuendoes while he just enjoyed the lilting cadence of her voice flowing over him; like music, soft and lyrical, her accent exotic and soothing and making him think of warmer climes and starry skies, and of other, more physical pleasures that he'd long denied himself.

Reaching the second-floor chamber, he tapped softly on the door, then opened it, and she turned to look at him, clad in a blue silk dressing gown trimmed in gold. A fire burned in the grate and warmed the room, casting gold and orange light that seemed to catch in her loose hair. It fell about her shoulders, a dark fire cloud of ringlets framing her face. Her lips were slightly parted and moist, and a small pulse beat in the ivory hollow of her throat. He could see it, could feel her indecision, and the blood in his veins rushed hot and swift.

She waits for me. . . .

He moved into the room, the door swinging shut behind him, and crossed the thick rug to reach her, taking her cold hands between his own. She stared up at him, eyes as deep and green as a woodland pool, fathomless so that he felt for an instant as if he were drowning in her gaze. How could she be so lovely? So soft and sweet and alluring?

He drew her to him, saw her eyes widen as his head lowered, but gathered her close and buried his hands in her wealth of hair, fingers crushing the curls as he tilted her face up to his. A groan caught in his throat when he touched his mouth to her lips, tasted her sweetness and soft surprise. He couldn't help himself, had no desire to stop.

Need thundered through him, powerful and relentless. So long, so long, and the softness and sweetness in his arms was so very tempting . . . he yielded to it, to the drumming impatience that had driven him for the past weeks. His mouth moved from her lips over the slope of her cheek to her ear, and she shivered when his hands coasted downward to her shoulders, fingers bunching the cool silk in his palms, pushing it aside. Her head fell back, a moan drifting past his jaw, and he ignored it, intent upon the fastenings of her dressing robe and gown. So many sashes and hooks, impediments to the prize beneath, and he stifled the urge to rip it all away.

At last he had her dressing gown open, edges falling away to reveal the gentle swells of her breasts beneath the fine lawn nightgown. Darker circles pressed against the ivory bodice, taut little buds of her nipples sending another hot beat of his blood surging through him. He cupped her breasts, raked his thumbs over the points of her beaded nipples, and she clutched at his arms with her hands, fingers digging into kerseymere sleeves.

"My lord . . ."

"Julian," he muttered, and bent his head to her breast, lips closing on the tempting shadow beneath the lawn. It was erotic, potent, the barrier of material only heightening his anticipation, and he drew her nipple into his mouth and heard her shaky intake of breath. So sweet, God, so sweet, and he had to curb the desire to rip away her gown and toss her to the floor. He'd played the game of seduction before, knew better than to rush what should be slow and tantalizing.

When he finally lifted his head, breathing harshly, she clung to him with almost desperate strength. "The bed," he murmured, and bent to lift her, but she eased away from him before he could, slipping away like an elusive dream.

"Wait . . . please." She stared up at him, trembling, her eyes so wide and dark in her pale face that he paused in reaching for her. "I . . . the agreement."

If she'd dashed cold water into his face, it couldn't have been more effective. His eyes narrowed, and he schooled his protesting body into restraint, hands moving behind him to keep from touching her again. Damp patches of material made the lawn transparent, her nipple rosy and far too tempting. He dragged his gaze back up to her face.

"Yes?"

She flushed, and pulled the edges of her dressing gown around her. "You specified that we would . . . you did not want . . . have you changed your mind, my lord?"

For a long moment, he just stared at her. Several possibilities flashed through his mind, the chief one being that perhaps she'd expect more money in return for bedding him. Is that what she wanted? Yet somehow, he didn't think that was it. She looked . . . distressed. He reminded himself that she was, after all, an actress, and this could all be a ploy to wrest concessions of some kind from him, but he didn't think so. Didn't *want* to think it could be true, and he smiled wryly at that, understanding now how the Duke of York had found himself gulled by Mrs. Clarke.

"What do you want?" he asked bluntly and Laura's eyes widened even more, then sparked with anger.

"Want? From you? I have all I want or even expected. I'm just not certain what it is that *you* want, my lord."

That damnable *my lord* again, his title and proper form of address a barrier between them that he recognized, and under different circumstances and with anyone else, demanded. But not with her. No, not with her.

"For tonight," he said after a moment, "I want only to sleep. Tomorrow, we'll discuss our agreement." He knew better than to try and think clearly when his body still ached for ease, when he wanted only to lift her onto the wide bed and follow her, to pull off that damned gown and see her soft curves, to put himself inside her and find peace and comfort and sweet release.

Awkward and frustrated, he took a step back, and his gaze fell upon a chaise longue near the fire. A fat pillow and coverlets were neatly stacked on the foot, and his brow shot up.

"For me, my lord," she said quickly, obviously following his gaze, and he shook his head.

"No. Sleep in the bed. I'll take the chaise."

"But you're so tall, and the bed is much more comfortable—"

He swung toward her, barely keeping his temper in check, spurred by the ache in his groin and the knowledge that he'd caused his own problems with that damned agreement. "I was in His Majesty's Navy and have slept on much worse, dammit. I'll take the chaise."

She promptly nodded, holding the open edges of her dressing gown close around her as she backed away a wary step. Julian wondered if he looked as tense and violent as he felt at the moment, and decided distance was the better part of valor. He managed a stiff half-bow in Laura's direction.

"I'll leave you to your privacy for now. Good night."

The solid *thunk* of the door banging shut behind him gave him only mild satisfaction. He'd outsmarted himself now, by God. Too bad Malcolm wasn't here to share the blame, but it was all his to shoulder and he knew it. Damnation. How could he have known that he'd actually want to bed her? He did. Oh yes, he certainly did, and it was an ache that time and distance wouldn't ease quickly. Maybe he'd try some of Belgrave's thirty-year-old brandy. That should do the trick. For a little while, anyway.

Laura blinked when Julian banged the door closed behind him. She was still trembling with reaction, not to his temper but to his touch. She'd wanted him to go on, not to stop holding her or kissing her or igniting that heavy pulse

Take A Trip Into A Timeless World of Passion and Adventure with Kensington Choice Historical Romances! —Absolutely FREE!

Enjoy the passion and adventure of another time with Kensington Choice Historical Romances. They are the finest novels of their kind, written by today's best-selling romance authors. Each Kensington Choice Historical Romance transports you to distant lands in a bygone age. Experience the adventure and share the delight as proud men and spirited women discover the wonder and passion of true love.

4 BOOKS WORTH UP TO $24.96— Absolutely FREE!

Get 4 FREE Books!

We created our convenient Home Subscription Service so you'll be sure to have the hottest new romances delivered each month right to your doorstep—usually before they are available in book stores. Just to show you how convenient the Zebra Home Subscription Service is, we would like to send you 4 FREE Kensington Choice Historical Romances. The books are worth up to $24.96, but you only pay $1.99 for shipping and handling. There's no obligation to buy additional books—ever!

Save Up To 30% With Home Delivery!

Accept your FREE books and each month we'll deliver 4 brand new titles as soon as they are published. They'll be yours to examine FREE for 10 days. Then if you decide to keep the books, you'll pay the preferred subscriber's price (up to 30% off the cover price!), plus shipping and handling. Remember, you are under no obligation to buy any of these books at any time! If you are not delighted with them, simply return them and owe nothing. But if you enjoy Kensington Choice Historical Romances as much as we think you will, pay the special preferred subscriber rate and save over $8.00 off the cover price!

4 FREE

Kensington
Choice
Historical
Romances
(worth up to
$24.96)
are waiting
for you to
claim them!

See details
inside...

‖‖.‖.‖‖....‖‖.‖.‖.‖.‖.‖.‖.‖..‖‖.‖.‖‖.‖.‖.‖‖...‖

KENSINGTON CHOICE

Zebra Home Subscription Service, Inc.

P.O. Box 5214

Clifton NJ 07015-5214

that throbbed between her legs, but to do something about it. That's what she really wanted. Desperation had driven her to bring up the agreement, but she was sorry it had worked so well.

Shakily, she reached behind her and found the bedpost, clinging to it to keep from sliding to the floor in a puddle of silk and misery. What should she do now? There was nothing she could say without sounding foolish or dishonest, and she didn't want to risk either. Tomorrow morning, she'd talk to Celia, and perhaps together they could think of a way out of this mess. She wanted so badly to confide in Lockwood, to tell him about Aubert Fortier and her mother and the French general, but how did she do that without sounding like part of it? For a man so dreadfully betrayed by his wife, he'd surely think she would betray him as well. If she waited too long, he'd hear it from Fortier, for she couldn't give him the outrageous amount he demanded. She'd bought only a little time with the few hundred pounds received for the pearl necklace. Once back in the city, Fortier would be at her door again. She had to find a way to get him to leave her—and the earl—alone.

Celia would know what to do. Celia always knew what to do. So she'd worry about all of it tomorrow when she could come up with a solution. Now, she'd go to bed and try to put Julian Norcliff, the sixth Earl Lockwood, firmly from her mind.

Her gaze fell upon a small carafe placed on the bedside table. Becky's touch, no doubt, her effort to please so evident. The girl learned fast, and she'd put on weight in the past month, become more confident. The change was remarkable and gratifying. What would happen to Becky once Laura was gone? Maybe she could take her to Virginia. She hated to think what would happen to her if she went back to the earl's house and that nasty-tempered Cook.

She washed her face, brushed her hair, and cleaned her teeth, then stood uncertainly for a few minutes in the middle of the room. It was so quiet in the house, the sound of the wind like a soft sigh outside, the pop and crackle of wood in the fireplace comforting. She looked at the chaise, then spread the coverlet over the cushions and plumped the pillow. Then she stepped back and gave it a considering look before moving to the tall bed against the wall. Heavy velvet bed-hangings had been pulled back, and a thick coverlet turned down. It looked inviting. And lonely.

Oh God . . . she was doomed.

She must have slept. Laura awakened in the high bed to the sound of a log being put on the fire. Peeking over the edge of the warm coverlet, her heart lurched when she saw Julian at the hearth. She'd not even heard his return, slept so soundly that she never knew he'd come back and slept so close by . . . only a few feet away, stretched on the chaise longue that couldn't be very comfortable.

Flames leaped to life, and he stood up, light playing over the sculpted planes of his chest and shoulders, bare skin a tawny gleam. He wore only white breeches, unbuttoned and hanging loosely around his narrow waist. Feeling wicked but unable to stop staring, Laura curled her fingers tightly into the velvet covers, heart thudding so hard she knew he must soon hear it. It had never occurred to her that the male form could be beautiful. He took her breath away, splendidly strong and masculine, powerful and potent, as magnificent as Michelangelo's statue of David.

There was such strength in him, of bone and sinew, but more importantly, of character. It was so obvious, even moreso among his peers. She'd watched him at dinner, compared him to his companions and found them all lacking. Only Lockwood possessed an innate courtesy, though Belgrave's occasional rudeness was more from carelessness than malice. Langston, she took an immediate dislike to, for he was crude to the point of vulgar, and the others seemed shallow and more intent upon their own appetites and comfort than on the feelings of the women at the table. Granted, perhaps they weren't viewed by them as "ladies" but it gave them no right to be cruel. As soon as possible, she and Celia had escaped upstairs, not wanting to remain in the company of the men or the women.

"We're just as snobbish as the lords," Celia had lamented, shaking her head, "but if I hear Ivy Tremayne say one more time that Drummond's as big as a horse, I think I'll choke her with my wool scarf."

Laura had laughed, but felt much the same. The ladies were so coarse, the men vulgar, and she'd flinched several times at the turn of the conversation, unable even to look at Lockwood. Did he think the same? Had he come to her after dinner because he thought she'd be easy to seduce? Just another harlot, purchased and paid for, body and soul? Oh God . . .

Closing her eyes tightly, heart thudding painfully, she still heard him moving about the room quietly as if unwilling to wake her. Finally she peeped through her lashes again, and saw him moving toward the wash bowl on the stand. It was a curious male ritual, the shaving of a beard, and one she recalled watching her father do when she was only a small child. Papa had kept long whiskers on the sides, but scraped clean his chin, leaving only a small mustache. The earl's side whiskers were shorter, but still extended down nearly to his jawline, with the rest of his face kept smooth. Fascinated, she watched him peer into the small mirror over the wash basin, wielding a razor in swift, expert swipes, whisking away soap and beard in clean strokes. Still bare to the waist, his muscles flexed as he worked, lithe and lean and drawing her rapt attention.

Then he wiped his face dry, dried his hands, and dressed. He seemed to have no trouble attaching his own collar or arranging his own neckcloth, tying it with swift, careless flips of white linen around his neck. He wore leather breeches and knee-high top boots polished to a high sheen. A scarlet coat and top hat completed his hunting attire, and he left the room silently, pausing in the open door to glance toward the bed where she watched him beneath her lashes. She froze in place, afraid he'd know she'd been staring at him, but he didn't speak, only studied her for a long moment, then shut the door softly. She heard his steps fade quickly on the thick hallway carpet. He was gone. And she felt suddenly bereft again. . . .

When Julian reached the dining room, breakfast had been set out on the walnut sideboard. Footmen served kidneys, scones, eggs, bacon, and fish, a hearty meal for men planning to brave the cold air. It was the best season for foxhunting, when the skins were at highest perfection. The sun had not yet risen, and they would be horsed by the time the hounds were at the cover. He did love the bracing air and feel of a good horse beneath him, the thrill of the chase always appealing more to him than the actual capture. It was invigorating to hear belling hounds, the huntsman's horn, the thundering hooves. He felt alive when on the hunt. It was his nature, he supposed, to love the hunt. Maybe that was part of the reason he much preferred an elusive female to those who fell simpering into his arms, though he'd never before encountered one as maddening as Laura Lancaster.

She should have already fallen into his arms. That she hadn't, was disconcerting.

Langston leaned close, eyes still bleary from his night's drinking. He reeked unpleasantly, and Julian leaned away as the man leered, "I must say, I'm surprised you're joining us so early this morning."

"Are you. Why would I not?"

Langston grinned. "I wagered a crown you'd be abed late, after a lively night a'twixt the sheets."

The other men chuckled at the ribald comment. Julian's brow rose. "You've lost your wager, Langston. We shall see if you lose your seat as well, once on the course."

Hoots of soft laughter made Langston's face flush. It was a fact that he'd lost his seat and fallen headlong into a mud puddle the year before, nearly drowning before he could be pulled from the muck, causing much merriment among his comrades and embarrassment for himself. Julian's oblique reminder shut Langston up at once.

It would have caused no end of laughter if Langston knew where he'd really slept, that he had a mistress he didn't bed. The chaise had proven to be uncomfortable enough that he'd been glad to rise early after long hours in the dark, tossing and turning. More uncomfortable than the short, horsehair-stuffed longue had been his acute awareness that Laura lay only a short distance away in the wide bed. He wanted her, and he'd signed away his right to her at his own foolish insistence. He must have been utterly mad.

"Off we go then," Belgrave said merrily. "I've a crack pack of foxhounds at the ready. The local yeomen are paid well for use of their land, and we've got a good chase ahead of us!"

Julian accompanied them outside. Maybe a good, rousing hunt would take his mind off Laura for a time. How would he have felt, he wondered, if it had been Laura whom his father arranged for him to marry instead of Eleanor? An intriguing thought.

CHAPTER 12

Eleanor, still Lady Lockwood though Julian had treated her most shabbily, sat forward in the coach. Familiar buildings loomed beyond the line of docks nibbling at the edge of the Thames, and the river itself was littered with crafts of every kind—coal barges and passenger skiffs, and tall-masted French, Dutch, and Spanish vessels separated into different quarters. It was exciting and dirty and so familiar. Home at last. And well in time to prepare for the next Season. Soon social functions would begin, escalating into springtime and the height of the Season. By June, most would begin the annual trek to their country estates, and she'd make her decision then.

Julian would regret his desertion of her. How dare he! It was bad enough that he'd made it plain how he felt about wedding her, adding to her humiliation, but then he'd thrown her to the mercy of the gossipmongers. Now she had to skulk into the city like any commoner, when she'd long been accustomed to deference. But before long, she'd be back in favor again. She had a plan to show Julian just how wrong he'd been. And how it felt to be cast out of the fold. Oh yes. He'd rue the day he'd been so cruel.

The little house on the fringe of Mayfair was shabby and unpretentious, offering discreet lodgings that would be private enough until she wished to make her return known. Still, it was an insult to one who had always known only the best. Annoyed, Eleanor gave her maid a sharp slap when she took too long in unfastening the hooks of her cloak.

"Clumsy girl! Must you dawdle?"

"Sorry, ma'am," the girl mumbled, sniffing a little to hold back tears.

"And so you should be. Witless rabbit. Here now, I'll be expecting a guest soon and you'd best have everything ready or you'll be sorry indeed."

Eleanor looked around her with ill-concealed dissatisfaction. It was shabby. How did he think she could exist in such a hovel? Surely, a better house could have been found for her, one with a bit of style. Still, after the sunshine and warmth of Italy, few lodgings would compare to those whitewashed villas open to the lovely sea air.

It was late when he arrived, and Eleanor was fuming at the delay, turning around to glare at him when the maid showed him into the small parlor.

"My lady," he said warmly, walking toward her with a smile, but she quickly banished it when she demanded to know why he hadn't come at once.

"Didn't you get my message? I sent a boy straightaway from the dock once I got off that wretched, wallowing tub— yet it's taken you all day to attend me!"

Jerking to a halt, the smile disappeared and brown eyes regarded her warily. "Your ship was not due to arrive until tomorrow, my lady."

"Yes, well, so we wouldn't have except for a nasty storm that nearly blew us to the North Sea. The captain said it did us a good turn in the end, however, getting us here much earlier than planned. I thought you'd be eager to see me."

Lowering her lashes over pale blue eyes, she gazed at him long enough to see his face flush with a mixture of chagrin and pleasure, and smiled before she turned away, patting a stray blond curl into place, then putting her palms out toward the fire to warm them.

"Oh, I am, milady, most glad to see you! Of course, I am. You must know . . . you must be aware how you've been missed since your departure."

"Have I really? And my husband? Did Julian miss me as well, do you think?" Silence answered her, and her fingers closed into fists. Turning back, she gave him a harsh glance. "I see that you've no ready answer for that question. How telling."

"His lordship mustn't suspect you've returned. He'd be furious."

"Would he?" She smiled. "How unfortunate. For him. He'll know when I'm ready for him to know. Until then . . ." She shrugged. "No one will know. It shall remain our little secret."

There was another silence, but she recognized doubt in his eyes and laughed when he said, "Your return was a bit . . . precipitate."

"So it was." Amused, she moved to the small settee and sat down with a graceful drift of her skirts, artfully arranging them to drape over her legs. There were times men could be such fools. Necessary evils, and most frustrating. Still, she could see that he was distressed and needed to be soothed. "Really, my dear Malcolm, how long could I be expected to remain among such peasants? Impetuous, sultry, attractive peasants to be certain, but not at all English."

"No," he said after a moment, "not at all English. The Italians are said to be passionate, but still . . . the scandal over that young man was most intense. It quite eclipsed the rumors from Vienna."

Irritated, she snapped, "It was hardly my fault the young fool was deranged enough to hang himself. Italians are so impetuous! What was I to do? Remaining in Florence was utterly impossible after that. Surely Julian will see the sense in my return."

"Yes, madam, perhaps he will once he understands your reasons. However, I'd advise you to approach him with subtlety and caution until you know his mood."

"Would you? Hm. I daresay you may be right." She stirred her tea, frowning. "Do sit down, Malcolm. You're exhausting me standing there. We need to discuss how best to approach

Julian over his ridiculous insistence that I remain an exile from my own home."

Stiffly, Malcolm sat on the settee opposite her and gazed at her with the same kind of sad expression Vincenzo had worn at times, a rather hopeless infatuation that made her hide a smile. Oh yes, he was most useful. An efficient secretary, steward of the household accounts—and with access to Lockwood wealth. How very fortunate indeed.

Leaning forward, she allowed Malcolm an unobstructed view of her breasts in her low-cut gown as she lifted a teacup and pressed it into his hand. His eyes looked a bit glazed as he accepted it, belatedly dragging his gaze from her bosom to her face.

"Malcolm, tell me what Julian has been up to since I left England. Still a pompous bore?"

"At times." Malcolm's cup rattled on the saucer. "There was a bit of a stir after you left, of course, and some nasty rumors that had to be squelched. I took initiative there, and now there are rumors of a very different sort."

"Are there? Excellent! You've done quite well, Malcolm. I'm exceedingly pleased. What is the nature of these rumors?"

"Lockwood has taken a mistress. An actress from Covent Garden. A *Colonial*."

"An American?" She clapped her hands together. "Capital! An entirely unsuitable creature, I'm certain." It couldn't be more perfect, she thought. She'd threaten him with ruin if he's foolish enough to think he could keep her from her rightful position as his wife. Perhaps she may not be received in some houses, but there were plenty of those in society who'd understand once they saw how she was driven away by a cruel husband. She'd soon have her place back. Very soon.

Lunch after a hunt was always a big affair. Julian went upstairs, expecting Cranford to be in the room to assist him as always, taking his muddy clothes away to be cleaned and providing him with proper attire. To his surprise, instead of Cranford, Laura lay upon the chaise, a cool cloth over her eyes.

"Hullo," he said, pausing to look down at her, and she lifted one edge of the cloth to peer up at him, "are you ill?"

"A headache, my lord. Nothing more."

"Oh." He stood there uncertainly for a moment. He wasn't familiar with female complaints at all; he and Eleanor had never shared quarters, nor had he spent much time with her. The other women in his life had been few, and he'd never lingered for more than a night.

"Do I importune you, my lord?" Laura sat up. She looked pale, eyes huge and bright in her face as she gazed at him.

"Not at all. I take it Cranford is elsewhere."

"I believe he went to fetch something, my lord."

Irritation knifed through him. "For pity's sake," he snapped, "must you 'my lord' me to death? I've told you my Christian name. Use it."

He instantly regretted his outburst. If anything, she grew even paler, and her hand shook slightly as she pulled the cloth from her forehead. Tiny damp ringlets clung to her skin. He felt like smoothing them back, and curled his hands into fists at his sides to keep from touching her.

"I take it the hunt didn't go well," she said after a moment, and he smiled wryly when she didn't use any name or title.

"The hunt went well enough until that fool Langston failed to clear a fence. His horse balked and he nearly came unseated."

"That must have been awkward."

"For Langston, and nearly for Belgrave. He almost didn't make it around him in time." He hooked a finger into the knot of his neckcloth and tugged it loose, then fumbled at his high collar. "It could have been a real mess. As it was, a minor dust-up."

"Shall I help you, my—I mean, you seem to be having trouble unbuttoning your collar."

"Damned thing. Where did you say Cranford went?"

"I didn't say." She stood up, setting aside her damp cloth

and coming to where he stood near the fire. Gently pushing aside his hands, she reached up, her gaze focused on the tiny buttons that held his collar to his shirt. "He left a few minutes ago and didn't say why. I thought perhaps you had summoned him."

She smelled of rose water, soft and alluring, a scent that reminded him of Shadowhurst and warm summer days in Kent. There was a ripeness about her, an earthy promise of peace and ease and pleasure. Her hands were cool, fingers swift and competent as she unfastened his collar and took his neckcloth, folding it neatly and putting them both atop a small table.

"You'd make an excellent valet," he said with a faint smile. "Should I warn Cranford?"

A smile pressed at the corners of her mouth, forming delightful dimples. He stared at her, fascinated.

"I have a feeling Cranford would not be impressed were you to tell him of my dubious qualifications," she said, and he grinned.

"Nothing impresses Cranford."

"So I understand. He's quite imperturbable."

"Yes, he's always been that way. A bastion of English dignity and reserve."

"Save for a just cause," she added, and his brow rose.

"A just cause? I was unaware that Cranford is inclined to lose his dignity for any reason."

"Oh, he never lost his dignity," she assured him, "but apparently took offense when your cook overstepped her bounds with one of the kitchen maids. He gave her quite a scold."

"Really." Julian stared at her. "No one told me."

"I imagine not." Laughter gleamed in her eyes. "He can be formidable, and instructed it not to be mentioned again. If Becky hadn't come with me, I'm sure I wouldn't know about it at all."

Julian nodded. "Yes, I can see Cranford dealing harshly with anyone who oversteps their bounds. He's done it to me often enough. You seem surprised. He's been with me since I was a lad in leading strings, and expresses himself freely. Too freely at times, in my opinion."

She was still smiling, and he found himself smiling back at her. Lingering irritations faded into memory, and his tension ebbed. What was it about this woman that so appealed to him? It wasn't only her fresh beauty, though she was lovely indeed. There was just something about her that intrigued him. He'd found himself thinking about her far too often, and had barely missed getting tangled up in Langston's near-disaster himself. If not for a good horse and his own quick reflexes, he could have taken a nasty fall, and it would have been his own fault for not paying proper attention to the course and hounds. Instead, he'd found himself thinking about spending the morning in bed with Laura, as Langston had so vulgarly insinuated.

Not a bad idea at all. In fact, a damned good one.

Lost in a pleasant reverie of whispers and ivory flesh beneath the velvet bedhangings, he was shaken rudely free when Cranford said, apparently not for the first time, "My lord, please be so good as to allow me to assist in removing your boots."

He saw then the elderly valet's austere face staring down with something close to a frown between his brows, a bootjack neatly placed at his feet. He looked down, and hooked his heel in the jack shaped like a woman's spread legs.

"This is not our jack, I trust," he said, and Cranford said in tones of grave disapproval, "Indeed not, my lord. Alas, it seems to be the only one available."

Looking up, he saw Laura's startled expression. A high flush stained her cheeks, and she looked quickly away.

Rather grimly, he muttered, "Belgrave has questionable taste."

"Indeed, my lord."

Laura drifted away, moving across the room to the tall windows that looked out over the back garden. Pale light filtered through blue velvet drapes swagged over leaded glass. Snow lay in sketchy clumps on the wide sill outside. Framed by the light beyond, a fuzzy halo gave Laura the appearance of a snow angel. Garbed in white velvet with a deep green ribbon sash, she seemed ethereal and virginal and beyond his reach. He stared at her, only vaguely aware of Cranford's attendance and the obscene bootjack.

"Shall I continue, my lord?"

"Um, what?" He glanced at Cranford, who stood immobile and patient, waiting with clean linen draped over his arms. "Oh . . . I see. No, not now. Lunch isn't for an hour yet. I'll ring for you when I'm ready."

"Very good, sir."

Feeling as if every sense was awake, Julian moved across the room to where Laura stood at the window. She didn't move or acknowledge his presence at first, and after a moment said in a soft tone, "I remember snows in Virginia. The first snow of the year was always the best. It was so clean and pure, and I loved to stand outside and try to catch the flakes on the tip of my tongue. They felt so good against my face, and when the fields were covered, I felt as if I were in another land. It looked so different, so beautiful . . . and I used to pretend I was far away. Now . . ."

When she lapsed into silence, he ended her sentence for her, saying, "Now you'd give anything to be there."

She turned, looking up at him. "Yes. Oh God, yes. But it's been so long, and it won't be the same. I don't know if I can ever really go home again."

He didn't say anything for a moment. He could have told her she was right, that she'd never be able to go back to what it was when she was a child. He didn't even have to know the details of what had taken her from Virginia and across the Atlantic to know that one could never go home again after a long absence.

Finally he said softly, "I know just how you feel. No, it's true. I was gone for a long time from the one place I love more than anywhere else, and after five years away, when I finally went back it wasn't the same at all. Everything had changed. Some of the familiar faces were gone, and it felt . . . foreign."

"Were you able to feel at home there again?"

"Yes, after a while. But it took time, and it will never be like it was when I was young. I'd seen too much, knew too much. And of course, by the time I went back, I'd inherited the title and it was mine. I'd been at war for five years, aboard His Majesty's *Prometheus*. All I thought about while I was gone was Shadowhurst. I dreamed about it at night, thought about it during the day when I should have been tending to other duties. When I finally got back, nothing was like I'd remembered or dreamed about. I was angry and disappointed."

Reaching out, he touched one of the curls on her forehead. It was glossy and soft, and still damp from the cloth she'd held to her head.

"But I finally realized," he said, "that Shadowhurst hadn't really changed at all. I had."

"Shadowhurst. It sounds lovely."

"It is, if you like sheep and fields and cottages instead of crowded city streets."

"I think," she said after a moment, "that if I never see another city street, I'll be happy."

It struck him then, that he'd found one more reason to keep her close. He smiled. "We have much in common. I feel the same way most of the time."

His gaze fell to her bare throat, creamy skin displayed by the low bodice of her gown. He couldn't resist dragging a fingertip over the fragile bones that winged toward the hollow in her throat. "You should wear the pearls to dinner tonight," he murmured, thinking of how lovely they would be against her skin, with the ivory rose dipping down to nestle almost between her breasts. "You did bring them with you?"

"I . . . no, I'm afraid I didn't," she said, and looked up at him with shadowed eyes.

"No matter. If you don't like wearing them—"

"Oh, they're lovely! A wonderful gift. I just . . . they . . . I didn't bring them."

His eyes narrowed slightly. High color rose in her cheeks like flags, and she didn't meet his gaze. He frowned.

"Why didn't you bring them with you?"

For a moment she didn't answer, then she took a deep breath and let it out again. "I no longer have them."

He stared at her. "Did you lose them?"

She shook her head, and her chin dipped low as she turned away from him, staring out the window as she said in a whisper, "No, I . . . sold them."

"Sold them?" Anger ripped through him. "God above, madam, do I not meet your every financial need? Why would you sell a gift?"

She turned back to look at him. "They were a gift, were they not? Mine to do with as I please?"

"Yes, of course, but—"

"I'm not comfortable coming to you with my every need, my lord. There are some things I feel I cannot ask of you. So I sold them to meet a . . . debt."

"Damn it all, you should have told me you needed more money." Disgruntled, he scowled at her, regretting the loss of the pearls more for her sake than his own. They meant little enough to him, but had been so lovely on her. He studied her face for a long moment. She could have lied to him but she hadn't. She'd confessed that she sold his gift, when many would have pretended to have misplaced them. If nothing else, he had to admire her honesty.

"Tell me when you have needs," he said brusquely. "You need not tell me why if you so choose, but I'll not have you selling gifts to pay tradesmen's bills." When she didn't reply, another thought struck him. Had she a lover on the side? Someone she supported? No, of course not. Yet he couldn't help but recall Rex Pentley, the infatuated smile on his face when he looked at Laura, and ugly doubt wriggled its dark way into his brain. What, really, did he know about her save the information Malcolm had ferreted out? Little enough. Caution warned him not to trust unwisely, reminded him that he had been a fool once before, but instinct contradicted any suspicion that she would be dishonest. She could have lied so easily about the pearls and he'd never have known the truth. No, he knew he could trust her. When she was ready to confide in him, she would.

Lifting her chin with a finger hooked beneath the softness, he met her eyes. "You never have to worry about telling me what you need, Laura, or what causes you distress. If I can help you, I will."

To his surprise, her eyes filled with tears. She blinked them away, drops clinging to dewed lashes as she lowered her gaze. "There are things I cannot confide in you right now, but you've given me hope for the first time—Norcliff."

He smiled. It was a start. Resting his hand on her shoulder, he let his fingers smooth over the soft velvet nap of her gown. Beneath the material her skin would be even softer. Devonshire cream was no sweeter than her smooth flesh, and he schooled his body into restraint. It was heady to be this close to her without yielding to the rising need to feel her beneath him, to taste her lips with his own. Fever spread through him in a drowning tide, until he floundered with it and could not bring himself to move away from her.

They stood silent for several moments, the heat beating through him while snow began to drift from the sky outside, powdering the window ledge. It was, in a way, a restful peace even with the need inside him so fast and furious. How strange . . .

His brief peace was shattered at her next words: "Tell me about your wife."

"There's nothing to tell. She's in Vienna. No, Italy now, I believe." The words came out harsh and brittle, and he took his hand from her shoulder and clenched it behind him. Heat ebbed, to be replaced by icy chill.

"How sad, that you'd be estranged from her."

"There's nothing at all sad about it. It's a relief." He cleared his throat, staring at Laura and wondering if Eleanor had managed to come between them after all. Why should she? It'd never been a real marriage. Yet the world saw it as one. He'd kept up the pretense because it had benefitted him once, kept him safe from any other arranged marriage.

"A relief? How could it be a relief?" She shook her head, her brow furrowed. "You're wed for life, and must make some kind of peace with her no matter the problems."

He looked beyond her out the window, unable to look at her face and think of Eleanor at the same time. He should tell her the truth, tell her how he'd found Eleanor with her skirts up and another man between her legs only an hour after the nuptials. But it was humiliating. Even the memory of his shock and outrage had the power to shame him. He should have withstood his father's insistence that he wed Lord Drumley's daughter, but he hadn't. He'd let the old earl have his way despite his better judgment, let his father's ill health and need for an heir override caution. And look what it had cost—his reputation, his future, and the heir he'd never have. He'd never even been in Eleanor's bed. Their marriage had never been consummated, though no one but he and Eleanor knew that. She'd tried every trick she could to lure him to her bed, but after finding her with her skirts over her head under a stairwell, he had no intention of getting a child on her. How would he ever know for a certainty it was his?

"I'm afraid," he said softly, "there will be no peace with Eleanor. Not for me. There are—other reasons."

It was as far as he was willing to go, and he thought with no small chagrin that Laura had been much more honest than he was being with her. He saw no reason in burdening her and shaming himself with a lengthy recital of Eleanor's sins. It would change nothing.

After a moment, he took a step back and away from Laura, putting distance between them in an effort to regain control of his emotions. He wanted to assure her that Eleanor meant nothing to him, but how did he do that without telling her why? It sounded so . . . tawdry.

Looking up at him, Laura held his gaze for a moment, diffused light behind her and the snow and her white gown giving her such an ethereal glow that it was like looking at an angel. He had the irrational thought that like an angel, she could grant him peace on earth.

Then the vision vanished as Cranford rapped sharply on the chamber door and stepped inside, intoning, "The first bell for luncheon has rung, my lord. Do you desire to attend?"

"Yes," he said without taking his eyes off Laura, "we'll take luncheon with the others."

CHAPTER 13

Luncheon had been awkward. Seated beside Julian, Laura felt clumsy and far too aware of him at her side, a seating arrangement she'd not expected. What had he meant about his wife? She should never have asked about her. It had just burst from her mouth before she could stop. She had retreated to their chamber again after lunch, pleading a headache. It wasn't a lie.

Everything seemed to be happening so quickly, and she had no control over any of it. Celia had followed her upstairs, and they devised a plan of sorts to stop Fortier. It would, of necessity, involve Rex Pentley. She had no choice in that. But if it would rid her of the fear that Aubert Fortier would ruin the earl, she'd willingly enlist the aid of whomever it took.

"Are you certain Rex won't mind?" she asked anxiously.

"Rex will love it." Celia smiled wickedly. "It's just the sort of thing he does so well. He loves to outwit the swells, and this Fortier sounds like a particularly nasty bit of work, he does. Oh no, Rex will enjoy himself immensely. Of course, you could always tell the earl. I daresay that Lockwood would also enjoy dispatching Fortier."

"I could never tell him. It's too . . . shameful."

"That the man is attempting to bleed you dry with extortion? Hardly, ducks. Oh no—you mean something else, don't you? Your mother?"

Laura stared down at her hands. Heat flushed her face so

that even her ears burned. It was true. Oh God, it was so true. She was ashamed of her mother, ashamed that Maman gave herself so freely. How had it happened? Had Papa known? Perhaps he had, perhaps that was why her grandparents had never seemed pleased when a letter had come from France, though they'd not said anything. They must have known. So long ago now, and she could understand why Maman fled Paris during the Reign of Terror, why she'd wed Papa and come to America with him. But Fleurette's heart had always been in France, and after Papa died—home meant more to her than her small daughter. Perhaps that was what Laura could never truly forgive her. . . .

"Here. Take this. It's mint, you little goose. Charley gave me an entire box of them. They're quite good." Celia popped a mint into her mouth and sat beside her on the longue, the box of mint bonbons between them. After a moment, she said, "Trust Rex. He'll take care of this Fortier for you, and you'll not have to worry about him again."

"Thank you." Laura managed a smile. "I just want this all behind me. I want—to be at home again."

Silent, Celia patted her hands. They sat for a moment as light coming through leaded glass windowpanes thinned into dusk, and shadows gathered in corners of the room. Lamps were lit, the fire on the hearth warm and cheery, warding off the early fall of night. Snow still fell, hitting the windows in a soft whisper.

"Have you made up your mind, then?" Celia finally asked, breaking the silence.

"About Rex?"

"No, ducks, about Lockwood."

"I don't know what you mean."

Celia smiled slightly. "Yes, you do. Think about it. You're here with him, aren't you? You said yes to his proposition. Are you ready to say yes to everything?"

"Why do you keep on at me about it?" Laura jerked to her feet, crossing her arms over her chest to move to the window and watch the snow fall on bushes and trees. "The earl is married."

"As I told you, the best kind of protector. Listen, ducks, do you truly think you can ever go home again and have it like it was? Marry some farmer or merchant and be a wife and mother, be respectable? You can't. I know you want to, and I wish it would happen for you, but it's not going to—I know that well enough. There will always be a Fortier just waiting to betray you. You can't live a lie. I could, quite easily. That's my nature. But *you* can't."

It was true. Oh God, it was true. Laura closed her eyes, shivering. Even if no one knew, she'd know. She'd know the truth of her mother's life, and she'd know the truth of how she felt about the earl. . . .

"Can you honestly say you don't want to be with him?" Celia pursued. "Can you? You know you do. And at least here in England you'll have people who care about you. If you return to America, you'll have only an uncle who offered you nothing but passage across the Atlantic. It won't be what you want, Laura."

Celia was right. Lockwood knew it, too. He'd felt the same yearning, and had gone home only to be disillusioned. *It will never be like it was when I was young. I'd seen too much, knew too much,* he'd said. And she knew he was right. Her uncle didn't want her there, and she had no home in Virginia, no one who cared about her.

"Yes," she said finally in a choked whisper, "you're right, Celia. It's not what I want. Not any longer. It's just that . . . I had nothing else these past two years, nothing but a dream of going home again. It's hard to relinquish now."

"But now you have a dream within your reach, ducks." When Laura turned to look at her, Celia smiled. "It's true. He's downstairs, and will be coming up soon. Don't lose what you have by wishing for the impossible."

Laura thought about that once Celia was gone, leaving her alone in the room with only the fire and lamps. Julian Norcliff,

Lord Lockwood, was just as impossible a dream as going home again. Did she dare risk all?

It was nearly dark when Julian went back upstairs. He'd won several hundred pounds at cards, putting Langston into a black mood. The others were affable enough, but young Langston needed a good set-down. He'd still not recovered from nearly losing his seat and becoming a butt of their jokes. Ah well. Trials taught patience. Langston must surely learn a great deal of patience if he continued on his heedless course in life.

God knows, he'd certainly learned patience the hard way. A lifetime of trials had tempered his former impatience into the ability to control his reactions. Service in His Majesty's Navy had done its part in teaching him self-control as well. Then Eleanor . . . the hardest lesson of all to learn. Betrayal cut deeply. It wasn't that he'd loved her, but that she'd cared so little for her position and him that she'd risk it all for a fling with a baronet. There had been a taut moment when he'd had to fight the urge to kill her. It would have been so easy to put his hands around her slender, vicious little neck and wring the life from her . . . and there were times he still fought the temptation.

Pausing in front of the chamber he shared with Laura, he reflected again on the difference between the two women, Eleanor faithless and selfish, Laura loyal and generous. Even Cranford had unbent enough to mention her without the tone of disapproval he used for most people. That in itself was a revelation.

When he opened the door, Laura turned away from the window to face him. Dying light seeped through the glass, subdued and filtered by falling snow, but brightness seemed to center on her, on her lovely face and white gown, and the rich, silky fall of fiery hair onto her shoulders.

"Did you enjoy your card game?" she asked, but he heard

only the thundering beat of blood pounding through his veins as he shut the door behind him.

"Your hair is loose," he said, an inane comment that somehow seemed relevant. He wanted to bury first his hands in that glorious mass, then his face.

"Yes. I had a headache . . . all the pins. I took down my hair—are you unwell?"

"No. I've never felt better." He took three strides toward her, then halted. She stared up at him as if she knew what he wanted, could hear the thud of his heartbeat and the need coursing through him. Her lips parted slightly, and the pulse in the hollow of her throat beat swiftly. Green eyes dilated, and her breath came in soft little drags of air like the hum of a swallow's wings. He cast aside restraint, ignored years of hard-won control, and reached for her.

She yielded.

Putting her face up, she made a soft little sound like "oh!" as he pulled her hard against him and bent to cover her lips with his mouth. Oh God, she was so sweet, tasting like mint and smelling like roses, a sugary confection he could no longer resist.

Caught by the tactile sensation of her mouth opening under his, he explored lightly with his tongue, still holding her, suspended in gray light and the brightness that was Laura, open and trusting in his arms. He felt her agitation, the fluttering of her hands against him as if she didn't know where to rest them, then they settled on his shoulders, fingers sliding over his coat to hold him in a light grip.

Untutored, her lips opened for him, her tongue a hesitant duel with his, erotic and heated and oh so delicious, and the hunger rose in him so strong he had to curb the impulse to press her down to the floor. Exerting subtle pressure, he guided her toward the bed, wide and comfortable and waiting, a bower of blue velvet and goose down pillows.

There was no protest from her, just that soft surrender he'd seen in her eyes, and at the edge of the bed, he paused,

Lisa Higdon

reveling in the sensation of her body pressed between his and the bed as his knee braced against the wood frame. Breathing raggedly, he held himself in check, his hands moving up to cradle her face between his palms and stare into her eyes.

"I won't hurt you," he said thickly, and she nodded.

"I know."

Those two simple words of trust struck him with the force of a hammer. For a moment he was too paralyzed by her faith in him to move. It was a monumental gift, something to be cherished and protected. He stood for a moment, then bent to press his forehead against hers, let his hands drift down through silky curls tumbling over her shoulders in a cape, lower to press his opened fingers into white velvet draped over the curve of her hips. Bunching it in a fist, he drew it slowly upward at the same time he lent his weight to press her backward. The high mattress met her spine, gave way when he half-lifted her onto it, cushioning their bodies as they fell in a tangle atop the coverlets. Her hair spread beneath her just as he'd envisioned it, a riot of curls beneath her head, bright against the soft blue coverlet.

It took all his restraint to go slow with her, his hand sliding over her curves lightly when he wanted to rip away her garments, see in the flesh what he'd dreamed of so many nights. His fingers brushed gently over her breasts, then slowly drew up the velvet along the slender length of her shapely legs. White clocked stockings were held at the knee with a pink garter and he closed his eyes briefly. When he opened them again, she curved her hand behind his neck and drew his head down to hers.

As her mouth closed over his, he knew he was lost, that his tenuous grasp on control was slipping away. He kissed her back, savagely, relentlessly, tangling his hands in her hair. He meant to be gentle but wasn't; he knew it, with a distant part of his brain that whispered caution, but the violence of his kiss was contagious. She kissed him back just as fiercely, her hands holding on to him, fingers digging into the cloth of his coat. Braced on his hands still wound in hair flowing over the velvet covers, he pressed closer to her, shoving his body between her legs. Exquisite pleasure shot through him at the contact, even cushioned by layers of fabric between them.

It was sweet torment.

Lifting away from her, he sat back, legs bent beneath him, and begin to unhook her gown. There were no bulky buttons, only tiny hooks set within the folds of velvet. Sliding his hand down through them, he soon freed her gown to leave her clad in only a thin chemise and her stockings, those impossibly sheer, snowy stockings with the delicate clocking that fit closely to the curve of her calves and thighs. Untying the garters, he slid the stockings away to bare her legs, heard her faint gasp, and looked up. It was nearly his undoing.

Half-reclining, she propped on her elbows to watch him, hair tumbled into her face like a sultry goddess. A Greek siren. Thick lashes nearly hid her eyes from him, and her lips were wet and still slightly swollen from his kisses. Tempting swells of her breasts rose above the lacy edge of her chemise, with her nipples pushing against the silk. She watched him, her rapid breathing making the lace quiver. If he wasn't careful, he could fall in love. . . .

He slid from the bed to stand beside it, his eyes holding her gaze as he pulled off his coat, neckcloth, and shirt, then unfastened his breeches. The bootjack . . . where was the damn bootjack?

She should feel shame, or some kind of guilt, but Laura felt only a combination of heat and chill that made her shiver. Inside she was burning up, yet her flesh prickled with cold and reaction, and she watched as Julian crossed to the obscene bootjack near the chaise longue, hooking his heels in it to swiftly divest himself of the boots. When he turned back to the bed, he moved with a soft tread that made her think of a huge, tawny cat, all lithe and graceful and predatory. Another shiver rippled through her.

Then he was there, leaning over her again, lamplight gleaming on his flexed muscles and in his spun-gold hair, on the tiny dark hairs with gilt tips that curled across his chest. Reaching up, she stroked a hand through the thick pelt, watching in fascination as it curled around her fingertips. From there, she boldly reached up to touch the strong angle of his jaw, scraping her nails lightly over the dark beard shadow with a soft, rasping sound, her heart thumping madly. It grew so fast, when only this morning she had watched him shave. . . .

Grateful for his stillness, she danced her fingertips over the outline of his mouth, smiling when he nipped at her hand, a teasing light flaring in his smoldering eyes. He watched her so closely and carefully, as if she might bolt, and somehow that knowledge made it easier. Her hand dipped lower, following the column of his throat back over his chest, coasting over ropes of hard muscle only lightly furred with hair on his belly. Then she paused, felt his tremor, saw his mouth go taut at her hesitation, and the thick brush of his lashes lowered when she slid her hand farther down to touch him *there*. Oh, it was so different! Not at all as she'd thought, and she jerked her hand away as if burned.

He laughed softly. Gently taking her hand in his, he brought it back to him, curled her fingers around him and held her a moment, bending lower to whisper into her ear that it wasn't so bad, that it was just as nature intended it to be.

It amazed her that he was shaking, that she felt him quiver, that though he smiled at her, his muscles shuddered at her touch. A feeling of power swept through her, and emboldened by it, she experimented with strokes that finally earned a groan from him.

"Enough," he muttered at last, and looked up at her through his lashes, fine white lines dug into each side of his mouth. "Now it's your turn, my lovely winter rose."

There was no time then for anything but surrender before he lowered his full weight on her and pushed her deeper into the bed. One leg wedged between her thighs, and his palms coasted up beneath the hem of her chemise in an agile move that lifted it up, fingers twisting in silk to pull it over her head and send it sailing through the air. Heat flushed her entire body when he stared down at her a moment. Then he looked up, and there was such emotion in his eyes that she couldn't move.

It seemed to reach down inside her and touch something she hadn't known she could feel, a surge of deep emotion welling up that obliterated everything but him—Julian Norcliff, sixth Earl of Lockwood. Oh God . . . she loved him. She knew it now, knew why she felt as she did, why she no longer felt the urgency to go home to Virginia. He was the reason.

But then there was no more time to think, only to feel, as he moved over her, his breath hot against her cheek, his whisper thick as he told her he'd not hurt her, only wanted to give her pleasure, his mouth trailing fire down her throat to her breasts, tongue and lips teasing her into a rising sense of urgency.

The urgency melded into excitement, overwhelming her as his full weight lowered atop her to push her deep into the mattress. Heat swamped her and yet she trembled as if chilled, unable to stop, her body rising to meet his almost as if compelled. Pleasure shot through her when his body touched hers intimately, a slow drag that made her shiver, then he slid forward. Braced with his hands on each side of her, he came fully against her and her eyes popped open as the hot pleasure turned swiftly to pain. She cried out sharply and he went still, hovering over her, looking down at her again with something like surprise in his golden gaze.

"Oh God, Laura . . . " His thick whisper sounded so raspy, as if torn from him, then he bent to kiss her again, his mouth moving over her lips, then her cheek, then back to her mouth. He held still inside her until she began to relax again, until she kissed him back, then began to move at last. It didn't hurt, not like that first sharp pain, but there was none of the promised pleasure, either. A low vibration like a great cat purred in his throat, then he finally shuddered and went still, and she lay beneath him as he collapsed atop her, her hands stroking his bare back.

So this was it. This was what she'd thought would be beautiful. It had *hurt*. Where was the pleasure that must come with the act? Why would women do this if there was no pleasure?

Holding her in his embrace, he kissed her gently on the cheek. His breathing was harsh and ragged, and he moved to one side, still holding her as he dragged edges of the coverlet over them.

"It will be better for you next time," he murmured.

"Next time?" She must have sounded as disgruntled as she felt because he laughed, and lifted to prop himself on his elbow, staring down at her with obvious amusement.

"Sweet treasure, for whatever reason, nature decreed that a woman's first time be uncomfortable. But now there should be only pleasure. Do you recall how you felt before it hurt? It will be much better than that."

"I liked the before," she muttered rather ungraciously, but already the discomfort had gone and she liked the way he held her, his hand stroking over her beneath the coverlet, the warmth and intimacy between them displacing the brief sense of betrayal she'd felt at the pain.

"You'll like it again," he assured her, and she believed him.

It felt so right to be here with him like this, to be held in his arms with snow falling outside and a warm fire inside, soft lamps lit and blue velvet bed hangings enclosing them in a world of their own, private and intimate. Oh yes. It felt right.

Whatever came after, she'd always have this memory to hold dear, of Julian holding her in his arms and whispering in her ear, of feeling warm and safe and cherished. *Always*.

* * *

Time ticked slowly past, marked by the soft clucking from the ormolu clock on the mantel. Julian held her close, heard her breathing soften into slumber, knew she slept at last. He closed his eyes but couldn't sleep, could only cherish the warmth of her in his embrace. She felt so delicious, lush and reassuringly close. Amazing, the emotion that stirred inside him, a complex blend of need and tenderness.

He'd hurt her and he knew it, but she hadn't blamed him, only stared up at him with that funny little expression of dissatisfaction that had caught him between chagrin and a need to reassure her. This was what it was supposed to feel like between a man and a woman, he thought then, this sharing of one another, not just bodies but emotion. Tenderness. The desire to give her everything he possessed just to see her smile.

It occurred to him that he was in trouble. He'd never be able to let her go. He wanted to make her his, when he knew that it was impossible. Even if he wasn't already married, the barriers between them were so great. But when had he ever faltered at obstacles? He'd divorce Eleanor. It wasn't unheard of, though frowned upon. His enemies in Parliament would make the most of it. And he wouldn't be the first titled earl to wed a woman of lower class—oh God, what was he thinking? It would ruin him. Ruin all he was trying to do in Parliament. These past years he'd immersed himself in causes, anything to keep from thinking about his faithless wife. Now he stood prepared to throw it all away for a woman.

Not just any woman—Laura. He opened his eyes, turned his head to look at her, lying beside him so sweetly. Would he really make a difference if he risked his influence by igniting more gossip? He thought of the reality of his situation, the reality of English politics. It was a disheartening realization that nothing in the world he inhabited had changed, or was likely to. There would always be dissension in Parliament, always be a war with France, or the Colonies, or Spain or India . . . unrest in some part of the world that would require military action. Unrest in England, too, with the Luddite rebellion that destroyed the industrial machines taking jobs from English laborers. Laws needed to be passed to counter the fears and desperate plights of so many . . . and well entrenched MPs feared change. How could he get them to see that change was not always bad, that adherence to tradition could be deadly?

An impossibility.

Yet with Laura at his side, defeat would be bearable. He felt he could risk anything with her beside him. How young and foolish she made him feel, invincible. He was reacting like Randal would do . . . with his heart instead of his head.

And right now, he didn't really give a damn.

Sliding the coverlet down, he put his hand beneath the soft weight of her breast, lifted it, then bent his head down to savor the sweetness of her, his tongue washing a path over lush flesh that smelled of rose water. Still sleeping, she made a faint sound and shifted restlessly. His tongue teased the tip of her breast, circled it, then his lips closed over it. After a moment, she moved again, awake this time, a fine tension tautening her muscles. With his mouth still at her breast, he looked up through his lashes and saw her watching him, her lips parted and her breath coming more quickly.

Fire leaped deep in his belly. He slid over her, pressing inside, saw her eyes widen with wonder but no pain this time. His hand rose to cradle her other breast, his mouth moving between them both, and heard her moan softly, not with pain but something else, a whimpering sound. It was insanely arousing. She arched beneath him after a moment, offering herself, and he took her with deep plunges that intensified with every thrust of his body inside her. This time she moved with him, her breath coming in swift little pants, her hands moving over his shoulders, chest, arms, fluttering little brushes of her fingers as light as butterfly wings across his skin.

Closing his eyes, he kissed her mouth, his tongue emulating the sex act, heard her soft cries in his ear, focused on bringing her the pleasure denied her earlier. He moved his hands lower to caress her, eliciting more gasps and faint whimpers. Release hovered for her, tension rising, then rolling through her quaking limbs. She dug her nails into his biceps, eyes widening as she wrenched free of his mouth, gasping for air and calling his name. It sounded so sweet on her lips as she said it over and over:

"Julian . . . Julian . . . oh, Julian . . ."

He couldn't have answered her, lost in the heat of the moment, and when he heard at last the sound of her release, that distinctly feminine cry of pleasure, he forgot to breathe, forgot to do anything but answer the driving urgency of his own body until he exploded into release in a blinding burst of heat and light.

Drifting downward, he slowly became aware that he was lying atop her still and she was holding him, her arms folded around him, her breath soft against his ear. He turned his head to look into her eyes, those lovely, sea-green eyes that held no shadows now, nothing but warmth and awe.

"I never knew," she whispered, and he kissed her.

"Lie still, love," he said after a moment, cradling her against him as he turned onto his side with one arm draped around her waist, the other beneath her. Sleep beckoned, and he pulled the coverlet over them both, wrapping them in warmth and satisfaction. Drugged with it, and with the knowledge that he'd never let her go, he slept at last, sinking into blue velvet and oblivion.

An insistent tapping jerked him awake, and he blinked against the darkness broken only by a small glow from the hearth. The lamps had burned out and night had completely fallen. Lethargy made him slow to react, and before he could answer the knocking at the door, it swung open.

Silhouetted against hall lamps behind her, Celia Carteret stood framed for an instant in the doorway, light behind her giving her blond hair a fuzzy halo. A slice of light speared the room's shadows, falling across the bed and occupants.

"Oh. Hullo! Well. Bad time, I see. Sorry, ducks." She didn't sound at all sorry; there was a cheerful tone in her voice that told him she approved.

"Please be so good as to inform the others that we won't be down for dinner," he said, his voice gruff with sleep.

"I don't mind at all. No, not at all." With a soft laugh, she shut the door again and shadows reclaimed the room.

Glancing at Laura, he saw she still slept. He smiled, and rested his head on the cushion of her soft breasts, breathing deeply and contentedly. Oddly enough, he felt as if he'd come home at last. How strange.

CHAPTER 14

"Who the devil are you?" Aubert Fortier stood with nostrils flared, anger and fear alive in his dark eyes. Light from the mouth of the alley glittered on his face, brittle and sharp.

"An excellent analogy. The devil I am, indeed, and you will soon see hell if you don't heed my warning." Rex Pentley took another step closer, the footpads he'd hired forming a half-circle behind the Frenchman. Fortier's breath steamed in front of him in frosty clouds like the breath of a dragon, erratic puffs that revealed his fright. Rex smiled. "Do not bother the lady again or you'll see hell before the sun sets. Am I clear?"

"*Lady*? Do you mean that daughter of a whore?" Fortier laughed harshly. "Your threats are worthless. I'm not the only one who knows who she really is."

"But you are the one I'll blame if she's caused any unnecessary grief." Anger ripped through Rex in a scouring tide. "She's a friend of mine, and I don't like to see my friends hurt."

Taking a step back, Rex jerked his head toward Fortier and four of the footpads closed in on him with grim purpose. The Frenchman fought back but he was outnumbered and quickly overpowered. It gave Rex great satisfaction to watch, though he'd promised Laura he wouldn't touch him. He'd not, however, promised he wouldn't enlist others to touch him, and he'd seen the same sentiment in Celia's knowing eyes. She'd only smiled, her silence a tacit approval.

When Fortier was bloodied and barely conscious, Rex

knelt down beside him in the filthy alley not far from King's Theater. "You see," he said in a reasonable tone, "that's only a small taste of what hell can be for those who harm my friends. Be wise enough to heed the warning. If I visit you again, you'll not survive our conversation."

The only reply was a guttural groan, and Rex nodded. Rising, he stepped over the prone form of the Frenchman and left the alley. The footpads faded into the cold mist, already paid well for their work. Yes, this should do the trick. And if not . . . well, he'd warned him. He had no compunction whatsoever about doing what was necessary. As he'd told Fortier, he took care of his friends. And Laura Lancaster was a most special friend. He found her beautiful and fascinating and far beyond him, but that didn't mean he'd allow anyone to cause her harm. Even if the man was a French count's son—or an English earl.

"Who is it?" Eleanor looked up with an irritated frown. "Malcolm just left. It can't be him again."

"I don't know, ma'am. It's . . . a gentleman of sorts." The maid retreated a step, shivering at the anger in her mistress's eyes and voice.

"Of sorts? You stupid little goose, why must you be so unbearable? In all this city, it'd seem Malcom could have found me a servant with some sense! Did the caller give you a card, girl? Or say his name?"

"N-n-no, ma'am."

"Stop that stuttering. Show him in. If he's a tradesman, I'll box your ears for you, you sly little wretch."

Heavens, the trials she had to endure! Returning to England had been uppermost in her mind since she'd had to flee both Julian and the gossipmongers, and now, at least, there were new topics to occupy her former friends. Brummel was in disgrace, said to be deep in debt and living only on borrowed time, having insulted the prince. She knew what it was to be an outcast, and could tell him how it felt, but apparently, he didn't consider himself disgraced enough to speak to *her*. He'd given her the cut direct when she'd chanced upon him in Bond Street, and the insult still rankled.

Just as bad, Julian apparently flaunted his new mistress, an insipid creature with no breeding, some silly Colonial with red hair—Judas hair, the same bold color as the man who had betrayed Christ. What nonsense that Julian would take up with her. If the old earl knew . . . it was too bad he'd died before she could repair the damage she'd done with that baronet. If she had any regrets, it was that Julian had chanced upon them in the stairwell. Too much champagne, and a handsome man who looked at her with desire instead of duty . . . enough of that. Just who was this man with a battered face coming into the parlor? He was rather good-looking, in a bruised sort of way.

"*Bonjour, madame,*" he said, taking the hand she offered him and bowing over it, his dark eyes knowing and appreciative. "Your beauty was not exaggerated, I see."

She allowed a faint smile to curve her mouth, and her eyes narrowed speculatively. His manners were good, his accent proclaiming him to be French. He dressed impeccably, though his face could belong to a pugilist.

"Pray, sir, what brings you on a visit?" She withdrew her hand from his grasp, saw his gaze move over her body boldly, then return to her face.

"A matter that will be of great interest to you, I think."

"I hardly think we have anything in common, sir. I do not even know your name."

He bowed eloquently, his black hair gleaming in the gray light coming through the parlor windows. "Aubert Fortier, Comte du Soulange."

A French count! She drew in a sharp breath. Was he a real count, or one of those who had been dispossessed by the revolution that killed so many French nobles? They littered the London streets like beggars, most penniless, their titles meaning nothing but a sentence of execution. Not even Napoleon had managed to restore them to their former glory. Indeed, he had sounded the death knell of the French aristocracy.

"Comte du Soulange . . . you are . . . exiled from France?"

A thin smile carved his mouth, and something swift and dark flickered in his eyes. "Only by distance, madame. My title survived due to my father's diligence."

"How extraordinary." She gestured to the chair opposite the small, shabby settee in front of the fire. "Do be seated. I'll ring for tea, and you can tell me what has brought you to visit."

"Lockwood," he said, and she paused in reaching for the bellpull. He smiled at her startled glance. "I believe we have much in common, madame. It has come to my attention that you are, shall we say, *estranged* from your husband at the moment, and he has taken up with a former acquaintance of mine. Perhaps we can form an alliance of sorts."

"Really, Comte, you presume too much," she said coolly, but inside, hope leaped to life. At last! An ally in her struggle to regain what was rightfully hers. The pittance Julian had settled on her wasn't enough to support a scullery maid, and her own funds were of little consequence. If he knew of a plan that would gain her desire more swiftly, then she was most eager to hear it. She arched a brow, and he nodded. Oh yes, he understood her. And better, she understood him.

Here was a man who would not hesitate to do what must be done to gain his own ends. It was time she met a man of courage and wit. Far too many were spineless wretches who thought only of a moment's pleasure, not the long-lasting sweetness of vengeance.

Leaning forward so that he could view her breasts beneath the round muslin neckline, she said softly, "But I am always willing to listen to intelligent ideas."

"As I had hoped—a woman of intelligence to match her great beauty."

Oh yes, this promised to be a beneficial association indeed. . . .

* * *

February's brutal cold eased into a wet, chilly March, and Laura thought she'd never been more content in her life. Not even the whispers that always attended her appearance on Julian's arm at the opera or theater or the occasional outing in Hyde Park, marred her happiness. Celia had been right, after all. She was deliriously happy with him.

The only flaw was a rising tension in London due to the sharp increase in food prices since passage of the Corn Laws. Julian exhausted himself working to ease the tension and find solutions to the problem. He fumed that those of his class, the wealthy landowners, had no sympathy for the farmers or those who lived in towns now beset with much higher prices, rendering it difficult just to subsist. It brewed unrest, he'd warned them, but his predictions fell on deaf ears. In Manchester on the twenty-third of February, a resolution by manufacturers had been passed against the Corn Laws. The laws had been originally passed to ensure domestic profits by imposing a duty on imported grains. During the wars, farmers had greatly expanded to produce more wheat and corn, but now that the wars were ended, grains that had sold for a hundred and twenty-six shillings a quarter, sold for only sixty-five shillings a quarter. Disastrous.

Despite Julian's argument, Parliament responded by passing a law permitting the import of foreign wheat free of duty only when the domestic price reached eighty shillings per quarter. Rumbles of riot threatened, and he'd not been able to convince Parliament to amend the law.

Most nights, he arrived on Frith Street weary and disgusted, and she soothed him as best she could. She could handle political troubles well enough, but the night came that she'd long dreaded.

Days were a bit longer now, March winds whipping debris along the streets and cold gray clouds streaming through the skies, and she met him at the door as she usually did, happy until she saw his face.

"Julian—" She put out her hands, heart thudding at his expression. "What is it?"

He didn't reply until he was in the parlor, dwarfing the settee with his long, lean frame, taking the brandy she pressed into his hand. "Eleanor's back in London."

Eleanor. His wife. Oh God . . . with a slightly shaking hand, she sipped her own brandy, tiny sips that burned down her throat and into her stomach.

He looked up at her, nodding. "It surprises me as well. I spoke with Brummel today. He said he saw her in Bond Street a couple of weeks ago. I wonder that she hasn't made demands. It isn't like her to be discreet."

Finding her voice, she said, "You haven't seen her?"

"No, thank God." His hand tightened on his crystal glass, his eyes narrowed. Staring at the fire, a muscle leaped in his jaw. She felt his tension, along with her own. He never spoke of her, and since the day she'd asked him about his wife, she'd not mentioned her either. Now she wondered, as she had many times, if the rumors about Lady Lockwood were true.

"Shall I have Becky serve our evening meal?" she asked when several silent minutes went past, and he turned his head to look at her, as if surprised to find her still there.

"Dinner . . . oh, yes. If you like. There's so much—*damn* Eleanor. Of all times to come skulking back into London, she chooses now when I'm trying to think of good arguments to put before Parliament." He shook his head, a wry smile touching the corners of his mouth. "If not for this damnable mess, we'd go to Shadowhurst." He paused, frowning, then shook his head with a heavy sigh. "No, impossible. Not now. Later, perhaps, when some of the furor dies down. All the shopkeepers and citizens are up in arms, with such high bread prices and angry rumblings. Would you like to visit the country, Laura?"

She smiled. "Oh, yes. Very much. You've spoken so often of Shadowhurst that I can almost visualize it."

Weary lines creased his brow and dug grooves on each side of his mouth, yet his eyes lit up at her reply. He held out a hand and she crossed to the settee, sinking down beside him to put her head on his shoulder. This was her favorite part of the day, when he came in and sat down to discuss the day's events, sharing his world with her. He often asked her opinion and always listened to her reply, even encouraging her at first when she'd hesitated. It was so important that he consider her as more valuable to him than just someone to warm his bed.

He pressed a kiss on her brow, and she slid an arm over his chest, holding him. He smelled of wind and brandy, masculine and oh so achingly familiar. Her heart lifted every time she saw him coming up the steps of the house.

"You lived in France," he said after a moment, and if he noticed her sudden start, he chose to ignore it. "What do you think the French would do if Napoleon were not exiled to Elba?"

She hesitated, then said slowly, "You must understand, I lived in France over two years ago when Napoleon was still very much in power. He could be very charming and persuasive. Liberties that were won by the people during the revolution were retained. After the regime of the Directory, it was a welcome relief. France did not view him in the same light as did England."

"And if Napoleon returned? If he left exile to be emperor again?"

Pulling away from him, she stared at him with wide eyes. He met her gaze calmly, but she felt his tension in the arm still resting atop her shoulders.

"Has he?"

"Yes. Word came that Napoleon left Elba on the twenty-sixth of February, and landed a few days ago in France. He's on his way to Paris. Already, several regiments have rallied to his standard."

"Oh, no," she whispered. "War again?"

Grimly, he nodded. "It's inevitable. Louis may not be the most ideal ruler, but he's not as avaricious as Napoleon. Louis is content just to sit on the throne, not conquer the world."

"Louis is fat and slothful." When his brow rose, she shrugged. "It's true. But I cannot think France is ready to go to war again, either."

"Neither did I. Apparently, we're both wrong."

The contentment she'd felt earlier in the day evaporated as if it had never existed. Peace was so fragile. A thought struck her, and she curled her fingers into his sleeve, staring at him.

"Will you . . . have to fight?"

He grinned, weariness edging his eyes but amusement evident. "No, little goose. Not that I wouldn't rather like a go at old Boney. Wellington will soon have him in hand, I predict. Come here." He pulled her close, kissed her forehead again, then her eyelids, lips closing them before he kissed the tip of her nose, then her mouth. Here he lingered, tongue gently probing between her lips, insistent and tasting of rich brandy, potent and heated.

After a few moments, she forgot the Corn Laws, Eleanor, and Bonaparte, thought only of Julian, his mouth and hands, the magic he created every time he touched her. Even dinner was forgotten for a while, and they went upstairs to her cozy little bedroom and wide, soft bed, undressing each other feverishly, caressing and stroking, kissing as they tumbled backward onto the mattress, coming together in quiet joy. It was absolution, consolation, and affirmation. He'd never said he loved her, the words had never passed his lips, but his actions proved it every day. It was all she had to cling to, that silent reassurance, and most times, it was enough.

But in the quiet after their lovemaking, when she lay looking up at a ceiling illuminated by a low fire in the grate, listening to Julian's soft, regular breathing, she thought of his wife and her return to London. What did she want? Her husband? Did Lady Lockwood know about her? Did she know that her husband spent nearly every night in this little house instead of in his elegant, spacious house in Mayfair? And if she did—what would she do?

How selfish she was, worrying about her own dilemma rather than national security or the plight of the poor. But she couldn't help how she felt. To her, Julian was the world. Events had moved so swiftly since their time at Belgrave's country house. She'd fallen deeply, hopelessly, in love with Julian. Now, instead of nights at the opera or theater, most nights were spent alone together. The last weeks had been tense for him, and he found comfort here in the peace and tranquility of this little house. As did she. It was precious to her.

Thoughts of home and America held no pain for her now, the memories sweet and not sharp. She even thought more kindly of her mother, and had considered writing her. Impossible now, of course. Even though Fortier had been made to leave her alone, she didn't dare risk any contact with her mother in light of these latest events. Napoleon's return made it too dangerous. The political climate was volatile and there didn't need to be any hint of an affiliation with the French, or Julian could be ruined. No, best to leave it for now.

Events would be resolved, she told herself, and she could go on here as usual, hiding away from the world with Julian. Yes, it would be all right.

On the ceiling, shadows flickered, orange, gold, and gray, forming strange patterns, and she suddenly shivered as if seized by a cold hand. Her throat tightened. She closed her eyes and buried her face into the counterpane, holding tightly to Julian.

No no no, nothing bad will happen!

But she knew that fate had a way of playing tricks just when life seemed to be going well. She could only pray that whatever happened, she could still be with Julian.

* * *

Julian stared grimly out the windows. A mob stormed the houses of Parliament, shouting threats, demanding repeal of the Corn Laws. Bloody hell, he'd warned them. He'd told them the citizens were not known for their patience when bellies were empty. The fools. Armed troops had been called to stop the riots in Westminster. Mobs roamed the streets. And across the Channel, Bonaparte rallied the French army to his standard. Louis XVIII had fled Paris. Disaster loomed.

Pondering his options, he decided to take Laura to Shadowhurst. It would be safer there. Until this was over, at any rate. Rubbing a hand over his brow, he pivoted on his heel and stalked down the high, echoing corridors and out into the damp mist settling over London like a cloud. Noise instantly assaulted him, the King's Guards brutally pushing back the mob, back toward the abbey and down wet streets, clubbing those who fell, marching over them relentlessly. Pinched, angry faces, open mouths howling outrage and hopelessness, and there was nothing he could do for them. Only a handful of men were enlightened enough to realize the impact the Corn Laws had on the citizens, or perhaps it was just that only a handful of men cared. So few of them, so many others stubbornly set in some feudal idea of *noblesse oblige* gone awry.

England was on the verge of great change. He sensed it, saw the future before them like some great, shining, golden fleece, a prize to be cherished. It was inevitable. He wanted to be part of it, wanted to be instrumental in changing England for the better.

And he intended to start with Eleanor.

Eleanor turned angrily when the maid sidled into her room. Always sneaking about, like a shadow, cringing every time she spoke to her.

"What is it?" she snapped.

"You've a caller, ma'am. He . . . he s-s-said he's your husband."

Eleanor dropped her hairbrush, heart lurching. Julian. *Here?* Oh God, she hadn't expected him, not now, not ever . . . yet he had come to her here!

"Well, come here, you witless goose," she hissed, "and help me with my hair! Did you show him to the parlor?"

"No . . . I . . . I left him in the hall. I didn't know—I've never seen—"

She slapped her smartly, then sent her below to see to Julian. The wretched girl. My God, why was Julian here? Finally! If only Aubert were here . . . but no. This was better. There was still a chance, slim though it might be, that he'd come to make amends. Thank heavens she'd put on her most flattering gown earlier, expecting the count to come by. Oh yes, she looked very fine, very fine indeed. Her blond hair curled fetchingly around her face, caught up in the back by a delicate mesh net entwined with flowers, the latest fashion. A little rice powder brushed over her face to hide the tiny flaws . . . there. She looked superb. He'd have to notice. And she would be cool at first, until he realized that she was beyond his reach. Then, of course, she'd be more accessible.

Straightening, she pressed her hands over her flat stomach to still the fluttering, then sailed down the stairs to meet Julian. At last.

Oh my . . . the past year had made him no less handsome. He looked regal, tall and golden in the light streaming through the bow window. Yet there was no welcome in his eyes when he saw her, nothing but that same steady regard that had always seemed to judge her and find her lacking. It was annihilating. And despite her earlier resolve to be cool and haughty, she turned vicious, as she always did when faced with any hint of censure.

"Well, the wayward husband. Tell me, how is your latest doxy? I hear she has hideous red hair, and is no more than a common actress. From *America*. Really, Julian, your father would turn over in his grave if he knew. Think of his shame."

"You'd be more familiar with that than I, Eleanor." A faint

smile tucked one corner of his mouth. He found her amusing! Damn him!

"My father is not dead."

"Your father has the good sense to stay in Yorkshire and not subject himself to the latest *on-dits* about his daughter. Why are you here? I expressly forbade you to return to London. You have a generous allowance—do you strive to end my generosity?"

A brittle smile settled on her mouth, and she affected carelessness as she sauntered across the parlor to the fire, then turned with her back to the mantel, an arm draped over the wood shelf in a casual pose.

"How did you know I returned?" Malcolm had promised not to tell. He'd never betray her but still . . . one could never be certain what men would do if cornered.

"That hardly matters. I know now. Rumors are following you, it seems. Something about a young Italian foolish enough to hang himself—is that why you fled Florence?"

She flushed. "Ridiculous! I had nothing to do with that. People will say anything. You know that. You have rumors of your own. Dalliance with first your steward, and now this tawdry little actress. I daresay, next you'll be said to sell military commissions in bed."

"Hardly. And you will leave Laura out of our conversation."

Her eyes narrowed, but her smile remained fixed, though it felt stiff. "Will I? Why should I do such a thing? Tell me, Julian—have you considered her background? An American actress. Do you think she'll ever be accepted—especially if people know you met her at Mme. Devereaux's infamous brothel?"

It was a telling shot. She saw it strike home at once. His eyes glittered, and his mouth thinned into a taut line. He vibrated with anger, and her smile turned feline. "Ah, people will talk, you know. They might even think—she's an American spy."

"Eleanor, your nasty innuendoes are patently false. Malcolm has investigated and found nothing out of order about her. She was in France when the war began. And even if she was here, she's not had access to government secrets."

"Oh no, of course not." Clever Malcolm. He'd not divulged what he knew. It would be so lovely. Now she and Aubert had only to put the last plan into place, and she'd bring Julian down.

A pity, really. He could have made a fine husband. A fine politician. She'd ruin him, and then he'd have no one to turn to, no one and nothing but his money. He'd slink back to that dirty estate in Kent, and she would remain in London, a sympathetic figure who'd known nothing of her husband's perfidy. Why, she'd been out of the country! How could she have known? Oh yes, if she was to be denied her rightful place as his esteemed wife, she'd take her place in society as a woman who scorned her treasonous husband.

"I've seen a solicitor, Eleanor," he said, and her lovely dream of vengeance evaporated. "I plan to get an annulment."

"Don't be ridiculous! We've been married far too long. You can't get an annulment without grounds."

"Failing to consummate our marriage should be grounds enough," he said dryly, and she shook her head, raking him with a scornful gaze.

"Fool, I'll swear you've had me six ways from Sunday, that we copulated atop every table in your house. Do you think any magistrate will believe that a man didn't consummate his vows?"

"Possibly. If I have signed testimony from a certain baronet that he had you in the stairwell before we ever reached the marriage bed." He smiled at her soft gasp. "And even if he doesn't, I'll divorce you. Whatever I have to do, I'm willing to do it. I'll settle a small sum on you, then you can go back to Yorkshire and your father's farm."

"I'll never do it! You can't be rid of me that easily, Julian! I'll fight you every step of the way, I swear I will!" Panic bubbled, nearly strangling her. If he divorced her, if he got that fool baronet whose name and face she couldn't even recall to swear against her, then she'd be put aside with a pittance and no decent house would ever receive her again. Oh no . . . she'd planned this so carefully, she and Aubert, planned to create sympathy for a wronged wife, one who'd been shunned by her husband in favor of a low-born actress. A woman wronged . . . a traitorous husband. It was so perfect. Of course, Malcolm would have to be silenced. He fancied himself in love with her, but his usefulness would soon be at an end. She'd offer him a large sum of money, but if that would not suffice . . . Aubert promised he could terrify him into silence. Yes. She was so close now. So close. They'd have to hurry before Julian could get a divorce, or it would all be ruined.

"You'll soon receive papers from my barrister," Julian said calmly, "and I advise you to be clever enough to sign them. If you fight me, I'll cut you off without a penny. If you do not, I'll be generous. It's your choice."

Disaster yawned before her. She had to think, had to delay . . . she looked down at her feet for a moment, then lifted her face to gaze into his eyes with a dignity and composure she didn't feel at all.

"Very well, Julian. I'll certainly consider your offers. There's the matter of my dowry, of course, and my mother's property I inherited."

"Retain your own barrister as counsel," he said, "and it will be done fairly." He paused, a slight frown settling on his brow as he regarded her thoughtfully. "We never had a true marriage. I would have kept our vows had you made it possible."

"I know," she said calmly. "You are an honorable man." His frown deepened. Obviously, he hadn't expected her swift capitulation. Good. She'd caught him off guard. Just as she meant to catch him for the final *coup de grâce*. Oh yes. He'd soon see that he couldn't cast her off like a used shoe.

His downfall would begin—and end—with Laura Lancaster.

CHAPTER 15

"What beautiful countryside."

It was a warm, soft day, with sunshine and a south wind that swept up from the coast and over the Kentish fields and roads. Laura curled her fingers over the reticule in her lap and smiled.

"Do you think so?" Julian returned her smile, a lazy curve of his mouth as he regarded her with sleepy eyes. "I've always loved it here. It's far enough from London to be distant, yet close enough to return in a day if need be."

Maidstone lay thirty-five miles south, and only ten miles south of the county seat lay his estate: Shadowhurst. Just the name conjured up images of pleasant vales, and Laura anticipated their visit with great pleasure. They passed fields of hops, and vast orchards with buds promising gentler weather. It was a rare day, the sunshine so bright and the skies so blue, fat clouds stacking up on the horizon as the carriage crested hills and the road dipped down and away toward the sea. Raw weather would return soon enough, and she intended to enjoy this respite while she could.

With London far behind them, Julian looked more relaxed than he had since Belgrave's country fête. She could almost see his muscles loosen, the tension in him ease, slipping away and leaving him at peace. The past weeks had been horrendous. Parliament, Napoleon, now the riots, all had combined to weigh upon him heavily. Only his wife remained unmentioned. Had he seen Eleanor? She wished she knew, wished she knew how he truly felt about her. He never spoke of his wife at all, not since he'd said she'd returned to England. Perhaps it was just as well.

Steep hills gave way to broad vales, sunlight glinting on dry stone fences and hedgerows that bisected fields of yellow rape from apple and cherry orchards. Neat houses were staggered over the landscape and at the roadside, cattle and black-faced sheep grazing in green fields. She thought of her lamb, transported to Shadowhurst the day after the play ended.

"Will Phoebe be at your farm?" she asked idly, hand tangling in the strap attached to the side of the carriage as the vehicle rocked precariously over ruts.

"Your lamb? It is my understanding that Tommy, my steward's son, is most taken with her and even begged that she be allowed into the parlor." Laughter edged his voice, and she looked at him with a smile.

"I trust he was refused."

"Most certainly. We're not so lax in the country that we allow farm animals at the table."

Sitting across from her, sprawled on the comfortable seat cushions, his knees occasionally bumped into her skirts. She felt brief nudges, subtle reminders of his presence even when she stared out the windows. It was hard not to watch him, to keep her gaze averted when she wanted to study him, drink in the way shifting light played over the angles and planes of his face, glittered on gold shirt studs, tiny flashes like controlled lightning. She was far too aware of him, senses heightened with him so near.

So soon, and she was hopelessly in love with him. How could it have happened in only three months? Amazing. Two years of yearning for home had evaporated, banished by something she didn't quite trust to last, but dared to reach for despite her reservations. It was the most daring thing she'd ever done, more daring than leaving Virginia for Paris, more daring than fleeing her mother's home for the unknown. Truly, she must be mad to hope.

Her first glimpse of Shadowhurst came as dusk settled on the land in soft purple shrouds. Built on a hill overlooking meadows and wood and the thin silvery ribbon of the River Medway, fading sunlight bathed the house in crimson so that it glowed like a jewel on green velvet. Her breath caught. It was magnificent. Unfamiliar with proper architectural terms, she still recognized the symmetry of construction, the Palladian front with graceful arches, and a beautiful Corinthian portico. The river lapped against massive stonework along the green banks, and a Palladian bridge winged over the glittering water.

Julian seemed to be waiting for something, his expression intent, and she turned to him at last. "It's beautiful. I cannot imagine why you would ever leave."

"Nor can I." He sat back against the squabs, a faint smile curving his mouth. "I'm always impatient to return. There are more changes I wish to make, but all in good time."

"Has it changed so very much from your childhood?" she asked after a moment. What was he like as a child, she wondered, running loose on the grounds rebelliously or had he been a quiet, obedient boy? Somehow she doubted the latter.

"Subtle changes. Mostly in the order of things, not so much in improvements. I'm looking into adding gas for lighting and cooking. Damned expensive, but much more efficient and cleaner than coal and oil."

When the carriage crossed the bridge and turned into the long, curving drive leading to the house, she sensed the excitement in him, the relief and pleasure it gave him to be home. *Home.* At times she still felt like an exile, still felt like a leaf in the wind, blown hither and yon, with no place to settle. As lovely as Shadowhurst was, it was his home and not hers.

Some of her pleasure dimmed, but she smiled brightly when Julian leaped down from the carriage without waiting for a footman to open the door, and reached up for her hand.

"Welcome to Shadowhurst," he said, and she knew he meant it.

They went inside where servants lined up just inside the

door to greet them. He knew them all by name, greeted them with just the right blend of reserve and cordiality; maids dipped in brief curtsies and some of the men touched their heads where once they'd have tugged on forelocks in attitudes of respect and servility.

"And this is Thomas," Julian said, indicating a man garbed in neat clothing, "whose son Tommy has taken ownership of Phoebe to heart."

"I'm very grateful," Laura said when Thomas respectfully inclined his head in greeting. "I hated to see her misused after she'd been such a pet for so long."

Thomas hesitated, then nodded. "She's a fine lamb but much grown of late. We've marked her with a bell so she'll not be mistaken."

It was obvious he thought the lamb as a pet was rather silly, but would never make his sentiments known. Laura hid a smile.

Their footsteps echoed in the cavernous entrance hall. The main portion of the hall was narrowed by low, marble-faced walls niched with small shelves holding busts and statues, some of which towered over them like avenging Greek gods. On the galleries, veined columns of alabaster supported coves with painted ceilings. At the far end of the hall, a graceful flight of stairs led upward, giving her a glimpse of rooms off the main gallery. Gilt trimmed the ceilings, and she had impressions of rich colors, carvings, and gilding as they passed up the stairs and onto the gallery level. Open doors revealed rooms that opened out of each other, doors placed so that it gave one a feeling of airy vistas. A few rooms were dark, but most newly painted with white, some walls of stucco, some covered in damask. Fireplaces were marble, with columns, pilasters, and narrow marble mantel shelves that supported a second story mantel. Hunting scenes were carved into some of these, Greek figures in others. Ornate, lovely, and a bit overwhelming. It was a relief to reach the third floor and the bedchambers.

"You'll have your own chamber if you like," Julian said, and if he thought it unusual that he should be the one to show her to her room, he gave no indication. His hand on her arm was polite but possessive, and though she knew the servants must wonder—or be aware—of her true position with the earl, he treated her with respect.

She stepped into a room that looked out over the back gardens, a sweep of clipped lawn and hedges fashioned into animal shapes; a fountain cascaded water into a rectangular reflecting pool. The room was light and airy, pale green and white, with graceful furniture instead of heavy, dark pieces.

"It's lovely," she said, and felt him right behind her, his warmth seeping into her even through the wool pelisse.

"It was my sister's room as a girl."

"Your sister?" She turned to face him, surprised. "I thought you had only your brother."

"She died. A fever when she was barely sixteen." A muscle leaped in his jaw, and he stared past her to the windows swagged with pale green brocade. "I was at sea. I didn't know about it until we docked in Tripoli and I received my mother's letter. Not long after, she died as well."

Laura put a hand on his arm, silently comforting. She knew what it was to lose those you loved, knew they left behind voids that could never be filled. Others may come to take their space, but none could ever take their place.

Sliding his arm behind her back, he held her for a moment in silence. Darkness already claimed the woods behind the house, shadows crept over the lawns in an inexorable march toward nightfall. Lamplight saved the chamber from darkness, and a fire in the grate cast gold and orange patterns on the thick carpet. Finally he shifted, and pressed a kiss above her ear.

"Dinner is earlier in the country. You've an hour to rest before the first bell rings."

Then he was gone, leaving her standing alone in the room that had once been his sister's. She thought of him coming here after leaving the sea, coming back to a house that must have echoed with happier memories, and finding everything changed. Perhaps he'd changed as well, but it must still have been difficult for him at first.

And then she thought of Longacre, the home where she'd spent her happiest years, the lovely rolling hills of Virginia remarkably like these, wooded and fenced, with spring a promise in tiny buds on tree limbs. She could never go back. It belonged to her uncle now, a dour man who'd seen no necessity in providing for his brother's child. He'd cast her out summarily, much to the distress of the lawyer who'd stammered that it was understood Laura was to remain until she was of her majority. Without written confirmation, an intent her grandfather had never carried out, there was no legal compulsion for Peter Lancaster to offer her shelter. Moral responsibility was for fools, he'd said, but grudgingly gave her money for passage to her mother in Paris. She'd not been wanted at Longacre, nor, she discovered, was she truly wanted in Paris.

Fleurette D'Arcy Lancaster told her lover that Laura was only thirteen, shaving four years off her age without a qualm, and insisted that her daughter maintain the deception. For three years, Laura had remained silent, until the night Aubert Fortier came to the house.

She'd known the instant he said it that her mother had sent him, though she'd not wanted to believe it. How could she? How could she betray her own daughter like that?

Now she was in the same position as her mother, a mistress without marriage lines. There was no going back. She had only the future, and the hope that Julian would love her as she loved him.

Two weeks passed in pleasant hours spent exploring the grounds of Shadowhurst, with Julian often at her side. Sometimes he met her clad in soiled shirt and trousers, mud clinging to him as he enthusiastically explained crop rotation and a new method of draining marshes. At night, they slept most often in his bed, his chamber adjoining hers. The master suite remained empty, a reminder to her of her true position. She tried not to dwell on it, focused instead on him, and on now instead of later.

Away from London, he became someone different. Cynicism and reserve were replaced by laughter and teasing. Laura thought that she'd never been so happy in her life as when she was with him, and it didn't matter if they were inspecting pig barrows or the rose garden.

Twice, he went back to London, riding swiftly on one of his magnificent horses instead of taking a carriage, and when he returned after a brief absence, he reported that the city was still in an uproar. It was safer in the country, and she was glad. She loved it at Shadowhurst. And loved it most when he was with her.

"Come along," he said one morning early, "I'm to take a basket to some of my cottagers. We'll ride. You did say you can ride?"

"Oh . . . yes, of course I can, though it's been so long."

He grinned. "I'll have Sims put you on a blind mare, then."

"Not *that* long," she said indignantly, and he laughed.

Two splendid mounts were saddled for them, and she acquainted herself with the mare she was to ride, a lovely bay with huge, dark eyes and a gentle spirit. "You're lovely," she murmured, scratching the whiskery chin with her fingertips, breathing softly into the horse's nose as she'd seen her grandfather do so often. The mare responded with a soft nicker of greeting, lips flexing as she stretched her head for more scratching. Laura patted the graceful neck, and the mare bobbed her head eagerly.

A groom helped her mount, putting a block on the ground beside the horse for Laura to step up and seat herself in the sidesaddle. Clumsy things, and she thought with longing of the days when she was a child and had dared ride like a man.

Her grandmother had scolded her roundly for it, saying ladies never rode like that, it was unseemly. It was dangerous to ride with one's weight so unevenly distributed, Laura had argued, to no avail.

Now, hooking her leg over the curved horn and settling herself back in the sidesaddle, she took up the reins and looked up to meet Julian's smiling gaze.

"Are you ready, then?"

She nodded. A basket was handed up to him, and they rode away from the stables and across the arched bridge at a sedate pace, the day lovely if a bit cool, clouds far to the south and the wind whipping briskly. Narrow roads took them between neat fields and wooded copses; the smell of fecund earth rose rich and damp in the air. Birdsong heralded the approach of spring. It lent a sense of expectancy, age-old and eternal. Life renewed after deep slumber.

Laura rode mostly in silence, relishing the knowledge that she was here with Julian, that when she was with him, nothing could harm her. She hadn't felt this safe since she was a small child.

As they rode, he pointed out sites of interest: a field he'd newly installed with drainage ditches to seep away flood waters; a pump house that would drain them quickly; and over there, a new strain of cherry trees thought to be more resistant to disease. While the topic was not of huge interest to her, the sound of his voice flowed like music over her and she smiled and nodded at the appropriate times. He took great pride in his estates, and cared for his tenant farmers, she saw, the cottages neat and solid if not grand, the children seeming well-fed and rosy-cheeked.

When she remarked upon it, his brow arched. "I've found it's more productive to have healthy workers in my employ rather than hungry, shivering men barely able to hold a scythe. If a man knows his family is cared for, he's more liable to work well and willingly. Those few who do not care to work, ccase their employment with me."

"You turn them out, then."

"Swiftly and irrevocably." He shrugged. "I have my limits. A lazy man has no place here. I imagine he'll find it the same elsewhere, whether in a bobbin factory or on the docks."

He reined his horse to a halt in front of a neat stone cottage only a few feet from the road. A woman came out, an apron pinned over her plain brown dress, two children peeking out from behind her skirts. She bobbed a curtsey, smiling as the earl handed her the basket.

"I trust the new lodgings are satisfactory, Mrs. Brewer?"

"Oh yes, my lord." She tucked loose strands of hair back beneath the muslin cap atop her head, her gaze sliding past to touch briefly on Laura before returning to the earl. "Very good they are indeed, my lord."

"You'll find bread, salt, and cheese in the basket. I believe Cook included some sweets for the children. The church has provided for you as well, I see."

"Yes, my lord. After the fire . . . we thought all't were lost. Very good, everyone has been, very good indeed, my lord." Her voice had quivered slightly at mention of the fire, but steadied at the earl's encouraging nod. "Clothing were found from the charity box that will see us well and through the season. We've a roof o'er our heads now, and food for our bellies, too."

New thatching covered the roof, and it looked as if new stones replaced old in the chimney; charred timbers lay stacked to one side. A scorched area indicated where the fire had spread, no doubt caused by sparks from the chimney.

Julian verified it when they left, riding leisurely back down the narrow track cutting through woods and fields. "Burned half the house before it could be extinguished. They lost most of their clothing, but thankfully, escaped unharmed. I had workmen fashion a cap for the chimney that should help prevent sparks escaping, but there's always a chance it could happen."

"It's a cozy little house," she said. "I'm sure they're glad to have it."

"Brewer's a good worker. His family has been on the estate nearly as long as mine."

"And how long would that be?" She slanted him a curious glance. "Have there always been Norcliffs in Kent?"

"Hardly." He laughed softly, grinning at her. "You'll not find this difficult to believe, I'm sure, but the first earl was once a privateer for King Henry VIII. He did quite well for himself, apparently, but it wasn't until Queen Elizabeth that he managed to gain a title. She took a fancy to him, the story goes, and he repaid her by delivering an entire Spanish galleon filled to the topdeck with booty. In appreciation, she gave him this estate in Kent, formerly taken from another baron who displeased her so much he lost his head for it. My ancestor was a bit more politic. He managed to die in his own bed. The second earl was not as fortunate. He was killed in a skirmish with the Spanish—rather fitting, some might say, since his father had killed so many Spaniards. As for the third earl, he died in the struggle between Cromwell and King Charles. The fourth and fifth earls led rather quiet lives, I'm told, managing to keep their heads firmly attached. Now here am I, surviving to the ripe old age of thirty-two, and I still have my head as well. It looks promising."

"So you descended from a pirate!"

"I knew you'd appreciate that fact most. We try not to mention it often, especially in polite company. Randal and I thought it most agreeable, but my mother forbade us to speak of it. Then her youngest brother moved to New York, and from all accounts is still doing well and quite content. That's also a family skeleton we don't rattle. My mother considered it particularly horrible when he sent a painting of himself wearing feathers and buckskin. It's in the portrait gallery on the second floor. It's my favorite of all the rest of the pompous faces I had to memorize as a child. As a boy, I once created a stir by announcing that I was going to America to live with my Uncle David and be a red Indian."

Laughing, she put a hand up to hold onto her hat, as the

wind had picked up and threatened to tear it from her head. "Yet you're still here. You must live with regret every day."

"Every hour of my life. I think I'd have made a properly ferocious Indian."

"I see you more as a pirate. A cutlass in your hand, standing in the bow of a ship with the wind in your hair."

He grimaced. "I've had enough of the sea, thank you. It was weeks of tedium broken only by hours of stark pandemonium and terror." Nudging his horse closer to hers, he bent his head toward the trees at the side of the road. "A storm is brewing. We'd best hurry back or be caught in it."

Indeed, tops of trees thrashed, bare limbs clacking loudly, but sunlight still lit the road and air. Only in the south, toward the Straits of Dover, did clouds stack ominously, much closer now than they'd been earlier. Even the horses sensed an approaching storm, dancing nervously over the rutted track, snorting.

The air felt damp, heavy. It crackled, as if lightning threatened, and they rode swiftly over the next hill and down into a broad vale. Clouds swept overhead, blotting out the sunlight. Fat raindrops began to fall, spattering onto her gloved hands and the brim of her hat. She blinked as rain pelted them mercilessly, turning the roadway to muck and slowing the horses, drenching her lovely velvet riding habit and wilting the feathers on the crown of her hat so they hung down in her face. Pushing them aside, she peered through the slashing downpour, following Julian as he shouted at her to stay close.

It was difficult keeping her balance as her mount slid in the mud, stumbling once so that she tilted precariously forward, grabbing hold of the mane to keep from pitching to the ground. Then Julian halted, dismounting to come to her and take her hand, and she saw through the heavy rain they were at a cottage. The door hung open, and when he led her inside, she saw it had been abandoned, the cottage dusty and deserted, yet retaining a certain charm.

"There's some kind of lean-to out back. I'll put the horses

in it and see if I can find some firewood," he said, squeezing her hand once before he disappeared back into the rain. It drummed against the wooden window shutters. She shivered, chilled to the bone. Velvet clung to her in heavy, clammy folds, and she gingerly removed her hat.

The feather hung dispiritedly in tattered ruins. She set the hat on a shelf, looking around the abandoned cottage. Earthenware jugs lay scattered, some broken, only a few intact, and it looked as if the occupants had left hastily. Moth-eaten blankets still hung on a cot in one corner; cracked dishes set upon a shelf near the fireplace. Once this had been a comfortable residence, but now it lay forgotten. Yet there was glass in the windows, and sturdy beams, and the fireplace was well built. Black soot marks darkened the back firewall, indicating much use.

Had the residents been turned out? An air of desolation hung thickly in the musty room; overhead, timbers were half-floored, obviously a sleeping area. Rain hissed against thatching. But here, near the fireplace, it was dry though definitely musty and dank-smelling. She wrinkled her nose, shivering again with chill. The earlier warmth of the day had been deceptive; now she felt an icy tinge in the wind that filtered through chinks in the walls.

Julian returned with an armload of wood and what looked like barrel staves. He tossed them to the floor by the hearth, and gave her a frowning glance. "I should have remembered how quickly storms can blow up this time of year. Give me a few minutes, and I think I can get some kind of fire going with this dry tinder."

Bare-headed, his pale hair was plastered in a dark cap to his head, dripping into his eyes as he knelt by the blackened hearth, searching for something. After a moment, he made a soft sound and then piled dry tinder against the firewall, stuffing bits of straw beneath pieces of kindling. He took up the flint he'd found near the hearth, struck it several times until sparks flew, and after a moment, the dry straw caught, flame flaring brightly. Nursing it, he blew gently until the slivers of wood began to burn, then built a stack of wood until a nice blaze spread heat and light into the damp gloom.

Still crouched, he pivoted on his bootheels to look at her with a raised brow. "That should warm it up a bit. Maybe we can dry out while we wait for the storm to blow over."

Nodding, she unfastened the snug Spencer, part of her riding costume she'd thought so frivolous when still in London, but appreciated more now. Lifting her velvet skirts, the green hem dragged across the bare floor. She lifted it to stare in dismay at her half-boots covered in mud as well. All ruined.

Peeling away clammy, wet garments, she draped them over a broken chair, then sat gingerly on a solid wood block of mysterious purpose to remove her boots. Unlacing the boots, she pulled them free, wiggling her damp toes, loath to walk on the hard dirt floor. She sat shivering near the fire in her chemise, drawers, and stockings, blessedly free of her half-corset.

Julian rose to fetch one of the tattered blankets from the cot, spread it like a carpet on the floor. As the fire rose, smoke hung in a heavy layer that slowly drifted toward the roof. It scented the air, stung her nose and eyes, and Laura coughed. Julian went back to the fire, manipulated a lever until the flue began to draw smoke up properly through the chimney. After a moment, he turned back to look at her. Her eyes watered from the smoke, and she coughed again, choking a bit.

"Here," he said, and moved her away from the hearth, "sit on this straw. It doesn't look too bad. At least it's dry." Kneeling in front of her, he looked up, a half-smile curving his mouth. "I should never have brought you with me today."

"Don't be silly." Lifting her hands, she raked them through her hair, loosening the coil at the back to let it fall free around her shoulders to dry. "I've been much more uncomfortable, I can assure you."

"Not with me." His eyes found and held hers, his hand

cupping her stockinged foot in his palm. "I vowed you'd never be cold or hungry again."

Her fingers stilled in her hair. Her heart thudded erratically. He was so serious, his tone soft and somber. He'd made a vow about her? He cared . . . he truly cared, and about more than just his own desires. He cared about *her*.

Closing her eyes, she sat for a moment while he massaged her feet, first one and then the other, fingers strong and sure. Competent. Heat washed over her, not just from the fire, but from his touch, the warmth of his concern comforting.

Outside, the rain beat against wooden shutters, the wind gusted and made a low, keening sound. Julian's hands moved from her foot to the calf of her leg, fingers working magic, rubbing over ribbed stockings and muscles, upward to her knee. She sighed with contentment, head tilted back, hair loose and swaying freely in damp curls that were cool against bare skin. The low, frilled neck of her linen chemise dipped low in the back, and barely covered her breasts. Cool air wafted over her, and she shivered again.

"Cold, sweeting?" His murmur was so soft, his hands so gentle, and she opened her eyes to find him gazing up at her through the thick brush of his lashes, gold eyes lit with reflection from the fire—or perhaps something else. Her breath caught.

"Yes—no," she breathed at last, the words coming out on a gush of air that she'd held too long, and he seemed to understand the effect he had on her, smiling a little at her confusion.

"This is not, perhaps, the prettiest place," he said, "but it's private." His hand slid up to the garter tied at her knee, fingers dextrously working it loose, his palm smoothing over the bare skin of her calf in a light stroke. "Very private. No one will come looking for us. We're quite—alone here." He untied her other garter, pulled her stockings away, rolling them down her legs in a tight coil, then slid his hands up under the cuffs of her linen drawers to flick open the buttons with a snap of his fingers. "So many layers of clothing . . . it's like plucking the petals from a rose."

Very still, she said nothing as he bunched the hem of her chemise in one hand, drawing it slowly upward. He'd taken off his own coat, but was still garbed in his shirt, neckcloth, and boots over his snug-fitting trousers. It felt wicked to be so bare when he was still clothed, wicked and somehow arousing. Then her chemise floated free, pulled over her head and discarded so that she sat on the blanket-covered straw in just her drawers.

Still kneeling in front of her, he spread her knees with his hands, leaned between them to curve his arms around her back, caressing her bare skin with slightly abrasive palms as his mouth moved to capture the peak of her breast between his lips. She gasped, arching toward him as fire shot through her like a bolt of lightning. He cradled her in his arms, mouth hot and searing against her chilled skin, suckling and nipping and kissing until she could barely breathe, until the cottage felt ablaze with steamy heat. Somehow, her hands were in his hair, holding his head to her, her own head thrown back as desire coursed through her in pulsebeat after pulsebeat, that insistent drumming throb below growing stronger.

His hands moved between her legs, stroking her through linen, finding the source of that exquisite pleasure that made her shudder, and the rough sensation of linen over tender flesh was arousing and heady. Gasping his name, she clung to him, crying out when white-hot spears of ecstasy rolled over her like ocean waves. She was drowning, drowning, and nothing else mattered but the moment, but *this,* Julian and how he made her feel, how he brought her body alive and filled her with sweet yearning. How he loved her. . . .

"The rain's stopped." Julian lifted to one elbow, looking down at Laura, who lay with her eyes closed, long lashes like tiny wings shadowing her soft cheeks. He'd spread his mantle atop the straw, a makeshift bed that had no doubt ruined his expensive mantle but was well worth it. He couldn't keep his hands off her, it seemed, nor did he want to try. Why? She was all he wanted and needed, and it was the most damnably unbelievable luck that had brought her to him.

Frightening, to think how easily he could have missed her among the multitude in London. If not for Malcolm's insistence that he find a fraudulent mistress, he'd not have found Laura. A fey, elusive creature, for all that she seemed happy enough. Yet there was something she hadn't told him—and he was certain he knew what it was.

Laura's lashes lifted, her eyes hazy and green as she smiled up at him. "I rather like it here for the moment," she murmured, dragging her fingertip along his jaw. "It's cozy."

He grinned. "Only you would find this hovel cozy. Anyone else would think it drafty."

"I have the advantage of being here with you. You make everything right."

"Do I?" He took her hand, pressed his mouth to her slender fingers. "You're easily pleased, I see. Come along, then. Thomas will have the grooms and stableboys out beating the bushes for us if we aren't back by dark. The days are still short."

It took her much longer to dress than it did him, and he watched with some appreciation as she drew her stockings up along the slender curve of her leg, tying them at the knee just below the dainty buttoned cuff of her linen drawers. It was with some regret that he observed her fastening the last button of her Spencer, becoming once more the elegantly clad female with only a hint of the delicious mysteries beneath layers of linen and velvet.

A rosebud furled against the world. He smiled mockingly at his own whimsies, and held out a hand to her.

"We aren't too far from Shadowhurst, sweeting. We should arrive soon enough."

"May we come again, Julian?" She put her gloved hand in his, fingers a light pressure in the cup of his palm. "I rather like this cottage. It seems much less—forlorn—than it did when we arrived."

"I daresay. You manage to brighten any hovel. But why on earth would you want to come back?"

"It's—quaint. And it reminds me that life is not all gilded walls and satin cushions. I don't ever want to become complacent."

Complacent. That was it. That was what he'd been trying to drum into the heads of those who never seemed to believe that there were human beings on earth who didn't have enough to eat or silk stockings to wear. They let their complacency delude them into viewing the rabble as choosing their own lot in life rather than having no escape from it.

Squeezing her hand, he nodded. "You may come here whenever you like. I give it to you."

"To . . . to me? You give this cottage to me?" She stared at him. "Just like that?"

"Just like that." He smiled. "It's been abandoned for a while now. It belonged to my old nurse, but she died several years ago and I never did anything with it after her son took all her personal belongings and went back to Nottingham. He works in the textile mills there."

A tremulous smile wobbled on her mouth, and her face flushed with pleasure. "I . . . I don't know what to say, Julian."

"Say nothing. It's a gift. I'll have Malcolm or Thomas draw up the papers for you."

He helped her mount, lifting her atop the mare, his hands remaining around her slender waist for a moment longer than necessary as she settled her skirts in a graceful drape down the side of the horse. He'd never really appreciated female garments until lately. The green velvet of her riding habit made her eyes greener and brighter, complemented the lush auburn hue of her hair, neatly wound into a coil on the nape of her neck again, though her hat was ruined beyond repair.

When they rode across the arched bridge, Julian caught a glimpse of a carriage pulling into the stableyard. It looked familiar, and when they were near and he saw the crest, he lifted a brow. Randal? Here? He hated the country.

But it was, indeed, his brother, waiting for him in the second floor parlor, impatiently pacing in front of the fireplace with a snifter of good French brandy in one hand.

"Good God, where the devil have you been?" Randal demanded when he saw him, then saw Laura close behind and paused, mouth slightly open. "Pardon, Miss Lancaster. I was talking to m'brother, of course."

"Of course, Lord Faraday," she said, smiling. "Do forgive my haste, but we were caught in the rain and I'm chilled."

Randal's gaze moved over her, lingering for a moment on her face. "Raining hay, was it?"

"Hay?"

"There seems to be straw in your hair."

Laura's hand went to her hair, her face reddening as she pulled a wisp of straw from the coil on her neck.

"Don't be an ass, Randal," Julian said calmly, "though I realize you find it amusing. We took refuge from the storm."

"Of course. Did I say otherwise?" Randal turned innocent eyes toward him, but a smile slanted his mouth. "That would be the intelligent thing to do in such a case."

"Which is why you'd never think of it, I'm sure. Pay no mind to him, Laura. He's got a devilish knack for saying the wrong thing."

"Or stating the obvious," she said with a faint smile, then nodded toward Randal and left them alone in the parlor. Julian turned to his brother.

"What brings you to Shadowhurst? I'll admit, I'm amazed you'd come all this way when I know how you hate the country."

"Julian, there's trouble." Randal turned serious, moving to shut the parlor door before turning back to face him. "Damnable trouble."

"You've always loved melodrama." Julian poured brandy into a glass, lifted it to his lips, but there was something in his brother's eyes and stance that alerted him. "What is it?"

"Treason."

"Good God. Who's the traitor?"

Randal stared at him, hazel eyes wide with apprehension. "You."

CHAPTER 16

"You're utterly mad," Julian said calmly, but a knot of tension grew tighter in his belly as Randal shook his head.

"No, it's true. There are rumors—it's being said that Miss Lancaster is passing military secrets she gets from you on to the French."

"Ludicrous."

"No, listen, Jule—there's a basis of reason for it. It's being said that you're angry at the Whigs for thwarting your efforts on the Corn Laws, and that Miss Lancaster's mother is mistress to General Laborteaux, consul to Napoleon."

"Bloody hell."

"Bloody hell, indeed," Randal said grimly. "I came as quickly as I could. I wanted to warn you before anyone else could get here."

"Anyone else? Who?"

"The King's Guards."

Julian's fingers tightened around the brandy glass. "It's gone that far, has it? You know it isn't true."

"Of course I know that! I'm not the fool you like to think me," Randal said testily, and shot him a frown as he crossed back to the fireplace. Bracing his hands against the marble mantel with the scene of Diana the huntress and a coursing hart, he stared into the flames. "Who could be doing this to you, dammit?"

"There are legions to choose from, I imagine. Anyone I've crossed in Parliament. A few who've taken exception to an angry exchange of words. Friends of Eleanor, though those would be blessed few—" He paused. "Randal, have you heard anything about her of late?"

"Eleanor? God, no. She's still in Italy, I suppose. Why?"

"She's not in Italy. She's in London. I saw her a few weeks ago, right before I brought Laura here. I thought it safer this way, and when the riots began, we left immediately."

"You saw Eleanor in London?" Randal blinked his surprise. "If she's back, why isn't she making some kind of fuss? It's not like her not to push herself forward, going where she isn't wanted, leaving a trail of discarded lovers—sorry, old boy. Guess I shouldn't remind you of that."

"No, you're quite right. Have you heard any news of Lord Drumley?"

"Eleanor's father? No, not lately. Still in Yorkshire with his pigs, I presume. He's a batty old gent. Guess it's better that way, not knowing what his daughter might do next. Do you expect him to be in London?"

"No, but Eleanor has to have some kind of financial support." He frowned. "Malcolm would know where to deposit her funds. Why didn't he tell me it had changed, I wonder. I think I should have a talk with him."

"Look, Jule, this is all very distracting, but has nothing to do with rumors of treason."

"Oh, on the contrary, Randal. I think it has a lot to do with it." Julian smiled grimly. "It'd be just the sort of trick Eleanor would pull if she could. The question is, who would listen to her? She had to tell someone, she has to have the ear of some official or MP. Who started the rumor?"

"Really, Malcolm, you look dreadful. What took you so long to get here? I've been waiting for hours!" Eleanor pushed out her lower lip out in a pout, glancing up at the steward through her lashes, a calculated effort that got the immediate result she desired. His smile wobbled.

"Those cursed mobs . . . the Watch has them under control, but getting through the streets can be difficult. Never mind. I'm here now, and with good news indeed."

"I hope so. This has taken much longer than it should, and really, I was about to think you had forgotten all about helping me."

"Never! Oh, never!" He stared at her fervently, brown eyes intent and hungry. She smiled prettily, and his lips parted. Oh, very good, just the reaction she wanted.

"I knew you'd not betray me. Not after everything. After all, we're really in this together now that you've kept your silence about me, aren't we, Malcolm?"

"I suppose we are." He looked dismayed, but said valiantly, "I'll not fail you, I swear it."

"Good." She leaned forward, lifting her tea from the small table in front of the settee, giving him an ample glimpse of her snowy bosom, revealed by the low vee of her neckline. He ogled, as she'd known he would, and she hid a smile of satisfaction. It was going much better than she had hoped. Malcolm had access to the ears of the influential—a word here or there, and the servants would know long before anyone else. It had no doubt gone through London like a fire, greedily leaping from house to house. Aubert had been right, after all. Malcolm was the perfect tool. But then, he always had been.

"What is the good news you brought?" she asked, leaning back against the cushions.

"Though there's talk of arrest for treason, he'll not be arrested, but he'll be called upon to give a proper account of his actions and justify his relationship with Miss Lancaster."

"Won't he? Be arrested, I mean. I'd rather hoped—but then, that might not suit after all, I suppose. We do need him for the present. Or at least, access to his accounts. You've very clever, Malcolm, to hide your manipulation of his money. He'll never know."

Shifting uncomfortably, Malcolm looked down at his

hands, fingers meshed together so tightly his knuckles were white. "Manipulation? That's rather—*strong*, don't you think? You've been paid handsomely this past year and a half, quite handsomely. I trust you were frugal with the . . . extra funds."

Alarmed, she sat up straight. "What do you mean? Can he cut me off? I've not a penny saved, and you must know it! Handsomely, indeed, I've had to live like a pauper on the pittance he granted, even with the extra you included. Malcolm, you must know how very much I've come to depend upon you. As always. You're so clever, really, and when this is all over—why, all the misunderstandings can be resolved at last."

He lifted his eyes to hers. "I trust they will be, indeed. All that nasty business with the man who broke in on you—a dangerous misunderstanding."

"Of course it was—are you implying otherwise?" Her tone went sharp, eyes narrowed on him. Really, there were times she suspected he was more loyal to Lockwood than she'd thought him, but then—if he was, why would he have helped her all this time?

"No, of course not, my lady." Malcolm's eyes slid away from hers. "It was a terrible time for you, a complete misunderstanding. And, of course, your decision to leave quietly after all was most wise of you. I commend you for your foresight."

"It wasn't foresight at all, as you well know," she said coldly. "I had no choice in the matter. Julian intended to throw me to the wolves if I didn't agree to exile. If not for assurance from you that I'd not be banished without proper recompense, I daresay I'd have starved to death in Newgate by now."

"I hardly think his lordship would allow that."

"Only to save his precious reputation!" She drew in a calming breath, studying Malcolm for a long moment. Aubert was right. The man could be a problem if she wasn't careful. He had access to Julian's ear, and though he seemed to be infatuated with her, was he really? He'd never said an improper word, never so much as touched her hand, just gazed at her with that calf-eyed stare that could be annoying at times. What a puzzle he was, sitting so primly across from her like a marionette jerked by strings.

"Whatever the reason, my lady, you were saved from the ordeal of a coroner's inquest. It could have been *most* unpleasant for you."

"There. You've said it again. Do you think I killed Fielding?"

He looked astonished. "I've said no such thing, my lady!"

"Not in words, but it's in your tone. You think I killed him when he became inconvenient, when he threatened to make our assignations public. You *do,* don't you!"

His eyes fixed on her face. "I know you are innocent, madam. It was all a terrible accident just as you said. . . ."

"Of course it was." Somewhat mollified, she relaxed back into the cushions. "He hit his head when he fell down the stairs, just as I said. Drunken fool." Toying with the lace cuff of her sleeve, she frowned slightly, then glanced up again at Malcolm. Really, Aubert was right. The man knew too much. Once he was no longer useful, he must be made to go away.

As if reading her mind, Malcolm rose to his feet, inclining his head respectfully. "There is much yet to do, madam, so I'll take my leave for now. His lordship will no doubt return from the country as soon as he hears the rumors, so all must be made ready in his household."

"Still off with that little tart, I presume," she snapped, and Malcolm's wooden expression eased into the faintest of smiles.

"Indeed, madam. So he is. They reside at Shadowhurst for the moment."

"How convenient." Damn Julian, how dare he? When he'd never wanted to be with her, he spent so much time with this . . . this Colonial trollop! And how utterly delicious vengeance would be. Oh yes.

When Malcolm had gone, she paced restlessly before the fireplace. Aubert was late. As he usually was, never arriving when he said, always when she'd given up expecting him. A most infuriating man. Infuriating and strangely exhilarating, a man with—unusual tastes. Continental in his nonchalant manner. He'd taught her a few things in the past months. Some of them were not so very pleasant, but then, the French were said to be peculiar and very loose when it came to the bedroom. Still, he'd managed to quite shock her at times. Some of his pleasures bordered on pain and violence. Very unusual, she thought, but oddly intriguing. Perhaps she'd become more jaded than she'd ever imagined.

It was well past dark when Aubert arrived, smelling of rain and gin. She wrinkled her nose at him, and he seemed only amused by her disapproval.

"Tut, *ma chérie*, you're becoming an annoying scold. For that, you shall be punished. But later. Now, I am too weary." Sprawling on the settee, he gazed at her with half-lidded, dark eyes that regarded her with bored indifference. Her heart quickened when he smiled slowly, one side of his mouth curling upward. "Perhaps you can think of something to enliven the evening, heh? Tell me, did our good friend Malcolm do as we wished?"

"Yes, of course he did. He's very resourceful. I wonder, however, just how agreeable he would be if he knew about you."

Waving a languid hand, Aubert dismissed the steward as if unworthy of more thought. "It hardly matters. All is set into motion. Once the earl is imprisoned, you will be left with his great fortune at your disposal."

"Yes," she said tartly, stung by his indifference, "at *my* disposal. Perhaps then I will find my pleasures elsewhere. There are other gentlemen in London, you know."

Moving swiftly as the strike of a snake, Aubert had her by the wrist, his grip painfully tight, fingers nearly crushing the fragile bones as he ignored her gasp. "Yes, *chérie*, there are other gentlemen in London, but none such as I who know how to please you even when you cry for mercy."

Quivering, she stared up at him, into black eyes that looked fierce and predatory. It was impossible to resist, impossible to retreat, and she knew even before his head lowered to kiss her that he would hurt her. But it didn't matter. He cared. He wanted her. He'd never share her with anyone else, and he'd told her so many times. A shiver went through her as his hand closed on her breast and his mouth took hers, and then she thought of nothing else but Aubert.

"Impossible. I refuse to even consider it."

"Very well, Julian. If you prefer to see her in prison alongside you—or since she's not English, hung on Tyburn Hill—then keep her with you. Excellent notion."

Julian glared at Randal furiously. Damn him, he made sense. What a devil of a mess to be in, and it was even worse for Laura. He felt like hitting something. Rage boiled up inside him, hot and consuming. He closed his eyes, struggled for self-control, until finally he could speak without shouting.

"I'll have to protect her, of course," he said evenly, turning from the fire to look at his brother. Randal stared at him with frowning concern.

"How do you propose to do that? I can take her with me, if you like, but that's only a temporary situation. If the magistrates decide she's under suspicion, then she's likely to go to—"

"Don't say it." Julian put up a hand to stop him, tone low and fierce. "I cannot bear the thought of her going to prison, especially because of me. She's blameless in this. My enemies are ruthless, it seems, willing to use the innocent for their own purpose."

"They seek to cast blame for the recent riots elsewhere. As you're the most relentless, you must bear the brunt of their efforts. You have to refute their charges as soon as possible, Julian, or they may well take you down."

He snorted. "They'll not do it. They'll try, but I'm damned if I'll give them the satisfaction of crying foul. I have my own methods of reprisal, by God. But you're right about Laura. She has to be protected first."

Blowing out a heavy breath, he raked a hand through his hair, turning to lean back against the mantel and let the fire warm his back and shoulders as he contemplated several options. None was appealing, nor entirely foolproof. While he was certain there was no real evidence that Laura was involved in any plot, even an innocent letter could be misconstrued. He had to do what he'd held off doing these past months. He could delay no longer.

"Julian," Randal said when he pushed away from the mantel and started across the parlor, "you know you'll have to send her away, don't you?"

"Yes. Dammit all, yes, I do," he said without turning to look at his brother, the awful truth unable to be denied, and more awful because of it. It was too damned close to surrender. Too damned close to admitting defeat. Yet he had little choice if he was to keep her safe.

How could he tell her? She'd insist upon staying if she thought he was in trouble. Could he convince her to leave England for her own safety? Did he have the strength to force her to go?

CHAPTER 17

"Becky, you're an angel." Laura smiled blindly, eyes closed as she luxuriated in the slipper bath, hot scented water lapping about her shoulders, her head resting against the rear of the tub. "I don't know how you knew I'd need this so badly."

"It were plain to me that ye'd be chilled and wet after the storm," Becky said, pouring more hot water from a brass kettle into the tub. "I had a footman bring up most of the water."

"You've done well." The hot water eased muscles aching from her ride. It'd been so long since she'd ridden, her muscles protested the unfamiliar activity. Bubbles frothed, and she opened her eyes to cup a mound in her palm, the sweet, slightly spicy fragrance filling the water closet. A fire burned on the grate, and layers of steam slithered in the air. She'd washed her hair and piled it atop her crown, securing it with pins.

Becky gasped, and Laura turned to see Julian in the open doorway. He seemed surprised, then a faint smile curved his mouth. "I should have knocked, I see, but the door was ajar and I heard you speaking, so didn't."

"And now you're sorry for it?" she teased, and he grinned.

"Not in the least." He leaned against the doorframe, crossed his arms over his chest, and leisurely let his gaze rove over her. "In fact, I'm most glad of it."

"What a rascal you are, to be sure."

"Oh yes, to be sure." His eyes shifted to Becky, and she

bobbed a clumsy curtsey, then skirted him to sidle out the door and disappear.

"Now you've run off my maid, so you'll have to wash my back in her place." Laura held out a cloth, and after a moment's hesitation, he pushed away from the door and came to the edge of the tub.

He removed his jacket, then rolled up his shirtsleeves before taking the cloth from her. "I don't think I've ever done this, so don't be surprised if I'm clumsy at it."

She closed her eyes and leaned forward. "I cannot imagine you being clumsy at anything."

Warm water lapped around her breasts, and she shivered when he dipped the cloth into the scented bubbles and then drew it down the curve of her spine in a slow motion more like a caress than an effort to clean. Not that she'd actually expected him to scrub her back. It had been impulse that prompted the suggestion.

She sat quietly, immersed in thought and scented water, eyes drifting shut in contentment. If only the moment would last forever. . . .

"We're leaving for London in the morning," he said softly, and her eyes snapped open. "I have work to do that will occupy me greatly. My enemies have found a new way to strike at me."

Her heart lurched. She turned to look at him, but his expression was impassive, showing nothing of emotion. She shivered. "What have they done?"

"There are—rumors. Suffice it to say, I know them to be false, but it could be dangerous to ignore them. I have to take action." The cloth sloshed warm water over her shoulder, slid down her upper arm, and he lifted her hand into the air as he soaped her elbow down to her wrist, not looking at her.

"What action must you take?"

His eyes lifted to hers; the cloth stilled, though he held her hand in his palm. "It's imperative that you leave England."

"No!" The word burst from her without thought, sharp in

the soft, warm air. Her fingers closed over his palm, held him when he started to pull free. "No, I won't leave you. There's nothing we can't overcome together—you cannot ask me to part from you, Julian!"

"My dear, you are not being given a choice in the matter. You're in more danger than I, and it's necessary."

"I don't care!"

"I do." His tone was cool, remote, and faint white lines bracketed his taut mouth. "As long as you remain in England, you'll be a danger to me as well. A liability, if you will."

If he'd struck her across the face, it could not have hurt more. She sucked in a sharp breath, felt the blood drain from her face to leave her chilled despite the warm air and water.

"A—liability?"

Julian pulled free of her hand, dropped the cloth into the water and rose to his feet, looming over her, suddenly so different, detached, and remote again as he'd been when first she'd met him, aloof aristocracy instead of her passionate lover.

"We've had a splendid arrangement, but it's ended now. Everything must end eventually."

Each word sounded a death knell in her heart. She stared at him, trying to find emotion in his flat tone, searching for denial that wasn't there. He turned away from her, crossed to the small fire in the grate, toed a glowing ember back onto the hearth tiles. Shivering, she reached for her robe draped over a stool, stood up, and stuck her arms into the sleeves as she stepped from the tub onto a thick towel spread on the floor. Not bothering to dry herself, she tied the sash tightly about her waist, so tightly it gave a painful pinch that still didn't abate the cold anguish inside.

"Very well, my lord," she managed to say coolly enough, though it felt as if she spoke too loudly, that her pain had to be evident. "Shall I make the arrangements?"

"I've taken care of that. Randal will accompany you to London tomorrow morning, and he'll see that Malcolm has proper instructions for your passage. A first-class accommodation, of course. You'll also have ample funds deposited into your account so that you can draw upon them at any time."

He spoke not to her, but to the carved marble figurines in the single-shelf mantel, a scene depicting Poseidon and the Sirens, fanciful and graceful, with sea waves rising up in curves and curls. She felt as if she were drowning, being sucked under by waves of grief as cold and relentless as the marble carvings.

"Thank you, my lord," she said, but it came out a husky whisper that she wasn't certain he heard. He continued to stare at the burning coals in the grate, until he pushed away with a violent motion that made her take a backward step, swinging around to face her.

"Don't look at me like that! We both knew we couldn't go on as we were forever. It was inevitable that things would change."

"Yes, of course. I'm—grateful for all you've done for me." Oh God, could one hurt this badly and remain alive? To keep breathing, the heart still beating, the lungs still taking in air . . . was it possible to live through such agony?

"*Grateful?*" His eyes burned like hot embers, his mouth twisted to one side in a horrible imitation of a smile. "That's lovely. I suppose we expected too much of one another. I'll not see you again after tonight, Laura. It would be—futile."

"Yes, I suppose it would."

For a long moment they stood staring at one another, the only sound the coals hissing in the grate—and she thought he must surely hear her heart breaking in that deadly silence, but he only nodded once, gave her a last smoldering glance, then moved past her to push out of the door—and her life.

It amazed her that the world did not come crashing down around her in a thunderous roar.

* * *

The weather had turned nasty again. Winter made a last swipe at England with cold wind and icy rain, freezing buds on fruit trees, turning roads to brittle frost. Laura sat on the carriage seat across from Julian's brother, and Becky huddled in a corner, sleeping noisily. Maidstone was behind them, London only twenty miles distant now. They should reach it before dark.

"Is she always so noisy in sleep?" Randal asked, indicating Becky's open-mouthed snoring with a nod of his head.

Laura shook her head. "I've never noticed if she is. But then, she usually sleeps elsewhere and not near me."

"She'll sleep alone the rest of her life if she sleeps this loudly," he grumbled, but there was no malice in his tone, only the awkwardness of a man in a difficult situation. She understood. She felt much the same. Conversation had been scarce and stilted, Julian's absence more marked than his presence would have been. He'd left before daylight, she'd been told, taking his swiftest mount to reach London, leaving her to follow with baggage and servants—and brother.

Shrugging, Laura murmured, "Perhaps she's more fortunate than she knows."

Randal's eyes rested on her for a long moment, his brow lowered into a frown, but he had no reply for her observation. What *could* he say? Julian had ended their relationship without a qualm, without more than a cursory explanation and vague words of danger, and there would be nothing his brother could say to ease her shock and pain. She knew that. She expected nothing from him. She'd expected everything from Julian.

Misery tightened into a hard knot in her chest. The carriage rocked hard to one side as a wheel dipped into a frozen rut, throwing her against Becky, who woke with a snort.

"'Ere," she said in alarm, blinking sleepily, "w'at is it?"

"Nothing terrible," Laura soothed, "only a rut in the road. Rest while you can. We're still some distance away."

Becky nodded, wiping her mouth with one hand, glancing

shyly toward Randal. Laura hid a smile. Julian's brother was quite handsome, though not, in her opinion, the equal of the earl. He was young yet, his strength of features still forming, but he had the same strong jawline and the promise of great character in his countenance. One day he'd be formidable, just like his brother.

Closing her eyes, she suppressed the knife-thrust of pain her thoughts of Julian summoned. He had left her, just when she'd dared to trust, dared to think there might be a future, dared to be happy. To no avail. Brief contentment had burst like so many soap bubbles. Squeezing her eyes tightly to hold back the memories, she thought of days long past, of Virginia and green fields and blue skies. It would be warm when she arrived, with flowers in bloom and soft sunshine to greet her. She'd purchase her own home, something small and cozy, like the cottage at Shadowhurst, a place of her very own, a place where she'd feel welcome and not miss England at all. No, not at all.

She must have slept. Becky's snoring woke her, and she opened her eyes to see Randal gazing at her with a faint smile. Sitting up, she flushed slightly.

"Do I snore?"

"Oh no, Miss Lancaster. Even if you did, however, I shouldn't be able to hear it over the droning of your maid. Good God, she near burst my ears with it."

"She's a good girl," she said defensively, and he nodded.

"I'd hope so. Just give her a room far from anyone with half-decent hearing." Stretching leisurely, he peered out the window. "We're nearly there. I'm to make arrangements for you. Did Julian tell you?"

Her hands tightened in her lap. "Yes. You're to make arrangements for my passage to America. Do you—think it will be soon?"

"Yes. Commerce with America has opened back up quickly, and not even Bonaparte has been able to affect shipping."

"Oh. That's—fortunate."

"Do you really think so?"

She glanced up in surprise at his dry tone, and saw him smiling at her. "Of course. Why would I wish for England's shipping to be affected?"

"That's not at all what I meant. You're not happy to be going home to America, are you?"

"No. You look surprised. Did you expect me to lie, to say that I'm glad to be leaving your brother? I'm not. You must know that." Irritation made her tone sharp.

"Yes, I know that." Randal studied her for a moment, hazel eyes narrowing slightly. "You love him."

"Yes, I do love him. Apparently, the sentiment is not returned."

Randal smiled. "Don't be too certain of that, Miss Lancaster. There are circumstances at the moment you cannot understand. Julian has never . . . loved a woman before."

"Not even his wife?"

She thought she'd made a valid point, but Randal snorted derisively and said, "Especially not his wife!"

Startled, she stared at him. "I know it was an arranged marriage, but why would he be so upset with her for creating scandal if he didn't love her once?"

"Frankly, he wouldn't care if she bedded half of England as long as she was discreet, but discretion has never been part of Eleanor's vocabulary. Not even in today's risqué society, is it acceptable to bed another man an hour after the nuptials, however? It puts rather a pall on the marriage, as I understand it."

"She didn't!"

"Oh yes, she certainly did. Julian has no idea that I know, but the baronet foolish enough to get so drunk he lost all his sense fled London afterward. When I happened to see him again, he asked if my brother was still angry at him for it. The gudgeon. If I were Julian, I'd have called him out, but then, that would have immediately set tongues wagging and created scandal. Julian chose discretion. For my father's sake more than his own, I think, as the old man was ill and eager for an heir." Shrugging, he crossed one leg over the other, resting his boot atop his knee as he gazed at her with an enigmatic expression. "Divorce was always out of the question for that reason at first. Now, I wonder if it's still an issue with him."

Confused, Laura stared at Faraday. What was he trying to tell her? She shook her head.

"I don't understand."

"I think you do." Randal's smile reminded her of Julian's, a wry curve of his mouth. "Just don't give up on him, Miss Lancaster."

"I think he's given up on me, my lord," she replied softly. "It's no longer my choice."

It was appallingly accurate. Julian had abandoned her.

"I received a note from Lord Lockwood to wait here for your mistress, so step aside and let me in!" Celia gave the footman barring entry into Laura's house a stern look, and he stepped aside at once, allowing her entrance. "She should arrive soon so you'd best prepare tea and a light supper," she added as she swept inside and untied the fastenings of her cloak.

If the footman thought it unusual, he said nothing, but took her discarded cloak and then promptly disappeared into the back of the house. Celia set about removing the dust cloths from atop the settee and chairs, bustling about and making herself busy as she tried to sort through the dozens of questions that had occurred to her since receiving the earl's note a short time before. It had been a brief missive, just saying that Laura was due back at her house late this afternoon and would need her friend's support. He'd signed it, sealed it, and sent it with a courier to her house, and she'd replied that she would go at once. Belgrave, bless him, hadn't argued at all, indeed had seemed rather relieved to end their heated discussion about the rumors he'd heard.

All nonsense. Laura would never be so foolish. Frowning, Celia tapped a forefinger on her chin thoughtfully. It certainly seemed convenient that Lady Lockwood would return to London, and Aubert Fortier would arrive from France, and then these dreadful rumors would spring up about the earl and his mistress. Was there a connection? Belgrave had said that was nonsense, that Lady Lockwood wasn't received at any decent house, so she'd have no opportunity to repeat any false tales. But neither did he think Lockwood guilty of foolish indiscretions. Indeed, what vital military secrets could he know to pass on to her? He'd been out of the city for some time, not long after Bonaparte had left Elba, so as yet there could be nothing of great import that he'd be involved in, he was quite certain of that. There was protocol, after all.

Staring at her, drawing himself up into a stiff knot of indignation, Charles had said as if it quite proved his point, "Lockwood would never turn traitor. He's *English,* for God's sake!"

Celia dusted off a lamp while the footman brought coal for the parlor fire. Belgrave may be a bit pompous at times, but he was also intelligent. He considered the rumors false, but would a magistrate?

Using a lit taper, she lit the parlor lamps, lost in thought and worried for her friend. Lord Lockwood would doubtless be exonerated; there may be a bit of a furor and investigation, but he had the money and position to escape relatively unscathed, while Laura did not. She'd be a scapegoat. What a bloody disaster this could be. . . .

It was late afternoon when Laura and her maid arrived. Celia went out to greet her, unable to wait a moment longer, anxious that Laura know she wasn't alone. A footman had opened the carriage door, and Laura stepped down to the paving stones, looking sad and weary. Her little maid emerged a moment later, followed by a tall, younger version of Lord Lockwood. Celia gave him a cursory glance as she hurried to Laura.

"Celia! Oh my . . . how fortunate that you're here. I longed so to speak with you." Laura seized her arm, squeezing tightly. "Can you stay?"

"Of course. That's why I came."

"Devilish convenient, I'd think," the young man drawled, and Celia turned her eyes to him with a cool stare.

"Not so convenient, sir. I was told she'd be arriving today and came to greet her. Do you object?"

An engaging grin split his face and he shook his fair head. "Not a'tall, not a'tall. Just a bit bemused by your timing, Miss—"

"I daresay you're often bemused."

Laura interrupted. "Celia Carteret, this is Lord Faraday, Lockwood's brother."

"Ah, the infamous viscount." Celia nodded coolly. Really, he needn't look at her as if he could see through her clothes! What a rake, just as his reputation claimed him to be . . . and he stood there grinning at her so charmingly she could see how he easily earned it.

"Yes, indeed, Miss Carteret, though rumors of your beauty have not been exaggerated, I see. Belgrave is a lucky man."

"I'm sure he'll be most gratified to hear it. Now, if you'll excuse us, Miss Lancaster looks ready to swoon at any moment and I'm certain you're eager to go home as well."

If she'd thought to dismiss him so easily, she was mistaken, it seemed, for he insisted upon accompanying them inside. Her first reservations gave way to grudging acceptance when she saw that Faraday was genuinely concerned with Laura's welfare. He sat across from her on the settee, speaking softly and earnestly.

"You'll be just fine once this has all blown over, as I assure you it will. London loves a good scandal, but there's always another one to replace it soon enough."

"But I don't understand," Laura broke in. "What scandal has happened to come between us like this? I thought—I thought he no longer wanted me with him."

"Oh ducks," Celia said, going to her at once and putting her arms around Laura while the viscount stared at her with what seemed to be genuine surprise, "you really don't know?"

"No!" Laura turned to look at her, exasperation erasing some of her weariness. "Julian did not reveal anything to me other than that we must keep to our agreement."

"Agreement?" Faraday broke in, but was ignored by both women.

"That cod's head," Celia said irritably. "Why must men be so foolish? Look, ducks, there's a terrible rumor going about that Lockwood relayed military information to you, and in turn, you gave the information to your mother to help Napoleon. It's said that she's mistress to a general in his command."

Laura paled. She stared silently at Celia, then glanced at Faraday, who nodded agreement. "I see," she said after a moment. "Why wouldn't Julian tell me this?"

"I think I can answer that—my brother has noble intentions. I've been instructed to put you on the first ship leaving England in order to spare you any nastiness. It's his method of dealing with vicious rumors. He takes it all on his own head."

"That's so idiotic," Celia said, and to her dismay, Laura burst into tears. "Oh there, there, ducks, it's all right, truly it is. If Lockwood intends to spare you, let him. You've wanted to go home for so long, and now you'll go in style—don't cry so, ducks."

Faraday looked appalled, and she held Laura to her, saying over her head, "Go find that jackanapes who was supposed to bring tea and tell him to be quick about it!"

Looking relieved to escape, the viscount abandoned the parlor at once and after a moment more, Celia patted Laura's back comfortingly and said briskly, "Do pull yourself together, my dear. This isn't so dreadful after all, now is it?"

"Yes!" Laura sat up, dabbing at her eyes with a handkerchief Celia provided. "He should have told me. I'd never leave him to face this alone."

"Which is quite probably why he didn't tell you. Don't be foolish. Lockwood will escape with only a little damage to his reputation, but you're liable to be imprisoned or deported. Or even hanged if the magistrate isn't convinced of your innocence. Someone will have to pay the piper for this mess, and it's most likely to be you. That's why you must do as the earl wishes and set sail at once for America. If you stay here—well, it won't be pleasant."

"Oh, you're probably right. That's what he meant when he said I was a liability." Laura gave a helpless shrug of her shoulders. "It's just that I thought . . . I thought he cared more for me. I thought he'd want us to always be together. Oh, I know he can't marry me, but at least we'd be able to be together."

"Don't count on that," Faraday said, coming back into the parlor in time to hear her last words, "for Eleanor is a vicious bitch. Sorry for m'language, but it's true. I'm sure she has a hand in this somehow."

Celia nodded. "Yes, that's what I thought, too. It's such a coincidence that she's back in London, and Fortier is here, and suddenly there are these rumors—"

"Fortier? Aubert Fortier?" Faraday's brows snapped together when she nodded. "How is he involved?"

"Well . . . I hear things," Celia said after a moment, aware of Laura's sudden tension, "and it came to me that he has been seen in Lady Lockwood's company. It's all very furtive, of course, but you know how servants talk. Fortier is said to be a most disagreeable man."

"He's a scoundrel and a scapegrace, and fancies himself a buck of the first head. He cheats abominably at cards, and was caught out by none other than Alvanley not so long ago. If he'd not passed it off as a mistake, there would have been pistols at dawn. Fortier claims to be visiting, but my suspicion is that he's left France for other reasons. It's not such a great leap of logic to assume him capable of helping Eleanor if he thinks there's profit in it for him." His mouth tightened into a grim line. "If he's out to do harm to Lockwood, I'll see to it that he rues that decision quickly enough. And as for Eleanor . . . maybe it's time I had a family discussion with her."

Celia looked at Faraday with new respect. Perhaps there was more to him than pursuit of frivolous pleasures after all. "Yes," she said, leaning forward, "if she thinks you're on her side, she is quite likely to reveal more than she should. Do you think—you could speak with her?"

Looking up, hazel eyes took on a golden sheen, and a feral smile curled his mouth. "Oh, I think I most definitely *shall* speak with my sister-in-law, and very soon."

"You see, ducks?" Celia said, giving Laura a comforting pat. "All will be well. Just give it time to sort out, and I think perhaps your trip won't be necessary at all."

And to be safe, perhaps she'd send Rex Pentley to learn what he could. Rex was a master at ferreting out truth, even when he didn't care to tell it himself.

Darkness fell, shrouding the house across the narrow street in shadows. Leaning back against a brick wall, hidden behind an iron fence railing, Rex Pentley watched Aubert Fortier leave Lady Lockwood's house and get into a hired cab. A faint smile curled his mouth. She was busy tonight. First, that young viscount he'd gulled so neatly at Laura's request had come to visit, then Fortier arrived right after he left. Neither man stayed long.

Very interesting. A most intriguing situation, indeed. Fortier must have seen Faraday's coach out front, for his cab had pulled up down the street and waited until the viscount left before moving forward. Fortier's time inside had been quite brief.

As the cab rolled away from the curb, Rex strode across the street. A cold wind blew down his collar, but he ignored it. He slipped around the side of the house, and let himself in an unlocked back door. A young maidservant whirled around, gaping at him, and he moved swiftly to put a hand over her mouth.

"Hush, girl. I'm here to see your mistress. I'll not harm you unless you force me. Do you understand?"

She nodded mutely, and when he took his hand away she whispered, "Ye'll find the spiteful old blowen in the front parlor, ye will. Give her a good cuffing if ye like, an' I'll not say a word to anyone about it."

"A favorite of yours, is she?" Amused, Rex moved past her down the hallway, stepping into the parlor. Lady Lockwood sat on the edge of a chair near the fire, her shoulders hunched forward, blond hair straggling loose down her back. He paused, then strode across the carpet to stand at the side of her chair. She looked up with a sudden start, and he saw the reddened imprint of a hand across her face. Apparently someone had already given her a good cuffing, and his coin was on Fortier as the culprit.

"Who are you?" she demanded, leaping up from the chair to face him, blue eyes glittering with tears and anger. "Did he send you already?"

"He? Ah, Fortier," he guessed, and saw from her face that he was right. "And if he did send me, m'lady?"

"I'll not allow it! He cannot threaten me like that. My father is a baronet, after all, and I'll not be treated shabbily by anyone!"

"And who has treated you shabbily?" Rex let his tone soften. "My guess would be Fortier struck you, am I right?"

She stared at him, some of the anger fading from her eyes. Her chin lifted slightly in that familiar haughty gesture Rex had seen the aristocracy use with those they considered beneath them. "It's really none of your business. State your purpose here, then leave. Did Aubert send you here?"

"And why would he do that?"

"Don't toy with me, sir. If you won't answer my question, I'll have a footman show you out immediately."

"Now you toy with me. You have no footman on duty tonight. If you had, I would have seen him."

Her brows snapped down. For the first time, he saw disquiet in her eyes, but she hid it well with a shrug and toss of her head. Hair loosened from a coil atop her crown shivered at the abrupt motion, pale and silky-looking, gleaming in the lamp and firelight.

"My maid—"

"Has been silenced for the moment. Now come. We must have a discussion, and I'd advise you to be perfectly honest with me. Those who are not, quickly come to regret it."

A flicker of fear crossed her face and she put out her tongue to wet her lips, backing away a step. "What . . . what do you want?"

"Answers. Correct answers, to be precise." He smiled ominously.

"What the devil did you do that for, Randal?" Julian glared at his brother seated near the fire in a wingback chair, but with no visible effect on him. A cool stare was the only reply. Shaking his head, he muttered an oath, then blew out a sigh. "I'm certain she was not accommodating. Eleanor has her own version of the truth most of the time."

"I'm convinced she's behind the rumors."

"It seems likely. Damned difficult to disprove, however, even if it comes from a scorned wife. I should have divorced her two years ago after that incident with Fielding. What a farce."

"Fielding's death was ruled accidental. Are you saying it wasn't?"

Julian gave his brother a wry glance. "I'll never know for certain, but my suspicions have been that he had help falling down those stairs. His head was cracked open like an egg."

Randal was quiet for a moment. "Then he didn't break into the house. He was there to see Eleanor. She said—God, Julian—do you know what that means?"

"Murder? Yes, of course. But I can't prove it, and it would only have caused more talk. If Fielding hadn't been there with my wife, it would never have happened."

"So you sent her away."

"Yes."

"Just like you're doing Laura Lancaster."

Julian's eyes narrowed. "Yes. But for a different reason. A much different reason. I sent Eleanor away to protect the Lockwood name. I'm sending Laura away to protect her life."

"Eleanor hates her, you know. And she hates you, but if you were to go back to her, she'd take you gladly."

"That's unlikely to happen."

"So I told her. She didn't . . . take it well."

Julian smiled. "Eleanor doesn't like being told no. I learned that fairly quickly."

Randal stood up. "Maybe we're wrong about sending Miss Lancaster away. Just send her back to the country, perhaps, or . . . or to Scotland or Ireland. All the way to America—she may never return."

"No, she may not. Why do you care if she does or doesn't?"

"Because, dammit, she's in love with you. A blind man could see it. Surely, *you* can!"

"Unfortunately for both of us, love is not always enough to prevent disaster. In fact, it's probably caused more disasters than ever it's prevented them. If I hadn't kept her with me so long she'd not be in danger now, yet—"

When he halted, unable to vocalize his emotions, Randal grinned. "Yet you love her and couldn't let her go. By God, I never thought I'd see it!"

"Don't be an ass, Faraday." Using Randal's title name distanced him effectively enough, but had little effect on his brother's immediate good humor.

"Oh, it's not me being an ass—*Lockwood*. It's you. You can't send her away now. It's too final."

Moving closer to him, Julian said slowly and distinctly, carefully enunciating each word, "I fully intend to send her to

America, Randal. She won't be safe any closer. Once all this is settled, if she wishes to return—if she wishes to come back, we'll deal with that then. Don't interfere. If you don't wish to secure her passage, then I'll have Malcolm take care of it. In fact, I think I'll do that anyway."

"Stubborn as an ass." Randal shook his head sadly. "You have influence, Julian. You're a peer of the realm. Do you not think a magistrate will take your word over Eleanor's? Especially after she's done nothing but create scandal since you were married? I hardly think this will be as desperate as you seem to think. Just wait until you've talked to a barrister before you send her away."

It was tempting. God, he wanted to keep her close, but it was risky. No, better to know she was safe than to chance her being arrested. Damn Randal for dangling temptation, and for his interference with Eleanor. He shook his head, looked up at his brother, his tone gruff.

"I've already contacted a barrister, but you and I both know there are different rules for different classes. Laura could take the brunt of Eleanor's mischief, and I've no intention of risking it."

It was too true. When he thought of her standing in the box under accusation, a feeling of desperation swept through him. He couldn't take that chance. No matter what it cost him, no matter what he had to do, he'd keep her safe.

CHAPTER 18

"Do you know who I am?"

Laura stared at the woman standing stiffly in the parlor. Blond, petite, lovely, she gazed back at her with frosty blue eyes. She'd have known who her visitor was even if she hadn't heard Becky gasp behind her, "Lady Lockwood!"

Sweeping past Laura as if she had every right to be there, Lady Lockwood moved to the settee, her elegant skirts lifted slightly as if they'd be contaminated by touching the floor. "Get rid of your maid. I wish to speak with you privately."

Although Becky was already slinking toward the back of the house, Laura turned to her and shook her head. "Please finish what you were doing, Becky. Then you may go."

"Y-y-yes, miss." Nervous, the little maid clumsily polished the brass firedogs, her cloth dragging into the embers as she glanced over her shoulder toward the countess. It began to smolder and she gasped aloud, slapping the polishing cloth against the hearth to put it out.

"It's all right, Becky, you may go," Laura said kindly when the fire had been extinguished, taking pity on the unnerved girl.

"She needs to be dealt with harshly," Lady Lockwood commented idly. "A sharp slap would do her good."

"Yes, I'm sure you think so. May I ask why you are here, my lady?"

"Oh, I think you know. You needn't pretend innocence. It doesn't suit you."

Laura held her tongue, though a half-dozen retorts sprang to mind as Lady Lockwood looked around the small, cozy house as if it were infested with vermin, her nose wrinkled in distaste. A heavy silence fell between them, and finally Lady Lockwood broke it, sounding impatient.

"You seem to have quite a nasty little army ready to spring to your defense. I find it most amazing. And enlightening."

"I beg your pardon?"

"As well you should!" Turning sharply, the countess glared at her, almost quivering with some emotion at which Laura could only guess, for the lovely lips trembled alarmingly. "No less than three persons have presented themselves at my door to demand I cease some foolish notion of vengeance against you. Yet no one ever rose to my defense when I was so horribly accused of a crime two years ago—not even my noble, honorable husband."

She said the last words with a sneer curling those lips, but beneath the anger, Laura saw the pain. Guilt scoured her, guilt for being with Julian when he was wed to another, guilt for being a part of causing anyone anguish. Didn't she know well enough how that felt? Why had she not considered that the countess was in love with her husband, that it was an emotion not returned? It had been far too easy to dismiss her as a wayward wife, when perhaps she'd felt driven by reasons Laura had not known or guessed. Even knowing that Lady Lockwood had been unfaithful to her husband on the very day of their wedding did not absolve her of her own guilt.

"I'm sorry to hear that, my lady," she said softly. "It must be terrible to feel so misused."

"Yes." Lady Lockwood stared at her. "It does. So please stop sending your friends to plead your cause, for it will do you no good. I've nothing to do with the rumors."

"I've sent no one. If you've had visitors on my account, it was of their own volition, not of mine, I assure you. My lady— this may make no difference to you, but Lord Lockwood and I have parted company."

"Have you. I'm not surprised. Julian loses interest quickly once he has the prize in hand. He always said he preferred the chase to the capture, and it's been proven true. Not that it matters at all to me. I bear him no love. Indeed, it's well that I don't, as he's turned traitor, it seems. Were I you, Miss Lancaster, I'd look to myself, as Julian will be of no help to you soon. England may forgive aristocracy many sins, but treason is not one of them."

"The rumors are quite false," Laura managed to say calmly. "There is no evidence of either my guilt or his. I've not had correspondence with my mother in over two years."

"Really. Perhaps you'd best save your argument for the magistrates. Rest assured, they have a way of getting to the truth of a matter."

Laura didn't respond as Lady Lockwood moved past her toward the entrance hall, the feathers on her stylish hat bobbing slightly with her light steps. At the door, she turned back, a gleam in her blue eyes as she smiled.

"I expect not to see you again, Miss Lancaster. Good day."

When Laura closed the door behind her and turned, Becky stood only a few feet away, her eyes wide. "Oh, miss! She—Lady Lockwood—she took something from your desk! I saw 'er, I did—she took it before ye came downstairs."

"Took something? What did she take?"

Becky shook her head. "I don't know, miss—truly I don't, but I saw 'er, I did."

Laura turned toward her desk, a small walnut secretary against the far wall; she'd been going over tradesmen's bills earlier, but why would the countess care about that? Puzzled, she moved to the desk, but nothing seemed amiss. Everything seemed to be in place—her sharpened quill, the stack of bills, pot of ink, blotting papers . . . where was her small seal? The one she used to fasten the folds of paper? It should be right there, but she didn't see it. Surely, the countess had not taken it. Why would she want a plain seal such as those anyone could purchase at one of the stationer shops? It wasn't remarkable at all.

Except that it was hers. Of course. The countess meant to prove that Laura had written to her mother recently. She'd fail. There had been no correspondence at all, though she'd thought about it. Well, Lady Lockwood would find the seal quite useless if she attempted to match it to any incriminating letters.

But now that she knew the countess would go to such lengths to be rid of her, it was time to leave England. She shouldn't risk remaining here any longer. She was, as Julian had said, only a liability to him now. If she left, the furor would die down.

Calling for her footman, she sent him down to the ship's pursers to obtain passage for her on the next ship leaving for Virginia. She drew on her letters of credit at the Bank of England, the money Julian had provided so generously for her, and with a heavy heart, made plans to pack up what she would take with her. There was so little she wanted, for it all reminded her of Julian.

The tall case clock in the downstairs hall chimed twice; darkness blanketed the house and all was still and quiet. A noise woke her, and Eleanor rolled over, blinking exhausted sleep from her eyes.

"Aubert? Is that you?" No one answered. She hadn't really expected him to stay; he rarely did. Where did he live? she wondered. He'd never said, and her one attempt to find out had been met with savage reprisal, a night she hadn't forgotten. Her entire body ached from tonight's time with him, his appetites demanding more and more violence until she felt ravaged and unsettled. He didn't care that he hurt her, that he left marks on her soft white skin, red weals that were slow to heal. Damn him. As soon as this was over, and Julian properly put away and his whore hanged or deported, she'd get rid of Fortier. He was a liability. He drank too much, gambled too much, said too much—just tonight she'd told him that he was depraved, and he'd only laughed. But there had been a look in his eyes when he took her to bed that made her regret her angry words soon enough.

Groaning slightly, she sat up, groggy with sleep, fiercely glad he was gone. He frightened her. One day he'd go too far, and might do irreparable damage to her, or even kill her. No, soon she would think of a way to get rid of him. He'd almost served his usefulness.

Sliding from the bed, her bare toes curled up from the chill boards. A chamber pot should be close, if that silly girl hadn't forgotten it again. If she had, she'd be sorry soon enough! Now, where was her robe? It should be close at hand; she'd put it over the end of the bed, but Aubert was so rough that the sheets were nearly on the floor. Fumbling in the dark with only the faint glow of the low fire providing any light, she finally found her robe in a wad on the floor.

When she stood up to put it on, something cool whispered over her bare back, like a gust of wind. Whirling around, she cried out sharply, "Who's there? Who is it?"

There was no reply and she thought she must be just nervous. She'd let Aubert get to her, with his thinly veiled threats, his vicious retaliation in the form of sex that was more pain than pleasure. Shivering, she turned the robe, searching for the sleeves, and ended up throwing it about her shoulders to cross to the fire. A few thrusts with the iron poker, and it flared enough to catch more coals ablaze, shedding light and warmth.

It was so cold yet, icy winds rattling windowpanes. Italy was lovely this time of year, with sun and blooming flowers . . . soon she'd be there again, once she had Julian's money. Then, not even those vicious old tabbies at Almack's could cut her, for she'd be far away from their wagging tongues and disapproving sniffs. Damn them.

As she rose to her feet, she felt another breath of cold air, as if a window had been left up or as if—as if someone was behind her. Alarm shot through her as firelight picked out a shadow outlined against the scant light coming through the window.

"Who—"

Something struck her on the side of her head, like a man's fist, and she reeled backward, slamming half against the fireplace, her robe sliding from her shoulders to puddle on the floor as she staggered to maintain her balance. Dazed, she flung out an arm, and encountered a man's chest beneath her flailing hand. Aubert?

She must have said it aloud; knuckles crashed into her lips. The salty taste of blood filled her mouth. She moaned. Why would he beat her like this? He never touched her face, always kept the bruises and marks hidden below her garments. "Badges of passion," he'd called them, but the novelty of his passion had faded more quickly than the bruises.

Yet another blow caught her other cheek, sending her to the floor. She began to crawl away, desperate to escape his punishing blows, but he followed her, straddling her bare back, his hands tangled in her hair to jerk her head up. Oh God, what was he doing? Why was he hurting her like this? She tried to tell him that she'd never tell, that she loved his touch, but the words came out mushy and garbled, disjointed sentences that sounded strange above the roaring in her ears.

Then his hands moved to her throat, circled it, fingers tightening like iron bands to cut off her air. Panic set in and she began to struggle violently, nearly dislodging him from her back so that he had to catch his balance. Stumbling, he righted himself and his hands grew even tighter.

"Faithless bitch," a low, sobbing voice grated in her ear, "you deserve to die!"

As the fingers tightened, lights exploded in front of her eyes and a sense of doom and despair swallowed her up in black, black shrouds, until there was nothing else.

CHAPTER 19

Laura nodded encouragement at Becky. "That's the last one. Now you can rest."

"Yes, miss." Becky's face reflected her unhappiness as she tugged the straps tighter on the wooden chest holding Laura's clothes. "Must ye go?"

"I'm afraid so, Becky. But Miss Carteret has agreed to give you employment, and she's quite kind. You'll like being in her household, I'm sure."

"Yes, miss." Becky stood up, dusting her hands off on the apron pinned to her dress. "Ye were kind to ask me to go with ye, miss. If I weren't afeard of water and ships—I'd like to see America, I would."

"That's quite all right, Becky. I understand, truly I do. It's rather a long voyage, and the seas can be very rough. Once I reach Virginia, I'll find a new maid. I'm leaving in such a hurry, and time is so short—but there, don't cry or you'll have me weeping as well!"

"Oh miss, it's just that no one has ever been so good to me as ye've been, taking me in like ye did, when I were so unhappy havin' to deal with Cook at his lordship's . . . I can't bear to see ye leave England!"

Laura fought back her own tears, determined not to surrender to emotion. Not now, not when she was so near the edge of yielding to complete misery. Instead, she said firmly, "It's for the best, though I'll miss you dreadfully. And I didn't 'take you in,' Becky, you work hard."

"Yes, miss." Becky sniffed audibly, and wiped her streaming eyes with the hem of her apron. "If ye say so, miss."

"I do say so. You're very industrious, and I daresay that one day I'll hear that you're the ladies' maid to a duchess, or even housekeeper at some great estate. You're quick and bright, and getting quite pretty. Even Charlton notices you when he delivers messages or . . . or supplies."

There would be no more messages, not from Lockwood, and the footman's visits had been few of late. But she wouldn't think of that, wouldn't think of the earl at all if she could keep from it, would concentrate only on what she had to do. If she dwelled on Julian, she'd dissolve into tears and regret.

Blushing, Becky ducked her head and mumbled that she thought Charlton very handsome, then peeked up at Laura through her lashes. "Miss, would ye take it amiss if I were ter tell ye something?"

"Of course not, Becky, what is it?" Laura moved to the small fire in the bedroom grate, lit to chase away the chill and gloom of the rainy day.

"Charlton says that his lordship is in a dreadful tear since he came back from the country, not like hisself at all. Charlton says, as how his lordship misses ye most turrible, that even stuffy old Cranford is near despairing at the earl's temper. Charlton says he's got a bit of a rest since the earl's left London on some errand, and Malcolm says as how no one's to say yer name ever again. Says it puts the earl right off, it does. Charlton says that's 'cause the earl is in love with ye."

Laura rested her forehead against the cool shelf of the mantel and closed her eyes. Oh, if only it were true! If it were true, he'd not be letting her leave, would want her with him no matter what the gossips said, despite all the vicious rumors. They'd fight it together instead of surrender so easily. Oh, if only it were true. . . .

She must have said it aloud, for Becky stepped forward, her tone earnest. "But it's true, miss, it truly is! Charlton allus tells me what goes on when he comes."

"Well, if it's true, it's not helping either one of us." Straightening, Laura turned to face her little maid, smiling faintly at Becky's wide brown eyes full of hope. "I leave tomorrow morning on the *Persephone*. A rather prophetic name for a ship, I think."

Indeed, it seemed fated. She'd thought of herself as Persephone trapped in the underworld by accepting Julian's proposition, and found instead that she was trapped by her own desires. If it weren't so tragic, she could acknowledge the irony of her situation.

"I still wish ye wouldn't go, miss," Becky said with a heavy sigh. "Ye'll be missed here."

"As I will miss all of you. Enough of this now, or we'll grow too maudlin to continue our work. There's still much to be done before I embark on my voyage, and very little time left. I'm expecting Celia to come around shortly for our farewells, so do be cheerful when she arrives or we shall all be in a dreadful state. Come along, now. Let's put these things with yours to take with you to your next post, shall we?"

Becky brightened, and she gazed at the stack of warm pelisses, India shawls, and French muslin gowns Laura had given her. Warm stockings of knit cotton and wool were included, and she lifted a pair almost reverently, smiling with delight.

"Ye're too good to me, miss."

"Not at all. You'll need good clothing for your day off. You can wear the blue-striped muslin with white bodice to visit your mum. It should impress her greatly."

Fingering an India shawl of worsted, Becky said hesitantly, "Would ye mind very much if I was to give me mum a warm shawl, miss? She gets so cold these days."

"They're your things to do with as you wish," Laura said gently. "I think it would be quite generous of you. Oh, I believe I hear Celia . . . do go and let her in, Becky."

A sharp rap on the door sounded below, and Becky went at once to greet Celia while Laura put a nightgown into the valise she'd saved until last. Her silver-backed hairbrush and mirror would go in this, kept close to her for safety's sake. The brush and mirror had been her grandmother's, and were very dear to her. She'd saved them all this time, even through dire need, and now they would be returning to Virginia with her.

Straightening, she looked around the cozy bedchamber, tried not to recall nights spent in the wide bed with Julian, tried instead to think of springtime in Virginia, with lovely buttercups in wide green fields, and the warm sun shining down on prim white houses and towns with wide streets. She shut her eyes tightly, but images of Julian bled into visions of green Virginia fields. It was no use. Only time would ease the pain, and nothing would ever ease the memories.

She left her bedchamber and started down the stairs, meeting Becky halfway. The girl blocked her descent, eyes wide with fright.

"Miss?"

"Yes, Becky, whatever is it that has you looking so—oh, it's not Lady Lockwood here again, is it?"

"No, miss—it's . . . it's the police!"

Police? Laura looked up and past the little maid, and saw a man standing at the foot of the stairs looking up at her with a scowl on his face.

"Come down here, if you please, Miss Lancaster. I'm most curious to know why you think Lady Lockwood would be comin' here to visit you again."

"Newgate!" Celia stared in horror at the weeping maid. "When?"

"Not an hour ago, miss. Oh, it were awful . . . they took 'er away, they did, barely let 'er get a warm cloak to take with 'er—she said I was to tell you straightaway, miss, that you'd know what to do."

"Yes. Stop that sniveling now, and tell me what was said—*exactly* what was said!"

Hiccupping, Becky scraped the heels of her hands over her cheeks and caught her breath. "The officer said as how she had no proper explanation for where she was last night, and that she was already known to be the earl's mistress. And 'e said as how with all the talk goin' about, that she was the likely suspect, especially since she planned to leave England tomorrow—"

"For heaven's sake, girl! *Why* did they arrest her? Treason?"

Staring up at her, Becky gulped. "Murder, miss. They say she killed Lady Lockwood."

"Good God." Sagging, Celia plopped down on the settee and stared blankly at the fire for a long moment. Laura, arrested for murdering Lady Lockwood. Oh, it looked so bad. She had to think what to do—she'd go to see her at once, of course, and enlist the services of a barrister to defend her, but the police were known to be overly enthusiastic at times, and more than willing to arrest the first likely suspect. They got paid handsomely for convictions, and weren't above lying to a magistrate to ensure their prompt payment.

"What of the earl?" she asked, turning to look at Becky again. "Has he been notified?"

"He's gone to the country. There's no one to 'elp 'er, miss, no one but you!"

As the maid collapsed into weeping again, Celia thought frantically. She'd take Laura money to pay the warden for better lodgings in prison, but she couldn't get her out. Belgrave might help—no. Faraday. He would help. He already liked Laura, and he'd do it. If the earl was out of town, then he hadn't . . . no, of course he wouldn't have killed his wife. Would he?

Never mind. That wasn't her task. She had to help Laura, and she had to work swiftly, or she may well end up just as dead as Lady Lockwood. First—she would enlist the help of Randal, Lord Faraday.

"Do as I tell you," she instructed the maid, rising determinedly to her feet, "and tell *no one* anything about Laura, do you understand?"

"Yes, miss." Becky gulped. "What must I do to 'elp?"

"Get her warmest cloak and gowns, two of them, plus heavy stockings and boots. Also, I'll need food for her. An entire basket of it. Wine, cheese, meat—whatever you have here."

"Will she need it all, miss?"

"Not if we're fortunate. It's to bribe the wardens. Hurry now. She'll get short shrift indeed if they think she has no one to come to her aid."

Soon, Celia had warm clothes and a heavy basket tucked into Belgrave's tilbury, and was on her way to Faraday's town house. She hoped he was in residence, as it was still afternoon and a young buck of the town rarely left home this early. Unless he was in Hyde Park, impressing the ladies, but more usually other young bucks, with his horsemanship. An idle life, and wasteful.

Luck was with her, for Faraday's butler looked down his long nose at her and informed her that his lordship could not be disturbed. Ignoring him, Celia brushed past, startling the man.

"Inform the viscount that this is a matter of extreme urgency concerning his brother, and be quick about it," she said sharply, and the butler hesitated briefly before inclining his head and moving up the staircase at a speed that matched a snail's pace. Celia wanted to scream at him, but had already presumed too much. Servants, especially butlers, could be more haughty than any lord ever considered being. So she waited, standing in the entrance hall without even the courtesy of being shown to a parlor, and in a moment, Norcliff came down the stairs to greet her.

"Miss Carteret. I'm surprised to see you here. What—"

"May we speak in privacy, my lord?" Celia shot a narrow glance at the disapproving butler who hovered behind the viscount. "I'm afraid I have dire news."

The smile that had curled his mouth disappeared immediately. "This way, if you please."

When they were in the parlor with the door closed behind

them, Celia said without preamble, "Laura Lancaster has been arrested for the murder of Lady Lockwood."

Staring at her, he blinked in surprise, but said nothing for a moment. Still silent, he moved to a small sideboard and took up a decanter, splashing brandy into two crystal goblets. He came to her and held one out, and she took it gratefully, glad for the liquid courage.

"What do I need to do?" he asked, and she arched a brow at his swift comprehension.

"Get her out of Newgate. That will take some time. I have supplies for her. You'll need to speak with a magistrate and barrister and see what can be done to free her. It will take someone with influence."

"Does Julian know?"

"Not to my knowledge. He's said to be out of the city at the moment. If we wait until his return—I suppose I don't have to tell you about conditions at Newgate."

Faraday grimaced. "No, you don't. I've heard Elizabeth Fry's cries for prison reform. She paints a vivid picture of deplorable conditions. If she weren't wife to a prominent banker, she'd no doubt be ignored, but she has the Lord Mayor's ear."

"Then we shall hope someone of your position and influence will have even more effect upon the Old Bailey magistrates. Hurry, my lord. We've no time to lose."

Nodding grimly, the viscount looked suddenly older. "I'll not fail Miss Lancaster. Nor my brother. Do you have enough coin to bribe the gaolers for better conditions?"

"Yes." When she set down her brandy and turned toward the door, he came to her and put a hand on her arm, snaring her instant attention. Her skin tingled where he touched, his fingers burning into her though his grip was not hard. Hazel eyes stared at her intently from beneath a thick brush of dark lashes, and she noted distractedly that his eyebrows were much darker than his blond hair. His voice was low, husky.

"Do you think she did it?"

"No. Laura would never have hurt her."

He released her arm, nodding. They stood for a moment, staring at each other, measuring the other's intentions. The air crackled with tension. Then he broke it, taking a step back and away from her.

"You'd best hurry, Miss Carteret. I'll do the same."

Safely back in her carriage, it occurred to Celia that Lord Faraday had not asked how his sister-in-law died. Nor had he expressed shock or regret. It seemed that Lady Lockwood would not leave much sorrow in her passing.

Noise reverberated off dank stone walls; a heavy stench layered the air. Screeching voices of raddled prostitutes, the shrieks of iron gratings, the constant babble of catcalls and laughter beat against Laura's ears. She huddled in a corner, knees drawn up to her chest, face pressed to her skirts as she tried to blend into the shadows and remain unnoticed. Without coin to pay, she'd been shoved into a huge, damp, cold chamber with over two dozen other women and children. Babies cried, toddlers wailed, and older children sat stoic and huge-eyed beside their mothers. The smell of gin and offal was ripe.

Laura had no illusions about her fate. Sessions met once a month, and the prosecution was called upon to present its case, while the accused must plead for a hearing before the judge. There were times it was denied, and the accused went to the gallows or deportation ships without being given a chance for a defense. People were hung for stealing; she'd find no mercy for charges of murder.

Despair sat like a stone in the pit of her stomach. Bars of murky light striped the filthy floor and illuminated the toes of her shoes. She'd nearly lost them when a particularly noisome gaoler shoved her rudely, demanding she pay for the privilege of residing in the Female Quarter. Pearl hairpins had been given in place of the shoes, quickly relinquished and grudgingly accepted. Everything here had a price. If she'd given up her shoes, she might have purchased some bedding, but as she had no intention of sleeping and chance being robbed for her clothing, she'd been lucky enough to find an unoccupied corner in which to hide. Nearby, a half-naked woman with a babe at her breast leaned against the wall, staring blankly into space. The infant had cried weakly at first, but was silent now, and so still Laura feared it must have died. It lay limply in its mother's arms, a piece of cloth draped over the tiny form.

Sobs rose up in her throat, and she pushed them down, knowing that to surrender to it may lure trouble. Already, women cast narrow glances at her, greedily eying her muslin gown and long-sleeved pelisse. Others stood at the barred entrance to the cell, reaching arms through to pluck at the sleeves of those passing, clamoring for money, offering to trade bodies for comfort, or a bit more bread for them or their children. It was a nightmarish place. If she stayed too long, she'd go mad, she truly would.

Burrowing her face into the angle of her crossed arms, she tried to block out everything but the fierce hope Julian would come for her, that he'd appear at the bars and the doors would open and he'd say her name, and she'd stand up and walk out a free woman. She could almost hear him calling her. . . .

"Laura! Laura Lancaster, are you in here?"

It was so real, hope so strong, she lifted her head and looked up, almost expecting to see a tall, golden-haired man opening the cell doors. Of course, there was no handsome knight come to rescue her, only the quarrelsome rabble at the bars, women screeching and shoving one another, elbows and fists flying.

Then the door opened, and a burly gaoler cuffed several of the women aside, snarling at them to back away and let the lady through, and Laura's heart leaped when she recognized Celia. Springing to her feet, she surged forward, sliding a little on slimy straw as she pushed through the other prisoners to reach Celia.

"Oh, thank God you've come, thank God you're here, oh Celia . . . Celia. . . . " She knew she was babbling but couldn't stop, clinging to her friend tenaciously. "I don't know what to do or if I can stand this much longer."

"I know, ducks. Come along, now. I have you your own cell. I know. It's not freedom, but at least it's better than this. It took quite a bit of talking—not to mention coin—but at least you'll not have to worry about having your throat slit while you sleep. Hurry, ducks, before that bouncer raises the price again. He's a greedy sod—fah, it smells like a bog house in here. Let's hope your cell is above ground."

While it wasn't exactly comfortable, her new cell was at least private, with a high barred window set into the wall. Celia had a footman bring in a heavy basket, grumbling about the good wine being confiscated by the greedy gaoler as she put out cold chicken, some cheese, and bread.

"I brought bedding for you, too, a few blankets that should be lice-free, and some coins so you can bribe the wardens if need be. Lord Faraday is doing what he can to see the charges dismissed, but you know how the police are. It's much easier to convict the most likely person and not search for the true culprit. Oh, I brought scents for you, and some soap to help wash away the stench, but I doubt you'll get a tub and hot water in here. You'll just have to do the best you can with that bucket."

Laura managed a smile, though she couldn't stop shivering. Celia stared at her, catching her lower lip between her teeth, and neither of them voiced their real fears. It was too possible.

"When Lord Lockwood returns from the country, he'll be able to convince them you're innocent, ducks," Celia said at last, and they both nodded. It was the only hope she had.

But when Celia was gone and she was alone, save for the muffled shrieks and shouts from other prisoners, Laura couldn't help but wonder if he'd come for her. Would he think her guilty of killing his wife?

Perching on the edge of the straw-filled mattress, she hugged her knees to her chest and squeezed her eyes tightly shut, praying that he'd not abandon her, that whatever else, he'd not think her a murderer. Whoever had killed Lady Lockwood may very well have killed her chances of ever knowing if Julian could have loved her.

"What do you mean?" Julian stared at Cranford, who met his gaze with some concern. "I was only out of London for two days, and now this? I don't believe it. It doesn't seem possible. Are you certain that's what they said? "

"Quite certain, my lord. The authorities are below now, and they wish to speak with you."

Slowly wiping away soap residue from his jaw, Julian braced his hands on the edges of the washstand and breathed deeply. "Tell them I'll be right down."

"Yes, my lord." Cranford hesitated. "May I offer my condolences?"

"Condolences for my loss?" Julian's mouth twisted wryly. "Sadly, Eleanor's death is no loss to me at all, Cranford. As you well know."

"My condolences were for your other loss, my lord."

"Other loss?"

Cranford arched a brow. "The rather impetuous, perpetually hungry young lady who was here so briefly a few months ago. I was given to understand that she is leaving the country."

"Yes." Julian slid his arms into the coat Cranford held out for him, frowning. "As soon as I can arrange it. I've instructed Malcolm to see to the details."

"Indeed, my lord. Now you should be quite content."

"What do you mean by that?"

"Only that you'll have it as you always said you wished, your life empty of all annoying females." Cranford's expression was carefully blank as always, but his tone held subtle irony.

"Devil take you, Cranford. You know that's not what I want now."

"Yes, my lord, *I* know that, but I wasn't certain you did."

Before Julian could offer a sharp retort, the elderly servant withdrew, closing the door behind him. Curse him, he always seemed to have the last word these days.

Now he must go and convince the authorities he was saddened by his wife's death, for no matter how she was viewed in life, death always lent a certain respectability to the recently departed. There would, no doubt, be great speculation about Eleanor's death, and he realized he hadn't even asked Cranford how she'd died. Was it accident or murder? Whichever it was, there would be an inquest. And more talk, more gossip, more rumors. It was a good thing Laura would soon be gone. Nothing could touch her then.

Two police officers were accompanied by a gentleman he recognized from his efforts to gain reform in the justice system. Patrick Colquhoun inclined his head gravely. "Good morning, my lord."

"Not so very good for my wife, I understand. Can you tell me what happened?" Gesturing to a chair before the parlor fire, he took a seat opposite Colquhoun.

"Constables are still investigating, my lord. It seems that she sustained a broken neck."

"A fall?"

"No, my lord. There are . . . marks around her neck that indicate this was deliberate."

Julian stared at him. That Colquhoun had troubled to accompany the police officers here indicated trouble; there had been much talk lately of "blood money" given to police for arrests that resulted in convictions, especially on capital charges. The presiding magistrate was authorized to give a parliamentary reward of forty pounds, a veritable fortune to most underpaid officers. It tempted some to deliberate perjury.

"I see," Julian said calmly. "It's murder, then."

"I'm afraid so, my lord. John Townsend asked me to accompany these officers to speak with you. We thought it best to question you here rather than at Queen Square. I trust that is satisfactory."

"Yes, of course." Julian nodded. Townsend had nearly thirty-five years experience with the Bow Street Runners, though the last few years had been spent squiring the Regent to Brighton or on jaunts through the city. Still, the man kept his hand in matters of the law, working often for the Bank of England and wealthy individual prosecutors. If he'd sent Colquhoun, the matter was dangerous.

The police officers asked the usual questions, where he'd been last night, who could verify he'd been at home besides his servants, and if he knew anyone who might have killed his wife.

"There are numerous candidates, I believe," he said dryly, "for Eleanor was not known for her docile nature."

John Lavendar, one of the officers, looked up at him. "You said you had business in Kent, and did not return until this morning—is that correct, my lord?"

"It is."

"How did your brother, Lord Faraday, get on with your late wife?"

Julian paused. Dammit. Had they somehow got wind of Randal's visit to Eleanor? That'd hardly look good, unless Randal could verify his own whereabouts after leaving him.

"Lord Faraday rarely saw her, I understand, though if Lady Lockwood ever needed him, I'm sure he'd do what he could for her." It bordered on the truth. And it satisfied the officer for the moment, though he had the look of a man who'd seen far too much and knew human nature too well.

By the time they left, Julian had the distinct impression that he was a suspect. He stood for a long moment, staring at the fire, discarding several options for action before finally giving in to the inevitable. As difficult as it would be to see her again, he had to personally warn Laura and get her on the next ship leaving England. It had been important before; now it was imperative.

* * *

"Silly chit, stop that wailing and tell me where your mistress has gone!" Julian's patience faded swiftly, and he had to use great restraint to keep from giving the sobbing little maid a good shaking. She was near incoherent.

"Gone . . . bobbies . . . oh, it were awful, my lord." She hiccupped, and dragged the hem of her apron across her wet face. "They came and got 'er, milord, police dragged 'er right out o' the house without a by your leave!"

Christ. He was too late.

"When?" he demanded tersely. "When did they come for her?"

"Gone two days now, m'lord. Took 'er right to Newgate, they did. . . ."

Two days in Newgate. Dear God. Laura, incarcerated with prostitutes, thieves, murderers, and worse. . . .

CHAPTER 20

"We have letters of proof, my lord." The prosecutor gazed at Julian speculatively, as if trying to decide if he was guilty of treason, as rumor had it. He held up a sheaf of papers. "These came into our possession, letters written to a Madame Fleurette D'Arcy, who happens to be the mistress of General Laborteaux, consul to Napoleon. I believe they are written in code, and we've not yet been able to decipher all of it, but we will."

Julian gazed at the frog-faced little man, whose appearance may be ridiculous, but he had a shrewd mind and the reputation of being tenacious. He'd best be careful in how he conducted himself, or he could endanger Laura.

"How do you know Miss Lancaster wrote them?"

"They have all been sealed with the same unusual seal. We found it in her desk, hidden in a pigeon-hole. It's a most unusual seal, very distinctive. Apparently, your wife was able to intercept these letters, and Miss Lancaster killed her for it."

"It was my understanding my wife was strangled. Do you think Miss Lancaster capable of overpowering Lady Lockwood?"

Shadwell frowned. "Your wife was a small woman. It might be difficult, but hardly impossible, my lord."

"This entire situation is preposterous. Miss Lancaster would do no such thing."

"Miss Lancaster had purchased passage on the *Persephone* right after Lady Lockwood was killed. Fleeing justice is hardly the action of an innocent woman."

Raking a hand through his hair, exasperated and alarmed, Julian managed to say calmly, "I sent my secretary to purchase her passage back to America, her home."

"Really." Shadwell's heavy-lidded eyes widened a little. "Yet your secretary did not do so. Miss Lancaster's footman purchased passage at her direction. You have been duped, my lord."

Frowning, Julian bit back a reply. No, it was impossible. He'd sent Malcolm to the purser to buy passage for her before he'd left London. And he'd only left the city to keep from yielding to the temptation to stop her departure.

Trying another tactic, he said reasonably, "How would my wife have intercepted letters from Miss Lancaster? They were hardly friends. One does not usually keep company with the wife of one's protector, Mr. Shadwell."

"Yes, that's quite true, but often these women have more than one protector. Apparently, Miss Lancaster was no exception. We have it on good authority that a former acquaintance of both Miss Lancaster and her mother is from Paris and has been seen visiting your wife—and your mistress. We're interrogating him as well. He must know something about these letters. Perhaps he informed your wife of his suspicions."

"And so Eleanor took it upon herself to investigate, perhaps confront Miss Lancaster? I hardly think so," he said dryly. "Her style would be to start rumors, which she did, that I passed on state secrets to my mistress. I'm sure she was hoping I would be arrested for treason."

Shadwell coughed, a maneuver that didn't fool Julian for a moment. His mouth tightened. "Do you intend to arrest me for treason, Mr. Shadwell?"

Rather blandly, the prosecutor demurred, "No, indeed, my lord. From what we've been able to determine, any information contained in those letters is old and useless. No doubt culled from old papers of yours. It's not as if you've been privy to matters of military movement of late, or called into the war council, so there was very little for Miss Lancaster to glean from your person. Only from your desk, perhaps."

"Do you think me a fool, Shadwell?" Julian arched a brow, leaning forward with both palms braced on the man's cluttered desk, until his face was only inches from his, and said with soft menace, "Any attempt to charge Miss Lancaster with treason against England is futile. She's not an English citizen. Nor would she be fool enough to sell worthless secrets to the French. You are obviously seeking a motive for her arrest, when it would serve your cause better to find the real murderer of my wife."

"A disgruntled Colonial seeking vengeance in the form of espionage is hardly futile cause, my lord," Shadwell said tightly. "There's no need to search for your wife's murderer when we have her in Newgate at this very moment. And we have a witness against her, prepared to swear that she's involved in the selling of information to the French."

"Rubbish! Who is your witness?"

"Aubert Fortier."

Julian leaned back against the cold stone wall, arms folded over his chest, as the police set about questioning Fortier. He'd demanded to be present, and to his surprise, Shadwell agreed. An officer leaned forward, punching his finger in Fortier's face.

"All right, mate, tell us how you know Miss Lancaster."

"Certainly." Fortier slid a glance toward Julian, a mocking smile tugging up one corner of his mouth. "We were close acquaintances in Paris. Her mother was my father's mistress for some time. Laura and I became quite—close, as well."

"She was your—"

"*Petite amie,* yes," Aubert said smoothly. "A lovely girl. How could one not fall in love with her a little bit, heh?"

"But you parted company and Miss Lancaster came to England."

"Alas, yes, it is true. A small misunderstanding, and she fled. A lover's quarrel, no more, but she has always been—impetuous."

Anger built up in Julian at the man's lies. He claimed to have been her lover, when Julian knew he'd been her first. If Fortier lied about that, then his entire tale was nothing more than a lie.

"So when you met her again here? Did she send for you?" the officer continued.

"No, I came for a visit, and chanced upon her at a playhouse where she was an actress. I did not know then that she had become Lord Lockwood's mistress. I soon discovered it, however, after we had—renewed—our acquaintance. Of course, I broke it off with her as soon as I knew, but by then, I'd also learned of her plan to get rid of the earl's wife. She thought once the lady was out of the way, she could wed the earl, you see. She intended to incriminate her with letters she'd written to her mother. I informed Lady Lockwood of this diabolical plot against her, and we decided to first secure the proof necessary, then bring it to the authorities. Apparently, Laura—Miss Lancaster—learned of our plan and killed poor Lady Lockwood. A dreadful thing, sir, a most dreadful thing."

"Indeed, sir, it is." Shadwell looked over at Julian with a gleam of triumph in his eyes, and a smile stretching his mouth.

As the police officer asked for details of how they'd secured the letters, Julian watched Fortier, convinced of his guilt. It was likely that he'd killed Eleanor, that he'd been her latest lover and probably strangled her in a fit of rage. Eleanor had a way of driving a man to the brink. He knew that well enough. But the prosecutor obviously had his mind made up about Laura's guilt. Unless he could prove Fortier was lying, there was little hope for her.

* * *

Laura stared at the broken seals in bewilderment. "These aren't mine. I mean, this is not my writing, and my seal is not like this at all. It's very simple, one that is plain, not elaborate like this one. How would I know any of these things? Troop movements? Wellington's position?"

"That is what they're claiming I told you," Julian said dryly, and she looked up at him with horror. "Your former acquaintance, Fortier, claims also that you've kept in contact with your mother, and that you swore him to silence, even paid him not to betray you. Yes, it looks very bad for you, I'm afraid."

"And—you? Will you be arrested?"

Rubbing a hand across his jaw, Julian grimaced. "Since the information is old and not very important, it's supposed that you must have gone through my old papers. I've been exonerated."

"I see." She twisted her hands together. "I'm glad for that."

"Laura . . . sweeting. Tell me again about Eleanor's visit to you right before her death."

"Oh, I've told you everything—we didn't quarrel, really, she just told me that . . . that I should stop sending people to annoy her, and that you tired easily of a woman after the chase ended, and that . . . that you'd be accused of treason soon and I'd best look to myself."

"Did she do anything odd while there, perhaps, or threaten you?"

Laura shook her head. "No. Oh, Becky did say she'd stolen something from my desk, but the only thing missing was my seal."

"Your seal?"

"Yes, the small, plain one I used to seal letters. I don't know why she took it, when they sell them quite inexpensively at any stationer's shop."

"Laura, the police found a seal in your desk. An elaborate one used on those letters."

She went very still. "Impossible. I never purchased anything like that."

"Perhaps Eleanor did. And perhaps she left it in your desk to incriminate you."

Lifting her eyes to his, she said a little breathlessly, "But how would we prove that?"

Julian rose to his feet. "I'll question her servants. By the way, who did you send to speak with her?"

"Me? I sent no one. I have no idea who she meant."

Rather grimly, Julian replied, "I think I do."

"My God—who?"

"My brother."

Julian found Celia Carteret visiting Randal, both of them looking far too cozy and familiar in the parlor when he arrived. His brow rose.

"I see you have company. Have I come at a bad time?"

Rising to his feet, Randal grinned. "Not at all, though I see your busy little mind is churning out all kinds of possibilities. We're just discussing alternatives for Laura's defense."

"Were you. Don't you think you've done enough harm?"

Randal's grin vanished. He straightened, eyes narrowing slightly. "Harm? What are you talking about?"

"Your visit to Eleanor. She went to Laura to complain, and now it looks very bad for her. The police think they discussed this ridiculous espionage contrivance Eleanor concocted."

Celia Carteret cleared her throat. "My lord, I fear that I may have also caused problems."

"Did you visit Eleanor as well?" he asked dryly, and she shook her head.

"No, but I sent a—friend of mine."

"Good God." He crossed to the small table bearing a cut-crystal decanter and glasses, and poured himself a generous amount of sherry before asking, "Who?"

"Rex Pentley."

Both brows shot up at her reply. "Pentley—the card sharp?"

"Rex is a man of many talents. Ah, perhaps I should tell you a few things, my lord. I'm willing to wager that the police are unaware Aubert Fortier tried to blackmail Laura. Am I right?"

"Go on," he said, fingers tightening on crystal, his eyes narrowing.

"He came to her one night after the play ended, and threatened to tell about her mother's situation if she didn't pay him. Of course, she didn't have the amount he wanted, so she—she sold a necklace in order to buy time. She didn't know what to do, my lord. She didn't want you to know about her mother, that she's a courtesan, for fear you'd think less of her. I tried to tell her that it wouldn't matter to you, but Laura was just so upset. Anyway, after we left Belgrave's fête in the country and returned to London, I enlisted Rex's aid to make Fortier go away."

"Did you." Julian walked across the room to the fire, turning with his back to it to lean against the mantel and regard Celia coolly. "And am I to understand that Pentley succeeded?"

"Yes, well—" Celia slid a glance toward Randal and sucked in a deep breath before saying softly, "apparently, he succeeded in frightening him away from Laura, but not Lady Lockwood. I took it upon myself to have Rex go to your wife to learn what he could about the rumors she'd started. When he arrived, he saw your brother just leaving, but so did Fortier. He went into the house and didn't stay long, and when he came out, Rex went to talk to her. Fortier had struck her, for she had the mark still upon her face. They were lovers as well as conspirators, my lord."

"I'm not surprised." He took a sip of sherry, frowning. "What did Pentley learn from her? Anything of use?"

"Lady Lockwood denied any involvement, but said she had proof Laura communicated with her mother. She said she'd use it when she pleased, and that . . . that after you were executed for treason, she intended to leave England for good. She'd have your money then—though, of course, the title and estates would go to your brother if they weren't confiscated by the Crown."

Staring in astonishment, Julian said, "And how did she think she'd manage to get money? I hardly think the Bank of England would allow her to draw upon my accounts without my express permission, even—or especially—if I were in prison."

"Rex wasn't certain, but he thought perhaps that Fortier was practiced at copying your handwriting, and intended to forge bank drafts and letters with your signature and seal."

"Good God." Julian shook his head. "Both of them are mad. Or were—so tell me, this Rex Pentley, would he be willing to testify on Laura's behalf?"

"Indeed he would, my lord." She smiled. "Indeed he would."

The view from her cell was bleak. Laura stood at the window and peered out, desperate for a glimpse of sunlight and clouds, anything but the desolate gray walls of her prison. She had to stretch to her toes atop her bunk to see, fingers digging into cold stone or curling around iron bars for balance, but it was better than going mad. She felt she would at times, felt the world closing in around her as if the walls were narrowing, felt black despair settle like a death shroud. Hope had become buried under an avalanche of accusations, until they were piled so high against her she'd no defense left.

Someone had killed Lady Lockwood. While there were many who disliked her, no one but Laura had sufficient reason to kill her, the prosecutor argued, and the damning evidence of those awful letters was proof. That they'd not been posted didn't seem to matter. They'd been written, and signed with her name, a seal found in her own desk affixed to them. Of course she'd claim it wasn't her seal—any murderer would do so.

Tiring at last of the strain of standing on her toes to peer out, Laura sank back to the cold comfort of her bunk. Dear Celia, so faithful in providing for her, and Julian—his face when she'd confessed to knowing Aubert Fortier had not changed expression, but she knew he must wonder. How could he not? She should have told him. She should have told him all months before, but it'd seemed as if Fortier had given up on her and gone away. She should have known better. Oh yes, she should have known he'd not go quietly, that he'd come back to haunt her. One could never escape one's past, it seemed.

How ironic that she'd considered writing her mother yet not done so, and was convicted of it now. Did Maman know of her troubles? Would she even care? They'd quarreled so heatedly about Aubert, and she'd left without farewells. Perhaps she'd write her one last letter. It could be delivered after . . . oh God, she couldn't bear to think of it!

The day before, there had been an execution. She'd seen it out her window, horrified at the sight, and immediately flung herself to her cot and pulled a pillow over her ears to blot out the sounds, though nothing could entirely obliterate her brief glimpse of men with muslin over their heads and faces, a hangman's noose around each neck. Bolts were drawn, the trapdoor fell open, the collective gasp of the watching crowd—and then the strange gurgles and gasps that followed, the straining creak of the ropes in that sudden, awful silence.

She couldn't think of that anymore or she'd go mad. They'd find her gibbering in her cell, wild-eyed and unkempt. Oh God . . . what was going to become of her?

Sir John Silvester, Recorder of London and an Old Bailey judge of considerable authority and influence, was to hear evidence against her produced by Mr. Shadwell. He'd spent a dozen years on the bench, and was unlikely to take at face value her protestations of innocence. Yet Sir John was her only hope. Would he even hear a defense from her? Julian had hired a barrister for her, but the man seemed hesitant, at least to her, quoting laws and penal codes, pompous in his white wig and robes, looking to her more like a judge than a barrister for her defense. Still, Julian said Mr. Wilberforce was very good.

Light slanted sharply through the bars of her window, heralding the approach of dusk. Days were longer now, with April nigh. It would be warmer soon. When summer came, the days would be soft, the nights cool, and she could almost see the grass growing taller in the fields that surrounded Shadowhurst, in the small copse that held the cottage where she'd spent her last hours of contentment with Julian. She had that memory to hold onto in the long, dark hours spent in this hell where no one ever slept, where screeches and cries could be heard all day and all night, chains clanking, and metal spoons rattling against bars, the moans and sobs of hopelessness echoing her own bleak despair.

"Here now, miss, come for me pay now, I have," a voice said from her cell door, and she looked up to see the gaoler peering at her with an avaricious grin. He fit a key into the lock and turned it with a loud metallic grate, then swung the door open to step inside. "It'll cost ye a guinea today."

"A guinea!" She stood up, irritated but wary. "You were paid only two days ago. Why do you think I have more now?"

Shrugging, he advanced into the cell, his eyes moving from the nearly depleted basket of food to her bedding, then to her. "It's the way o' things here. Ye pay for privilege o' lodging with us. And then ye pay for the privilege o' leavin' us, ye do."

"As you can see, I am still here, and you've been paid for my week's lodgings," Laura said coldly. "I've no coin left."

"No? Then ye'll no' be goin', I daresay."

For an instant, Laura's hope flared, then logic prevailed. The man was trying to trick her out of more money. In her week in this horrid place, she'd lost nearly everything to gaolers and wardens. They were a greedy lot, always with their hands out, demanding and usually receiving what they wanted. The alternatives were grim. She couldn't imagine what she would have suffered had she been left in the common area below.

Crossing her arms over her chest, Laura said calmly, "I'm expecting a visitor. When she arrives, I'll pay you then."

"Yer visitor is already here, only it's no 'she' that's come ta take ye out. It's a bleedin' swell, come with some squint-eyed bastard to demand yer freedom. It'll cost ye, and I won't wait fer it, no I won't, not and be beat out o' me just due."

Julian? Had he somehow found a way to gain her freedom? The *squint-eyed bastard* could only be her barrister, Mr. Wilberforce. Hope flared anew, and she didn't realize she'd been holding her breath until she heard Julian's familiar voice in the corridor outside. Breath left her lungs in a whoosh of air, and taut muscles went suddenly limp when he stepped into her cell and said, "You may come with me, Laura. You're free."

She took a step forward but her legs refused to obey her commands and she collapsed in a heap on the straw-littered stones, the world wheeling around her at such a dizzying speed she felt as if she were caught in a miller's wheel.

Free, free, free. . . .

CHAPTER 21

"Will she be all right?" Celia asked, meeting the physician just outside Laura's door. "How ill is she?"

"A bit of a fever is all. Common enough for those unfortunates incarcerated in Newgate. I daresay she's most fortunate not to have remained any longer than she did. So many don't survive in that cesspool." Large and portly, the doctor had a kind but weary face, and he smiled at Celia. "Your friend is much stronger than she looks, m'dear. I've given her something to make her rest. Be sure she has good food and plenty of sleep, and within a few days she should be quite herself again."

Glancing with relief toward Lord Lockwood and Randal, Celia managed a smile. "I'll tend her myself. I trust there will be no objections?"

Lockwood was stone-faced, but his brother looked as relieved as she felt and nodded. "It will be better for her, I should think. Unless you have objections, old boy?"

The earl, who had already strenuously voiced his objections to Laura being taken to his brother's house instead of his or even her own, only nodded woodenly. It was plain he didn't like not being in charge, but it would have complicated matters far too greatly if his mistress were to be taken to his house so soon after the earl's wife was murdered. There had been too much talk already, too many rumors, and it had been with the greatest of difficulty that Lockwood had been able to affect Laura's release.

If not for Rex Pentley, and his swearing to the magistrates that he'd witnessed Fortier at Lady Lockwood's house, and seen the marks upon her face that he'd caused, Laura might still be in prison. As it was, her release may only be temporary. The police were looking for Fortier, and, of course, he was expected to deny everything. Lockwood had hired a former Bow Street Runner to find Fortier and gather evidence against him. Pentley was convinced Fortier had killed the countess.

"I'll go sit with her," Celia said, and left the brothers in Randal's parlor to go upstairs and wait beside Laura's bed for her to wake. She didn't want her to wake in a strange place and be frightened, not after all she'd gone through. Laura would be safe here. Fortier would not dare come to the viscount's residence for any reason.

Letting herself into the darkened room where Laura slept, Celia moved a chair near the bed and sank down onto the tufted cushion. Wine-dark draperies hung over the bed, and the high mattress required a step stool to reach it; Laura lay in the middle, face a pale blur against the mane of her hair spread over a snowy pillow. Faint bluish circles looked like bruises under her eyes, and her lips were slightly parted, breathing deep and regular.

A clock on the mantel ticked softly, and a low fire burned in the grate. Rain beat against the windowpanes, a sudden storm springing up from the south. It was so quiet, the door left ajar so she could hear if anyone came to visit. She half-expected Rex to arrive, or even Belgrave, who had been quite supportive during these past weeks. Poor Charles. He wanted to avoid any undue gossip, and was anxious to remain distant so as not to cause problems at home with his wife. And, of course, the aristocracy closed ranks at a time like this, publicly mourning the loss of a countess while privately relieved that a quarrelsome, unsuitable member of their number could cause no more scandals. No, perhaps Belgrave wouldn't come after all. He'd not want to be connected in any way with this affair. She couldn't blame him.

There was a slight rustle behind her and she turned, smiling slightly when Faraday stuck his head into the room. "She still sleeping?"

"Yes. Where's the earl?"

"Gone."

That surprised her. "I'd not thought he'd leave yet, not until he sees her again."

Drawing near the bed, the viscount snagged a small chair and straddled it, resting his hands atop the chairback. "He has much to do yet, and I don't think he wanted to see her like this. He's devilish torn up about her."

"She'll be fine. As the doctor said, she's much stronger than she appears."

"It's not her health that he's so worried about, I think, as the rest of it. We were fortunate to find a magistrate sympathetic to our family. Sir John is fair enough, and trying to bring justice to London as well as rid the streets of crime."

"Is he." Her brow rose in amusement. "He's set himself quite a task. As long as he doesn't sentence Laura to hang, I'll be satisfied."

"Yes." Faraday rested his chin on his folded hands. He gazed at Laura, sleeping peacefully in the middle of the wide bed, and after a moment, said softly, "Julian will do what has to be done to keep her safe. Even if he has to send her away."

"Send her away?" Celia shot him a worried glance. "Will that be necessary now?"

"It's possible." He looked at her steadily for a long moment. "If Fortier isn't found, or if he refuses to tell the truth, then the prosecutor may insist that there are grounds enough to arrest Laura again for Eleanor's murder. If that happens, I think Julian plans to get her aboard a ship before she can be imprisoned."

Celia put a hand to her temple, frowning. Her head throbbed. She thought of Laura in that horrible cell, and shuddered. "Is he making the arrangements just in case?"

"I'm sure he will." Faraday looked troubled. "Julian rarely leaves anything to chance."

* * *

Silence pressed down on him like a heavy cloak, enveloping and smothering. Julian leaned back in his chair, staring across the shadowed study at the far wall, seeing nothing, aware of every trick of light. Lamps cast soft pools of light, muted and subtle, and the fire on the hearth gave off a leaping dance of yellow and orange shadows.

Several choices occurred to him. He could hope John Townsend's man found Fortier and convinced him to tell the truth, perhaps even confess to Eleanor's murder, or he could send Laura to the country, or he could even defy the courts and send her to America. Townsend relied on expert Bow Street Runners to get results, and the best option was probably to wait until Fortier could be run down. Then, of course, the police would interrogate him. What were the chances that he could question Fortier first? He had a feeling he'd be more successful in getting answers.

Drumming his fingers atop the desk, he tried to concentrate. Some small detail eluded him. What was it? There was something he needed to find out, or use . . . something Laura had said to him while still in prison. It was about the letters—no, the seal. That was it. She'd said she never used an elaborate seal, that her stamp was common, like those found in any stationer's. If that was so, why hadn't the police found it in her desk? The only seal they'd found was the silver stamp in an ornate L-shape.

L for Lancaster. L for—Lockwood. God, how could he have been so blind? Eleanor's seal! Of course. He should have seen it at once. She'd simply switched seals with Laura the day she'd come to visit her. That meant the seal belonging to Laura may very well be in Eleanor's desk. He could only hope that she hadn't thrown it away, that she'd taken it home with her.

Rising from behind his desk, he strode across the room to the bellpull and gave it a sharp tug. His mind raced. He had to talk to the police—no, the Bow Street Runner hired by Townsend to find the truth. That man would be able to go to Eleanor's home unremarked and look for the seal. Eleanor's family suspected Julian of being involved in her death since news of Laura's arrest had been made so public. Her father had arrived in London to see to his daughter's funeral, not at all amenable to any overtures from Eleanor's husband. Not that he blamed him. It was hardly the time to inform the old man that Eleanor had been a faithless wife.

He returned to his desk and drew out paper and a pen, then scribbled furiously and blotted and folded it, sealing it with his own seal pressed into the hot wax. Another L for Lockwood, this one plain and masculine, not fussy and flowery as Eleanor's—as the one she'd tried to pass off as Laura's.

"You rang for me, my lord?"

Looking up, Julian nodded. "Yes, Malcolm. Be so good as to see that this message goes to John Townsend. This must be kept private. It's vital. Is that clear?"

"Yes, my lord. Quite clear."

"Good man." He frowned. "Malcolm, are you all right?"

"Yes, my lord, perfectly well, thank you for asking."

Malcolm didn't look perfectly well. In fact, he looked quite ill, pale and thinner, his dark eyes sunk into his face as if he'd aged ten years in the space of a few days. Perhaps it was just that he hadn't paid much attention to his secretary lately, had not been home enough to do so since returning from the country. Still, if Malcolm didn't want to divulge any weakness, he'd not force him.

Handing him the letter, he said evenly, "See that this is delivered to John Townsend as soon as possible. I expect a reply."

"Yes, my lord. I'll take care of it personally."

"Excellent. And Malcolm—" When the secretary turned back to face him, he said, "You'd do well to get some rest. This has been a very exhausting time for all of us."

"Yes, my lord, I appreciate your concern, my lord." Malcolm

hesitated, then inclined his head respectfully and withdrew from the study, leaving Julian alone again.

He moved to the windows that looked out over Bruton Street, staring through drapes that hadn't been drawn, watching rain slide down windowpanes and run along the glazing in tiny, thin rivulets. It made a soft, hissing sound that sounded like a feminine whisper. If he closed his eyes, he could almost see Laura that day in the cottage, hear her soft laughter, her sultry whispers. Feel her arms around him, smell that sweet, delicate fragrance that always seemed to envelop her . . . he thought of roses, white buds like those she'd worn in her hair the first time he'd seen her at Mme. Devereaux's fête. Laura—his own white rose, pale and lovely and summer-sweet.

To save her, he had to give her up. It was the only solution, the only certainty, and the bitterness of it overwhelmed him. Even if her innocence were proven, she'd never be accepted in society. If nothing else, Eleanor's parents would see to that.

For himself, he didn't care, but he knew how cruel those of his station could be, the snubs and set-downs ruthless and devastating. He didn't want to expose her to that. Better to let her go back to America, to her beloved Virginia, than to subject her to scathing gossip. It had already taken so much from her. But this time, instead of sending her away without explanations, he'd go to her and tell her how he felt about her, tell her that he loved her enough to let her go, and that she'd always remain a beautiful memory to him.

This time, he wouldn't be such a bloody coward.

Laura woke slowly, blinking at the light coming through the windows across from her bed. How strange . . . her windows were at the side, not opposite . . . oh, but she wasn't even in her own bed but a huge, curtained affair, with heavy wine-red velvet drapes at the corners and overhead, tied back to the posts with braided ropes. She sat up abruptly, head swimming.

It all came rushing back, the horrible days in Newgate, her release, the physician . . . and now she was at Lord Faraday's house. Safe. Free. But not exonerated. Oh God.

Throwing back the covers, she put her legs over the side of the bed but it suddenly seemed too far down; she was up so high. Her feet dangled, and she stared at her toes as dizziness caught her by surprise, hands on each side of her tightly gripping the coverlet to keep from falling. As she swayed slightly, she heard voices in the hall, and looked up to see the door ajar. An empty chair by her bed indicated someone had sat there recently.

The voices drew nearer, and she recognized Julian's deep rumble: "Dammit, Randal, of course I see the danger. What would you have me do—risk her life?"

"It seems to me that you'd be risking it by sending her away. What if she's caught? They'll think her guilty for certain, then."

"I know. Oh God, believe me, I know. But no one's found Fortier yet, and when they do, we have no guarantee we can get him to tell the truth. He had to be the one who killed Eleanor, and he's certainly involved in the plot to have Laura and me tried for treason. Laura's seal was found in Eleanor's desk. It matches a tradesman's bill we found in Laura's desk, so it's evident they both plotted against us."

"Just one more reason to have killed her," Randal said quietly, and Laura shivered.

That was so true . . . the nightmare wasn't over, after all.

"It'll be better when Laura's gone," she heard Randal say, and froze, her hand curling into the velvet covers. Breathless, she waited, heart drumming loudly in her ears, hoping to hear Julian say he wanted her to stay, that he wanted her with him.

"Yes," Julian said gruffly, "I suppose it would."

"Damn—you're not considering letting her stay, are you? Tell me you're not that foolish!"

"Speaking of foolish, just what is this game you're playing with Belgrave's mistress? Do you think he won't notice that she spends more time with you lately than with him?"

A moment of sizzling silence shocked Laura, and she sat back on the bed, drawing the coverlet up to her chin. She should let them know she was awake, make some kind of noise or cough or something, for she shouldn't be privy to this conversation. Celia and Faraday? No, it couldn't be. . . .

"For your information, Julian," Randal said coldly, "Celia has been here to see Laura, not me. Her main concern is her friend. Don't try to distract me. What are your plans for Laura?"

"At the moment, to talk to her. Be so good as to step aside, or—"

"Or what? You'll move me aside?" Randal's laugh was angry. "You'd best think about it before you do or say anything you'll regret, old boy. Not to me—to Laura. She loves you. And you love her. What will that matter if she's thousands of miles away?"

"Randal—"

"Yes, I see you're in a temper. I'm moving aside. Just remember what I said, Julian. Haven't you had enough regrets in your life without adding more?"

There was a moment of heavy silence, then the door pushed open and Laura saw Julian in the opening, looking weary and so handsome and beloved . . . her heart lurched, and she closed her eyes for a moment to compose herself. When she opened them again, he stood right next to the bed, only an arm's length away.

"Hullo, sweeting," he said softly when she looked up at him, and she managed a smile.

"Hullo yourself. You look—wet."

He grinned. "It's raining again. April is always wet."

"It's April? I thought—oh my."

Pulling the empty chair closer to the bed, he sat down on it and reached for her hand. Her fingers were swallowed in his large, strong palm, and she felt the strength in his touch. Damp hair clung to his forehead, and a fine mist glowed on his face and in his lashes. She wanted to kiss him, to tell him that she loved him so dearly, that she didn't want to leave England and him. How could she? Now? When she'd found her heart's desire at last? When everything she wanted was right here? Oh, she couldn't go, couldn't leave him, and she prayed he'd not ask it of her.

"You've been through so much lately," he said, and his mouth tightened a little. "I brought you something to—to have."

To remember him by? Oh no . . . a lump formed in her throat as he sat back and fumbled in his coat pocket, withdrawing a small, flat box. He held it out.

"A token of my great . . . affection for you, Laura. Open it."

Slowly, she lifted the lid. Her eyes widened. Nestled on pink satin, a diamond-and-emerald necklace glittered beautifully. Tears sprang to her eyes as she lightly touched the rosebud formed by diamonds, emeralds creating leaves around it, the delicate piece dangling from a strand of more diamonds interspersed with emeralds.

"Whenever I see a white rose," he said softly, "I think of that first time I saw you, with the white roses in your beautiful hair. I'll never see another rose without thinking of you."

It sounded like a farewell, and she couldn't look up at him, could only keep staring at the necklace as her vision blurred and her eyes stung so that she couldn't even see it anymore. It was his way of saying goodbye, his way of sending her home and far away, and she didn't think she could bear it. She wanted to shout at him, to stamp her feet and insist that he listen to her, to say that they could get through anything if they were together, but the strange lethargy produced by the medicine and her ordeal kept her from it.

Instead, she stared silently at the necklace and let the tears fall, blinking furiously so he wouldn't see her weep.

"Do you like it?" he asked after a moment, and she nodded.

"It's lovely." Her words came out in a husky whisper, and he reached out to put a finger under her chin to lift her face. His eyes met hers, and she recognized the same misery in them as she felt. His mouth twisted.

"Ah, sweeting—don't cry. I can bear anything but that. You see, don't you, that I've got to keep you safe? It drove me mad to think of you in Newgate, to know that all my money, my name, my influence, might not be enough to save you. I won't risk that again. I can't. I . . . care too much for you to chance your safety."

Reaching up, she curled her fingers around his hand and held him, his fingers still caressing the side of her face. She turned her head to press a kiss into his palm. Then she looked deeply into his eyes, finding courage in the certainty that he loved her.

"All my life I've had people arrange events for my own safety, Julian. First, my mother, by leaving me with my grandparents. Then my grandparents, by keeping me from joining my mother in Paris, and then my uncle, who sent me to join my mother—for my own good. For the most part, they were quite correct. But it's time now for me to choose my own fate. I'm not that scared, foolish girl I was when I fled Paris and Fortier. I should have stayed, perhaps given my mother the chance to explain, but I didn't. I'll probably never know if she truly sent him to me, or if he lied. I ran before learning the truth. I'm weary of running, Julian. I want to make a stand. I want to stay in England. I want to be with you."

He stared at her, his golden eyes reflecting lamp light and indecision, then finally shook his head. "No, Laura, it's too big a risk. As long as you remain here, you're in danger. Go for now, and when Fortier is caught and charged with Eleanor's murder, then you can return. I have men looking for him. They'll find him. Until I know you're safe, I want you far from London."

"Then I'll go to Shadowhurst. You promised me that cottage. I'll go there." Her fingers tightened when he tried to draw his hand away, and she held him fast. "It's my choice to make. It is my life—and I've made my choice."

"Dammit, Laura—you aren't considering the risks!" His eyes flashed angrily at her, but she refused to retreat.

"I've considered the risks. But if I flee now, I'll be running the rest of my life. I've got to stop running, Julian." She took a deep breath. "I won't leave you. I love you."

There. She'd said it. There was no return now.

"Yes," he said, "I know. My brother is much more perceptive than I am, it seems." He rose to his feet, raking a hand through his hair, moving to lean against the side of the bed and gaze down at her. "Randal changes his mind more than the wind changes direction lately, but he's right about a few things. The only thing that seems to have remained the same is that you'll be safer in America than England. God, I've tried to think of other solutions, tried to reason that justice will prevail and Eleanor's killer will be caught, and we'll all live happily ever afterward, but it doesn't always work out that way, I'm afraid. I'll regret it, I know I will, but if I'm wrong and you're sent to the gallows—I could never live with that."

He hadn't said he loved her, but she saw it in his eyes, heard it in the anguish of his voice, and nodded understanding.

"It's not your choice, Julian. It's mine. Any regrets will be mine as well. I'll not go to America, but I will leave England if you insist."

"Where will you go?"

"Paris. To my mother."

CHAPTER 22

"I thought he be a lumper at first, sir, or maybe a mudlark or scufflehunter got caught wadin' in the water 'neath a ship ter catch goods thrown down to smuggle ashore, but 'tain't. Th' River Police says as how this cull's a swell o' sorts, and since I knowed yer huntin' fer a man o' his description, I fetched ye ter see him fer yerself."

Reeking of dead fish and marine life, the man bobbed alongside like a fishing cork as they walked down the quay toward the docks. A sea of masts swayed in the evening mist, and vessels looked eerily like ghost ships in the haze. They stopped near the side of a stone buttress, and he jabbed his hand toward a covered form stretched out on the dock.

"This is him."

Rex Pentley pulled back the edge of the blanket carelessly thrown over the bloated corpse fished from the River Thames earlier in the day. Even bloated, he recognized him, and nodded. "You did well, Grimes. There's a guinea in it for you now, there's a good man. Another guinea if you'll get him loaded onto a cart for me. I need to take him to Queen Square."

"Queen Square! Cor, then 'e must be worth more than a few guineas, sir."

Rex grinned affably, but there was a light in his eyes that told the other man he'd best not push his luck, and he backed away, muttering that he'd see to the body being loaded up right quick for him. Yes, this certainly put a new wrinkle in the case, Rex thought as the corpse was loaded into an empty cart. How had Aubert Fortier ended up floating in the Thames?

It was a relief to be back in her own parlor, Laura thought, looking around the cozy little room with a faint smile. Julian had first refused to let her return for her trunks, but she'd insisted. What was the harm now? Once Fortier was found and questioned, she'd be exonerated of any involvement. Then she could return to England. Paris wasn't that far, and it was time she confronted her mother. She had to know, even if the answers weren't what she wanted, she had to know why Maman had betrayed her as she had.

The house echoed emptily. Becky was already at Celia's, and the footman had gone to fetch a carriage for her trunks. She'd miss this little house. She'd felt safe here, especially with Julian, and felt at home. It had been so long since she'd felt that way, not since she was a child.

A knock at the door interrupted her musing, and when she opened it, she was startled to see Malcolm. He seemed distraught, stepping past her when she held open the door for him, his hands fretting the brim of his hat. Damp evening mist came in with him, and she closed the door.

"Forgive the late intrusion, Miss Lancaster, but there's been a new development. You're to come with me at once. I have a hired hack outside."

"Come with you? Now? Why? What's happened? His lordship, is he alright?"

"He's fine, miss. But you're in danger—Fortier is dead. You need to leave England at once or you're likely to be arrested again. The earl has made all the arrangements for you. Please do not tarry."

"But my ship doesn't leave until tomorrow—"

"You're to go to the country, miss. To his lordship's estate. When it's safer, you can go from Dover to Paris, perhaps, or return to London. But you must come with me *now*."

"Well, really—this is all so sudden. Did he send me a note?"

"No, no, there wasn't time. You must hurry, miss. I fear the constable will be hard on my heels as it is. Take only what you must—that valise there. It has enough for a day or two, hasn't it?"

"What? Oh yes, I suppose—I intended to have it in my cabin with me. I'm not at all sure about this. Is it wise? I mean, to flee to the country? How did Fortier die? Did he confess to Lady Lockwood's murder before he—died? Oh, I know that sounds callous, but if he did confess, then there's no need for all this haste."

Drawing himself up to his full height, Malcolm looked her in the eyes, his dark gaze flinty and cold. "If you do not hasten, I have been instructed to be—forceful. Believe me when I say I should not wish it to go that far, but that I am quite capable of it, Miss Lancaster."

There was such a hard note in his voice that she believed him capable of anything at that moment, and she nodded. "Very well. I'll leave a note—"

"No, there's no time. We must hurry."

"Oh. I see. Only give me time to visit the . . . the necessary, and I'll come right with you."

"In light of your peril, I shall accompany you. As far as the door, if you will."

"Really, I hardly think that's at all required of you!"

"Yet I do."

In the end, he followed her to the door of her bedchamber upstairs, and she left him just outside while she went in and pulled out a chamber pot to use. Satisfied she'd be safe in the room, he closed the door to give her privacy. He acted so strangely, was so intent and tense, that she wondered if he had not taken it upon himself to get her to safety. Was there something he hadn't told her? Was Julian hurt somehow? Arrested? Why all this haste?

Celia was to visit her this evening, a last night together before she left for Paris. If only she could talk to her first . . . but

Malcolm was so adamant that she leave immediately. Moving quickly, Laura took a piece of dead coal from the uncleaned fireplace and used it as a pen to scratch a note on a scrap of wrapping parchment, then placed the clean chamber pot atop the scrap. Becky would no doubt find it, a last farewell and promise to return soon.

Then she went to the door, straightening her skirts as if she'd used the pot, and Malcolm gave her a sharp look before accompanying her downstairs. His air of haste made her nervous, and she wondered again if matters were not much worse than he'd said. Perhaps the magistrate had already issued an order for her arrest. Or worse, arrested Julian. Rumor had it that Lord Drumley had all but accused his son-in-law of being responsible for Lady Lockwood's death—had he been charged?

"Why are we in a hired hack?" she asked when they were seated in the vehicle and it lurched forward. There was no light inside, and dark shadows blanketed the interior so that he sounded far away when he replied.

"There's less risk if his lordship's carriage is not seen leaving your house."

"Do you think I'm being watched?" She frowned. "Why would they watch me instead of arrest me?"

"I have no idea, miss. I am simply acting upon instructions."

That was true. It was unfair of her to blame him for doing his job. The hack reeked of old cushions and other things she'd rather not dwell upon, and she thought of the vast differences between this vehicle and Julian's well-kept carriages. Dampness seeped inside, chilled her hands and feet, and the poor old cob that drew the hack had looked bony and thin. The seats were hard.

She nearly pitched off the seat onto the floor when the hack turned a corner, and braced herself by clinging to a well-worn strap dangling from the interior frame.

"The driver seems to be in a hurry," she commented, straightening the hat that dipped low over her face with one hand. "Is he taking us all the way to Kent?"

"He's been employed to take us to our destination, yes."

She wished she could see Malcolm's face. The darkness was only occasionally broken by street lamps that cast light inside as they passed. He seemed so remote sitting across from her, his silence a bit daunting.

"Is Malcolm your given name?" she asked after a few minutes. "I've never known if it is your first or last name."

After another moment of silence, he said curtly, "Malcolm is my last name."

"Ah, I rather thought most men of your position were referred to by their last name, but it's one of those names that can be either a Christian or surname, isn't it? Cranford, for instance, is definitely a last name, but Becky, being an under servant and female, is called by her given name. There are so many rules, even in the service class, that I cannot keep them straight."

She knew she was babbling, but Malcolm's silence made her nervous, and the situation of fleeing into the night as if she were a felon only made it worse. Her valise bumped against her legs as the hack turned another corner. A streetlight flashed illumination inside, and she couldn't help a gasp as it splashed across Malcolm's face.

His expression was sharp, predatory, lips curled back in a snarl and his eyes like two hot coals, burning into her before the darkness swallowed him again. It was unexpected and terrifying, and panic shot through her. She jerked upright, shrinking back into the seat cushions.

Celia met Randal at the door. "She's gone. Becky found this upstairs—why would she flee to the country now? Oh, this is so frustrating! What is Lockwood *thinking*?"

Pressing the scrap of paper with blurred writing into his hand, she paced back and forth in the small parlor, concentrating fiercely. Randal read the note, a frown knitting his brows; then he looked up at her with a shake of his head.

"This is—unusual. I don't think Julian would send her to the country at all. Do you think she went there on her own?"

"Why?" Celia rounded on him, throwing her hands up in the air. "Why would she do such a foolish thing? It was all decided—she was to go to Paris, visit with her mother, or just tour the countryside and wait until Fortier confesses and is arrested. Then she'd be sent for, and could come back again. A simple solution that should have worked quite well. Why would she suddenly decide to go to Kent? It seems more likely that the earl sent her, as she says, but why?"

"Perhaps we'd find out more quickly if we ask him. Come with me. Tell me again how it is you came to find her gone."

Once in the carriage, Celia said a bit impatiently, "I was to see her before she leaves tomorrow morning. When I arrived, her footman was there, bewildered because she was gone. He had been sent to fetch a carriage for her trunks. Since she'd been staying at your house, her usual carriage had already been sent away as it would no longer be needed. It was Becky who found the note, however, when she went upstairs searching for Laura. It was under a chamber pot."

The viscount stared at her incredulously. "Under a chamber pot? Good God, why?"

Leaning forward, Celia said, "That's what bothers me most. If she wished to leave me a note of her own volition, why not just fold it and leave it downstairs on the mantel? Or give it to the footman? Why would she *hide* it? It doesn't make sense unless—unless there was someone whom she didn't want to see her leave it."

"Julian? But that doesn't make sense—oh God, what if it's Fortier? Dammit! Julian told her not to come back here, but she insisted, said she wouldn't be alone."

A chill went through her and she shuddered. "She wouldn't have been if I'd come on time as I was supposed to do. Oh, this is my fault—I took too long getting ready, then dawdled about instead of hurrying. I suppose I just dreaded saying goodbye, but now she may be in danger and if I'd only been on time—"

"If you'd been on time, Fortier may have abducted both of you," Randal said grimly, and leaned forward to put a hand on her arm, fingers curling around her wrist. "I couldn't stand it if both of you were in danger."

Blinking, Celia felt a rush of surprise and pleasure. He looked so intense, eyes gleaming in the murky coach lights, and the breath left her lungs in a whoosh of air. This was crazy, this heat that swamped her, that made her feel breathless and giddy and more alive than she'd ever felt before, and she stared at him with her heart tripping so madly she was certain he must hear it.

"Celia—I have no right to say anything, Belgrave and all, and he's a decent chap, but if ever . . . if ever you should part company with him, I'll be right there."

"Would you?" she said faintly. No, no, she never yielded to impetuous young men. They were too impulsive, too fickle, and she preferred stability and security. Older men may be boring at times, but they were appreciative, gentle, and less demanding.

Yet Lord Faraday made her heartbeat quicken and her breath come more rapidly, and sent the blood racing through her veins in a way not even her late husband had done, and she'd been so young and foolish and in love then, she'd thought he was nigh perfect. Poor Billy, hung at Tyburn for stealing a purse or two, leaving her alone and desolate and determined never to be hurt like that again. But this man could hurt her. He had the devil in his smile and eyes, despite his easy manner. Oh yes, he'd tire of her quickly and move on, leaving her grieving just like Billy had done six years ago. If she yielded to the insidious whispers that promised he'd be different, she'd find out to her sorrow that he wasn't—and then where would she be?

Freeing her arm from his grasp, she sat back in the cushions and managed to say coolly, "I appreciate your concern for me, my lord. However, we'd best concentrate on finding Laura at the moment."

"Of course." He sat back, too, gazing at her steadily. "We'll find her. Then perhaps you and I should talk."

"I hardly think that necessary."

He smiled. "But I do."

"Julian, Fortier abducted Laura!"

Startled, Julian whirled around to see his brother racing toward him, Celia close behind. Randal came to an abrupt halt, panting a little in the damp air. Julian put up a hand to keep his coachman from putting away the carriage. "When?"

"Only a short time ago, no more than an hour at best. We came straight here to find you."

"Really. An hour ago? I believe that's impossible."

"Dammit, listen to me—she's gone! She left a note saying you'd sent her to Kent."

Julian shook his head. "That's two impossibilities."

Randal grabbed the front of his coat. "Will you listen to me? Fortier must have taken her!"

"If he did, it'd be a most unpleasant miracle. Fortier is dead. And I most certainly did not send her to Kent. Now release my coat. Cranford will be apoplectic if you crease it." Brushing off Randal's hands, he frowned. "Tell me about this note."

Angry, Randal thrust a scrap of paper into his hand. "Read it for yourself!"

Celia, Julian has sent me to Kent for safety. Laura.

It was smudged, and nearly illegible, looking as if it'd been written in soot, but he made out the gist of it and looked up, alarm tingling in every fiber. "Where did you find this?"

"Now I have your attention, I see. What makes you certain Fortier is dead?"

"Because I saw his corpse. A damned unpleasant sight. He'd been in the river for a while. Shot between the eyes— we'll take my fastest horses."

"Where are we going?"

"Kent. If Laura said she was going to Kent, that's where we'll find her."

He didn't know if she was in danger, but a sense of urgency filled him, and he looked up at his brother and saw the same grim apprehension mirrored in his eyes. Someone had Laura, and he didn't know who—or why. Fortier was dead. Who else could it be?

"Wait! What about me?" Celia Carteret demanded, grabbing Randal by the arm as he turned away. "What should I do?"

"Go back to Laura's house and wait there in case she returns." Slanting a glance at Julian, Randal put an arm around Celia's waist and yanked her close, whispering something in her ear that made her face go red, then he released her. "Take my footman with you for safety."

"Yes, I will," she said, somewhat flustered, and Randal sent his footman with her to the waiting carriage, then went to speak to his coachman.

"I'm not going to ask you what that was about," Julian said when Randal came back, and his brother grinned.

"Excellent. Then I won't have to invent a lie. Is a groom bringing around our mounts?"

"Yes. Come inside and I'll loan you a pair of my boots. If we hurry, we may catch up to her, though God only knows who she's with, or even how she's traveling."

It was the truth. How would he know where to look? He could only hope that whoever she was with, Laura was safe.

CHAPTER 23

"This isn't the way to Kent." Laura clung to the leather strap, bouncing on the slick seat as the coach picked up speed. "Where are we going?"

"It'd be far too easy for anyone following us to guess our destination were we to go by the usual routes, Miss Lancaster. There are many roads to Kent."

Uneasy, she subsided into silence again, though that dark, niggling feeling of disquiet that had dogged her since he'd shown up at her door grew stronger by the moment. They'd gone far to the west of London, and were now in Hounslow Heath, an area rife with footpads and thieves despite efforts of the police. It was a bleak and open area, with rolling grasslands full of heather, gorse, and furze, and where thickets formed good hiding places. A few abandoned gibbets still sprouted on the roadsides as a reminder of the days when the grisly remains of highwaymen hung there as a warning to those who might be tempted to join that old and dishonorable profession.

Malcolm lapsed back into stubborn silence, a dark and brooding presence far too close, and she shuddered. There was something terribly wrong. What could she do? She suspected now that Julian hadn't sent her from London at all, that for some reason, Malcolm was behind this. But why? What could he possibly want from her?

When the hack turned off the main Bath road and onto a track that ran alongside a narrow, winding ribbon of water, she tensed. Malcolm sat forward, and as they rounded a sharp curve, he rapped smartly on the roof of the hack.

"Stop here."

Laura stared out the window with dismay at dark fields with no sign of life. "Why are we stopping?"

Without bothering to answer, Malcolm opened the door and swung out, landing lightly on his feet on spongy ground. The scent of heather mixed with the distinctive smell of a marsh. He moved to speak to the hack driver in low tones, then came back to lean in and grab her valise.

"This isn't Shadowhurst," she said firmly, "and I'll not get out. Take me back to London at once, or I'll be forced to tell Lord Lockwood of your actions!"

"Step down, please, Miss Lancaster. Do not make me pull you out. It would be most uncomfortable for both of us, but if I'm forced to it—you do understand, don't you, that this is for your own protection?"

She wanted to believe him. It would be so much easier than to think he meant her harm. But since she'd seen his face in the light of a street lamp, she'd known he was not what he seemed to be. Nor was she fooled now. What could she do? Perhaps if she lulled him into thinking her compliant, she could seize the first opportunity to flee.

"Yes, of course. It's just that this is all so irregular and frightening. You did say, after all, that we were going to his estate."

"His lordship owns this land, and that cottage on the hill. He also owns that gunpowder mill in the distance. You might recall, as his secretary, I'm aware of his holdings and interests. If you please—?"

He held out his hand and she reluctantly accepted his help in stepping from the hack. Out of the vehicle, she saw a cottage outlined against a deep-hued sky, looking desolate atop a barren hill. No lights shone in the windows. She began to shiver uncontrollably.

Malcolm led the way up the hill, through a thin path overgrown with thistles; moor grass waved in the wind that blew up from the river, the pungent scent of wet earth strong. Oak and birch trees clustered in a staggered line along the riverbanks. A fox yipped in the brush, then went quiet.

"It's not elaborate, but better than Seven Dials, I should think," Malcolm said as he swung open the cottage door for her to precede him. "That *is* where you lived when the earl found you, am I correct, Miss Lancaster?"

"Near there, yes. Are you certain it's safe here?"

"Much safer than the rookeries. There's nothing out there to harm you."

No, she thought, *the real danger is right here with me now.* . . .

The thunder of hoofbeats behind them made Julian rein his mount to one side, slowing a bit to see who rode at night in such haste. It wasn't completely unknown for highwaymen to risk all for a fat purse, and he and Randal rode obviously expensive horses. His hand went to the butt of the pistol he'd tucked into the waist of his trousers, and he saw from one corner of his eye that Randal had done the same. They exchanged glances.

As the rider passed them, his lathered horse wheezing, some of the tension eased from his taut muscles and Julian relaxed slightly. Then the rider halted abruptly, looking behind him.

"Lockwood?"

Frowning, Julian rode close, then recognized the Bow Street Runner whom Townsend had sent to look for Fortier. "Your horse is a bit hot, Stewart."

"Indeed, my lord. Rex Pentley sent me after you. He spoke with a young woman who informed him you're in pursuit of Miss Lancaster."

"Yes, I am. So why are you here?" Curbing his restive mount with one hand, he sidled closer to Stewart. "Do you know where she is?"

"Pentley said she's in Hounslow Heath."

"Hounslow Heath! Good God—why?"

"It seems that your secretary has taken her there."

"Malcolm?" Julian stared at him in the faint light of a sickle moon. "Why would he do that?"

"I can't answer that, my lord, only suggest that you come with me. We're to meet Pentley on the Bath Road."

Waiting impatiently on the road that led from London to Bath, Rex Pentley braced against the leaning post that had once been a gibbet. It had been several years since highwaymen had been hung here as a warning, but he could almost swear he still smelled the lingering stench of death. Dick Turpin himself had roamed here once, an infamous highwayman caught and hung for his crimes long before Pentley had been born, but he'd never aspired to such risky ventures himself.

No, he much preferred the more reliable method of fleecing the wealthy when possible, and they usually made it far too easy. Working for John Townsend smacked too much of labor for his tastes, and if not for pretty Celia's begging him to help find Laura, he'd have refused. But for lovely Laura—ah, there was a lady he most admired, but she was far beyond his reach. She'd end up the earl's lady, if he was one to wager on love, but that was always too fickle a bet.

Still, he would have come to her aid even without Celia's request. If only the earl would hurry along now, they could reach her in time. If he didn't arrive soon, he'd be forced to go it alone, and that could get dangerous.

When hoofbeats grew loud on the road, he eased into the shadows of the copse where his horse grazed on mat-grass. Hounslow Heath was perfectly suited to felony. Even with thin light from a sliver of moon overhead, it was dark as pitch, so that it wasn't until they were abreast of him that he recognized the earl and his brother, closely followed by Stewart. It had begun.

Leaping from the thicket, he shouted, "Stand and deliver!" as a jest, and was very nearly shot for his trick. In a motion faster than he'd thought possible, Lockwood had a pistol in his hand and the deadly bore trained on him, even while his horse snorted and danced sideways.

"Pentley," the earl drawled after a moment, "you do have the devil's own luck. I almost shot you."

"Christ. So I see." He sucked in a deep breath, and saw Stewart staring at him with a grin. "I wouldn't think it so amusing were I you, Stewart. I'm the only one who knows where they are. Unless you've managed to learn more than I thought."

"Where are they?" Lockwood leaned forward, and Rex noted he'd not put away his pistol. "If you know, tell me."

"A cottage near Isleworth."

Recognition gave the earl a start. "I own—"

"Yes, so I learned. Land, a gunpowder mill, and several cottages. Only one cottage is empty at the moment. I thought we'd start with that one."

"How did you find this out?" Lockwood asked when Rex had fetched his horse and mounted.

"Your secretary."

"Malcolm told you?"

"No, my lord. Malcolm is with Miss Lancaster."

"Then she's safe."

Pentley hesitated, then shook his head. "No, I'm afraid not."

"Dammit, man, what are you saying?"

"I'm saying, my lord, that John Malcolm killed your wife, and most likely Fortier, and will probably kill Laura if we don't get there in time to stop him."

Malcolm lit a candle and put it in the middle of the table, then turned to look at Laura. The light played eerily over his face, cast half in shadow, half in an orange glow. It gave him the look of a man wearing a mask, as indeed, he had done all this time.

"Why are you doing this?" she asked calmly, and he looked at her with a faint smile.

"You are my only hope. Odd to say that, but it's true. You're my doom, and yet I must use you to save me."

"I don't know what you mean." She edged closer to the door, tension knotting her muscles as she tried to keep him talking and his mind on anything but her slow progress. Closer now, only a few feet away . . . "Why am I your doom?"

"Did you know it was I who sent the earl to you? Oh yes. It was my suggestion that he take a mistress to stop the rumors." He laughed harshly, a short bark that made her jump. "It was also my idea to start the rumors, to take some of the attention off Lady Lockwood. She was so lovely, so sad, and I thought . . . I thought she deserved better than a loveless marriage. And thought she deserved better than the men who sought her."

"Including you?" Laura watched his face, saw the quick leap of chagrin that proved her suspicion to be correct. He took a swift step toward her and she froze, heart pounding with fear.

"You needn't prod me too sharply, my dear, for you're no better than I, and, I daresay, not as well-born or educated. Pah! For all the good it does a man of my station to be adept. I'm no more important than a chair, and much less important than one of those damned blooded horses he keeps in his stables."

"I'm sure the earl never thought of you that way," she began, but his savage glare halted her.

"The earl! He didn't even recognize Eleanor's worth. Eleanor . . . named for a queen, and he treated her most shabbily. Of course, now I know why—it has caused quite a reassessment of my former conclusions." He said the last bitterly, turning around to pace the small confines of the cottage. "I did it all for her—and thought her worth it. A countess, and she loved me. Me, a man of good birth but not noble, a man who worshiped the ground she walked on, who killed for her when she was threatened—oh, you needn't look so surprised,

Miss Lancaster. Eleanor never killed anyone. Fielding was a fool. He threatened to go to the earl and tell him that I'd stolen a great deal of money from his accounts if I didn't pay him off. I agreed to divide my gains, but soon realized he'd never keep his silence, not until he'd bled me dry. Then he made the unforgivable error of sneaking into the countess's bedroom at night. I learned it quite by accident. There was a rather nasty scene—I struck him with an iron poker, then pushed him down the stairs. If servants hadn't come so quickly, I'd have dumped him in the Thames and been done with it."

"But Lady Lockwood was accused instead of you."

Turning back to her, he nodded. "Yes. An unforeseen event. Most unfortunate. I did what I could to negate the scandal, but of course, she had to flee. The earl had already made up his mind to rid himself of her. Fielding's death was explained as an unfortunate accident, his family compensated, and the matter was ended. Yet the countess was banished by her husband. That's when I decided I must find a way to make it all right again, to clear her name, but she was so impulsive, so impetuous, and returned to England before arrangements and plans were complete. I tried to tell her—ah, she was so headstrong."

Laura dared another step closer to the door, tension vibrating through her as Malcolm continued to pace back and forth, pausing to glance out the front windows on occasion, as if he were waiting for something. Or perhaps someone.

"It must have shocked you when Fortier killed her. A terrible shock," she said, gauging the distance to the door, keeping an eye on Malcolm while she eased another step sideways.

"Fortier?" Malcolm turned around to face her and she halted. "That scurvy frog? No, he didn't kill her. He used her most shamefully. And she liked it. God, I heard them that night, up in her bed, the grunts and cries, the obscene acts—and she liked it. My lovely countess. She begged him for more, I heard her, the depravity—I knew then that I'd been wrong all that time. She was exactly what his lordship named her, faithless and incapable of love. I was such a fool. Such a fool."

When he moved closer, Laura shrank back, heart thudding so loudly it sounded like thunder in her ears. Pale light flickered over him, and in the murky shadows he looked quite mad, a sort of wild ferocity in features she'd always thought rather bland. Beneath Malcolm's austere façade, turmoil churned, emotions she had never guessed he possessed, and he terrified her. How did he know Fortier hadn't killed Lady Lockwood, unless . . . unless he had done it?

Staring into his eyes then, she knew the truth. And she knew he intended to kill her as well for some twisted, terrible reason.

"Malcolm, you have suffered greatly, and I'm sorry for it," she said softly, forcing her tone to gentleness when she felt like screaming. "You were deceived."

He seemed to come back from some brink, blinking at her, then schooling his features into the familiar calm mask again. "Yes, quite true. And now it is my turn to deceive. You'll be found here with certain papers—and the earl's monogrammed scarf wound around your neck. It will be supposed that he found evidence of your thefts from his accounts and killed you for it. And even if he's able to purchase his freedom by some miracle, with all the talk of late there will always be suspicion that he killed his wife, her lover, and then his own mistress."

"Why do you hate him so?" she couldn't help blurting. "He's trusted you!"

"My dear, he's used me. My allegiance was only hired. I gave ample recompense for his coin. By a trick of birth, he took all his wealth, his position, his influence for granted, as his just due, while I had to bow and scrape for every penny. I worked just as hard as he did, even harder at times, yet he received all the credit for my efforts."

Trembling, she took the chance of retreating another step, and felt the door so close at her back now, if she reached out she could touch it . . . could lift the latch and escape into the black night. . . .

"Move away from the door, Miss Lancaster," Malcolm said crisply, and came toward her.

Whirling, she grabbed at the latch, fingers scrabbling over the cold iron, and succeeded in wrenching open the door. A gush of cold air swept over her, then a hand closed on the neck of her gown and yanked her backward.

"Ah no, not yet, my dear," Malcolm said against her ear, his arm going around her in a firm grip to hold her still. "I must make this quick now. I'm afraid I find murder distasteful, if a bit necessary. Only Eleanor—I was so angry, I almost didn't mind killing her. She'd deceived me for so long, playing her game with Fortier, planning to be rid of me once I'd served her purposes. I heard her that night when I stood outside her chamber, the little gift I'd so foolishly brought her still in my hands. What a cuckold I felt. I almost had empathy with the earl then—no, no, don't struggle. I'll make this quick and as painless as possible."

He coiled something soft around her neck in a swift motion, and her hands went up to tug at it, fingers scratching at linen to pull it free. Lights flashed in front of her eyes, tiny pinpricks that danced against darkness, but beyond them, a steadier flame—the candle. Just there, beyond her reach, sitting in the middle of the table. Lurching forward, she pulled Malcolm off balance and he cursed softly in her ear, panting with exertion, the scarf tightening around her neck more, and she reached, reached, until her fingers curled around the fat candle and its holder. Jerking it up, she stabbed behind her with it, smelled burning flesh and heard Malcolm's high-pitched scream.

The pressure around her neck lessened; his arms fell away from her and he stumbled back, still screaming, holding a hand to his face. Laura darted for the door, her own breath coming in gasping sobs, the scarf still trailing from her neck as she dashed into darkness.

* * *

A deadly calm gripped him. Julian concentrated on the dark road, not seeing the sweeping fields or occasional cottage. All his attention was trained on reaching Laura before Malcolm did the unthinkable.

"Did you see that?" Pentley swore softly, and spurred his mount faster. "I saw a light flash. We're nearly there."

Four horsemen thundered over the narrow track that led up a slope to a dark cottage, and Julian tensed when he heard a piercing scream. Oh God, was he too late?

"Laura!" Her name ripped from his throat as he strained to see in the fickle moonlight. It was so dark, the night so black—a movement caught his eye and he swerved toward it, toward a line of birch trees, trampling heather beneath hooves, the sharp scent spicing the air.

Then he saw her—a flash of white threading through tall clumps of mugwort before disappearing. He called her name again while the others rode on toward the cottage, intent only upon her. If she was wounded . . . he didn't want to think that Malcolm may have shot her. The burst of light they'd seen quickly extinguished, but he'd heard no pistol report. Was he too late?

Cursing the darkness, he reined to a halt and flung himself from the saddle, following the swaying fronds of tall grasses. Then he saw her—a slender figure fleeing into the birch copse, a brief, dark silhouette against pale tree trunks.

"Laura! For the love of God, stop!"

The silhouette paused, outlined against the paper-white trees behind her, and he reached her in several strides, heard her faint gasp of relief followed by a welcome cry, and she was in his arms again, warm and familiar and trembling—but alive.

"Are you hurt?" He kissed the top of her head, crushed tumbling curls in his gloved palms and stuck a fist under her chin to lift her face to his, eyes narrowing in thin light to search her for signs of injury. "God, Laura, talk to me, tell me if you're hurt!"

"He—Malcolm—oh, thank God you came for me, Julian! I thought I'd be killed and never see you again. . . ." Her voice trailed into dry sobs of reaction, her slender body shivering in uncontrollable shudders, and he held her to him fiercely.

"I came as swiftly as I could, my love. My sweet love, my precious lady—I'll not let you go again, not without me, not to Paris or even Shadowhurst—you'll not be out of my sight!"

Looking up at him, eyes wide, her face a pale oval gleaming in the shadows, she said in a shaky voice, "Do you love me after all, Julian?"

"Love you? More than my own life, dearest heart." He kissed her then, fiercely, mouth moving over her parted lips to seal both their fates, to bind them forever. He meant it. He'd not let her go again, no matter what he had to do to keep her with him.

In the distance, he heard shouting, and keeping her tucked beneath his arm for protection, he turned back to the cottage. Malcolm must be dealt with. He'd have to confess, for he wanted no shadow of suspicion to fall upon either Laura or himself.

"No," she said softly, resisting when she saw where he was taking her. "He—he's still out there, Julian!"

"I imagine Randal and Pentley have matters in hand, or will soon," he said. "We have a Bow Street Runner with us as well. Malcolm can't go far. He'll be caught soon enough."

He heard the snap but had no time to react before Malcolm said softly behind him, "If I am caught, my lord, it will be because you are dead."

Turning swiftly, Julian shoved Laura behind him, facing his secretary and the black bore of the pistol he held in one hand. It was cocked, ready to fire. Moonlight glittered on the steel barrel in brittle splinters that made it look even more deadly.

"Don't be a fool, Malcolm. You're caught. Don't make it worse."

"Hung for one murder or five—what would be the difference? I'd be just as dead. I've not much else to lose now. Step aside and push her toward me. I'll take her with me and keep her alive as long as you don't give pursuit. Should I see you or the police after me, I'll shoot her between the eyes."

"Like you did Fortier?"

Malcolm's laugh was unpleasant. "He deserved much worse. It was too quick for him. If I could have, I'd have taken more time. Push her toward me. I've no time for conversation."

"No. You'll have to shoot me first, and when you do, the others will be on you so quick you'll never escape."

Laughing incredulously, Malcolm said, "You'd die for her? How novel. And futile. I'll shoot both of you right here, and be gone before they can arrive." The pistol muzzle wagged in a sharp motion. "Your last chance to save both your lives, my lord—I've a punt waiting for me on the river. I'll be gone by the time your friends find your bodies."

"You think you can escape by river?"

"I was captain of my rowing team in school, if you'll recall. Yes, my lord, I know I can escape by river—now *step aside*!"

As Malcolm took a step forward, reaching for Laura, Julian half-turned as if to push her toward him, reaching beneath his coat for the pistol still tucked into the waist of his trousers. He yanked it free and turned in the same motion, firing. Orange flame spewed brightly, the smell of gunpowder sharp and sulphuric, and two gunshots nearly drowned out Laura's sudden scream. A hot pain seared Julian's left arm and he ignored it, all his attention focused on his steward.

Malcolm stared at him in surprise, then looked at his empty hand where the pistol had been. Blood dripped, and he watched it with a strange expression on his face. Then he took a step back, shaking his head.

"I've one shot left," Julian said, leveling the pistol. "Don't make me use it."

"Damn you." Malcolm gave a bark of bitter laughter. "I'd rather be shot than hanged."

"It's your choice." Coldly, deliberately, he tightened his thumb on the second hammer of the pistol, aiming straight for Malcolm's heart. He'd caused so much pain, destroyed lives and nearly destroyed Laura, and all for greed—he wanted to kill him, wanted to watch him die.

"Julian, no!" Laura cried, gripping his arm so that he winced at the sudden pain from his wound. "You'll be no better than he if you kill him!"

Above the pounding in his head, the drumming urge to kill a man he'd trusted, he heard his brother's shout, heard Pentley and Stewart, and knew that if he hesitated now, the moment would be lost. He had to thumb the hammer, had to do it now, had to take his vengeance or be cheated of it forever. . . .

Sound and motion, shifting light and shadows, voices calling his name, all faded into a muted roar and there was only John Malcolm and him standing on the heath facing destiny, only the two of them at last, a moment frozen in time. He lifted his arm a little, saw Malcolm brace for the shot that would end his life—and saw a flicker of triumph cross his face. *He knew.* He knew what it was to be pushed to this, to feel the blood lust rise hot and high and overpowering—but there was a difference between them. One of them was a cold-blooded murderer. One was not.

Lowering the pistol, he heard Laura begin to sob and saw Stewart rush forward to take Malcolm into custody, arresting him in the Crown's name, and he let the pistol fall from his hand.

It was over.

"You're hurt," Laura sobbed, her hand coming away bloody from his sleeve, but he shook his head.

"A scratch only, my love." Holding her tightly to him, he looked over her head and saw Rex Pentley smile. Then Randal and Stewart bundled Malcolm away, and they all left him standing alone on the heath with Laura. For several long moments, he just held her close, savoring the feel and scent of her.

Then she lifted her tear-streaked face to look up at him, and he kissed her, gently, lovingly and with a promise for the future. She was his now. Nothing stood in their way.

"You're mine," he whispered, and she nodded, smiling as she pressed her fingertips to his mouth.

"Always."

EPILOGUE

"I always dreamed of you standing here," Julian said softly, smiling down at her, and Laura blinked in the warm sunshine flooding the rose garden. "Right here, among the white roses. You're more lovely than any of them."

Flushing with pleasure, she returned his smile, then closed her eyes to breathe deeply of the sweet scent of so many blossoms. June in Shadowhurst was a riot of color: roses—red, white, and pink, buttery yellow—so many of them, lovingly tended and nurtured. She felt pale next to them, but Julian thought her more beautiful.

"May I have some cuttings for my cottage?" she asked, and he laughed.

"Sweeting, you may have anything your heart desires. Do you truly intend to renovate that old cottage?"

"Of course. It's mine. I have plans for it. It's so lovely, with the ivy growing over it, and I see white roses entwined with the ivy, perhaps, trailing over the windows and even the door. It will be so welcoming, I think. It reminds me of Virginia at times, though the trees aren't as wild and dense."

His arms went around her, holding her with her back pressed against his chest, his jaw resting atop her bare head. "Do you miss Virginia very much?"

She shook her head. "Not anymore. What I had there is gone now. What I have here—is the rest of my life."

For a moment neither of them spoke. The wind was soft, the sunlight bright, the garden sweetly spiced; bees hummed from blossom to blossom, and a butterfly lit upon the open petals of a pink rose. A round wheel of herbs lent their scent to the air, and contentment shimmered around her. The muted clang of a bell identified Phoebe grazing among the other sheep in tall, green grass that dipped to the river beyond the gardens and house. Cattle lowed in the distance. Emotion rose suddenly and swiftly, bringing tears of utter joy to her eyes.

"Not everyone will accept you as my wife," Julian said into the silence, a gentle reminder of the differences between them. "Just know that those who matter most to me love you."

"It will be a small wedding. Do you mind so very much?"

"My love, I'd wed you over the anvil and be perfectly content. We shouldn't give in to the demands of our friends and family."

She laughed softly. "Your brother is most adamant we be wed properly, and Celia is happy to be my bridesmaid. And . . . and now that Bonaparte has been defeated at Waterloo, my mother will be attending. Her letter was quite surprising, and she wishes to make amends for the misunderstandings. While I'm relieved to know that she didn't send Fortier to me, I still rather wish she would wed her general instead of continue as his mistress."

"As her daughter is doing?" Julian's laughter was soft, his breath warm against her ear. "My love, you cannot direct the lives of others. It's enough that we have our own lives at last."

"Does that mean you'll stop admonishing Randal for his wild, wicked ways?" she teased, and he gave an exasperated snort.

"Not at all. He needs guidance. Investing his money in plays—he's courting complete ruin."

"Not with Celia as the star player. She's becoming quite famous, and will be the toast of London before long, I expect. A good thing, as she and Belgrave are no longer companions. She has always depended upon men for her support."

"Then it's time she learned to be independent, though Randal spends most of his time with her these days." His arms tightened around her. "Enough about them. Let's discuss our future. I see I'm to provide a gardener for your cottage—does that mean you wish to live there?"

Smiling, she turned to face him, looking up into his amber eyes, love and happiness and hope filling her heart. "No, I will always be where you are, of course. But I do think we should provide a happy place for our children's nursemaid."

His eyes widened, and she saw joy radiate in his face. "Laura, do you mean—?"

"Not yet. We shall have to work on that."

"Ah, and so we shall." He bent suddenly and scooped her into his arms, grinning at her laughing shriek. "In fact, I think we should start work on that right now."

Burying her face into the strong angle of his neck and shoulder, she sighed, "I hoped you'd say that."